DAREDEVIL

DAREDEVIL

LESLIE CHARTERIS

WILDSIDE PRESS

TO
JERRY DOWMAN

Originally published in 1929.
Published by Wildside Press LLC.
wildsidepress.com

INTRODUCTION

KARL WURF

First published in 1929, *Daredevil* is a standalone thriller from Leslie Charteris, the British-American author best known for creating *The Saint*, Simon Templar. Although *Daredevil* features none of the characters from that iconic series, it clearly foreshadows the charm, irreverence, and fast-paced action that would come to define Charteris's most famous creation.

The central figure of *Daredevil* is Christopher "Storm" Arden, a suave, clever adventurer whose devil-may-care attitude and flair for mischief would not be out of place in the later Saint stories. Arden's escapades unfold in a world of intrigue and danger, peppered with dry humor and daring escapes—trademarks of Charteris's early narrative style.

Leslie Charteris was born Leslie Charles Bowyer-Yin on May 12, 1907, in Singapore, to a Chinese father and English mother. He studied at King's College, Cambridge, though he left before completing his degree. His first novel, *X Esquire*, was published in 1927 when he was just 20. *Daredevil* came two years later, during a prolific period when he was experimenting with various forms of the adventure thriller.

Charteris achieved lasting fame with *Meet the Tiger* (1928), which introduced Simon Templar. But *The Saint* series didn't gain real traction until *Enter the Saint* (1930) and its successors. By the mid-20th century (thanks to television adaptations most famously featuring Roger Moore), Templar had become a pop culture icon through books, radio, television, and film. Charteris eventually became a U.S. citizen in 1946 and continued writing and editing Saint stories into the 1960s, although others began to write under his supervision. He died in Windsor, England, on April 15, 1993.

Reading *Daredevil* offers a rare glimpse into the early development of a major 20th-century genre writer—a snapshot of Leslie Charteris before *The Saint* took center stage.

CHAPTER 1

INTRODUCTION TO STORM

Probably Susan Hawthorne got a lot of her courage and independence from her father, old Smiler Hawthorne, who in his time had been nearly everything and nearly everywhere—a tall, grizzled man who was generally broke but always unbeatable. Anyway, wherever she got it from, she needed it all; for old Hawthorne crossed the Divide one night with the same reckless optimism as he had gone through life. He left her his name and thirty pounds, the rest of his fortune having disappeared only a week before, together with the promoter of a company whose sole asset was a diamond field wherein no diamonds were.

And Susan Hawthorne faced a blank future with a smile that was reminiscent of old Smiler's cheeriest effort, which you only saw when things were very black and the proposition to be tackled was exceeding tough. He was that sort of man, and she was his daughter.

She felt very much alone in the world. She had lost touch with her own friends in the accompanying of her father in his happy-go-lucky aimless globe-trotting; and most of the friends he had picked up himself—and they were legion—were scattered in odd corners of the earth. In any case, she was not one to look for charity. Wherefore she went to Lord Hannassay, because he seemed to be the only friend of her father's who was in England.

She went with some trepidation, and was not unpleasantly surprised, and more than a little nervous, when she found that he was not so inaccessible as his name and position seemed to indicate.

"I remember you—sixteen, weren't you?—queer kid—all eyes and legs. And your father?"

He had a curiously disjointed manner of speaking, conveying the impression that his thoughts moved faster than his mouth could frame them.

"My father died a month ago," she said.

His grim face softened for a moment.

"I'm sorry," he said quietly. "Your father was one of the few men I have ever really liked."

After a while she broached the subject of her visit. It was not a task she relished, for she was desperately afraid he would misunderstand.

His face remained inscrutable, but the blue eyes searched her face.

The fingers of his right hand drummed on the table. She learnt afterwards that this was a trick of his when he was embarrassed.

"What can you do?" he asked. "Shorthand—book-keeping—type-writing—anything?"

"Nothing, I'm afraid." She had realised all along the hopeless inadequacy of her qualifications, and felt unnecessarily small and foolish. "But I could learn."

"There are hundreds of girls who have learnt—still looking for jobs," he said. His fingertips played an intricate tattoo. "Listen—you're afraid I'll offer you money. Feel insulted if I do—probably walk out in a rage. Still, I wish you'd let me. I've got heaps. I like money—I'd like more—and I don't often give it away. But you're different. I'd have done it for your father, any day—why not for you?"

Strangely enough, she was not annoyed. His nervousness was so amusing. He was obviously as scared of making a *faux pas* as she was of his making one, and he didn't know how to do it without seeming to.

"I'm sorry," she said. "I'm looking for work, not outdoor relief."

"I know all about that," he said peevishly. "You wouldn't have minded taking it from your father."

"That's different," she said, and he was not foolish enough to attempt to argue the point further.

He turned over some papers, picked up a pencil, and played with it. There was an unusual quality about these little mannerisms of his: they were never jerky and inconsequent, like the fidgeting of a different kind of man. He seemed to employ material objects to assist his thoughts.

"I want a typist," he said at length. "You can get reasonably proficient in a fortnight if you work hard. No need for much speed, anyhow—no dictation. Copying letters, etcetera. You can have the job if you'll be my guest here while you're learning. That's not charity—you'd accept an invitation like that even if you weren't broke. Use the house how you like—I'm going to Geneva. League of Nations conferences—all rot. However ... housekeeper's always here. Your reputation's all right. But while I'm away—no wild parties, mind!"

He issued the order with such a comical seriousness that she all but laughed aloud.

"I'll try to reform," she promised gravely.

The time passed quickly for her. The work was easy and interesting, the hours short. Once or twice it occurred to her that her job was simply a disguise for the charity she dreaded, but her hint of this suspicion was received with such pained surprise that, not unwillingly, she banished the idea. Hannassay came and went, always courteous and correct. She grew to like him, for he thought she detected the sentimentalist masquerading in self-defence as the tyrant.

After a month she began to consider herself an authority on affairs of State, for Lord Hannassay held a high post in the Home Office. It took her nearly three months more to realise that she knew practically nothing.

She was returning from the Home Office one afternoon after delivering some papers when she discovered that she was not as friendless as she had thought, and the discovery was a cheerful surprise. She was walking back along Piccadilly when she nearly collided with a tall young man in a grey flannel suit.

He raised his hat absently, apologised, and was about to pass on when suddenly they stopped dead and stared at one another.

"Je-rusalem!" exclaimed the young man.

He linked his arm in hers in the most natural way in the world, and steered her out of the press towards the portals of the Leroy.

"It's just four," he remarked, "and therefore tea-time. I've not seen you for years, Susan—millions of years!"

They found a table and sat down on either side of it, inspecting one another. Then they both smiled.

"Christopher Arden," she said, "you'll do!"

"And you, by Jeremy! Susan, what do you mean by it? I've written you regularly for the last three years, and you haven't answered a line."

"I might have," she answered demurely, "if you'd put your address on your letters."

His jaw dropped.

"Didn't I?" he demanded.

"Oh, yes!" She smiled. "You put 'Morocco' and 'South Pacific' and 'Nassau' and that sort of thing. Only I didn't think you were notorious enough for that alone to find you."

He grinned.

"Sorry!" he apologised. "Tell me all about this and that."

She told him, and his brown hand went across the table and touched her fingers lightly.

He said nothing—that wouldn't have been Kit Arden, known as Storm wherever soldiers of fortune were gathered together. He hadn't altered. He had always had a manner which mocked the expression of words; and yet his unspoken sympathy meant more to the girl than any amount of fluent condolences. She found his old irresistible spell, that had captured her imagination even when he was a dashing youngster of twenty-four and she a girl of seventeen, as potent as it had always been.

Physically he was the same as ever, save that his fair hair had oddly greyed a little at the temples—a curious contrast to the unlined boyishness of his face. But that was the keynote of his appearance, those contrasts. His slim yet broad-shouldered figure, the forceful mouth that could smile with such an infectious gaiety, the square jaw and the artist's hands, the Saxon hair and gun-metal grey eyes. Storm, who was Storm—so perfectly did the name fit him that it was impossible to think of him as anything else—Storm, the reckless, daredevil trouble-hunter with the heart of a crusader....

"And where've you been?"

"Oh, here and there," he said. "I put in a bit of time with the Riffi—they made me a Kaid or a Pasha or whatever a Riff makes you when he loves you like a brother. Then that blew over, so I beat it to the Pacific and went pearling. Had a merry scrap with a Jap patrol, fishing on forbidden ground. That was nearly the end of my career! Then that got dull, so I toddled over to the Bahamas and set up as a bootlegger. Respectability's tame! A short life and a beery one—that's me! And then you can bury me under the foundation-stone of a brewery. Stevenson's verse 'll do for my epitaph—fine! You know it?

> *"Here he lies where he longed to be,*
> *Home is the bootlegger, home from the sea,*
> *And the moonshiner home from the still..."*

"You haven't changed a bit," she laughed

"Nor you—you're just as lovely as ever—more so! Your eyes, now. I love brown eyes——"

She stopped him with a solemnly upraised hand.

"What are you doing now?" she asked.

"Divers things, and, on the whole, nothing much," he said vaguely. "London's paralytic! I'm just wondering whether it'd be worth while going back to Paluna—you remember, I ran a one-man revolution there and made myself President about three years back. Being President of a South American Republic is some game, believe uncle!"

He was, as a matter of fact, doing rather more than divers things. When he left he returned to Scotland Yard and made his way to the office of the Assistant Commissioner.

"You can take it from me, Bill," he informed that gentleman, "that Hannassay's new typist's all right. I've known her for years——her father took me out of the workhouse and educated me. Incidentally, he started me on my adventurous career. I tell you, anyone who was brought up by Smiler Hawthorne and after that went in for stockbroking or market gardening or anything else respectable and dull would have been a blistering Robot!"

"I'm glad to hear it," said Bill Kennedy drily. "I'd already gathered that you weren't a Robot, laddie, from the fact that you took an hour and a half to find out about her when you'd known her for years. Now you can push off, because I work sometimes. See you later."

Storm went to his own room, and shortly after Inspector Teal arrived to make his report. "Well, Teal?" he prompted briskly.

"Nothing," said Mr. Teal sleepily. "The process of reformation continues. I looked up Lew Mecklen and Gat Morini this morning, and they greeted me like a long-lost brother—which isn't like Lew and the gentle Gat. They've been over for a month now, and they haven't made a joke yet. Birdie Sands has been out six weeks, and we haven't had a thing on him. And Prester John hasn't cracked a crib for two months—and I know he was hard up two months ago. Mr. Arden, when a lot of old lags all start reforming at once my nose itches!"

"Uh-huh," said Storm thoughtfully. "And they're only a few."

"With more coming into the fold every day," supplemented Mr. Teal.

He was a big slow-moving man, red-faced and sleepy-eyed, beginning to pay the price of his youthful robustness as muscle turned to fat and easy living irresistibly increased his circumference. He was invariably tired and invariably bored—it was an affectation of his of which he was intensely proud.

Storm stared out of the window.

"When I got into this job," he said, "I had ideas. I thought Special Branch dealt with active crooks—not the boys who'd turned good. This is more subtle than I'd like it to be."

Inspector Teal said nothing.

Rousing himself slightly with what seemed a terrific effort, he reached into a pocket and extracted a small packet therefrom. From this packet he removed a smaller packet, and from the smaller packet he detached the pink wrapper.

"If it wasn't so absurd," said Storm, "I'd tell you the only explanation I can see that fits."

Mr. Teal conveyed a wafer of chewing gum to his mouth and champed meditatively.

"Mr. Arden," he murmured drowsily, "if I hadn't heard things that make me want to offer that same theory, I'd say it was absurd. But I stood Prester John a drink this afternoon, and I picked his pocket. I ought to have been a criminal really—people wouldn't suspect me, because I look so innocent. Anyway, I found something interesting. Look at this."

From his waistcoat pocket he took something that glittered and laid it on Storm's desk.

It was a little silver triangle. In the centre a similar triangle was picked out in black enamel, and in the centre of this a silver alpha had been picked out in the enamel.

Storm looked at it closely, turned it over and inspected the back, and laid it down.

"What's this got to do with anything—if anything?" he demanded, and Mr. Teal shook his head. "That's what I want to know."

The bell under Storm's desk rang discordantly, and he picked up the receiver.

"Hullo... Speaking."

He listened for a moment, and then spoke insistently.

"Struth! No, I don't know anything about it—yet. Look here, Mr. Blaythwayt, will you wrap that letter up exactly as it came, envelope and all, and send it round at once by special messenger? ... Yes, New Scotland Yard.... Right-thanks!"

"I know that man Blaythwayt," said Mr. Teal, as Storm replaced the receiver. "He's manager—"

"Shut up!" snarled Storm. "I'm thinking."

He swung over to the window and stood looking down for some moments. Then, abruptly, he came back to his desk and pressed a bell.

To the man who answered the summons he gave the trinket that Teal had brought him.

"Go down to Records," he commanded, "and ask 'em for anything they've got in which anything like this figured."

It was only ten minutes before the man returned, bearing with him a small bundle of papers. Storm lighted a cigarette and went through them carefully, and at the end he looked steadily across at Inspector Teal.

"Listen," he said. "Just over three months ago a man was found dead by the railway between Priory and Kearsney—that's on the Dover-London line. There were no marks of violence, and since he had a ticket from Dover to Victoria it was supposed that he'd simply fallen out of the train. He was identified as Henri Francois Joubert, a Frenchman domiciled in England, who'd made his fortune on the Stock Exchange—jobbing, you know—about thirty years ago. There'd be no records of the case if it hadn't been for one curious thing. In one of his pockets was this!"

He tapped a photograph with his forefinger, and Mr. Teal peered at it with his habitual indifference.

It was a picture of a visiting card. In the centre had been sketched a design similar to that on the silver triangle of Prester John, and underneath was roughly scrawled, "*February, 1899.*"

"Mr. Blaythwayt," said Storm, "has just received through the post a similar card, and all that's written under the triangle is *Harchester.* What do you know about Harchester, Teal?"

"One of the biggest and best public schools," said Mr. Teal. "Joe Blaythwayt was educated there."

Storm leaned back in his chair and exhaled a thin streamer of smoke. Then he looked at Inspector Teal and smiled. Storm's smile was the most attractive thing about him. It flickered about his lips for a moment as though he didn't want to give it a chance, and then it broke out—irrepressibly boyish. It bubbled over with mischief.

Head back and a little to one side, eyes dancing, Storm smiled.

"Absurd be catlicked!" Storm said. "Teal, this is going to be Big!"

CHAPTER 2

TITTLE-TATTLE OF MR. TEAL

Inspector Teal was that unusual type of man who literally takes both pride and pleasure in his employment. Mr. Teal loved talking shop, and would do so for hours on end if he found a listener on whom his enthusiasm was not wasted.

He was never off duty. His leisure hours would always find him sauntering round the preserves of other divisions, listening to gossip in public houses and at coffee stalls, entering queer and unregistered "clubs," and paying friendly calls on eccentric gentlemen not unknown to the Records Office. Criminals, to him, were a race of children—interesting, amusing, and completely human, but occasionally in need of sharp correction. And when necessity demanded that they be chastised, he haled them to their punishment without resentment.

It was his boast that he knew every bad man in London, and he was probably right.

The morning following his discovery of the Alpha Triangle (already, with that queer instinct for the dramatic which few would have suspected beneath his prosaic exterior, he spelt it with capital letters) Inspector Teal flowed—there is no other word for his peculiar method of locomotion—in the direction of Kensington, for on the left-hand side of Church Street, behind a door over which hung three golden orbs, lived Mr. Eddie—more commonly known as "Snooper"—Brome.

He was a big, florid, shock-headed man with an alarming taste in fancy waistcoats. Also the reputation of being a receiver of stolen goods.

Mr. Teal considered himself lucky to find him in residence, for Snooper was a man of erratic habits and rarely attended to his business in person.

"Good morning, Snooper," said Mr. Teal affably. "How's trade?"

"Not too bad," said Snooper—trade, with him, was always either "not too bad" or "not too good"—"Have a cigar?"

The sample he offered was undoubtedly a weed of great price, and Mr. Teal sniffed at it suspiciously.

"Who gave you this?" he asked, and Snooper shook his head.

"I cannot," he said unhappily, "get rid of the idea that you suspect me of being a receiver."

"You might have made a worse guess," said Mr. Teal. "Quite easily. How are the crooks? Or is 'clients' the correct term? Comrades Lew and Gat are heading for trouble, you know."

"Don't know 'em," said Eddie.

"Interesting people, very," said Mr. Teal. "Especially the educated Gat. He has the most cherubic blue eyes. You'd love him." He stirred in his chair sluggishly. "By the way, Snooper, there's a friend of mine I'd like to bring along to meet you one day, if you'll let me know when you're at home. He's interested in criminals."

Mr. Brome shrugged.

"I'm afraid my acquaintance with the criminal fraternity won't help him. Still," he admitted, "like all pawn—er—financial agents, I have had stolen property offered to me. Naturally, I immediately notified the police."

"On two occasions," supplemented Mr. Teal. "And the total value of the stuff was exactly two pounds five shillings and ten pence."

"I can't help that. I wish it had been more," said Eddie piously.

"I believe you," said Mr. Teal.

He glanced round the room, his heavy-lidded eyes taking in afresh every familiar detail of unostentatious comfort—even luxury. There was no suggestion of wealth, but more than a hint of solid well-being. Looking merely at Snooper's waistcoats, one would never have suspected their inhabitant of possessing so artistically furnished a room.

"You do rather well out of pawn—er—financial agenting," remarked Teal absently, and went off at an abrupt angle. "Are you the philanthropist who's financing Birdie Sands?"

"Birdie's hands?" inquired the puzzled Mr. Brome.

"Birdie Sands," Mr. Teal enunciated clearly and distinctly. "Strange as it may seem, I was once educated."

"I have met a *Mister* Sands. Who's this 'Birdie' Sands?"

"A gentleman," said Mr. Teal, "who used to be on the whizz."

"On *what*?" demanded the startled Snooper.

"A pickpocket," explained Mr. Teal patiently. "Do you know him?"

If Mr. Brome did not squawk derisively, his elevated archidiaconal eyebrows rendered such a lamentable exhibition unnecessary.

"A low criminal?" he protested. "Now, I ask you, Mr. Teal, is it likely?"

"Taking things all round, I should say it is. Birdie Sands," went on the detective, apparently for his own benefit, "is, or was, the best whizzer operating in London. He was inside up—to about six weeks ago—that's about twice the time you've been financial agenting, isn't it, by the way? Since then we've had nothing on him, and he seems to have all the money in the world."

"He may be going straight," suggested Eddie.

"Go straight?" jeered Teal drowsily. "It's a physical impossibility. That man's a human corkscrew with all the twists case-hardened. He's a born crook—his mother was a crook and all his fathers were crooks, and Birdie was brought up as a crook, Borstal trained. Why, if you shot him out of a gun he'd tie knots in the barrel."

"What happened to the gun you were shot out of when you got that face?" inquired Mr. Brome vulgarly, but Inspector Teal failed to bite.

He heaved himself laboriously from his chair.

"I'm interested," he said, "because when a born-an'-bred crook earns a lot of honest money, it just ain't natural. I've got a nose for dirty work, and that same nose is worrying me now. When shall I bring my friend along?"

"Shall we say Sunday?" invited Mr. Brome. "At eight? Suit you? Splendid. Good-bye."

But he stopped Teal at the door.

"I hope you won't put any ideas into his head," he said anxiously.

Mr. Teal regarded him thoughtfully.

"What I'm afraid of," he replied, "is that he'll put ideas into yours."

With that his projected programme was exhausted, but he was destined to have an interesting morning.

On his way back to the Yard he dropped in at Walton Street police station, near the Brompton Road, for a chat with the divisional-inspector. While he was there a lank, saturnine man entered jauntily.

"James Mattock—convict on licence. I've come to report."

Inspector Teal surged across (as I have said, one has to use extraordinary words to convey his ponderous mode of progression).

"Hullo, Mattock," he said. "When did you come out?"

"A fortnight ago."

Mattock's manner did not encourage further conversation, but it took a lot to put off Mr. Teal.

"What are you doing now?"

The man's thin lips twisted.

"Working. Do you want to get me the sack by telling them my past record?" he sneered. "Because if so, you're too late. I thought I'd get in with it before you busies got a chance."

"I suppose you picked up that word in Wandsworth," said Teal. "Getting the slang already—a pity. Who are 'them'?"

"Raegenssen's. I'm head clerk and in practice semi-manager. They haven't got much of a staff."

"That's a pity, too," murmured Mr. Teal. "Temptation never did anybody any good; and you weren't built for a crook, Mattock."

"I'm glad of that," said Mattock, surveying Mr. Teal's girth pointedly.

Teal fingered his chin, his eyes on the other man's face. It was a refined face, lined bitterly. The man was educated—Teal knew that, for he himself had arrested Mattock for his first and only crime. Teal also knew what the court that sentenced Mattock for forgery never knew—why the crime was committed.

"Let's see," mused Teal. "Hannassay put you away."

"That's true."

"A cheque—you were his private secretary, weren't you? And he saw to it you got the full stretch—not even a first offender's chance. That's right, isn't it?"

"It is."

Mr. Teal's contemplative fingering of his chin continued. He would have been better pleased if Mattock had been stung to a storm of abuse and threats, for the only dangerous criminal is the one who hugs his grievances.

"You don't love him much, do you?"

"Would you?" countered the other.

"Possibly not," admitted Mr. Teal. "Did they ever recover the money you drew on that cheque? Six thousand, wasn't it? You must have a tidy bit put away—why go clerking? Or did Joan throw you over?"

"That's my business," said Mattock icily. "What exactly are you trying to do, Teal—rub in my disgrace, or persuade me to commit another crime so that you can make me a thorough old lag?"

Mr. Teal shrugged. His sleepy eyes were nearly closed.

"I'm sorry you're such a fool, Mattock," he drawled. "What I'm trying to do is to save you from making an utter mess of the rest of your life."

"Thanks," said Mattock curtly. "And now do you mind going and preaching to someone else?"

"I will," promised Mr. Teal. "Come along and have lunch, Mattock, and let's talk things over."

He rolled in to report progress to Storm later, and told of an unsatisfactory conversation.

"He thawed after a bit, but since he was liquid air to start with he wasn't much better than an iceberg even then. A card—he was a gentleman all right, once, and still talks like one. One of the Somerset Mattocks—they had pots of money once, and then went bust. Mattock fell in with Joan Sands, Birdie's sister. She got very ill. The docs. said the only way to save her life was to operate and then send her to the south of France for a long rest. Mattock couldn't pay, and Birdie was in stir and never had much money anyway. He was defiant and insolent in court, otherwise he might have got off a bit lighter, in spite of all the fuss Hannassay kicked up at the time about making examples and so on. He's the hottest man in the country on crooks, and they all hate him like a pussyfoot hates beer. My own idea is that Mattock begged

Hannassay to help him out and was turned down. Hannassay's as hard as tungsten, in any case."

"What about Snooper?" asked Storm.

Teal flicked his chewing gum through the window and replaced it with a fresh slab.

"The flavour *doesn't* last," he remarked with irrelevant irritation. "Oh, Snooper. We don't know much about him—he's a success so far. We don't even know where he lives. We had him shadowed once, to find out, and he spotted the tail and came storming in here swearing he'd bring a suit against us if it happened again. He'd have won his case, too—we can't tail people unless we've got anything definite to justify it. He's only been in business for about three months, and as far as anyone can prove he's as innocent as the day. What I *know* 's another matter—and that is that in three months he's become the first fence in London."

Storm nodded and pulled out a drawer, from which he took an envelope.

"Some more souvenirs have come in," he said.

One by one he spread out three small white caras on the desk. Each bore the same symbol in the centre, but the inscriptions differed.

One said simply, "*Harchester.*"

"That's your pal Blaythwayt's."

On the second was written, "*March 23rd, 1897.*"

"That was received this morning by the Home Secretary, Sir John Marker," said Storm.

The third similarly bore a date: "*December 2nd, 1899.*"

"That one went to John Cardan, editor of the *Record.*" Storm's faint smile played about his lips. "What do you make of it, Teal?"

Inspector Teal shook his head.

"Give me time, sir," he murmured. "A French-English stock-jobber, a bank manager, a Cabinet Minister, and a newspaper editor. And just dates, except one which has the name of a place. Where were they posted?"

"In different parts of London. There's not even a threat, you notice. Just dates and places, which obviously mean something to the man who sent 'em, and may mean something to the men who got 'em. I want you to push off on that trail for the moment, Teal. It mayn't lead anywhere, but it may. Find out what happened to Marker on March 23rd, 1897, anything important that happened to Blaythwayt at Harchester, and anything Cardan can remember about December 2nd, 1899."

Inspector Teal sighed.

"That sounds like a lifer to me," he groaned, and picked up his hat wearily.

He concluded an unproductive round of investigations by spending the evening at a house in the Finchley Road, where dwelt Joe Blaythwayt, manager of the Lombard Street branch of the City and Continental Bank.

Joe Blaythwayt was nearly as rotund as himself, but shorter by six inches. And, whereas Mr. Teal's eyes always seemed to be struggling with an overpowering desire for sleep, Blaythwayt's were always alert and twinkling.

These evenings, during which they played piquet and discussed crime and criminals, detectives and detection (these are four different subjects) were among the relaxations of Mr. Teal's life. Joe Blaythwayt had a crimson taste in fiction, and absorbed Mr. Teal's practical knowledge eagerly.

It is, of course, unusual for a policeman to be the especial friend of a bank manager; but then, Inspector Teal's friends were a queerly mixed crowd.

Blaythwayt was reading a novel with a distinctly intriguing cover, but he put it away on Teal's arrival.

"That book," he said, jerking a disgusted thumb in the direction of the offending volume, "that book is supposed to deal with the exploits of a master criminal, and already he's made four mistakes which even a policeman couldn't miss."

Teal grinned languidly and took his usual chair.

"You'd better write a book yourself and show 'em how to do it."

"I've started!" announced Joe. "Two minds, etcetera. It'll be the greatest detective story ever written. Everyone will buy it."

"Will anybody publish it?" inquired the practical Mr. Teal.

"How do you get a book published?" asked Blaythwayt.

"Send it to a publisher and enclose enough stamps to pay for him sending it back," pronounced the detective, and Joe's round face lengthened as he visualised the sordid difficulties of a literary career.

But he soon brightened up.

"It'll be great," he enthused. "I'm writing it in the first person, and I shall commit impossible crimes. I shall never be caught."

"Let's hope not," grunted Teal. "I'd hate having to arrest you. Besides, crooks are only romantic characters in fiction."

"It'll be in the form of a diary, and——"

"Where are the cards?" asked Mr. Teal slumbrously.

During the intervals of the game, he recounted his experiences of the day, for Blaythwayt was a great student of contemporary crime. Also, he delighted his friend by telling him that a real live criminal had consented to be at home when they called.

"I think you must peeve Snooper," said Blaythwayt. "You do try the magazine detective stunt—trying to make people think you know everything."

"Nearly everything," corrected Teal modestly.

"If you know everything you know nearly everything," said Joe sententiously, and Mr. Teal stared at him.

"You've been going to one of these modern plays," he accused.

"I've been studying the stage with a view to dramatising my book. That sort of thing goes well. Look at *Raffles*."

"You didn't write *Raffles*," said Mr. Teal crushingly.

They played out two more hands in silence, and then Blaythwayt looked up brightly.

"At least," he said, "I can stump you."

"Carry on," suggested Teal.

"Who is Christopher Arden?"

"My chief, *pro tem*. He got into Special Branch through the Assistant Commissioner, and he's all right—you can take that from me. He's one of these tough young soldiers of fortune. He'll never settle down. He joined up in the ranks at sixteen, and came out at the end of the war a captain. Ever met him?"

"No."

"You'd like him. He's big, and strong as they're made. He talks like a quick-firing gun, and he's got a nerve that'd make a refrigerator look like a quiet corner in hell. He's one of these cool, casual devils who could get on to a bus politely during the rush hour—and get on first!"

"That's off the point," said Blaythwayt, "I know all that. You've told me about him once before. I didn't ask *what* he is, but *who* he is."

"Christopher Arden," said Mr. Teal.

Blaythwayt smiled triumphantly.

"That stumped you! I came across it quite by accident, and if you hadn't mentioned the name I shouldn't have done anything about it. I scented a coincidence and I got one. Someone took him out of a workhouse at the age of two, but who put him in?"

"I'll buy it," said Teal.

"He's got a good bit of money, too, hasn't he? Well, he may have picked up a bit on his travels—according to you, he's tackled a few risky and paying jobs—but you can't go pearling or bootlegging or running revolutions without capital."

"I know that one," murmured the somnambulous Teal. "An uncle died and left him ten thousand. The solicitors traced him somehow."

"What was the name of the uncle?"

"I don't know, and it isn't my business," said Teal bluntly. "If Kennedy says a man's all right, he is all right. What are you getting at, Joe?"

"You ought to play about a bit in Somerset House," said Blaythwayt.

Mr. Teal blinked. It was the only evidence he gave that he was interested.

On his way home to his modest lodging near Victoria he dropped in at the Albany to report his discoveries, such as they were. He found Storm arrayed in a suit of wonderfully jazzed silk pyjamas and a staggering silk dressing-gown, seated in a comfortable armchair in front of the open window, his bare feet propped up on the sill and a slim volume of Kipling On his knees.

"What news, Teal?"

Mr. Teal pulled up a chair and accepted the proffered cigarette.

"Very little," he confessed. "Joe Blaythwayt says he never made an enemy at Harchester—in fact, he was very popular. Harchester's a great Rugger school, and Joe used to be a star three-quarter before he put on weight. Cardan can't remember a thing. Marker's the only man who could remember anything at all, and all he knew was that in March, 1897—he can't swear to the exact date—he got into Parliament at the Clayston bye-election, and got married a week later on the strength of it."

"It isn't much to go on," Storm admitted ruefully. "I'll talk to Marker tomorrow. I suppose we can look up who opposed him at Clayston, though I don't suppose there's much in that. Now look here."

He reached out for an envelope that lay on the table beside him, and from it he drew a card which he laid in Teal's hand.

"That came round from the Yard after dinner. Raegenssen brought it in—got it this afternoon."

The card and the sketch were by this time familiar to Mr. Teal. Underneath was the legend, "*April 1st, 1928.*"

Inspector Teal shook his head.

"There's been a mistake," he said. "That one ought to have come to me. April the First is my birthday!"

CHAPTER 3

ADVANTAGES OF RESPECTABILITY

Snooper Brome was not a man who was noted for his love of fresh air and exercise. In fact, none of his clients had ever seen him except in the small, comfortable room in Church Street, where he transacted business with the favoured few who were privileged to deal with him personally. He came and went secretly, and discouraged interest in his movements.

On this particular day, however, there was no furtiveness about him. He sauntered slowly through Kensington Gardens, an exceptionally brilliant waistcoat proclaiming his approach several hundred yards in advance of his person, emerged into Exhibition Road, and strolled on down that wide, barren thoroughfare. At least one man followed his progress, and Snooper permitted himself to smile faintly.

On your right-hand side as you walk down from the Park is a tube subway which leads to South Kensington Station. Into this wandered Mr. Brome, continued about fifty yards, and stopped to light a cigar—a process which took him some time.

Satisfied at last that anyone who was interested in his destination had hurried onto the station by the overground route to pick him up again as he left the tunnel, Mr. Brome turned about, left the subway where he had entered it, buttoned his coat over his fancy waistcoat, and made his way briskly into Queen's Gate. Just before he reached the entrance of a block of flats he stopped to relight his cigar, and took the opportunity of glancing keenly up and down the road.

Joan Sands was curled up on a sofa reading when he rang the bell, and she was not pleased when she saw who her visitor was.

"I don't remember inviting you," she said. "I happen to be alone, so you'd better go."

He pushed her aside without offence, and led the way into the sitting-room.

"This isn't much of a place," he remarked, glancing around him disparagingly. "Couldn't you and Jimmy have done better than this on six thousand?"

"You might leave Jimmy out of it, if you don't mind," she told him briefly. "Also, as I've already said, you weren't asked to come, so if you don't like it you know what to do."

"What's Jimmy doing now?" he pursued.

"Working."

"And what are you doing?"

She frowned at him contemptuously, and he laughed.

"No need to get annoyed, Joan. I've got some good news for you. There's a nice flat in Cornwall House waiting for someone to live in. It's big—there's a huge panelled dining-room, a sitting-room you could lose yourself in that cost six hundred pounds to furnish, and two bedrooms that'd make a queen happy. And the Apex is paying for it and offering you an allowance of two thousand a year for overhead expenses. How does that appeal to you, Joan?"

She nodded.

"I know. And he has a key and drops in any night he feels like it. No, thank you, Snooper!"

He was almost pathetically shocked at her frankness.

"No, no—not that—Good Lord, Joan! Wouldn't have dreamed of suggesting it—don't know what made you imagine such a thing."

"Brought up the way I was, you get that sort of imagination," she informed him coolly. "If it isn't that, what's the game? Don't tell me there's a philanthropist behind it, because I shall shriek with laughter."

He fidgeted while she sat down and lighted a cigarette. It was a side of him she had never seen before, and she would have mocked at the idea of a fence being so sensitive if his distress had not been so palpably sincere.

"It's the Triangle," he said presently. "We've got to have several places in different parts of London, and that flat'll be one of them. All you have to do is to live there and spend your allowance any way you like. In return, any member must be able to come and go as he pleases. The place is really two small flats knocked into one, so there are two entrances. If you like, you can lock yourself in half of it at night, and you can have both the keys of one entrance. I'll have a special lock put on the communicating doors, too, if that'll make you feel more comfortable. The only thing is to have some solid tenant—when big expensive flats aren't occupied the splits are liable to be a little curious, and we can't afford to take risks. Won't you think it over again, Joan?"

She looked at him through a wreath of smoke.

"Who is the Apex—who are the Triangle, for that matter?" she asked him directly, and his agitation froze into a menacing stillness.

"That doesn't matter to you," he said. "All you need to know is that you're part of it, Joan, and you do as you're told."

She stood up and set the long cigarette-holder carefully between her white teeth. Hands thrust down into the pockets of her boyish coat, she stared him straight in the eyes.

"My name happens to be Sands, with a Miss in front of it," she said steadily. "All this Joaning is getting on my nerves. And as for the Triangle—I don't suppose I shall ever go to heaven, but I certainly don't intend to go to Aylesbury! I'll do my gold-digging where I don't have to trust a lot of other crooks with my safety. I'll take on your job, Snooper, but listen to this: I came into this Triangle of yours on the understanding that the crooked side of it didn't touch me, and I meant it. If you'll have those locks fixed, you can billet your crooks on me, because I want big money, and I want it bad. I'll take a chance of the busies getting on to me, but they'll never get me inside even as an accessory. When do I move?"

"This afternoon," said Snooper shortly. "And you can drop the high-and-mighty tone, Miss Sands. It cuts no ice. You're a crook, even if they don't know you on the Embankment—your brother's hardly ever out of stir, and the pair of you come straight from a family of crooks."

She opened the door and waved her hand towards the tiny hall.

"I don't intend to breed a family of Triangles, anyway," she remarked, and closed the door in his face.

James Mattock, returning that evening, was informed that "Mrs. Mattock" had left, and read the note that was waiting for him uneasily. He found her already installed in the flat in Cornwall House, and looked around at the palatial furnishing perplexedly.

"What's this, Joan?" he asked.

"Oh, a matchbox on stilts," she said sarcastically. "What did you think it was—a tram?"

She was stretched out in a deep-cushioned chair, her kimono lightly sashed about her, her little bare feet pillowed in the deep pile of the carpet. Her fluffy golden hair was elaborately untidy. She was arrestingly pretty and attractive.

"Who are you waiting for?" Mattock demanded roughly, but she shook her head and held out a silk-sheathed arm.

"Only you, Jimmy. I'm sorry I was snappy just now. I've had rather a trying day."

"Poor kid!" He knelt down beside her and laid an arm about her shoulders. "But, Joan, who's paying for this? We can't afford anything like this—it must cost thousands!"

"No—it's bringing us thousands," she said. "Two thousand a year, and we need it. And all it means is letting a few men come in and out. I'll tell you——"

He stood up suddenly and clutched her wrists fiercely.

"Joan! *Joan!*" His voice was tense with agony. "Oh, my darling, what have you done this for? I've got a job. Good—good God, Joan——"

"No—no—*listen*, Jimmy! You've got it all wrong. Yes, it *is* crooked, in a way," she went on desperately. "It's some silly gang. I don't know what they're after, but I'm not in it. Only they want a place to—to come to, sometimes, and there must be somebody always living there, and as I'm one of them, they got me."

"But——"

"Oh, yes, I know! I said I'd given it up, but I couldn't. They've got a hold on me that I can't break—that you can't break. The only way to break it is expensive, and I've got to have that money. Look—doesn't that mean anything to you?"

She drew back the sleeve and showed him her forearm, holding it up close to his eyes. It showed the faint marks of several small punctures, but Mattock only shook his head.

"I don't know what it is," he said dully. "But, of course, I'm a fool anyway…."

He sank into a chair and covered his face with his hands. She went on her knees beside him and pressed herself close to him.

"Jimmy——"

"Oh, yes … Joan …"

He took her hand and fondled it, and then he pressed it to his lips.

It was a very long time before he spoke again.

"I'm sorry. I'm making a fool of myself. But I was afraid."

The words fell from his lips in a painful monotone.

"I'll go out for a walk. I'll feel better then."

Storm, following Susan into the Leroy that night, saw the hatless figure striding madly down Piccadilly and was puzzled.

"You *are* doing something," Susan accused him. "I saw you this morning with a detective—Mr. Teal."

"I was being arrested," he said solemnly. "The charge was barratry, champerty, and attempted gum-boils, with complications. I explained that I was a Quaker and had never eaten tripe, so after ringing up Carter Paterson's to verify my alibi they let me go."

"I know he was a detective, because he's been in to see Lord Hannassay. Have you become a detective?"

"Not yet," he assured her, "though I hope to rise to that later. At present I'm looking for a job. I suppose you couldn't get me a master carpenter's ticket or a wood-repairer's diploma, could you?"

"What on earth do you want that for?" she asked, and Storm laughed.

"I'm interested in a saw-mill," he said gravely, "and I want to get inside it. Unfortunately the owner discourages visitors—and I'm curious! I want to rubber round that saw-mill! Why have a saw-mill in Billingsgate? Why not in Tottenham Court Road or Bloomsbury? They're just as aristocratic."

That faint smile of his flickered on his lips provocatively, and she knew him too well to question him further.

"A man's been following me about all day," she told him later. "I don't know what he wants, but he worries me. He hasn't tried to speak to me or anything like that—just trails round behind me wherever I go."

"I'm being followed too," he said with a lightness he didn't feel. "And my man isn't a detective, either! I'll tell you—we're beautiful, and he's an artist. We shall be on the walls of Burlington House next year. Or have you been married secretly and are we going to be compromised?"

"Stop fooling, Storm," she commanded.

He grinned.

"My dear soul, what else can one do? I'll push your little playmate's face in if you like, but you'll only have another man in his place tomorrow. Everybody's being followed—it must be a new game! Raegenssen's being followed, and Sir John Marker's being followed, and Joe Blaythwayt's being followed, and John Cardan's being followed, and Sir John Marker's private secretary's being followed, and I'm being followed, and Inspector Teal's being followed, and——"

"Don't you know what's at the back of it?"

"I know what, but I'd perjure my soul to know who!" said Storm. "And I take back what I said the other day. Respectability's exciting! It's the fiercest sport in the whole wide world bar haggis-shooting! Everyone's turning respectable now, even the crooks, just for the fun of the thing. Just look over to your right—that little cherub at the next table but one. See him? He's my little pet! My name's Mary, and he's a scorching lamb. We're inseparable, like Castor and Pollux or Swan and Edgar."

He waved a friendly hand to the small neatly dressed man at the adjoining table, and grinned when his salutation was coldly ignored. The girl was mystified.

"Who's that?" she asked. "He looks the most respectable man in the place."

"Oh, yes, he's respectable!" said Storm caustically. "He's only killed eleven men! That, old thing, is Comrade 'Gat' Morini, and for exactly four years all the policemen in New York and Chicago have been aching to put him in a hard chair and run two thousand volts through his spine. He's a professional gun artist, and I'll say he guns well! I ran into him in Chicago about two years back, and we exchanged compliments. His compliment missed my heart by just over two inches, and mine missed his by exactly one inch, so I always tell people I won on points. He loves me all right—you can stake your socks on uncle!"

The gaiety of his smile was entirely unforced, and in spite of herself Susan shivered, although the steel showed behind his careless self-confidence. Even so, she was afraid, for she knew his cheerful recklessness too well.

"Can't you do anything about it?" she suggested.

"What?" he demanded promptly. "There isn't a word against him. If I printed what I've just told you there'd be a libel action within the week, and young Storm wouldn't win it! He's committed eleven murders, he's been arrested eleven times, and he's been released just that number. It isn't a crime to follow anyone about."

Morini rose a moment after they did, and Storm was amused to see him greet a loiterer outside with every appearance of astonishment. As Storm handed Susan into a taxi the two reunited friends also decided to charter a taxi, and Storm grinned again.

Lord Hannassay's house was in Hamilton Place, and Storm felt that his luck was in when he caught sight of the massive figure of Oscar Raegenssen coming down the steps, for Raegenssen was a man he particularly wanted to see.

As they alighted, another taxi crawled past and stopped in Park Lane.

He watched Susan let herself in, and then hurried after the Swede.

"Excuse me," he said. "I'm Captain Arden, attached to the Special Branch at Scotland Yard."

"Well? Please be prief! I hof an appointment for supper."

He was in evening dress, with a foreign-looking cloak over his shoulders, and his Viking beard overflowed the white expanse of his shirt-front.

"That card you received—does the date mean anything to you? Did anything important happen to you on April the first, or did you do anything important?"

"I know nothing!" said Raegenssen curtly. "It is my pusiness. I hof entrosted t'bolicemans wit rezearch. April first is day of all the fools. Thot is all I know."

There was nothing to be done. Storm shrugged, raised his hat, said goodnight, and strolled on.

In his flat he found the patient Mr. Teal consoling himself for a long wait with one of his host's best cigars.

"Mecklen is my shadow," said Teal, yawning. "He's outside now."

"I saw him," said Storm. "He's got company—Morini trailed me home. For sheer plodding industry, give me the Yankee gunman!"

He threw his hat and gloves into a chair and walked over to the side table on which a decanter and syphon stood.

"Been helping yourself to a drink, Teal?" he murmured.

"I don't drink," said Mr. Teal piously. "It's bad for my heart. Fat men didn't ought to touch alcohol."

Storm carried the decanter to the light, held it up, and inspected the level of the liquid carefully. Then he called to Teal, and that stout abstainer came lethargically.

"See that little scratch in the glass?" said Storm. "That's the level I always keep the whisky up to. And now there's about a quarter of an inch more than there was when I went out. Some little pal of mine's been kind by stealth. I love these subterranean chariteers!"

He moistened the tip of one finger with the spirit and dabbed it on his tongue. Then he went hastily to the bathroom and rinsed his mouth out thoroughly.

"Aconite, I think," he remarked pleasantly when he returned. "Still, we'll send a peg round to the Home Office Analyst in the morning to make sure."

He sat down on the table, forearms resting on his knees, the cigarette that he was never without pointed optimistically skywards between his compressed lips. He grinned at Mr. Teal, and Mr. Teal's mouth widened half an inch momentarily, which was about the nearest Mr. Teal ever came to smiling.

"They seem to think you're important," drawled the detective callously, and Storm nodded.

"I was about due for it. I saw Raegenssen tonight coming out of Hannassay's—didn't know they were friends! Dear old Olaf the Seabird was quite rude. All these people seem to hate having to try and remember their pasts. What can you remember about yourself thirty years ago, Teal?"

"I daren't tell you, Captain Arden," said Inspector Teal.

They were talking seriously about fifteen minutes later when the telephone buzzed a warning, and Storm picked up the instrument.

"Hullo... yes... Susan!... Yes?"

He listened impatiently for a few moments, and then hung up the receiver violently.

"Let's go to a moonlight picnic, Teal!" he crisped, and picked up his hat as he sprang past the languid detective.

He led the way at a breakneck speed down the covered alley towards the courtyard which opens on to Piccadilly, but Inspector Teal, showing an agility which one would not have suspected, kept pace with him fairly comfortably. Just level with the porter's lodge, Storm stopped for a moment and thumbed down the safety catch of his automatic.

"I'll bet it's Lew," he said, and stepped calmly out of cover.

They had just reached the foot of the steps when a spurt of flame leapt out of the darkness of Albany Court Yard, and something sang viciously past his head.

"Rotten bad shooting, comrade," he remarked mildly.

Mr. Teal, however, missed the last part of that observation, for as he spoke Storm fired. There was a scream of pain, and a police whistle sounded shrilly. The next instant Inspector Teal was deafened by the roar of an open exhaust. Storm was already at the wheel of his long silver Hirondel, and Mr. Teal climbed in beside him briskly, A crowd had already gathered in the yard, and Storm made his Klaxon howl urgently.

A uniformed man signalled them to stop, but stepped aside when he recognized the detective.

"Arrest that man!" shouted Teal, as they went past.

The Hirondel skidded hectically into Piccadilly, swinging straight across the nose of an omnibus. There was a screech of grinding brakes, a chorus of angry yells, and the silver car lurched across the road and headed west, gathering speed with powerful ease.

They sailed down the slight gradient towards Hyde Park Corner, cutting in and owl of the stream of traffic with a daring that made Inspector Teal grip the side of the car hard and temporarily suspend mastication of his chewing gum.

"Something funny happening at Hannassay's," Storm explained, raising his voice to make himself heard. "Secretary rang me up—two men trying to get in the back door, and Hannassay in his bedroom, locked in, and can't be woken. I heard a shot, and then the line went dead. Respectability—huh!"

CHAPTER 4

TALKING OF TRIANGLES

Susan Hawthorne saw the door of the library opening slowly, and her heart stood still.

The man outside was Morini—she saw his baby blue eyes above the white silk muffler that was bound about the lower part of his face. She saw something else that was blue, also, but by no means baby like, something that came up like the head of a striking snake....

The electric light switch was close to her hand, and she clicked it down and ducked swiftly. Even as she did so the sudden darkness was split by a streak of orange fire, and a deafening explosion battered on her ear-drums and left them buzzing painfully. The next instant she had smashed the heavy telephone twice against the delicate lever of the switch and efficiently mangled the mechanism.

She moved silently away along the wall, and the terrible hunt began. The girl was helped by her knowledge of the room, but Morini crept after her with an uncanny accuracy in spite of the impenetrable blackness. Her chest was heaving so that it seemed as if every breath she took must betray her whereabouts as surely as a siren. The door was a little ajar, and the lights in the hall were on. There was no escape that way, for he would see her as she was silhouetted against the glare, and she had already had enough evidence of the grimness of his purpose. Once she saw him step cat-wise across the pencil of light that the hall bulbs smudged across the room, and with difficulty choked back the cry that would have been fatal. Once he fired again, at random, and she only just had time to drop behind a couch out of the way of the more accurate shot that followed instantly on the echo of the first when the brief flash had given him his bearings.

From outside came a swelling drone that grew in volume with startling speed and then died into a breathless purr coincident with the muffled squeal of rubber tearing on asphalt. Hardly two seconds later the bell at the back of the house rang stridently, and someone pounded on the front door.

Through the half-open window came Storm's voice:

"Stand clear of the lift gates, please! This is where I damage architecture!"

She saw Morini slip through the door and out into the corridor, and then with a dreadful premonition she rushed to the window and flung up the lower sash. Storm and Inspector Teal were on the step, and Storm already had his automatic crammed against the Yale lock and his finger was on the trigger.

"Storm! Stop!" she cried, and he looked round. "Morini's in the hall and the back door's broken in—he'll get you as you come in and escape easily!"

He only hesitated for a second. Then—

"That be bullraced for a yarn!" he sang out recklessly. "All aboard for hell!"

She heard the explosion as she dashed across the room and opened the door wide. The two men crashed into the hall, but she did not look at them. She was straining her eyes into the shadows at the end of the passage which led to the servants' quarters, and, used as she was to the darkness, she saw Morini a space of time before they did ... saw his gun leap up ... and hurled the priceless vase she carried....

Three automatics detonated almost as one.

Morini was hit by the vase as he pressed the trigger, and his shot went high, splintering the transom above the front door. As Storm fired back he raced towards the servants' entrance.

Mr. Teal laid an unexpectedly gentle arm about the girl's shoulders and led her into the library.

"There's another light," she said, trying to keep her voice level. "I smashed the big switch. A reading lamp, on the table—it's lucky Morini didn't find it."

Teal, groping round, located the lamp and turned it on. A moment later Storm returned. He had rolled back his sleeve and was endeavouring to tie his handkerchief round his wrist, and to her surprise and disgust she said the conventional thing.

"You're hurt."

"Not a bit of it," he assured her. "Only a graze—dear old Gat's going off, and I think I must be, too. It's time some of us old soldiers retired—Gat and I wouldn't have missed each other in Chicago!"

"He got away?" said Teal.

Storm nodded.

"That's the day's safety bet—clean! He got through into Park Lane, and there was a fast car waiting for him. All lights out, so I missed the number. It was Morini, of course, but we couldn't get a conviction—the defence'd produce half a dozen small men with washed-out blue eyes that you couldn't distinguish from Morini if they were all dressed alike and had scarves spliced on their dials." He looked at Teal, and his gunmetal grey eyes were alight with challenge. "And this is only the opening chorus. You wait till the balloon goes up!"

Inspector Teal stroked his bowler.

"Where's Hannassay?" he asked prosaically.

"Je-rusalem! I'd forgotten him. The fireworks ought to have woken him if nothing else will."

Upstairs, after an unavailing assault on the door of Hannassay's bedroom, Storm went around to the adjoining bathroom, climbed out of the window, and edged his way perilously along a two-inch ledge with the assistance of a rickety drainpipe. He came back to report that the room was empty.

"He must be out," Susan said. "It never occurred to me, though—he generally tells me where and when he's going so that any important messages can be sent on."

"Did he always lock his bedroom?" asked Storm, and she nodded.

"He had a safe there with all his private papers. The room's always locked as soon as his valet has swept it out to make the bed."

"Let's hope it wasn't burgled," said Teal. "Didn't you say there were two men at the back door?"

They went round to the back, and the detective made an inspection with the aid of his pocket torch. The door had been burst open with a jemmy of a peculiar pattern, and Inspector Teal examined the marks with a professional eye.

"That's Prester John's work," he declared. "I know that jemmy of his—he invented it himself, and it's guaranteed to make a safe look like a sardine tin."

"Get back to the Yard and send an all-station call for Morini and John," instructed Storm. "Send Henderson up here for the rest of the night, and tell Rankin to be ready to relieve him at eight tomorrow. Find out where they took Mecklen, and ring me here. I'll wait till Henderson arrives…. There mayn't be another attempt tonight, but if there are any strategists on the staff of the Triangle there may be. Oh, and tell Henderson to bring some burglarious gadgets along with him—I want to see if that safe's all right. I can't get in through the window—there's a patent fastening inside, and not enough handhold outside for an athletic fly."

When the detective had gone, he made a careful round of the room, but found nothing. Then he turned to the girl.

"I don't know what it is you're supposed to have discovered," he said, "but there's a bad hombre in the background who seems to think you spoil the view! Can you remember anything unusual you've come across in Hannassay's papers?"

She thought for a moment.

"No…. Well, yes, a few days ago he made me search his files for something about a man named Mattock. Somebody who forged a cheque with Lord Hannassay's signature and was caught and sent to prison."

"Did you mention that to anyone?"

"I did, as a matter of fact, though I suppose I shouldn't have. It was an uncle of mine on my mother's side—I didn't know where he was, but in the City the other day I ran into Uncle Joe and he made me have lunch with him. He always was interested in crime, and of course he started talking about it almost immediately. Then I happened to mention Mattock's dossier, and he seemed awfully interested—but Uncle Joe's interested in the weirdest things."

"Uncle Joe who?" Storm asked.

"Blaythwayt. He's got a job as manager——"

"Of the City and Continental Bank, Lombard Street, which same firm is honoured with the account of Olaf the Seabird. Je-rusalem! Things do run in circles! Why isn't this Regent's Park?"

Just before Henderson arrived a call came through on the upstairs telephone, and Storm learned that Lew Mecklen had been taken to St. George's Hospital suffering from nothing more serious than a flesh wound in the thigh, and that a detective was already guarding him. So far he had refused to make any statement.

"I'll see him first thing tomorrow," said Storm. "Get hold of the Assistant Commissioner. Lew must be charged tomorrow morning."

He shook hands with Henderson and led the way upstairs. From the detective he received a small leather wallet of fine steel tools and reviewed them critically.

"Anyone might think I was going to smash a strongroom," he murmured. "Gather round for a demonstration of expert yeggship!"

It took him only a couple of minutes to manipulate the lock, and then he straightened himself and pushed open the door.

The safe was untouched, and nothing appeared to have been disturbed.

"This is not exciting," he remarked, and re-locked the door on the outside with his instruments.

They returned to the library, and he gave Henderson his instructions.

"Of course, it's all wrong," he concluded. "The Triangle are so keen on broadcasting their visiting cards—why haven't we got a memento of their call?"

While Henderson talked to the girl, Storm embarked on a fresh search of the house. He combed every inch of every room and corridor, and was raking the study upstairs when Lord Hannassay himself arrived. Storm heard the voices downstairs, and came down with the irritating belief that he had overlooked something. As a matter of fact, he had, for as he descended the stairs he saw something gleaming at the edge of the rug in the hall.

It was a silver triangle similar to the one Inspector Teal had showed him, and had obviously been kicked out of sight when they charged in—it was barely visible except when it caught the light in a certain way.

Susan was just telling Lord Hannassay her story when Storm stroked in.

"Look for the trade mark on every genuine article," he said. "I hate these anonymous presents!"

He held out the token in one triumphant palm as he spokes and the peer turned to greet him with a smile.

"Oh, Captain Arden——"

His voice trailed away, and they saw him suddenly go white. Henderson was just in time to catch him as he fell.

Inspector Teal stood on the threshold, a burly figure, hat in hand.

"I just dropped in——" he was starting to explain, and then he caught sight of the limp form in Henderson's arms and his jaw dropped.

Storm put an arm around Hannassay and brushed Henderson aside. Then he jerked the unconscious man from the floor and, heavy as he was, carried him without any apparent effort to the chesterfield.

He left the two detectives to apply restoratives, and led the girl over to the window.

Storm was the last man on earth she would ever have associated with nerves. He was too essentially virile—dynamic—and there was too much grim strength in every line of his lean, tanned face. His eyes were as cold and steady as chilled granite, and his every least movement showed the supple grace of the born fighting man. And yet the hand he laid on her arm trembled, and when he spoke she was amazed to detect the faintest unevenness in his voice.

"Hannassay fainted as though he'd seen a ghost, didn't he?" he said. "And I know the ghost. My God!—— Life's queer!"

"Was it the Triangle you showed him?" she asked.

He shook his head, and his white teeth gleamed in a mirthless smile.

"The Triangle brought it, but the ghost's name was Mattock!" said Storm.

CHAPTER 5

BLAYTHWAYT ON CLUES

In spite of the hour, the nucleus of a crowd had already gathered outside, with that peculiar instinct for the morbid which is the gift of crowds; and Storm had to fight his way to a taxi through the first batch of eager reporters.

He found the vanguard of another contingent sitting patiently on his doorstep when he got back to the Albany, and was instantly deluged with questions.

"I can give you no information at present," he repeated for the umteenth time. "Also, I want to get a couple of hours' rest before breakfast. Try your luck later."

Fifteen minutes afterwards he rolled into bed and fell at once into a calm, untroubled sleep.

He breakfasted at seven-thirty in his dressing-gown, already bathed and shaved, and he was looking as cool and fresh as if he had had nine hours' healthy slumber instead of two. The table was littered with newspapers, and folded sheets were propped up against every available support in front of him. He read while he ate. In spite of his own reticence, someone at the Yard had evidently talked unguardedly, for the stop-press columns were full of sensational hints in small closely set type.

"This will be all over the world in three hours," he said resignedly, and Inspector Teal, who had dropped in for a cup of coffee, nodded.

"I don't know that it matters much. The real point of advertising a crime is to call up the noses, and I doubt if there'll be much nosing the Triangle. Do you know, when they searched Lew he had five hundred pounds on him? You can't nose a gang who can pay that well."

Storm drove down to the hospital after breakfast to see the injured gunman, and found him confidently defiant.

"Ef yew think yew're gonna git a squeak outer me, yew sure gotten another guess comin', Cap."

Storm sat down by the side of the bed and lighted a cigarette. He had already surmised that it would be difficult to make Lew Mecklen talk, and he had the disadvantage of being on the right side of the law, which put the more obvious methods of securing information out of the question.

"I don't know what the law is in the States," he said, "and I don't know if you know what it is over here. Anyway, in England we have a thing called King's Evidence, and it's saved one or two people's necks before now."

Lew shook his head.

"Quit kiddin', son," he advised. "Yew cain't hang me fer doin' a bit of fancy shootin' around yore haid. Yew weren't injured any. All yew bulls c'n do is ter lock me up fer a time—an' then I've gotten yew all skinned a mile!"

The thought seemed to amuse him, for his big chest heaved with silent guffaws.

"You can get your sentence reduced by helping us to round up the rest of the gang," Storm pointed out. "And I can get you a longer stretch if you're obstinate."

"Yew c'n go ter hell any time," said Mecklen, and chuckled again. "Aw—mother! Take 'im outside an' tie a halo round 'is baby braow. Tell me good-bye, buddy, an' go home, or yew'll make me die laughin'! Put ole Lew in jail?" he scoffed. "I'm an Amurrican cidizen, bo, an' don't yew fergit it."

"Since when has America been using the slums of Leipzig as a breeding-ground?" inquired Storm mildly. "Mecklen, you synthetic Americans make me tired! In case you're interested, I'll say you're nothing more than a fourth-rate Hun thug, and your pal Morini's about as American as you are—which means he's a plain ornery Dago!"

He held a consultation with the house-surgeon, and was unaccountably annoyed at the report he received.

"Of course, if you insist, Captain Arden, I can do nothing; but I strongly advise against moving him."

"How long is it likely to be before we can take him away?" Storm asked, and the doctor spread out his hands.

"It may be any time," was his unsatisfactory answer. "I'll do my best to get him patched up as soon as possible—you can be sure of that. But if you move him now, you may be sued for damages later, and that wouldn't do you any good."

As Storm drove back along Piccadilly he saw that nearly every poster advertising the early editions of the evening papers bore an enlarged repro-duction of the Alpha Triangle. He bought a copy of the *Evening Record* and found the latest Fleet Street conjectures stunted across four columns and crowned with bloodcurdling headlines.

He rang up Susan from Scotland Yard, and had the disappointment of hearing that she was already engaged for lunch.

"Lord Hannassay leaves for a holiday the day after tomorrow," she add-ed. "He's going down through Spain, then to Teneriffe, and finishing up with a tour down the West African coast."

This was news to Storm, and, incidentally, an unexpected blessing for with Lord Hannassay out of the way a responsibility would be off his hands.

"Who are you lunching with?" he demanded jealously.

"Uncle Joe."

"Damn Uncle Joe!" snarled Storm, and her soft, amused laughter reached his ears before he hung up the receiver.

Joe Blaythwayt had come into his own. Few of the callers he interviewed that morning failed to make some remarks about the Triangle, and Joe made the best of the secondhand scraps of out-of-the-way knowledge he had acquired from Inspector Teal.

"I know criminals," he would say to the scoffers, with morbid satisfaction.

Nevertheless, the Joe Blaythwayt who discussed evil-doers and evil deeds with a Central Detective-Inspector in his leisure moments was a very different man from the Joe Blaythwayt who conducted the business of the Lombard Street branch of the City and Continental Bank. Still alert, eyes still ready to twinkle, frequent of laughter—yes. But eminently practical and business-like.

He was business-like when he held his usual weekly interview with Raegenssen in the snug little office to which the roar of traffic came but faintly.

It was a highly business-like occasion—one of those colossal moments during which the most unassuming man is justified in donning horn-rimmed spectacles and a cigar, sticking his thumbs in the armholes of his waistcoat, and generally adopting the accent and demeanour of the Man of Big Business. For Raegenssen was augmenting his account by a sum which exceeded even his ordinary weekly contributions—and they would have represented Blaythwayt's income for a year.

He dropped a wad of hundred-pound notes on the table as carelessly as a merely rich man might have paid in a handful of fivers. The manager counted them with a similar dispassionate air, and passed them over to the cashier as if they were so much waste paper; for Joe Blaythwayt was a stickler for the etiquette of his profession.

But, business over, he degenerated into a human being.

"Of course, you've seen the papers," he remarked.

The Swede nodded.

"It is ter pig bluff," he said.

He glared at the inoffensive Joe as though he suspected him of being in league with the gang.

"Plackmail!" he declared violently. "Ant I shall nod bay!"

Blaythwayt watched the departure of the huge Viking figure in its ill-fitting clothes thoughtfully.

Oscar Raegenssen drove back to Cockspur Street, where he occupied a palatial suite of offices in Scandinavia House. He sat over his desk for a long time, his big, capable hands toying with a ridiculously small pencil. Crag-like jaw outthrust, he stared truculently into space. His leonine head was set at an arrogant angle—he looked by no means an easy man to intimidate.

Presently he pressed the bell at his side, and there was a knock on the door.

"Gom!" he commanded curtly, and Mattock entered.

Raegenssen took the little bundle of pink slips from his clerk's hand and spread them out on the blotting-paper in front of him. With ponderous delib-eration he scrawled his thick untidy signature in the bottom right-hand corner of each; and when he had finished he gathered them up, counted them, and studied every one minutely.

"Two are missing!"

"I have them here," Mattock said. "I've written nothing on them—they're for large sums."

"Why?"

Mattock showed his teeth.

"You forget my reputation, sir," he said gently.

Raegenssen regarded his clerk inscrutably. Mattock met the stare bold-ly—almost insolently. Then, without a word, Raegenssen wrote out the cheques, blotted them, and handed them back.

Although Raegenssen's were vaguely described in the directory as "Agents," the City knew them very little. It was rumoured that the Swede was a gigantic speculator in foreign exchanges, and certainly large sums of exotic currencies passed through the Scandinavia House offices and between London and the firm's correspondents in Marseilles, Lisbon, Amsterdam and Genoa.

"Next week ter will pe ingoing monies. You will nodify Amstertam as usual. That iss all. Go!"

"There was something I wanted to mention, sir, if you'll excuse me," Mattock said.

"Gondinue—yess?"

"The safe you have in the office is of an old pattern. It would be child's play to an expert safe-breaker."

"Gondinue—yess?"

"Mightn't it be wiser, sir, to get a new safe—or, better still, keep the pa-pers at the bank? If anything should happen, the police would be after me at once. Once a man's made a break, they never let him go."

"Gondinue—yess?"

"They are rather private papers, sir?"

Cold blue eyes bored mercilessly into insolent brown ones.

"Hof you seen ter babers?"

"No, sir, but—"

"What mages you tink we hof anydings to gonceal?"

"Nothing, sir, but the private correspondence of any business—"

"Gondinue—yess?"

"That's all, sir," Mattock concluded lamely.

"Thang you. Go!"

Towards three o'clock Raegenssen rose, tidied his desk, picked up his battered felt hat.

The safe to which Mattock had taken exception stood in one corner of the room—a great massive affair that seemed to occupy half the office. It was eight feet high by three feet wide by three feet deep, and it was Oscar Raegenssen's especial joy. There was a glitter of amusement in his eyes as he comprehended its imposing bulk.

He locked the door of his sanctum and passed through the outer office where his two clerks and Mattock worked. Only Mattock was left, and he was at that moment drawing on his waterproof preparatory to departure, for Raegenssen's closed early.

"It's come on to rain, sir," he remarked. "Have you your car outside, or shall I fetch a taxi?"

"Ter gar is in St. James's Square. You will blease summon it."

Storm, endeavouring to appear interested in Inspector Teal's lengthy monologue on the psychology of the criminal, had been suddenly seized with what struck him as being an exceptionally brilliant idea. He took up the telephone and gave a number in the City.

"I want to speak to Mr. Blaythwayt, please.... Captain Arden of the Criminal Investigation Department."

He was unpleasantly conscious of Mr. Teal's curious gaze, and fervently wished that he had delayed putting his idea into practice until that portly sleuth had taken his leave.

"Hullo ... yes.... Can you see me almost immediately, Mr. Blaythwayt? This Triangle affair—it's an awful nuisance, I know; but it can't be helped.... You're just going out to lunch? ... No, I'm afraid I can't—I've got a lot of other things to attend to this afternoon. Look here, if I shan't intrude, will you lunch with me? ... Susan Hawthorne? Je-ru-salem, that's funny! ... Yes—known her for years! I remember now; you're her uncle, aren't you? ... No, I'm sure she won't mind. I'd tell you over the phone, but I hate invisible backchatters! ... I'll pick you up at the *Record* office in under ten minutes. So long!"

"She's a nice kid, that Miss Hawthorne," observed the somniloquent Mr. Teal, as Storm put down the instrument.

Storm was not inclined to be conversational on the subject.

"M'm. You know, sir, I always say a young man ought to get married. It kind of puts a kick into his work. And if there's kids, it gives him something to work for. Now, I was married when I was a youngster of twenty-two, walking my beat like any cub copper. Well, believe me, sir, it made a new man of me, and when we had our First—that was four months after——"

"Teal," said Storm awfully, "you're shocking me. Go away and blow froth."

He collected Blaythwayt at the bank, and they parked the car in Salisbury Square and proceeded on foot to the Fleet Street restaurant where Joe had arranged to meet his niece. She was surprised to see Storm, and, in his state of exaggerated self-consciousness, he thought she was a trifle displeased. Thinking things over, he realised the painful transparency of his ruse.

"I'm sorry to butt in on you like this," he said. "Fact is, it's important for me to see your uncle, and I shan't have ten consecutive free seconds this afternoon."

Joe Blaythwayt tucked his napkin into his waistcoat and beamed at them both impartially.

"Anything I can do for you, Captain Arden——"

This placed Storm in a quandary, for he hadn't the foggiest notion of an excuse for his presence. The timely arrival of an overworked waiter gave him a few minutes' respite, during which time his brain seethed frantically, and at the end of it he was prepared to be fluently plausible.

"Teal is always talking about you, Mr. Blaythwayt. He says you're a great criminologist."

"Well, I've read a bit about it," admitted Joe modestly. "It's difficult, of course, to do much as an amateur. Now, this Triangle, Captain Arden, is the very first time I've ever been mixed up in anything of the sort personally. I shall put it in my book—I'm writing a book, you know. Did Teal tell you that?"

Storm nodded. He glanced at Susan and then exerted himself not to meet her eye, for her initial annoyance had given place to quiet amusement. He felt her eyes upon him, and went hot and cold.

"And you absolutely can't remember a thing about Harchester that you could associate with the Triangle?" he asked.

"Not a thing," said Blaythwayt with a vigorous shake of his head. "Of course, some people must have been jealous—I was jolly good at Rugger in my time, and Harchester thinks more of brawn than of brains, so I became captain of the school rather out of my turn. But that's all so long ago I can't remember details. Certainly nobody disliked me to my face, whatever they may have thought."

"Who was the bird you cut out?"

Blaythwayt wrinkled his brow.

"I can remember him a bit. A big fellow, no good at games—he was so gawky everyone used to rag him about it. Bull-something ... Bull ... Bulsaid—that's it! He was brilliantly clever, I remember that. I often wonder what happened to him. He ought to have become a great scientist. But, bless you, Bulsaid never kicked. He was too quiet. One of the most easy-going fellows I've ever met."

Susan turned to Storm with a smile.

"Is Uncle's school life so terrifically important?" she asked sweetly.

"Fearfully," Storm assured her gravely.

She shook her head, and all mischief was in her eyes.

"You're forgiven," she said, and the simple Joe blinked uncomprehendingly at the laughter that followed.

The rest of the meal was delightful, and Storm listened soberly to the account of Blaythwayt's literary aspirations, interspersing the recital at intervals with the most innocent expressions of admiration.

"About this Triangle, though—seriously!" he said later. "There's going to be trouble, and it's going to be tough! You've heard what they've done already—tried to poison me, shot me up, and sent the gentle Gat gunning for Susan. And that's before they've committed a single crime against the men they've threatened. I say 'threatened,' although no threats have been put on paper in so many words. But I guess if I got one of those little valentines I'd look under my bed before I got into it, whether they said, 'This is where you get yours,' or not! What do you make of it?"

"Crime on a big scale," said Blaythwayt impressively. "It's a solid possibility, as a commercial investment, to a man with capital and genius."

Joe's simplicity was his great charm.

"As I see it, Captain Arden, criminals would never be caught if they didn't leave Clues. Consequently, in order to be a successful criminal, all you have to do is to master the art of not leaving Clues. And, as a detective, you will only run the Triangle to earth by looking for and following up Clues. The ordinary police methods of searching for Clues are inadequate. There are too many hindrances—you should be able to enter houses without search warrants, take people into custody and interrogate them on the slightest provocation, and adopt any means you choose in order to accumulate evidence. The Detective should be above the Law."

Storm shook his head.

"I'm not a pukka detective," he said, "and Teal owes me ten bob."

"Are you being funny," demanded Susan, "or is there likely to be more trouble?"

He looked at her steadily, eyes half closed, his cigarette between his lips.

"You're scared!" he said.

"Well, I'm not absolutely praying to be killed."

There was a short silence, for he had no wish to alarm her unduly. And yet, to minimise the danger would not be the thought of anyone but a born fool. He turned his eyes on Blaythwayt.

"Are *you* scared?"

"I can't say I've thought about it seriously," confessed Joe. "I really don't see that I have much to fear—far less, anyway, than I have to fear from bank robbers and kiters—that's an American word for bank swindlers," he explained unnecessarily. "Inspector Teal, my very good friend, always says that violent crime is foreign to this country. A few attempts by dagoes and suchlike, perhaps, but they can easily be rounded up. It's just a coincidence that a threat should have come to me. One can understand them being sent to the others. Public men are bound to receive threatening letters, but they very rarely come to anything."

Storm would have liked to point out the minor coincidences of alcohol diluted with aconite, and firework displays in Albany Court Yard and Hamilton Place, but refrained.

"What's your honest opinion, Kit?" Susan persisted.

"Oh, well, Mecklen's in hospital, and we've got Morini's description. There may be a bit of fun before he's found," he conceded easily, "but I don't think you need be afraid. I'd like you to stay with some friends of mine, though, while Hannassay's away. You don't want to be alone in that huge house—besides, it's so dull. You'll like 'em—Terry Mannering's a great lad. But don't go liking him too much, because he's already married!"

"You needn't be afraid of that," she told him coldly, and did not realise for five minutes why he smiled.

Blaythwayt pulled out his watch.

"I'm afraid I really must be off, Captain Arden. It's nearly a quarter to three—please don't think I'm rude, my dear fellow, but Business..."

When Joe Blaythwayt spoke of weighty matters he always gave the impression that he talked in capital letters.

In Salisbury Square he inspected every inch of the silver Hirondel with an almost childish awe.

"I wish I could afford a car like this," he said wistfully. "Can she Go?"

"Go?" scoffed Storm. "She's the fastest thing on wheels that you can use on the road! I've tried her up to a hundred and fifteen at Brooklands." He had an inspiration. "Get in and let's have a run—I'll be taking Susan home, anyway."

"Can we really?" said Joe, and Storm had shepherded him into the back seat before he had quite decided whether to accept the invitation.

He had, apparently, forgotten the calls of Business.

They whirled round Trafalgar Square, and Storm hesitated momentarily between Cockspur Street and the Mall. He decided on Cockspur Street, and to this day the thought of the far-reaching effects of that casual decision makes him gasp.

Oscar Raegenssen, waiting for the arrival of his luxurious Navarre cabriolet, saw a man whom he particularly wished to avoid sauntering down from Pall Mall. He looked up and down the street, but there was no sign of his car. With a slight gesture of annoyance he started to cross the road.

He stepped directly in front of the bonnet of Storm's car. The fine drizzle that was falling lay on the road like thin oil, and Storm knew at once that it would be impossible to pull up in time on the treacherous surface, for he was doing over thirty miles an hour. He wrenched the wheel over to the right as he braked, and one wing just caught Raegenssen as the Hirondel skidded round. Luckily the street was almost deserted, and the silver car turned completely round in a space of feet and fetched up against the kerb, facing back towards Trafalgar Square.

It was a magnificent piece of driving, but the most masterly driver in the world could not have saved Raegenssen from that blow.

Storm jumped from his seat and ran towards the stunned man, an excited Joe hard on his heels. He picked the Swede up in his arms and carried him to the pavement. He was loosening the clothes about Raegenssen's throat, with Blaythwayt trying ineffectually to assist, when a tall, oldish man elbowed his way through the crowd and knelt down beside him.

"Your boss, Mattock," remarked Storm briefly.

Raegenssen was not badly hurt. He was even then recovering consciousness. His eyelids flickered dazedly, and his lips framed an almost inaudible word.

"*Sylvia ... Sylvia...*"

"He's coming round," said Storm to the constable who had joined the group. "He stepped out right in front of me without looking where he was going, but I only grazed him."

"This gentleman is Captain Arden of the Special Branch," announced Blaythwayt pompously.

Storm was searching in his pockets for a card, and Susan saw that his jaw was tightened up so that the muscles stood out in faintly serrated knots, and his eyes were abnormally level.

Wondering, she looked at the others. Joe Blaythwayt was standing by importantly with a broad smile on his face, and yet he was trembling with excitement. Mattock had looked up from applying first aid to his employer, and was staring at one of the other two—she could not be sure which. His features were contorted, his mouth working, and there was a blaze in his eyes that set her heart pounding against her ribs like a trip-hammer.

CHAPTER 6

IMMIGRATION OF THE UNGODLY

Storm breakfasted with Hannassay on the morning his lordship left for his holiday. It was an unexpected invitation, but Lord Hannassay came to the reason of it without delay.

"I have made arrangements for you to be given complete charge of the case," he said. "You will probably get the official intimation when you reach the Yard."

His usual abruptness of manner was conspicuously absent. He spoke restrainedly and rather artificially, like a man who has planned out his speech in advance and intends to adhere rigidly to a premeditated sequence of words.

"You will have *carte blanche*, and you may use any means you think fit within—and, by special arrangement, without—the law to round up the Alpha Triangle. I am convinced that the menace with which we are faced is the greatest in the history of crime."

"I'm glad to have your support," said Storm. "I more than scent rodents myself! But I thought I was in for some job persuading the authorities I wasn't an alarmist."

The peer nodded absently and stirred his coffee. He seemed hardly to have heard Kit's remark, and when he spoke again it was in the same mechanical way as before, as though he neither anticipated nor required interruption.

"Strictly between ourselves, Captain Arden, I know the secret of the Alpha Triangle." He pushed away his plate and lighted a cigar. "That, I think, should surprise you. You will ask, also, why I do not place my information at the service of the police. There is a reason for that—a reason which I cannot explain to you now, but which will be clear to you when, and if, you run the gang to earth. The Alpha Triangle is an organisation which came into existence originally for the purposes of revenge—the purpose for which it was organised by a genius who, I sometimes think, is mad. You have, of course, been interested in the murder—it was murder, by the way—of Joubert, a few months ago. That was the first crime of the Triangle, and yet I offer for your contemplation the paradox that until five minutes before the murder there was no Alpha Triangle."

Storm sat without comment, although he was literally amazed at the confession he had just heard. Lord Hannassay, whose eyes throughout had been fixed vacantly on the opposite wall, after the fashion of a child repeating a lesson, looked at him suddenly and surprised that look of consternation.

"Exactly—I am deliberately admitting that I am, in a sense, an accessory," he said with a smile. "I must ask you to accept the extraordinary situation, the cause of which will be apparent to you at the successful conclusion of your labours. The Alpha Triangle, then," he went on, "from being a purely revengeful society, became an acquisitively criminal one. I ask you to take my word on that score, for although the Triangle has committed no acquisitive crimes up to date, I have every reason to believe that it will make up for the deficiency in the future. This transition, already an accomplished fact—in the spirit, if not in the deed—must have already occurred to you as a probability. What, indeed, could be more natural than that such an organisation, having established a powerful and unscrupulous society for taking its vengeances, should visualise the possibilities for material gain latent in such a society? The power is there—a power, Captain Arden, which, if you knew its magnitude and the utter, cold, superhuman inflexibility of the man who controls it, might make even you, in spite of your reputation for physical prowess and indomitable courage, turn back from the task you seem so eager to undertake."

For all the precise, calculated levelness of Lord Hannassay's voice, there was an earnestness behind his pedantic sentences that pricked the small hairs on the nape of Storm's neck like a chill wind. And yet this was a purely reflex sensation, for Storm smiled lightly and flicked the ash from his cigarette with leisured care.

"I'll take the risk," he drawled.

Lord Hannassay nodded slowly.

"I thought you would," he said. "You're the sort that would."

"And that's not what they call 'sand,' either," said Storm, and his mocking smile flitted elusively across his lips. "I'll give it you, Lord Hannassay, straight, that I'd rather tackle anything else under the sun than this Triangle business. And I could throw in my hand—I'm not a detective, and I'm not even in Special Branch regularly. I stay on simply because it's a challenge. I've got some sort of a reputation among disreputable people—*Storm won't be beat till he's buried, and maybe not then*, they'll tell you. And they've got it all wrong! It's pride—arrogance—conceit—anything you care to call it. But all it stews down to is just that I'm too bucked with myself—it'd break my heart to have to admit I was beaten! I'd sooner go down fighting, because if I'm beaten that way I'll never have to admit it."

He spoke without a trace of affectation, and yet it was an analysis he had never made to anyone in his life before. Later, Lord Hannassay knew the reason for that frankness, yet even at the time Storm's simple directness appealed to him.

The peer rose and held out his hand.

"I call that 'sand,'" he said quietly. "Captain Arden, you have my very best wishes. I'm—scared of that Triangle. It's got me jumpy—that's honest." He had relapsed into his old jerky style. "It's bigger than I ever dreamed such a thing could be. Queer thing: sometimes I don't care, sometimes I wish I could speak. Probably you'll be killed; sometimes I'm sorry, sometimes it doesn't seem to matter. Yet I like you extraordinarily. Look an easy man to frighten?"

Storm viewed the splendid physique, seemingly unimpaired by age, and his glance wandered to the masterful poise of the big head on the broad shoulders. He smiled as he shook his head.

"I'm afraid," said Lord Hannassay with a grim matter-of-factness that was more startling than any emotional outburst.

"Is that serious?" Storm asked incredulously, and Hannassay nodded.

"Same as you—I'd like to be out of it. Sooner or later, I think, I'll have to pay for my knowledge of it. And yet, if I placed that knowledge at your disposal, even on your assurance that it would go no further, I should be little better off. The Triangle is supremely callous—you understand that, Captain Arden? A human life—half a dozen, if you like—*that*!"

He snapped his fingers contemptuously. Storm concentrated on blowing three smoke rings interlinked with accurate symmetry.

"Who is Bulsaid?" he asked carelessly.

He had expected to create a sensation, and in this he was not disappointed. Hannassay froze into a rock-like immobility. His pale blue eyes were like chips of ice, brittle and glistening.

"Bulsaid," he whispered.

"Bulsaid—the man who was supplanted by Joe Blaythwayt at school, whose mean little soul conceived even at that age an undying hatred of those who passed him in the race. Bulsaid, the man whom Sir John Marker beat at the Clayston bye-election in March, 1897. Bulsaid, the scientist whose seriousness and anarchical views caused him to be ragged rather unmercifully at Oxford, particularly by a man named James Mattock—a man of good family but with too much money, a popular, noisy, carefree youngster whom Bulsaid came to add to the list of enemies his warped mind never forgot. Bulsaid, the man who has you, Lord Hannassay, in his clutches, and who will perhaps never let you go. Bulsaid, the brilliant scholar, the fanatic, the unforgiving hater, the embittered, half-mad genius—Hugo Arden Bulsaid, my father!"

The Under Secretary said nothing, but the ramrod set of his giant frame was now only superficial, for Storm saw that the whole man was vibrant with tiny tremors. Every line on that stern, dominant face was graven deeper and sterner, and little chips of hot steel glinted behind the icy blue eyes.

"Hugo Arden Bulsaid," said Storm slowly, "the man who made Oscar Raegenssen, and who will break him; the man who'll kill me one day, if I don't kill him!"

"So you know," breathed Hannassay. "And I needn't have been so secretive about my knowledge."

He placed his thin cigar between his white teeth and walked across to the window, whence he could look out on the green beauty of Hyde Park dappled with the golden glory of the morning sun.

"Yes.... I know," said Storm after a silence, and the peer turned.

"Captain Arden," he said, "do you hate your father?"

Storm shook his head.

"No—it's just the luck of the game." He paused. "But you hate him."

"I hate him, I think, more than I had ever believed it was possible to hate a man," said Hannassay with a cold gentleness that was like the caress of vitriol. "I hate him from the ultimate depths of my soul. I would kill him without compunction and without fear this day ... but for one thing."

Storm pitched the stump of his cigarette into a flowerpot and buttoned his coat. In those trivial actions he dispelled the tense gloom of the atmosphere as the dawning sunshine breaks up the miasma of a swamp—it was a quality born of his clean, fresh wholesomeness.

"I must be going," he said cheerily. "Hope you have a good holiday."

Lord Hannassay did not ring for the butler, but himself escorted his guest to the door and opened it. He held out his hand and took Kit Arden's in a firm grip.

"*Au revoir*," said Storm, but Hannassay's head made a slight, half-amused negative movement.

"*Adieu*," he said. "A premonition, Captain Arden.... We shall never meet again.... Good-bye!"

Storm drove back to New Scotland Yard, and found the indefatigable Teal waiting for him. That stout detective was working his jaws rhythmically, and a folded copy of the morning paper was propped up on Storm's table before him, while a litter of papers and printed forms of all colours were spread across the blotter.

"There's a few notes you asked for," he remarked. "I've been looking through them."

He rose ponderously, and Storm took his place at the desk.

"I can see somebody's been at them," said Storm gently, and proceeded to attempt to restore order. "Those files of the *Record* arrived yet?"

"They're at the bottom."

Storm swept the chaos to one side and opened the package which lay beneath. Then he smoothed out the two newspapers he found and began to skim methodically through the pages. It was some minutes before he found the passage he had expected to find, and then the form of it was entirely unsuspected. It consisted of the book reviews, and most of the space was occupied by criticisms of a certain work.

"You read this, Teal," he observed after a while, "and then tell Uncle Joe to give up literature as a career. He's no idea what budding authors have to put up with!"

The commentary was one of the most scathing Storm had ever read. At the head of it was the title *Devolution*, by Hugo Bulsaid; and, a little lower down, appeared the name of the reviewer—signed, as he had anticipated, John Cardan. There was one paragraph:

We are, frankly, amazed that a firm of such standing as Messrs. Barry and Stokes should have suffered such a fit of judicial aberration as to place on the market a work of such incredible worthlessness. We are equally astounded that a man of such scientific prestige as Mr. Bulsaid should have wasted his time in preparing it.

The article went on to discuss the worthlessness of the book in detail, and, judging by the quotations from it with which the remarks were interlarded, it seemed that there was some excuse for the reviewer's violence.

"Anyone but Bulsaid would have started a libel action," Storm murmured.

The tirade concluded with these words:

There is, we know, a great freedom allowed to the printed word, but this freedom was originated that social problems might be clearly and adequately discussed, and that reforms, where necessary, might be suggested without fear. It was not granted in order that such works as "Devolution" might be published. "Devolution" is not only a degrading book; it is a revolting book. The subject is unclean, the theme might have been adopted from the ravings of a lunatic, the treatment is of a coarseness unrelieved by the faintest sparkle of wit or logic, and to the mentality of the author can only be applied the adjective "septic." The only way in which one can regard this work is as a joke—and then the joke is in such poisonous taste that, one hopes, it would scarcely be tolerated in a Wapping taproom.

Storm passed the sheet over to Teal, and the stolid detective read it dispassionately.

"I hope you never read *Devolution*," Kit said when Teal had finished.

"I was a respectably married man by that time," said Mr. Teal virtuously. "And, anyway, what sort of jokes don't they tolerate in Wapping taprooms? I've never been into one—fat men didn't ought to drink."

"I seem to have heard that homily before," remarked Storm. "Anyway, not many people did read it—it was withdrawn shortly after that review. Here's the record."

He glanced through the second paper and finally folded it down at a certain paragraph and passed it across the desk.

"And yet it was all hot air," he said. "I've made inquiries, and as far as anyone can ascertain, Bulsaid led an impeccably moral life both before and after he married. I think that book marks the beginning of his definite insanity. Later, his madness turned into another channel, and consequently became far less obvious."

He collected the scattered documents which he had pushed aside, and began to run through them, classifying them as he did so, and discarding those which did not bear directly on his investigation. Then he drew a clean sheet of paper towards him and made some notes, and when he had finished he called Teal over to study the result.

"I know all about Bulsaid," he said, speaking slowly and quietly, as was his fashion when he was outlining his thoughts aloud. "But Bulsaid isn't the Triangle by any means! There are men in the Triangle who've been brought in to serve the ends of the Triangle, but who've become its masters. Not openly—that's not what I mean. But work's got to be found for them, and money's got to be found for them, or else they'll turn on their leader. Bulsaid started the Triangle, and now Bulsaid's the unconfessed slave of the men he leads."

It was a curious thing that, although it was Teal, acting on the suggestion of Joe Blaythwayt, who had revealed to Storm the identity of his father, the relationship had never since then been mentioned between them.

"Here's the list," said Storm, indicating the notes he had made, "of the crook emigrants into this country, as supplied to us by the American, French, and German police. I'll bracket them off: Con men"——he ticked one group with his pencil—"yeggs ... whizzers ... knockers-off ... blackmailers ... dope merchants ... jewel thieves ... and so forth and so on. All the usual bunch who come over in the season—and the numbers are about average. But look at these, who generally stay at home: eleven killers from Germany; sixteen ditto from Paris, Toulon and Marseilles; twenty-seven synthetic American gunmen. That makes fifty-four criminals who value the life of a man at approximately two cents——all in, or 'believed to be in,' London. Tell me why,

Teal! Here's the report of the Chief of the *Sûreté: 'Sans doute, quelqu'un a causé....'* Sorry, you don't talk the lingo, do you?

> "Undoubtedly, someone has been talking of the opportunities which presents violent crime in England. We have been able to trace some of the movements of this unknown, and we are convinced that his words have induced numbers of our criminals to quit our shores.

That's a literal translation. In England, old Lafleuve means that some coot's been touting for thugs!" He turned over other papers. "Much the same from Germany. New York says:

> "Knowing the rarity of violent crime in England, and the efficiency of the police in suppressing such as exists, we beg to suggest that you search for an organisation which contemplates an attack on London which might easily have disastrous consequences by reason of its very unexpectedness. Our information leads us to suspect the existence of some such organisation, since there is abundant evidence of the persuasive suggestions of some agent, whom we have been unable to trace and identify, and since it is unlikely that men such as those we name on the enclosed list would leave in a body without a definite plan in mind.

Teal, who said respectability was dull?"

"I'll put through an all-station call for these men—you've got the descriptions," said Teal conventionally.

Storm lighted a cigarette with a grace which he contrived to make inexpressibly cynical.

"Put through all the calls you like," he said languidly. "I'll bet you ten thousand bucks to half a secondhand Limberger you don't get more than six of 'em that way! Personally, I'm going to commit two felonies in the course of the next forty-eight hours, and I'll guarantee to find out more about the Triangle that way than you will in forty-eight years with the help of the *Police News* and the *Weekly List* and the rest of the bunch, and the whole dogstrung C.I.D. into the bargain!"

He cast around for an excuse to ring up Susan, and, finding none, called her number and hoped that the Lord would provide.

"Yes, of course I'm all right," he said in answer to her first question, and felt a pleasant tingle at the thought that this should have been her initial interest. "One reason I rung up was to find out if you'd decided to accept Terry's invitation to stay with them till Hannassay's back. I wish you would."

In the new spirit of selfishness that had come upon him in the past few days, this was an inquiry of minor importance; and yet, having made it, he was seriously concerned about the reply he would receive.

"I have accepted it," she told him, and he was relieved.

"I'd like you to move in today," he said. "I'm sorry if that rushes you, but you've got to realise that there is a certain amount of danger, and if you're killed or anything, I shall get it in the neck. I'll give Terry a ring, and he'll come round and fix everything for you. He loves work," added Storm mendaciously.

"I suppose it can be managed," she said, for in spite of his flippancy she recognised his determination, and knew of old the futility of opposing him. Also, when Storm gave orders he had an uncanny knack of being always right.

"Do we lunch with Uncle Joe?" he teased her.

"I shall probably lunch with Mr. Mannering," she mocked him back. "No, really, I'm sorry you're in such a hurry for me to move. I wanted to go to Moraine's and see the jewels."

"What jewels?"

"Haven't you seen the papers?"

"Haven't had time yet, I usually breakfast in pyjamas, if that personal detail interests you. Getting up so early to go out to breakfast spoilt my interest in the latest horrors other people have been suffering! I'll get hold of Terry now—and I'll be round with him. That boy wants watching!"

He hung up the receiver and took the paper from Teal's hand. The detective, with a perspicacity which indicated that he had not turned a politely deaf ear to the telephone conversation, had already found the place and folded the sheet so as to display it. It was an announcement that the final instalment of the Russian Crown jewels were to be sold by auction at Moraine's on the morrow, and would be on view from ten to four on this particular day, and for one day only. The regalia had already been broken up, and the stones alone, valued at something like four hundred thousand pounds, would be sold.

"That's a lot of money," murmured Storm thoughtfully. "Teal, get on the phone and find out how many men are watching Moraine's."

Mr. Teal obeyed heavily, and in a few moments he had the required information. He cupped one hand over the mouthpiece of the telephone and imparted the facts without interest.

"Eight?" repeated Storm. "That's a hell of a lot—I don't think! Tell 'em to turn out the reserves. I want fifty men at Moraine's in thirty minutes, and they've got to be armed!"

CHAPTER 7

ROBBERY OVER ARMS

"The car's in Cannon Row," said Storm, and led the way down the stone stairs.

Just before they came into view from the street he stopped in the corridor, fished out his cigarette case, and selected a slender cylinder with elaborate care.

"I think I'm considered the most important, Teal," he remarked. "So you'll stand in the doorway while I go down to the car—and you'll shoot first!"

Mr. Teal nodded, and Storm lighted his cigarette as calmly as though he was about to stroll out of a theatre during the interval. Then, with a gay wave of his hand to the grim detective, he stepped out into the bright sunlight and began to walk towards the Hirondel.

He fully expected that an attempt would be made on his life, but the manner of it came as a complete surprise. He had covered half the distance when he heard a warning yell from Teal, which, even in those circumstances, was unlike that placid gentleman; for Inspector Teal was accounted the best revolver shot in the Force. An instinct that had lain dormant since 1918 made him fling himself to the ground, and as he did so Teal's gun cracked viciously. Practically on the instant, there came a detonation that surged staggeringly, and clanged with savage force back from the stone walls of the building. Deafened and half-stunned, he sensed dimly a chorus of shouts and one shrill scream, and something hummed menacingly over his body.

Then he stumbled to his feet, mechanically brushing the dust from his clothes.

In the roadway was a Thing which, presumably, had once been a man. Inspector Teal was coming imperturbably towards him, pocketing his revolver with an air of duty well done. Further from the Thing were a couple of moaning figures, around which a crowd was rapidly collecting....

"A Mills bomb," said Teal unemotionally.

Two men who had been passing at the time were terribly injured, and an elderly lady was leaning against a convenient lamp-post having hysterics. Storm saw the ambulance arrive and superintended the removal of the wounded men, and then he made an inspection of the car. It had been between himself and the bursting bomb, and undoubtedly it had saved his life. The coachwork on one side was battered and torn in great gaping holes, but, miraculously, the tires and the engine had escaped.

He climbed in, lighted a fresh cigarette to replace the one he had lost, and Teal followed him.

"Like to insure my life, Teal?" Storm murmured lightly. "You might make enough to retire on in a few days."

"I'll go first next time, sir," said the sporting Mr. Teal, and the two men solemnly shook hands.

Storm drove the car to Moraine's and affected a sublime indifference to the curious glances which followed the progress of the damaged relic of what had once been a glorious shining Hirondel.

All the world knows Moraine's, the inconspicuous house where priceless art treasures change hands, and the bidding rises in thousands of pounds. To Moraine's come the wealthy connoisseurs and their resplendent wives, with a small sprinkling of gaping sightseers, awing themselves with the sight of so much concentrated wealth, and a few optimistic ladies and gentlemen of irregular notions anent the laws of property, whose dream it is that one day they will arrange a coup on the premises. That they do not is due to the foresight of the architect who designed the showroom—a lofty hall of glass and marble, roughly square in shape, and set in the centre of the building, with no windows for the cruder criminals to attempt to smash, too severely furnished for the more nimble to find cover in at closing time, too solidly built for the violent to break into with high explosive. It is a room of fearful silences, where every whisper rings out like a clarion, and the intruder moves delicately on the unpurchasable crimson carpet that hides most of the tiled floor—for fear of offending the giant flunkeys who stand statuesquely, one on each side of each of the three portals (it would be sacrilege to describe these masterpieces as "doors") in all the glory of their gold and scarlet livery.

But Storm and Teal had small leisure to absorb all this vision of magnificence. Outside they had seen little knots of variously dressed stalwart men standing chatting, men who scarcely spared them a glance; or, if they did, gave no sign of recognition. Inside, grouped about the doors, were similar men; and yet more moved unostentatiously about the room, peering idly at the glittering gems displayed in the long glass case that ran down the centre of the hall.

"Four hundred thousand pounds," said Storm. "Teal, wouldn't you sell your soul for the brains of the Triangle!"

Among the crowd Mr. Teal caught sight of an old friend, and flowed irresistibly towards him. The friend so recognised suddenly remembered an urgent appointment elsewhere, but the vast form of the detective effectively barred his path.

"Hullo, Birdie," he drawled. "How's trade?"

"You're making a mistake, Mr. Teal," said the little man with dignity. "I'm an honest man. Them jools"—he jerked a contemptuous thumb in the direction of the showcase—"them jools are beautiful, but my interest is solely that of the connosewer."

Birdie Sands was playing his "gentleman act," a device he adopted automatically when accused of anything. Mr. Teal, however, remained unimpressed.

"Oh, no, Birdie, you naughty, wicked man!" he said genially, "I won't believe you've degenerated that much. Not when you see as much of Snooper as you do. What does the Good Book say? 'Snooper finds some mischief still for Birdie Sands to do.' Birdie, go home!"

"As a lore-abiding citizen an' a man of edjucation," Birdie began haughtily—but Teal was in no mood for wasting time.

He signed to one of the "connosewers" who was loafing near by, and a protesting Birdie was taken gently but firmly by the arm and conducted towards the open air. Following which Teal, with intent to continue his clean-up, looked around him for a fresh victim.

He never accomplished his ambition.

Startlingly loud above the hushed whispering of the crowd a voice rang out in a curt command:

"Everybody will now stand perfectly still and keep silence!"

Teal swung round, his hand moving instinctively to his hip. It stayed abruptly, for he saw the means there were for enforcing the order. At one end of the room stood six men, in line, their right hands held high above their heads. And in every one of those hands was something round and black and shining.

"Shades of Mills!" breathed Teal.

The leader spoke again:

"These are Mills bombs. The pins are out, and at the first sign of resistance they will be thrown. Also, if any one of us is shot, his bomb will, of course, explode when he falls. Please be sensible. We do not wish to shed blood unnecessarily."

The detectives, uncertain, looked to Storm for their cue. He only hesitated for a second, and then he gave them their instructions in a clear voice.

"You will all obey that order. Carry on, Gat!"

Three of the men handed their bombs to their companions and moved towards the glass cases. The other three, now holding a bomb in each hand, stood motionless.

"Everybody will now move down to the far end of the room," said Gat Morini. "The officers of the law, except Mr. Teal and Captain Arden, will be at the back of the crowd. If a bomb has to be thrown, I should dislike having to hurt any policemen or any of my assistants."

Storm, standing well to the front, was coolly lighting a cigarette. That amazing young man was smiling, and the hand that held the match was coldly steady as an iceberg. He looked at Teal, and found that the detective was flushed and shaking with rage. Teal's vanity was an unsuspected tender spot, and there was no doubt that the barefaced effrontery of the gang in so holding up a squad of detectives was likely to strike him with apoplexy.

"Can't anything be done, sir?" he pleaded unsteadily. "There's about thirty armed men behind us, and we're helpless!"

"And there's about sixty civilians, male and female," Storm told him, "who'll get where the bottle got the cork if we start any funny stuff and bombs go flying about! And they will throw 'em—you can invest your hosiery in that!"

Teal shook his head despondently.

"This'll be the end of both of us," he said. "What in hell's happened to those dear friends outside?"

He did not say "dear friends."

Storm shrugged. A bag had been produced, and the three men in the centre of the room were gathering up the jewels and packing them quickly and carefully away. One by one they emptied the cases, and the bag grew heavy and bulging. They were working on the last case when an interruption occurred. One of the guards from the street came to the entrance.

The whole thing was perfectly planned. The three unarmed men hardly looked up from their task. One of those who held bombs turned with one arm threateningly drawn back as the detective, swiftly comprehending the scene, made a swift movement of his right hand. The other two continued to menace the crowd huddled together at the far end of the room.

"Don't shoot!" rapped Storm, and the man's hand fell to his side.

He was passed back to his comrades behind the crowd of frightened men and women, and the despoiling of the last case went on without a break. The Triangle had allowed for all contingencies, and every counter-move had been designed and rehearsed to perfection, so that the complete performance should move as cleanly and slickly as an exhibition by a perfectly trained *corps de ballet*.

It was all carried out with incredible speed and efficiency. Barely five minutes elapsed between the first intimation of the attack and the collection of every gem in the place in the bag the three operatives carried.

In the forefront of the crowd a keen-faced young man was writing swiftly in a notebook. His astounding unconcern stamped him immediately as a member of the only profession which would be detachedly interested in the end of the world.

Snooper Brome replaced the pins in the bombs he held, and one of his assistants did the same. The third man still held up his hands with their load of concentrated death. The three who had rifled the cases left first, strolling out one by one and conversing casually of what they had seen. Morini, carrying the bag, paused to deliver a mocking farewell.

"We shall meet again, Captain Arden," he said.

"In the Old Bailey," brisked Storm cheerfully. "So long, Gat."

He had no fear of being attacked then, for obviously the gang would be unwilling to alarm the people outside if it could be avoided. The whole thing was staked on the handicap of the crowd of people who would be involved in the fight if the police made a move. It was the most consummately daring bluff in the history of crime, and, granted police officers who felt responsibility for the safety of the general public, it was a bluff that could not be called....

Now only the last man was left, and he stood like a graven image while the hands of the big clock on the wall over his head moved slowly. A silence had fallen on the crowd, and the only sound was the restless movements of their feet. The reporter was still writing dispassionately.

And then, without the quiver of a nerve, Storm performed an act of reckless heroism that drew a great gasp from the crowd. He threw away the butt of his cigarette, and reached boredly to his pocket. Those who were near him saw something hard and blue-black leap out with his hand....

He fired, and as he fired he hurled himself forward, The man with the bombs sagged and crumpled with a little choking cry. Storm was upon him even before he fell, had wrenched the bombs from the spastic clutch of the dead hands, and was racing towards the door. Beyond that door was a long marble corridor which led to the vaults wherein the treasures offered for sale at Moraine's were stored at night. With a grunt he flung the two bombs far from him and jerked himself back into the room.

They detonated in mid-air, and he was only just in time to avoid the fragments of metal that came whizzing back on the earth-shaking reverberation. The tense effort left him gasping weakly, and the screams of panicking men and women came to him through a red haze. But it was only for a moment.

"Attaboy!" His cheery voice rose above the pandemonium. "Three shies a penny—*after 'em, you hounds of Hell!*"

The detectives, led by Teal, poured out of the other door which led to the street, and were met by the inrush of the outside guards who had heard the explosion. Storm watched them go, and then went towards the fighting, stampeding mass of people who were striving to follow them. At a glance he saw that the flying splinters of the bombs had done no physical damage, and he let his parade-ground voice go like a whip crack. He cursed and insulted them into silence, and barked them back into the room.

"You poor henripped sheep!" he snapped when he had cowed them into some sort of order. "There'll be no more fireworks. Form single rank, all ladies to the right, and go out quietly—not like a lot of milling white rabbits!"

He marched them out like a string of beaten dogs. Only one protested at this assumption of command, and he was a man whom Storm had marked down in the stampede—a gross, expensively dressed bounder, white and shaking with terror, who had striven to claw his way to safety through a mob of frightened women.

"I'll have the coat off your back, sir!" he fumed, his voice shrill with the reaction from fear. "You—you—you insolent young puppy, swearing at us as if we were the scum of the earth! I'll report you to your chief! I'll have you kicked out of the Force! You're a disgrace to the police, sir—a disgrace! You—you endanger our lives, and then you have the—the impertinence—the impertinence—I demand to know your name, sir! I shall go straight to Scotland Yard!"

"I am Captain Arden," said Storm coldly, and his lip curled. "Ask for Mr. Kennedy, who is my chief. And put a cushion in the seat of your trousers before you go, because he will quite certainly kick you down the stairs."

"I'll write to the papers about this outrage!" stormed the man. "I'll have you pilloried in the Press! I'll—I'll——"

"I'll tie you in three knots and push you under an omnibus if you aren't outside in five seconds," said Storm quietly, and there was such concentrated scorn in his voice that the man shrank away as though he expected a blow.

Storm was boiling with suppressed rage beneath his calm exterior, for the events of the past minutes had frayed his nerves more than he would ever have admitted. The reporter had watched the scramble with half-closed, amused eyes, and had gracefully taken his place at the end of the queue when peace was restored. He was the last to leave, and he held out his hand as he came to the door.

"I won't ask for an interview," he said, "because I don't want my head bitten off before I've written up this scoop. Here's my card. I'll see you through if that cow in trousers makes a fuss."

Storm's acid stare dissolved into a smile in response to the youngster's grin, and he shook hands heartily. They went out into the street together, and shouldered their way through the mass of excited people who had assembled. A uniformed man answered Storm's query.

"Your men are after them, sir, but I don't think they've much chance. I saw them all go, and they looked too innocent to be wrong; besides, there'd been no alarm."

Storm started up the Hirondel and the journalist, without invitation, joined him. Storm drove him back to Fleet Street and returned to Scotland Yard. He was feeling annoyed, for he had risked everything to allow the detectives to give chase with the least possible delay, and yet he knew the futility of attempting to allow even two minutes' start in London to a fast car whose number was unknown; and he did not doubt for one moment that the gang had provided themselves with every possible means of ensuring a good getaway.

Newsboys were rushing about with sensational posters in their hands, yelling indistinguishable captions, but he hardly noticed them. He had occasion to remember them, however, when he reached his room, for a letter was awaiting him and it was marked URGENT. He tore it open, and found a sheet of thin foolscap covered with neat writing. At the head of it was drawn the symbol of the Alpha Triangle, and just below this was a note:

> A copy of this Manifesto has been sent to all the London newspapers, and all News Agencies.

Then came the lines of writing headed in a way that was more audacious than any criminal proclamation—of which a few are issued from time to time, but of which nobody takes any notice—he had ever read. And the subject-matter of the manifesto would only a week ago have excited his derision.

FIRST MANIFESTO
by the Lord of the Alpha Triangle, in Council, to the Parliament and People of the United Kingdom.

WHEREBY it is announced as follows:

The Society at present known as the Alpha Triangle is the most powerful and the most highly-organised Institution of its kind the world has ever known. The Society is composed of those who, recognising the fact that Force is the law of Nature, and that the principles obtaining in International Politics are those which should have currency in Social Politics, have arranged to extract from the World the wealth which they desire by such means as they think fit to employ. Recognising, also, that they are declaring a War upon the Laws of the World, the Alpha Triangle wish it to be understood that no human life will be sacred to them during the duration of such a War.

IN ORDER, therefore, that much needless sacrifice of life may be saved, the Alpha Triangle takes this opportunity of announcing that it will declare an End of this War on receiving official Intimation of the acceptance by His Majesty's Government of the following Terms of Peace:

(1) THAT the Government above cited shall, within two months of the date hereof, pay to the Alpha Triangle the sum of £15,000,000 (Fifteen million pounds).

(2) THAT the Government above cited shall, upon making this payment, utter a proclamation freely pardoning the several members of the Alpha Triangle and fully indemnifying them from the results of any civil or criminal proceedings in connection with any felonies, misdemeanours or torts committed by the said members of the Alpha Triangle, up to and including the day upon which this payment is made.

(3) THAT the Government above cited shall make this payment in gold ingots, in a manner to be described upon our receipt of the notification of the said Government that they accept these Terms without any reservation or alteration whatsoever.

AND WHEREAS it is expedient that these Terms shall be complied with without delay, we further announce that until the aforesaid notification of acceptance shall be received by us through the medium of the Daily Press, we shall at intervals of three days inclusive assassinate the undermentioned members of the Cabinet:—

Sir John Marker (Home Secretary).
Hugh Anderby Neilson (Chancellor of the Exchequer).
Paul Hesketh (Foreign Secretary).
Lester Hume Smith (Secretary for War)
Lord Hannassay.
John Bayridge-Rand.

AND IN ADDITION, the criminal activities of the Alpha Triangle will continue with unabated energy. Of the efficiency of these activities the Public will be in possession of a striking example by the time this Manifesto appears in print.

FURTHER BE IT KNOWN that the lives of those who set themselves to track down the Alpha Triangle are forfeit, and this sentence will be first carried out upon the persons of Captain Christopher Arden and Inspector Claud Eustace Teal.

GIVEN by our Hand this Day,
(Signed)

For signature there was simply a small replica of the crest which commenced the sheet.

Storm read the rambling, arrogant proclamation through again, taking in all its pseudo-legal jargon, unnecessary capitals, and peculiar paragraphing. It was an amazing announcement, and yet he absorbed every word of it eagerly, for even though it was undoubtedly the work of a madman he had already had enough evidence that the madman had the brain of a genius and the organising ability to carry through his extravagant threats. And the men were there to serve him—the half-human, brutal, remorseless dregs of four or five nations, who would kill for him readily.... One thing only amused him, and he spoke of it to Inspector Teal when the plump detective arrived.

"You've discovered my guilty secret," said Mr. Teal sadly. "If I was on the staff of the Triangle, I'd have put the name of the man who suggested those names to my father on the list."

There was a silence. Then:

"It's incredible!" Storm said harshly. "Teal, if your pal Joe put this manifesto into his book every critic would tear it to pieces. And yet it's true! It's possible! A bughouse genius with an army of cheap thugs who'll obey him—this"—he tapped the paper—"this don't count a blue hoot! It only proves he's mad, and I knew that already. And God knows how to stop him. I know the Triangle, and I could arrest him in thirty minutes, but what court'd convict on all the evidence I've got?"

Teal shook his head.

"The Moraine's men got clean away—we hadn't an earthly." He fumbled in his pocket and drew out a pink slip. "This might interest you," he said casually, and strolled away to the window.

Storm read the telegram, and as he read he went cold.

Lord Hannassay found murdered on line near Kearsney.

CHAPTER 8

ANNOYANCE OF OSCAR

Nothing but credit can attach to Captain Arden, who is in charge of the case. Immediately he heard of the display of jewels, he ordered fifty officers in plain clothes to be armed and dispatched to Moraine's. The hold-up, however, was staged in a manner so unprecedented and so completely unforseen that, hampered as they were by a considerable number of sightseers, Captain Arden and his men were helpless. As it was, his prompt action in attacking the member of the gang who was left behind to ensure the getaway of the others was as courageous a deed as that which won him the D.S.O. at Mons during the Great War. It was not his fault that he failed to prevent the escape of the gang. Captain Arden also deserves special praise for the way in which he quelled the subsequent panic. A gentleman who was present has written us a strongly worded letter abusing the methods used by Captain Arden in doing this. Our correspondent apparently fails to realise that you cannot argue politely with a terrified mob, and that Captain Arden's vigorous measures probably saved several people from, at least, serious injury.

So spoke the *Daily Record*, after the first profitable crime of the Triangle.

The trouble about sensational crime, from the journalist's point of view, is that once the public has ceased to be interested in its committal, the news value falls several degrees below par. The Triangle mystery, however, suffered from no such disadvantages. The definite threat of further crimes effectively maintained popular interest at fever heat. The Triangle was the topic of conversation wherever two or three were gathered together, and those who at the first announcement had dismissed it as a hoax, prayed that their indiscretion might be forgotten.

Joe Blaythwayt was confidently pessimistic.

"I Know Criminals," he would say darkly, to the few doubters that remained.

Another man, personally concerned with the fate of the plot, was belligerently smug.

"I shall nod bay," he repeated with liturgical monotony.

He sat opposite Joe Blaythwayt in the Lombard Street office. It was not his usual day for calling, but his reason was costly enough to justify this departure from routine.

"Ter day afder tomorrow," he said, "I shall a cheque traw vor fifty tousand bounds. I shall require to pe baid in one bound notes. Led berbarations pe mate."

"Certainly, sir," said Joe Blaythwayt briskly, and made a note on his pad. "The money will be ready for you. In the morning?"

"Yess!" Raegenssen nodded violently. "That iss all. Thang you."

He rose.

"If I might mention something, sir," Blaythwayt stopped him. "That man Snooper—you want to be careful of him."

Raegenssen wrinkled.

"Snoober?"

"That Brome fellow—Edward Brome he calls himself. I saw him driving through the City in your car yesterday morning. Of course, it's really no business of mine if you give your acquaintance a lift, but Brome isn't—ah—desirable. He's a well-known fence."

"Fence?"

"'Fence,'" explained Mr. Blaythwayt with unction, "is the cant term among criminals for a man who buys stolen property. A receiver. Brome is a receiver."

Raegenssen stroked his chin.

"Tear me! That iss most disdressing—yess! Hof you seen him before? How do you know?"

"I Know Criminals," said Joe with an air.

"When you again meed him," said Raegenssen seriously, "dell him nod to gall on me again. I shall pe gross—yess! A griminal! I shall eggsdinguish him! He shall hof ter fire out!"

Blaythwayt was surprised at the man's vehemence.

"There's no actual evidence against him," he explained erroneously, "but the police know him for a criminal and they're anxious to get a conviction." In this he was nearer the truth. "It'd be unpleasant for you to be known as a friend of Snooper's. I thought I'd take the liberty of warning you."

The Swede nodded.

"I am gradeful. Thang you. Goot-pye!"

He left in his usual abrupt manner, and Joe Blaythwayt returned to his desk with a comfortable feeling of having at last found an opportunity of giving a practical demonstration of his knowledge of the criminal classes.

So escaped Snooper Brome, with three car-loads of detectives all but on his heels and four hundred thousand pounds' worth of gems in a shabby leather bag. And the armed men who prowled the streets of London searched in vain.

That evening, Oscar Raegenssen summoned his portly butler and his chauffeur to his study. He took the cocktail the butler shook for him, and threw two buff scraps of paper on the table.

"Tonight," he ordered, "you will go to der theadrigal enderdainments. Your tiggets! I do not wiss to disturbed pe!"

His servants accepted the tickets with murmured thanks, and exchanged a covert wink, for they were used to their master's eccentricities. Without warning or explanation he would disappear for weeks, and return, as though he had only been absent for a day, expecting to find everything running smoothly for him to drop back into. Often he sent them away for the night, with some such instructions as he gave them now. They put their own constructions on these habits of his, and they were quite wrong.

Raegenssen saw them out of the house, and then fetched a hat and stick and himself left. He dined economically at a small restaurant in Soho, and from there he went on to the Orpheum Theatre, where that bright entertainment *Bronx or Manhattan* played nightly to crowded houses. Not that Oscar Raegenssen was interested in snappy back-chat, negroid music, or chorus girls' legs; but the box of a theatre is a convenient place for meeting those whom you wish to see and speak with in private. There Storm, who was in the stalls, saw him dozing boredly during the first part of the show, for Oscar Raegenssen's friend was not due to arrive until ten.

Storm left in the interval, and strolled leisurely to the garage where his car was kept. He drove north and west—along Oxford Street and up Orchard Street, and when the gates of Regent's Park loomed before him he veered half left and went on up the Finchley Road. After a distance he turned right, drove on for about three hundred yards, and suddenly swung left into an unlighted track. The car bumped and jolted as he nursed it over the uneven ground.

At length he stopped, switched off all his lights, got down, and stretched himself.

The moon was new and feeble, and the sky black with hurrying clouds. Somewhere to the north rumbled the mutter of distant thunder, A summer storm was brewing.

He disappeared among the shadows. The darkness was almost complete, yet he picked his way over the rough path unerringly. On either side of him rose ghostly polyliths which resembled ruins in that faint light, and once he climbed over a wall in the interstices of which the cement was still soft. He was on a plot of land where a block of flats was being erected.

Presently he stopped and took a black silk handkerchief from his pocket, and this he pinned to the lapels of his dinner jacket. It erased the white blur of his shirt and made him practically invisible. A second black silk handkerchief, folded diagonally, he tied about the lower part of his face.

A six-foot wall barred his way. He scaled it like a cat, and dropped nimbly on the springy turf on the other side.

The house stood back from the road, in darkness. Storm was in the back garden, the high walls that enclosed it screening him effectively from the view of any possible outside watchers. He stole along in the shadow they cast. A car passed with a hoot and a blare as the latch of a window clicked open under his expert manipulation, and as the splutter of the car died away he raised the sash soundlessly and slipped over the sill.

Inside, the blackness was intense, with a tangible quality to it that was numbing to the senses. Myriads of silver specks whirled before the eyes in protest against the strain of attempted vision. The utter opacity was tactile, half fluid, like a fog. He crept through the room with a feline assurance, uncannily avoiding chairs and tables, crossed the hall, and opened a door on the far side, closing it behind him. Then he went over to the window and passed his sensitive fingers delicately over every inch of it, even as he had done to that by which he had entered—a touch light enough to stroke a butterfly's wing unfelt. Satisfied that there were no alarms fitted, he pressed back the catch and opened the window to its fullest extent, after which he drew the heavy curtains.

A beam of light stabbed the darkness, flickered over every part of the room, and rested at length on a Sheraton cabinet.

Unhurriedly he made his preparations. From an inside pocket he took a paper bag from which he scattered a coarse powder over the exposed parquet by the door, so that anyone attempting to enter would be bound to step on it. Next came a slim wallet of morocco leather which, laid open on the floor beside the cabinet, gleamed with the silvery sheen of fine steel tools. Lastly, he drew from his hip pocket an automatic pistol, and this he also laid on the floor beside him.

The cabinet hid a small safe of the most modern type, built like a battleship, yet he tackled it confidently. Patiently and skillfully he worked, and at last he had a rubber cup fixed securely to the metal about the lock. Into this he poured a viscid liquid from a rubber bottle, which he handled gingerly. Then he sat back on his heels, while the concentrated acid bubbled against the steel and gave off a heavy, pungent vapour.

Exactly three hours after he had entered the house the door of the safe hung open, disclosing rows and rows of documents tied in bundles of various sizes, neatly arranged on the metal shelves.

Holding the electric lamp between his knees so that its rays fell towards the floor, he ran through the packets rapidly.

It was then that he heard the snap of potassium chlorate—the safety powder he had sprinkled around the door detonated under foot like the tiny explosions of "cap" pistols. He caught up his automatic and spun around, just as a switch clicked over and the room was flooded with a blinding glare.

For a space of seconds there was a strung, pulsating silence. Then:

"Hullo, Snooper," said Storm, in a voice that was not his own. "How are things?"

It was a deadlock. Snooper Brome's big hand held an ugly revolver which covered Storm, and Storm's little automatic was steadily focused on Mr. Brome's rainbow waistcoat. So they stood without movement, with every nerve keyed and strained to humming pitch, while their eyes never swerved a fraction of a millimetre from each other's trigger finger. Moments passed with the glittering clarity of crystal drops falling in a bottomless pit....

"What are you doing?" asked Mr. Brome, though the question was rather unnecessary.

He looked pale, and his mane of black hair was more unruly than usual.

"I might ask the same question," remarked Storm.

Their eyes met over the blue-black gleam of their weapons—Storm's glinting metallically over his improvised mask, Snooper's blue ones cold and level. And Storm saw Snooper's first finger whiten over the knuckle ... saw the slight backward tremble of the hammer of his revolver.

"Don't be a fool!" he snapped tensely. "An automatic's quicker than an uncocked revolver. I can shoot a fraction of a second before you can, and I never miss!"

Snooper's finger relaxed, and the masked man rose slowly from his crouching position.

"That's why you'll drop that gat," went on Storm's monotonous, unrecognisable voice. It was perfectly level, and yet he was playing the most terrific gamble of nerve in his career. He was banking, betting, coldly and unruffledly threatening on the infinitesimal margin of time's advantage the difference of weapons gave him. "You're poaching, Snooper. Your business is to fence, not to crack cribs yourself ... taking the bread out of the poor burglar's mouth.... I shall have to report you to the Larcenists' Union, Snooper, really I shall...."

His voice trailed away.

Brome slackened the muscles of his forearm preparatory to making his own gamble, for he knew how desperate was his position. And yet he need not have been afraid, for Storm had taken one of those swift, inspirational, entirely characteristic decisions of his. But, not knowing this, Eddie Brome watched keenly for the faintest wavering of the gun-metal grey eyes…. He stirred slightly, and the *crack!* of another speck of potassium chlorate under his foot was like a gunshot in the stillness.

For a decimal of a split second it distracted his attention.

A fine tongue of flame licked out from the muzzle of Storm's automatic, and the roar of the explosion was shattering. The bullet struck Brome's revolver from his hand, and it clattered to the floor while his arm fell limply to his side, suddenly paralysed by the shock.

Storm dropped his gun into his pocket and leapt. His fist crashed into Snooper's face, and the big man slid limply to the ground.

Storm had his back to the drawn curtains, and behind him he heard, quite distinctly, a stifled gasp. In one lightning spring he was beside the window, his back flattened against the wall, watching and listening. No one entered, and he drew back the edge of the curtain a centimetre. There was nothing to be seen, but as he let the cloth fall back he caught the gentle crunch of stealthy footsteps on gravel.

He was across the room in a flash, had turned out the lights, and was back at the window. He slipped between the curtains and swung himself out, dropping to the path with hardly a sound. At the corner of the building a dim grey shape moved suddenly and vanished.

Storm jumped the path and raced along the turf to where he had seen the figure. There was no sign of it, but he could glimpse the small area in front of the house, and he saw the two black burly forms which pounded up the tiled approach, their lanterns dancing as they ran.

"Damn these police…. But it's no use getting rattled, Horace!" he murmured.

With which sound piece of philosophy he doubled back to the window and returned to the room he had left. His one shot had already raised the alarm, and he had much to do, yet he moved without flurry. On the floor in front of the safe he continued his interrupted task by the light of his torch. It was finished in a few moments, and then he closed the safe and replaced the wallet of tools in his pocket. As he crossed to the door he saw that Snooper had vanished and, on the strength of his decision, was glad that he had not hit the fence harder.

There was, however, small time for these reflections, for the constables outside were already thundering on the front door. He flitted upstairs like a shadow, temporarily unperturbed by the problem of how he was to escape, and made a speedy, methodical search of all the upstairs rooms. The door of one remained shut when he turned the handle noiselessly, and from within came a faint sound of cautious movement.

Coolly he twisted into the next room, and, looking out and down, he saw the policemen climb in through the window he had left open for his own bolt-hole.

"Jerusalem!" he breathed. "They've both gone in—the poor, damned boobs! I ought to take their numbers, really, and report them for incompetence.... However...."

He flung a leg over the sill and looked up, for although his way of escape was temporarily clear he was anxious to see the man in the adjoining room. Above his head ran a stout gutter, and, testing it with his weight, he decided that it would hold. He swung out into space and risked his way along the side of the building. In a few hair-raising seconds he could see into one corner of the lighted room, and then a loose section of pipe rattled in his hand, and the blind whirred down almost in his face.

Without hesitation he turned and made his way as swiftly as he dared back to the window he had left. He got his legs inside, and then grabbed the top of the sash and wrenched his body down and inwards with all his strength. Even as he did so, the shot he had feared and sought thus to dodge rang out, and something seared across his shoulder.

"Here—none of that, sir!" commanded a voice, and the next instant the lights went up.

Raegenssen stood on the threshold, cold murder flaming in his eyes. Behind him were the two constables, holding him back, and one of them was clutching the Swede's wrist to prevent him firing the second round he was wrestling and straining to loose off. He was in evening dress, with his mane of fair hair dishevelled and his Viking beard awry with the struggle.

"Take that man!" he screamed, and one of the constables released his hold and came towards Storm.

"Dear me," murmured Storm. "Siegfried, my Pelican, you seem annoyed!"

His hand went to his pocket, and whipped into view again immediately with a vision of snarling death. He fired in between the men until the magazine was exhausted, and for a moment they recoiled instinctively. It gave him his chance. With a light laugh he leapt for the little group in the doorway.

Raegenssen staggered back from the sideways smash of Storm's elbow, and in the same movement Storm hit one of the policemen regretfully but scientifically on the point of the jaw. An instant later he was sprinting down the passage.

He sprang to the banisters, and went whirling down, as the Swede fired again. The bullet sang harmlessly past Storm's head, and a whistle shrilled urgently. The three men came stumbling down in his wake, but he had the start of them, and he had ducked back into the shadows of the hall and vanished into the library before they could switch on the downstairs lights. They were still groping about when he passed through the still open window and scudded across the back lawn the way he had come.

He found his car, stripped off his disguise, and had his hand on the door when he noticed that there was someone huddled up in the front seat. He glanced keenly around him, and then kept his right hand on the gun in his pocket as he turned his electric flash on the face of the intruder.

"Hullo, Kit," said Susan calmly,

When he had disposed of the police Raegenssen collected the papers from his safe and studied each one of them closely. Then he replaced them and went to the kitchen at the back of the house, where he brewed himself some coffee, and, armed with this, returned to the library and lighted a cigar.

Half-way through the smoke he discarded the stump fastidiously and rose. At one end of the room was a small writing-desk, which he unlocked, drawing down the folding front. Then he took off his coat and white waistcoat and began to work.

A tiny reading-lamp on the top of the desk was all the light in the room. He looked a grotesque figure, his leonine head stooped over his work, his glasses perched precariously on the end of his nose, his protruding tongue following the movements of his hands, with the direct light bringing out his angular face in high relief.

It was two hours later that he heard the sound—the creak of a board under a wary foot. He laid down his stylo carefully and switched out the reading-lamp. On the threshold of the library he halted. The hall was in darkness. Facing him, though he could not see them, were three doors, and he had left each one of them slightly ajar. Almost certainly his study would be the goal of this new trespasser, he decided, and passed over the heavy carpet without sound. He was just outside the study door when he heard a curious noise—three deliberate claps. It was so obviously designed to attract attention that another man would have paused, but Raegenssen was a man without fear. He slid through the opening and stood with his back to the wall, every sense on the alert.

"Who iss that?" he demanded.

"Wouldn't you like to know?" boomed back a mocking voice.

It was disguised, yet there was something familiar in it which he could not place. His searching fingers located the electric light switch, but he flicked the lever over and back without results. The wires were cut—he found the loose ends hanging free a foot further down.

"What is...?" he said.

And then came a rollicking chuckle that, unemotional as he was, seemed to set a fine thread of ice vibrating in his spine.

"Maddock!" he roared uncertainly, and then he saw a shadow move, and stumbled forward.

He touched cloth, and with a deep-throated grunt he closed. The unknown struck at him with something that whistled as it fell, but Raegenssen bowed his head and the life-preserver thudded agonisingly into his shoulder instead of into his skull. He grabbed the striker's hand, and for a short while they swayed and panted in the darkness. His opponent was heavy and strong above the average, but he was no match for the giant Swede. Presently they fell together, and Raegenssen heaved himself astride the writhing man and sought to gather in the arms that struck viciously at him.

"Now we shall see," he growled, and then a chance blow crashed into his solar plexus and he rolled limply away, gasping in a torment of nausea.

It was some minutes before he could rise, his great chest heaving painfully, and by that time he knew that the unknown had gone. He reeled across the hall, bent almost double, and snapped on the lights in his library. Every drawer and cupboard had been hurriedly rifled, and their contents strewn on the floor, but he gave the damage scarcely a glance. From among the wreckage he retrieved a flashlight and went back to the study, switching on the lights in the hall on his way. He went over every inch of the room in search of anything his late visitor might have lost in the struggle, and it was quite early in his hunt that he saw something winking up at him from the carpet.

It was a little silver triangle.

CHAPTER 9

SPECIMENS OF JOURNALESE

Storm trod on the self-starter. The powerful engine woke to life with no more than a whispering purr. Like a long shadow the Hirondel slid out of the cart track and down the deserted road between ghostly files of street lamps.

He switched on his lights as he turned into the Finchley Road.

It had been a merry evening, and not without those thrilling moments after which his heart yearned; and it had left him with things to ponder. He wanted to know the reason for Snooper Brome's appearance in the home of Oscar Raegenssen, and he wanted to know what the hurriedly lowered blind in an upstairs room had hidden from him, but it was typical of the man that he accepted Susan's arrival as though it were the most natural thing in the world.

"Lucky you found me," he remarked. "Now I can take you along to the Elysion, and we can consume bacon and eggs."

He made no effort to discover the reason for her presence, but she enlightened him of her own accord.

"It's all Uncle Joe's fault," she explained. "I'd been to dinner with him, and—you've had some experience of him—you know what a bloodthirsty little man he is, and this Triangle business is meat and strong drink to him. He was lecturing me about it for hours after I ought to have gone home, and he kept dragging Raegenssen into the discussion and then forgetting what he was going to say about him. Then he told me Raegenssen lived near by, and promptly added that women shouldn't get mixed up with crime. So, of course, I had to butt in. Did you kill Snooper?"

She asked the question so dispassionately that Storm laughed.

"No," he said mildly. "Not tonight. It wasn't—er—expedient. One of these days I shall probably have to, but that'll keep. How much did you see?"

"You saw me."

"And," said Storm in pained accents, "you saw the police charging up the garden, and you didn't rally round to assist the getaway? Susan, you're going off!"

She smiled, and laid a cool hand on his.

"Old chap," she said, "that would have been unpardonable. You knew what you were doing, and you don't need lessons in looking after yourself. If I'd thought you wanted help, I'd have come——"

"Like old times," said Storm, and raised her hand to his lips.

He felt curiously exhilarated that night. It may have been due to the fresh food for thought which he had gathered from his adventurous and wholly illegal visit, or to the sudden bracing rush of swift action he had enjoyed to the full after overmuch peace and quiet. Or, on the other hand, it may have been due to the presence of the girl at his side…. Storm felt happily incompetent to judge. He knew, at least, that the old, gay recklessness had returned to him in all its reawakened daredevilry. The cool night air was grateful on his face: he drew deep breaths of it contentedly, and it went to his head like wine. He moved his arms ecstatically, for the pure sensuous joy of feeling the rippling suppleness of them. He laughed softly, irresponsible and proud, throwing back his head—a splendid animal glorying in its magnificent manhood.

"Oh, Susan, this is the life!" he said. "No dull safety for me! I only hope it doesn't end too soon."

"You get all the fun," she complained. "All I can do is to mooch around waiting to be shot up, and fill in the intervals lunching with Uncle Joe."

"Damn Uncle Joe!" exploded Storm, but this time without jealousy. "I'm sick of hearing about Uncle Joe! Forget him, kid, and listen to me. Susan, when this jaunt's over, and the Alpha Triangle's done the six-foot drop, you're coming away with me—I don't care where, so long as it's some place where you can still go gunning for people who annoy you. London's all right when there's a Triangle livening things up, but one day the Triangle'll toe the T in a whitewashed shed, and I hate stagnation! We'll start a young war somewhere, if you like. Any old thing suits me, so long as it's disreputable and dangerous…. Is that a bet?"

"I don't know," she said demurely. "You're so very unconventional…." And thereafter he only had one hand for the steering-wheel.

Storm breakfasted next morning with his usual litter of newspapers scattered on the floor all around him, but he was chiefly amused by the alarm of the *Daily Record*. To his mind, the crime reports in which the *Record* specialised were far more interesting than fiction, for that paper had a reputation for chewing more meat from tropical bones than any of its contemporaries.

WHERE ARE THE POLICE?
LONDON AT MERCY OF GANG OF MURDERERS.
GOVERNMENT MUST NOT SURRENDER.
FURTHER OUTRAGES ANTICIPATED.
LATEST NEWS OF GIGANTIC CONSPIRACY.

—and a lot more. The police, one gathered, were either incapable or afraid; the Government were meditating incontinent surrender; England was to be plunged into anarchy; neither life nor property would be safe.... Only the policy of the *Daily Record* was stemming the tide of disaster.

"These people aren't helpful," murmured Storm. "Stampeding sheep! Bring me some more toast."

"Yessir," said Cork.

Cork, Storm's valet, was a man with aggrieved eyebrows and a disapproving mouth. He had the expression of one who has looked on the wine when it was sour, and who has never quite succeeded in getting rid of the taste. But, at least, he went about his work with the efficiency of a superman whose head would be bloody but unbowed despite plague, pestilence, famine, riot, civil commotion, the fall of the Conservative Party, the dissolution of the British Empire, Act of God, or the agitation of the *Daily Record*.

"There is a man downstairs who wishes to speak to you, sir," he said, returning with reinforcements of coffee.

Sorrow was in every line of his pessimistic face, and he laid a faint emphasis on the word "man." Storm had never quite induced his servant to accept Inspector Teal as a human being.

"What's the matter with him, Cork?" asked Storm. "Leper?"

"I'm afraid not, sir," replied Cork gloomily. "It's the policeman who calls sometimes."

"Show him up," said Storm and returned to his newspapers.

Mr. Teal glutinated through the door.

"Good morning, sir."

"Morn'n," said Storm without looking up. "Sit down, Teal. English or Colonial breakfast?"

Inspector Teal frowned suspiciously.

"What's a Colonial breakfast?" he inquired.

"Oh, a horse's neck, a mutton chop, and a small dog."

"What's the small dog for?" queried Mr. Teal innocently. "And why a horse's neck?"

"The dog eats the mutton chop, and a horse's neck's a brandy and ginger ale——"

"Coffee—thank you, sir," said the shocked Mr. Teal. "Fat men didn't ought——"

Over a steaming cup he surveyed the cheery, comfortable room. There were well-filled bookcases, a grand piano, and an open secretaire strewn with scraps of paper and writing materials. On the walls were fencing foils, boxing gloves, an oar, and over the mantelpiece hung a couple of sporting rifles.

"Nice little place you've got here," he remarked. "I've always liked it."

"Not so bad! Listen, Teal. The papers say, *the police are believed to have a clue*. Why don't we contradict such wicked slanders?"

"It's better than Finchley," pursued Mr. Teal without emotion.

"And this: *A sensational arrest is expected at every moment.* Je-rusalem. My dear soul, how can even a great man like yourself make a sensational arrest at every moment? There aren't enough sensational people in London to maintain the supply. Besides, blokes'd start getting peeved."

"Raegenssen was peeved," said Mr. Teal sleepily.

Storm slewed his chair round so that he faced the detective, and searched for a cigarette. His gun-metal grey eyes were alight with mischief.

"Teal!" he protested. "Why must you be inconsequent?"

"Why must you burgle Raegenssen?" asked Mr. Teal.

That quick, flickering smile played about Storm's lips.

"How do you know?" he asked calmly.

"Your tire tracks were all over that bit of building ground. And I called at your garage on my way here and found dry mud caked all over your wheels. You don't collect that sort of mud in the streets." Mr. Teal blinked twice and yawned. He became almost awake, "Mr. Arden, why can't you and me work together?"

"That accusative makes me go all goosey!" complained Storm.

"You and I," Mr. Teal corrected himself. "Why not? We'd get on much better."

Storm exhaled a thin feather of smoke from the corner of his mouth.

"You might," he said. "But then, you're only a detective."

Inspector Teal accepted the proffered cigar. His mouth widened half an inch momentarily.

"I shouldn't compromise you," he pleaded.

Storm walked over to the window.

"How did you come to visit Raegenssen at all?" he asked.

"I was called early this morning," said Teal. "I haven't been to bed yet. So I heard all about the masked man and the fancy shooting, and then I remembered you'd promised to commit a few felonies. Besides, you can recognise a Hirondel's tracks—they've got a very wide wheel-base, and you can only fit Veloris tires."

"Bit off your beat, wasn't it?"

"No." The detective rummaged in his pocket and produced something that was familiar to Storm without a closer inspection. "Anything to do with Triangles is on my beat."

Storm took the trinket and stared at it. Then he paced quickly up and down the room, his eyes half-closed and his cigarette tightened up in his lips. He raised his shoulders and shoved his hands deep into his pockets, and then he stopped in his stride abruptly and turned.

"Did you get that from Raegenssen?"

Teal nodded.

"The burglar came back, and the second time he left that. He and Raegenssen had a fight, but the Swede stopped one in the tummy."

"Do you think I'm the Triangle?" asked Storm directly.

Inspector Teal jerked the ash from his cigar.

"No, I don't. But you know too much about it, and I wish you'd come across. There's an inquiry about that Moraine's stunt scheduled for this afternoon, and the Commissioner 'll be curious."

"I want the whole yarn," Storm said after a short pause. "As heard from Raegenssen."

"I can do better," said Teal. "A reporter who lives out that way was there even before I was. It was just ten when I came along Piccadilly, so I brought you in the midday edition of the *Evening Record*."

Storm took the sheet and grinned.

"You're an old cynic, Teal!" he reproved.

He lounged over to the table and rested on the edge of it while he read with interest the brief account of the happenings in North London of the small hours of that morning.

"An air of mystery surrounds the two attempts to burgle the house of Mr. Oscar Raegenssen, the well-known Swedish merchant, which took place last night.

"How does a house take place, Teal?

"Mr. Raegenssen had been to a theatre, and had thence proceeded to a night club—

"How shocking," murmured Storm.

"—from which he returned to his house in Marchmont Avenue at about 1 a.m. He went upstairs immediately and was undressing when he heard a suspicious sound in his study. A moment later a shot rang out. Stopping only to pull on a dressing-gown, Mr. Raegenssen hastened downstairs and found the window wide open and his safe broken open. Finding that the telephone wires had been cut, Mr. Raegenssen returned to his bedroom in order to don some clothes before summoning the police."

"Decency before duty," Storm drawled.

"Two constables who had heard the shot, however, had already arrived, and had entered the building by way of the window which the burglar had left open in his flight. Mr. Raegenssen, meanwhile, had heard a noise in the room adjoining his bedroom which led him to suspect that the burglar was perhaps still in the house. This, indeed, proved to be the case, and the two officers, assisted by Mr. Raegenssen, attempted to apprehend the man. The burglar, however, who was masked and evidently a dangerous character, drew a pistol and fired several times at his would-be captors without hitting them, after which he made a desperate and successful bid for safety.

"About two and a half hours later, when Mr. Raegenssen who had been too disturbed by the thrilling incident to return immediately to his bed, was working in his library, he heard a suspicious sound in his study and attempted to investigate it. He was promptly attacked with great ferocity by the desperado, who again contrived to make his escape, but who this time left behind him a silver triangle of a type which is by now familiar to readers of the *Evening Record*. During the time it took Mr. Raegenssen to recover sufficiently to rise, the library was in its turn the subject of the burglar's attentions.

"The extraordinary feature of the affair, however—

"That's three 'howevers.'

"—is the fact that in neither case—

"That's two cases.

"—was any attempt—

"That's four attempts, Teal. Beaver! ... Fifteen love.

"—made to abstract anything of value. The only things interfered with were the safe and a number of drawers and filing cabinets in which Mr. Raegenssen kept private papers concerning his business.

"Inspector Teal, who is working on the Triangle Mystery in conjunction with Captain Arden, has been called in, and he is said to have made an important discovery, which is at present being kept a strict secret."

"How much did you lend this reporter, Teal?" asked Storm accusingly.

"It will be remembered that Mr. Raegenssen had already been the recipient of one of the warnings of the Alpha Triangle.

"Good old Snooper!" said Storm cryptically. "I knew he'd get away with it somehow!" He pitched the paper into a corner and swung himself off the table. "And an inquiry. Well, I'll deal with the inquiry! But I wish I knew who Oscar's second friend was."

"It wasn't you?" Inspector Teal was incredulous.

"It was not. If you're really interested, I can prove an alibi; I was inhaling bacon and eggs at the Elysion, or beer *chez* Mannering—where Miss Hawthorne's staying—at the time."

Teal wrinkled his brow.

"Didn't I hear you mention Snooper?" he prompted, and Storm nodded.

"Snooper was at Raegenssen's last night. And I let him go—you can tell that to your Board of Inquiry! And now, if you don't mind, we'll leave the subject until this afternoon."

The Board assembled in the Chief Commissioner's room at two o'clock, and Storm took his place at one end of the table without a trace of embarrassment. Teal, who sat on his right, was less self-confident, for Inspector Teal was a conventional detective with a proper awe for the majesty of Higher Command. Bill Kennedy, the Assistant Commissioner, shook hands with Storm as he passed, although his usual cheeriness was singularly half-hearted. The Chief, Sir Brodie Smethurst, was the last to arrive, and with him came a man whom no one present with the exception of Storm had expected to see.

"What's the Home Secretary doing in this picnic?" demanded Teal in a hoarse whisper, and Storm shrugged.

"I asked him to come," he stated shortly.

The preliminary business was soon over, for in theory the Board had assembled to make an inquiry into Storm's failure to prevent the robbery at Moraine's; and then Storm rose to give an account of his progress with the main problem.

"I have no excuses to make for the Moraine's affair," he said. "On that score you may take what action you like. The second point is the double burglary at Raegenssen's early this morning. I was the first burglar, but I don't know who the second was—although I could name the man, with certainty, in two guesses. And I'll make you a prophecy: within the next forty-eight hours the man known as Raegenssen will either have disappeared or been killed! ... I have no excuses for the burglary either. It merely happened to be necessary. By swearing information I might conceivably have got a search warrant, but I decided that that course would be both risky and futile, because the issue of the warrant would alarm the man I was anxious to trap; futile, because it might have been necessary to repeat the search without the man being aware that an official search had been made. I was both lucky and unlucky. I found what I expected, to a certain extent, but the arrival of the police gave me no time to find out all that I wanted to. To this moment Raegenssen does not know that his visitor was not a common thief, and therefore he will be killed. If I had revealed my identity to the police, he would have recognised me, and *I* should have been killed. It was, you see, a matter of my life or—his."

They listened without comprehending.

"You suspect Raegenssen of having some connection with the Alpha Triangle?" suggested Smethurst.

"I *know*," said Storm carefully, "that the evidence I have secured from Raegenssen, together with what I have obtained from another man, will kill the Alpha Triangle. I could arrest the Apex today—but I won't!"

He heard the suppressed gasp that went up, and smiled faintly at Inspector Teal's muffled "Good God!"

"No one but myself," he went on simply, "has anything like the evidence necessary to secure a conviction—I even doubt very much if I could get one myself. You can be satisfied that it is a moral certainty, even if it would fail to convince a Grand Jury. But, at the instance of the late Lord Hannassay, and with the consent of Sir John Marker, I was given carte blanche in this case, and you must continue that support."

"*Must* is a strong word, Captain Arden," said the Home Secretary mildly.

"I am a strong man," said Storm.

He spoke quietly, not as a boaster, but as one who states a fact, and his cool assurance staggered the Board. Whereas before they had been scowling or incredulous, according to temperament, they were united in indignation.

"P-please make yourself p-p-plain," stammered Smethurst harshly.

"It's rather obvious already," said Storm calmly. "The Alpha Triangle is my father. You needn't think I'm giving away my secret, because I'm not! If you took the trouble to trace my father, you'd come up against a dead end. You'd laugh at the idea—just as you'd laugh if I told you openly now. But, anyway, I don't want you to try and trace him. I don't want this case messed up with a lot of flat-footed half-wits trying to take my place! You're at my mercy. Do what you like. Sack me. Keep me on under supervision. It won't help you, because in a few hours I shall be the only man who can hope to catch the Alpha Triangle. In time, I mean. Of course, I suppose there are plenty of other men who could mug along till they got him—but by that time the Triangle will have cost the country hundreds of thousands of pounds and many lives. You can take your choice...."

He had them stymied. Their world was reeling about their ears. Never within living memory had a man dared to address a Board of Inquiry in such an arrogant manner. Storm set at naught their authority, he was coldly indifferent to the fact that he laid himself open to prosecution, he had given them an ultimatum with all the casualness of a man to whom acceptance or rejection means nothing to speak of—and the chilled insolence of it dazed them.

And Storm, while they strove to collect their wits, was leisurely lighting a cigarette and smiling as affably as if he had merely made some commonplace remark about the weather, instead of handing out to Their Augustnesses the starkest slice of sheer frozen case-hardened nerve in their experience....

The atmosphere was electric. It seemed to have temporarily hypnotised all but two of them—Bill Kennedy—who was leaning back in his chair with a grin of pure delight on his ugly face, and Sir John Marker, who was tapping his teeth reflectively with a pencil and apparently considering Storm's proposition as seriously as he would have considered a question in the House.

"It is an extraordinary situation, Captain Arden," he admitted. "I can see your point—up to a point. But if, as you say, your father is involved, hadn't you better pass the case over to someone else?"

"No," said Storm steadily.

"Can't you be a little more explicit, then?"

"I can tell you this: I first suspected my man on a day when I had a slight accident." Storm spoke slowly and evenly, ignoring the stunned faces of the Board and addressing his remarks to the Home Secretary. He was standing erect, with the tips of his fingers resting on the table in front of him, completely at ease. "I was driving down Cockspur Street, and my car skidded and knocked Raegenssen down. There were present Mr. Blaythwayt, manager of the Lombard Street City and Continental; Mattock, a convict on licence employed by Raegenssen; and Miss Hawthorne, Lord Hannassay's secretary. Of those people, two were in a position to note the same thing as I did—the first piece of evidence against my father." He smiled again at their perplexity. "Acting on this, I burgled Raegenssen last night, and learnt something of the next coup planned by the Triangle. I also acquired a fresh suspicion, which I hope to verify soon. But that's all speculation. The solid fact," he said, watching them with a glimmer of amusement in his eyes, "is that one is always interested in a saw-mill which has recently received a consignment of machinery and materials that have nothing whatever to do with the sawing of wood!"

"Do we have to play at Sexton Blake when there aren't any reporters with us?" drawled Bill Kennedy.

Storm grinned.

"I must have notice of that question," he murmured, and sat down.

Then the bottled-up feelings of the Police Chiefs had their vent, and a hum of argument broke out like the snarl of numerous irritated bees. Marker remained aloof, taking no part in the discussion, but listening shrewdly to what his neighbours had to say. Bill Kennedy waved a hand to Storm and lighted a cigar, seemingly bored with the whole business.

Inspector Teal was shaking his head.

"Never," he muttered breathlessly, "never, never did I hope to see this day.... Kent Road's nothin'—he's knocked 'em on the old Embankment and he's got away with it...." His vast form vibrated with Titanic ecstasy.... "'Flat-footed half-wits ... you can take your choice!' ... Oh, Boy!... *Oh, BOY!...*"

"Teal!" whispered Storm reprovingly. "This mirth is nearly indecent!"

He himself was sublimely unconcerned, for he knew exactly where he had the Great Ones of Scotland Yard. He had them right where he wanted them, gently but firmly held down under his brogues, and he wasn't of the type to indulge in gloating on that account. It had simply been, in his opinion, necessary for him to stand on their necks, and he had done it. That was all. It never occurred to him to crow about it, any more than he gave a snide halfpenny for the consequences.

He finished his cigarette and extinguished it, and selected a second. The drone of dispute died away.

"Will you answer some questions?" asked Sir John Marker.

"Within limits—yes," Storm gave back without hesitation.

"Are you convinced that you know the Triangle?"

"Yes,"

"You based your conclusion entirely on two scraps of evidence?"

"Yes."

"Solely?"

"No. Only a born fool forms a theory on the basis of two scraps of evidence without applying the known facts to that theory and finding out how it wears."

"And you think your theory stands the test?"

"Beautifully."

"What chance would you give your theory in a court of law?"

"About as much chance as a very small icicle in a burning fiery furnace," said Storm carefully—"depending, of course, on the precise grade of imbeciles you chose your jury from."

The Home Secretary conferred in an undertone with Smethurst.

"Then you think," he said, his lips twitching at the corners, "that if you are allowed to go on in your own way. without question, you will be able to raise your theory to the standard of obviousness demanded by a jury of average imbeciles?"

"It's possible."

"And what about the crimes which may be committed by the Triangle while you are attempting to do this?"

"They will be fewer than if you took the case out of my hands."

"Then what are your immediate plans?"

"I'm going to confirm my theory to my own satisfaction, and—by way of an impartial witness—to the satisfaction of Inspector Teal; and then I shall find the Triangle, and——"

"And?"

"He will die," said Storm simply. "But it will not be on the gallows."

His even, unemotional tone held them all rapt. In spite of themselves, his personality had gripped them. His slim straight figure stood out above them; his level confident voice commanded their unwilling attention; he dominated the scene as surely as if he had sat in the Chief Commissioner's chair with all the authority of Parliament behind him.

"That," he said, "is the only reason why I do not intend to conduct this case in the normal way." He looked around him searchingly, and then his eyes returned to the Home Secretary. "I will now make my demands." They gasped again at that—his unassuming presumption was a paradox they needed time to digest. "You will permit me to go on with the case as I wish, with the assistance of Inspector Teal. You will ask for no information, nor will you follow up the hints I have given you this afternoon. You will keep secret my real name, which is now known to you, until I wish the fact to be published. You will allow me to take what counter-measures I think fit to meet the offensive of the Triangle. That may seem arrogant," he continued after a short silence, as though the possibility had just occurred to him. "As a matter of fact, it's only to emphasise my determination. Anyway, you wouldn't all mess about with the case, so my reticence won't hinder you. Mr. Kennedy and Inspector Teal will vouch for my competence. In a fortnight the Triangle will have ceased to be—I can guarantee that..."

He paused, while Bill Kennedy and the for-once-completely-awake Mr. Teal nodded their answers to the unspoken question of the rest of the Board.

"Finally," said Storm, "if Sir John Marker would like to come into a private room with me, I will tell him the name of the Apex of the Triangle."

The Home Secretary deliberated for a moment, and then led the way. They were absent for fully half an hour, during which time Bill Kennedy appeared to go to sleep and Inspector Teal stolidly shook his head and refused to answer the questions that were showered upon him.

When Sir John Marker returned his face was white and he seemed to be shivering.

"Captain Arden continues with the case, on his own terms," he instructed curtly. "I may say that I agree with his attitude in every way. But keep it dark ... I don't want trouble in the House."

The other members of the Board stared at him blankly, for they had anticipated nothing so decisive. There was an eerie chill in the air, born of Sir John Marker's ghostly pallor, that would have shaken less matter-of-fact men. The hint of something vast and menacing and incomprehensible loomed over them ... something bigger than even the *Daily Record* had ever dreamed of....

They broke up into little groups which converged on the placid Storm and the now weary Teal, while Sir Brodie Smethurst escorted the Home Secretary from the room.

As the Minister was taking his leave, the Chief Commissioner stopped him.

"There's been a lot of talk about that man Raegenssen," he said. "I've heard other things about him which make him interesting in a general way, apart from the Triangle. Can't I have that one question?"

The Home Secretary moistened his dry lips as he shook his head, and smiled crookedly.

"Oscar Raegenssen must have been reincarnated," he said flatly. "He's been dead two days..."

CHAPTER 10

RETURN OF AN EXILE

There was a thin yellow envelope which was familiar to the members of the Alpha Triangle, for it was in such envelopes that they received their weekly general orders, and in similar envelopes the lieutenants of the Apex communicated with their Chief, under one or another of his various aliases. It was one of these which caught the eye of Joan Sands on a certain morning when she entered the living-room for her belated breakfast. It lay beside her husband's plate unopened, for James Mattock was absorbed in the latest news about the Alpha Triangle, as purveyed by the *Daily Mercury*, and seemed to be unattached for the moment by the more intimate news which awaited his scrutiny.

He glanced up as she came in, gave her a perfunctory smile, and went on with his reading.

Joan took her seat and poured herself out some coffee. There were unbecoming shadows under her eyes; and, not yet rouged and powdered, she was unhealthily pale. The girl had altered during the past week, and Mattock had noticed the change without understanding it. There had never been any love between them—the old sophisticated Joan would have scoffed at the idea—but there had been Mattock's infatuation and the girl's readiness to accept anything that offered in the shape of easy money and a good time. He had done much for her—had served a term of imprisonment to save her life—and she was grateful. But love ... no. She was a gold-digger, and she was honest about it; she played the game by him, because her own peculiar code commanded her to. She would have given him what he wanted without the formality of marriage, because she was fond of him in a cynical way, and he had been very good to her in his unworldly, altruistic manner. Not that she was in any sense promiscuous; that was about the only form of gold-digging she barred, and that fact, perhaps, constituted her only virtue in the eyes of her victims.

It is difficult to analyse her mind. A child of the people, she had risen to the fringe of Society by reason of her beauty, wit, vivacity, and a certain acquired refinement, while her less gifted brother remained in the ranks of the petty in-and-out-of-"stir" sneak-thieves. She kept up her position because she was unscrupulous where money was concerned. And yet, incredible as it may seem, for all the wealth her foolish middle-aged admirers had offered her, she had come to James Mattock a virgin. So ill-assorted a couple were they—James Mattock, Oxford graduate and gentleman by birth, who had in his headlong course down-hill tasted all but the ultimate dregs of dissipation, unselfishly in love with a woman of the criminal classes whose chastity had been her only claim to his consideration....

He was at a loss, now, to interpret her changed attitude towards him. Ordinarily, she had been the ideal of a good comrade to him—not demonstratively affectionate, yet kindly sympathetic, loyal and trustworthy. Of late she had become rather distant. There was an awkwardness between them which exasperated Mattock and perplexed the girl herself.

"You've forgotten your letter," she reminded him as he drained his cup and rose to go.

"Oh, yes."

He was preoccupied. She could see the lines of worry on his face. He had been past middle age when he had met her, and prison had aged him; he had aged even more during the last few days. His unspoken trouble awakened the old companionship—shook for a moment the strange barrier of reserve which had separated them so incomprehensibly.

She fetched his hat and umbrella for him, and then put her hands on his shoulders.

"What is it, Jimmy?" she prompted. "You're so quiet lately."

"Am I? Oh, yes, dear, perhaps I am a bit. I'm not feeling quite myself." His voice was expressionless. "This—the whole thing's rather getting on my nerves, I think."

He had forgotten the yellow envelope in spite of her reminder, and she went back for it and placed it in his hands.

"Do you have to go on?" she said wistfully. "I wish—I wish you'd drop it, Jimmy."

"You wouldn't have this flat, then," he said innocently.

"D'you think that's everything in my life?" she broke out resentfully. "Didn't I marry you when you hadn't a bean—when you had to—to steal for me? Have we always got to have this life, with everyone's hand against us, and nothing in the future ... *nothing* ... unless it's Aylesbury for me and the Awful Place for you?" The wall was down now. "This silly feud of yours is going to cost us everything! That's the only idea you've got in your head—to satisfy your rotten vanity, and get your paltry revenge—and you'll go on slogging at it, and risking on it, and wasting your whole life on it! You've set it up as your god, and you'll sacrifice everything to it—sacrifice yourself—sacrifice *me*! ... You've kidded yourself that heaven's at the end of this road you're going, and you'll sweat for your worm-eaten heaven—you'll slave and slink and cringe and break your heart to feed this bloody thing that's gnawing away inside you—and what good'll it do you?"

"We've had all this before," said Mattock tonelessly. "I've got to go on. I'm sorry, Joan.... But you can get out of it—it nearly broke me up when I found you were in the Triangle, but it's been on my mind ever since. Get out of it, Joan, and don't fret. We'll pull through somehow."

She faced him accusingly, unshed tears in her eyes.

"If it costs you everything—in spite of all I've said, you're going on?" she flared.

He nodded.

"Even if you lose ... *me*?"

He stared at her.

"You, Joan? Why, how does it touch you? You can go—I've told you I'd prefer you to—and then, when it's all over——"

"Yes, *when*!" she blazed back. "And when that happens you'll be dead—dead! Don't you know that? You're playing skittles with dynamite, James Mattock—you're screwing your head into the mouth of a howitzer with a wild horse harnessed to the lanyard! You're mad!" She clung to him convulsively, her head buried in his shabby coat. "Jimmy, give it up ... don't go on asking for death!"

Instinctive actress though she was, her passionate outburst was desperately sincere, and Mattock passed a shaking hand across his forehead as if to brush away a veil that clouded his eyes. And yet, when he took her gently by the shoulders and set her from him, the dull blankness of his eyes had given place only to the glimmer of a fanatical light.

"There was Sylvia," he said. "I must go on.... She suffered cruelly ... I must...."

He spoke as one who repeats a prayer, and as she drew away from him it seemed as if the old insurmountable wall slid into the space between them. She must have realised it, for she made a last fierce effort to break through his armour.

"Are you blind?" she whispered tremblingly. "The strain's getting too much for me—and it's not myself I'm worrying about.... I've been blind too, and I've just realised it.... Jim"—a wonderful light was born suddenly in her eyes—"oh, Jimmy"—breathlessly—"Jimmy——"

And then, in the old caprice of Fate, the clock struck. The sharp chime of it perked Mattock from his throbbing expectancy, wiped the dawning comprehension from his face, lashed and wrenched and hammered and tortured him back behind the reef that had all but crumbled away—beat him back to the cold matter-of-fact reality of things and his madness.... Flung back into his brain the madness that had come to him one drizzling afternoon when he had sworn to set a Goal above all Prizes…. Gave him back the Ambition— the One Idea….

"I must be going," he said unevenly, for the hurt showed in his voice. "Can't afford to lose my job. Cheer up, Joan."

He kissed her—not perfunctorily now, but with all the frustrated longing of his heart. And then he strode swiftly from the place.

He saw little of Raegenssen that morning, for the Swede marched straight through the outer office without his customary "Goot morning!" to his clerk, and gave no instructions for the day's work.

Raegenssen locked himself in the inner office and lighted a cigar. He opened the big safe and took down from it a number of ledgers and a bundle of miscellaneous papers bound up with tape. Each one of the books and papers he went through carefully three times, as though memorising their contents, and then he tore out the pages which bore his scrawling handwriting, added the other papers to the pile, and carried the whole over to the fireplace. He watched them burn until every least scrap was reduced to brittle black flakes, and then with the poker he stirred and powdered the ash to a fine dust. Even this, to make doubly sure, he swept up into the shovel and threw from the window.

He was left with three photographs, and these he placed in the wallet he carried in an inside pocket.

Then he resumed his seat and sat through the time it took him to smoke another cigar, motionless except for the regular monotonous twisting of the pencil in his strong hands. It was nearing eleven-thirty when with a sudden movement of decision he snapped the pencil in half, pitched it into the waste-paper basket and rose. He picked up his battered hat, unlocked the door, and passed again through the outer office without a word or a glance to either side, and Mattock watched his departure with a puzzled frown.

He went to the City and Continental, drew some money, and made certain arrangements.

"I see you've had a burglar," remarked Blaythwayt when they had concluded their business.

"Yess. He debarted away!" The Swede's voice was lifeless.

"So the police haven't caught him yet?"

Raegenssen glowered.

"No!" he snapped. "Der bolice are fools! Why hof they nod ter Driangle abbrehented?"

He usually stayed for a short chat with his bank manager, but this morning he seemed curiously disinclined to be conversational. Joe Blaythwayt himself opened the door to his customer, and that simple soul was almost personally apologetic, for Raegenssen's comments on the Force seemed a direct slight on the lethargic officer who was wont on occasion to brighten the Finchley Nights Entertainments.

That same Teal, driving down Lombard Street in a taxi with a couple of unsuccessful jargoon sellers, saw the Swede leaving the bank and chuckled.

"You boys want to aim high," he said. "Fifteen million pounds for a few murders is better than a hundred for a white sapphire!"

Things happened to Mr. Teal in those days with the well-oiled precision of a detective story from a master pen. He was chatting downstairs in Scotland Yard that afternoon when a vast young man of incredible ugliness came hurtling down the steps three at a time.

"I want you, Teal," he crisped. "Where's Captain Arden?"

Teal came to attention.

"I don't know, sir. He hasn't been in all day. He said he'd be here about dinner-time."

"Get him on the phone."

Teal called the number, and was answered by the voice of Cork. He snapped out a curt demand, listened, and then snicked back the receiver.

"No good, sir," he said. "Captain Arden's been out since eleven this morning and his man doesn't know where he is."

"Hell!" snarled the Assistant Commissioner. "You'd better come along, then."

Bill Kennedy led the way to the waiting taxi, Teal following obediently, and it was not until they were turning out into the Embankment that the Commissioner explained.

"The Triangle's on the war-path again," he said. "Marker was shot this afternoon as he was leaving his house."

"Dead?" drawled the callous Teal, and Kennedy shrugged.

"The message didn't say. Did Captain Arden give you any idea what he was doing this afternoon?"

"He said he was going to commit another felony today. I wonder if he is the Triangle?" suggested Mr. Teal lusciously.

His inspiration being received with scorn, he maintained a dignified silence until the taxi drew up in Queen's Gate, where the Home Secretary lived. The usual crowd was gaping about the entrance, only restrained from closer investigation by the presence of two burly constables. The two detectives pushed their way through the mob and were instantly admitted.

The doctor who had been summoned was already preparing for an impromptu operation, and was inclined to be brusque.

"The bullet glanced off a rib and tore up his right lung," he said shortly. "I may be able to save his life, but it's very chancy."

The most coherent narrative was supplied by the chauffeur, who had been actually holding the door for his master at the time of the shooting.

"There were three cars close together—a Navarre limousine, a Carillon cabriolet, and a Hirondel sports. I couldn't be sure which it was, as I had my back to the street and didn't turn until I heard the report. I should say it was either the Navarre or the Hirondel—they were nearest when I looked round."

"Did you get any numbers?" asked Kennedy.

"No. They all put on speed immediately the shot was fired, and I was too busy attending to my master to look at them closely. Oh—I remember the Hirondel was very battered—looked as if it had been in an air-raid. ZY-something. There was a '2' in it, anyway."

"ZY 28822?" murmured Teal, and the man nodded.

"Something like that. It was the last car of the three, and they all raced into Cromwell Road, so that's the only number I got a glimpse of."

Kennedy dismissed the man and glanced at Teal.

"Captain Arden on duty," he said. "That looks like a thin time for Morini. It was the gentle Gat, of course."

"How're you going to prove it?" Teal wanted to know.

"Your business!" Bill Kennedy took his cigar-case from his pocket and offered it. "This isn't my case at all, really, only Marker's so deuced important."

"What about Hannassay?"

The Assistant Commissioner carefully charred the end of his cigar and then placed it in his mouth and lighted it meticulously.

"Hannassay's was his own fault," he said. "The man refused protection—-said he could look after himself, and that he wouldn't have his holiday messed up with a lot of detectives hanging round. He had a compartment to himself—I saw him off—and it was a corridor train. He must have been easy."

They waited to hear the result of the doctor's operation, for there was clearly nothing they could do for the moment. An all-station call for Morini had been out for days without result, and unless their luck changed the only hope was that Storm would be able to hold up the gunman.

A butler came in with a tray of sandwiches and offered them the use of the syphon and decanter in the corner. They talked on odd subjects, and it was just before they received their report that Bill Kennedy opened up a new line of thought to Mr. Teal.

"What we really need in a case like this is the German Razzia," he remarked. "If a wanted man's patient and really ingenious, he's as hard to find as water in the desert. All he has to do is to retire to the house of a friend, or to a fairly big residential hotel, and never budge out of doors. By simply lying doggo instead of trying to make a bolt for it, he could have the police rubbering till all's blue, and never be in danger."

A few minutes later the doctor arrived.

There was a hope—yes. Marker was a healthy man in good condition, and stood as much chance of pulling round as anyone. It had been a nasty wound, and the illness would be a ticklish business, but it would not necessarily be fatal.

"Well, that's a relief," Kennedy said as they returned to the street. "But it don't let us out, laddie. Morini must have been rattled—according to Captain Arden, that dago's one of the slickest gunmen in the world."

Towards eight o'clock that evening, when Storm had failed to put in his promised appearance, Inspector Teal huddled into his mackintosh and set out to walk down the Embankment towards the restaurant in New Bridge Street where he occasionally fed. He was a man who never complained of the vilest weather, seeming even to revel in it; which was fortunate for him, for the rain was pouring down in stinging clouds, drumming on the macadam like a stage effect. The sky was black and thunderous, and from time to time a crackling reverberation omened the continuation of the downpour. Such few pedestrians as there were scurried along under umbrellas with stifled curses and a drowned-rat-like aspect, but Teal plodded along with his shoulders squared and his face defiantly thrust out to meet the lash of the storm.

He was within sight of Blackfriars Bridge when he first noticed the tail lamp of a stationary car, and wondered that anyone provided with such a luxury should dally by the way on such a night. As he came abreast he saw that the driver was poring over a map, and as Teal passed he was hailed.

"Can you tell me the way——" began the man, and then the flickering light of a street lamp swaying in the wind fell across his face, and Teal let out an exclamation.

"You're Carl Schwesen," he said, "and you were deported six months ago for——"

So far he got before the driver's fist shot out and ripped into his face. Half-stunned with pain, the detective staggered back, tripped on the kerb, and fell. As he did so the car jumped forward.

He was fumbling for his whistle when he saw it had slowed up again, and he struggled to regain his feet. And then a heavy-calibre revolver thundered from the interior, and his hat went flying.

He got out his whistle and blew a piercing blast, but the driver of the car accelerated and dashed up the empty road into the obscurity of the streaming rain. He saw the car speed over the bridge, and knew that he had no hope of catching it, but the number was firmly imprinted on his memory.

Inspector Teal continued towards his dinner with a furrowed brow, for he well knew the brilliance and unscrupulousness of the erstwhile deported Austrian chemist. Without being able to give any logical reason for his suspicion, he had more than an idea that Schwesen's return was not unconnected with the sudden inrush of other dangerous men into London, and he wondered what this fresh activity of the Triangle might mean.

CHAPTER 11

EZRA SURCON DIGS

There was a man named Ezra Surcon who owned much land in London. He did not court publicity; there were no paragraphs about him in the gossip columns of the newspapers, and as a matter of fact his name was never mentioned, even in whispers, among the Real Estate Kings of the metropolis. He made his purchases quickly and without ostentation, and the fact remains that in the space of three days he acquired the freehold of no less than seven properties. There was a gloomy house in Buckingham Gate, and another, equally gloomy, in College Street. For a large sum he secured a vacant building in Great Windmill Street; the imposing mansion in Queen's Gate cost him less; and a modest erection in Orange Street was comparatively cheap. He paid reasonable prices for No. 94, Carter Lane and No. 53, Montague Street. In all, he must have expended five considerable figures of hard cash, but since he transacted his business under seven different aliases no one was startled by the magnitude of his investments.

He was a tall loose-limbed man of rising sixty, yet the elasticity of his gait as he walked down Constitution Hill that evening showed that the years had made only superficial inroads on his physique. The benevolence of his expression was emphasised by the large horn-rimmed spectacles he wore, and contradicted by the tightness of his mouth and the angularity of his jaw. A studious stoop took some inches off his height and the shabbiness of his clothes gave no indication of the wealth to which his lavish expenditures in other directions testified.

He passed behind the Victoria Memorial and entered Buckingham Gate. The residence of which he was the proud landlord stood only a short distance down the road—a gaunt and grimy affair having about it that indescribable air of forbidding unkemptness which is a seal upon the seats of the mighty. The blinds in all the downstairs windows were drawn, and there was no sign of life about the place.

For a moment he stood at the foot of the steps, and if the suggestion had not been so palpably incongruous one would have said he was listening intently for a sound he half expected to come from beneath his feet. Then he inserted his latchkey in the lock and passed inside.

The panelled hall was in twilight, and his footsteps rang out hollowly on the uncarpeted parquet. The soles of his shoes gritted on strewn earth, and sporadic cakes of dirt disfigured the rest of the floor. Peering into one room, he found it filled almost to the ceiling with a great mound of soil and clay.

A door at the back opened suddenly, and he was confronted by a burly man, stripped to the waist.

"Getting on, Torino?" queried Mr. Surcon shortly, and the giant nodded.

"Very well, *signor*."

From head to foot the man was stippled and plastered with mud, and the streaming perspiration had cut eccentric patterns in the mess.

He led the way through the kitchen and opened a second door. Before them yawned a flight of stairs which led down into the earth, shrouded in a half-light in which danced the beam of the Italian's flashlight as he guided his employer towards the cellars. The steps themselves were inches deep in trodden clay, and down one side ran two heavy insulated cables. From below them came a muffled thud and clatter.

Presently they met another man, half-naked like the guide, who bore on his shoulders a huge basket of earth, and almost on his heels came a second. Surcon passed them with a brief word of greeting.

They reached the cellars and made their way with difficulty across the layer of soil which cloyed their feet. At the far end of the vault yawned a circular hole, and it was from this that the sounds they heard came.

"We have done eighty yards," said Torino. "Another twenty will be sufficient. That engine is a marvel. Tonight we finish."

"There's been no difficulty?"

"None, *signor*. We have many men, and they are relieved before they tire. There are no complaints, for the pay is good."

They stumbled down the tunnel towards the bobbing light that showed in the distance. The roof was low, and they had to bow their heads; even so, Surcon cracked his head once on a buttress and swore softly. A third man, similarly laden with a muddy basket, passed them, and they caught the heavy tread of the two they had passed on the stairs returning.

At length they reached the end.

A powerful electric bulb swung from a stake driven into the earthen roof, making the tunnel almost as light as day. Right up against the ultimate wall was a thing of shining metal on a wheeled truck. The power cables connected with two large terminals on its outer casing, and over it hovered a wizened man with a rag and an oilcan. It thrummed and thudded with the quiet-efficiency of its compressed strength, and from its stern a stream of earth poured down an iron channel into the waiting baskets. Other men, stripped to the waist and sweating, snatched away the baskets as they were filled and rushed them away. From time to time the engineer slewed the truck round so that the machine attacked a fresh area, and once he adjusted a winch that raised it bodily on the truck to burrow at the height of the passage.

Surcon tapped him on the shoulder, and he turned drawing a greasy hand across his forehead.

"It gives no trouble?" he asked in German, and the man shook his head.

"*Nein, Herr.*"

"The dynamo runs well?"

"*Recht wohl, Herr.*"

"*Sehr gut!*"

Accompanied by Torino, he retraced his steps laboriously, for the tunnel had a distinct upward gradient from the point where the engine was working. He was glad to return to the comparative freshness of the hall, for the atmosphere below was close and almost insufferable.

They entered a room at the back of the house which had once been a beautiful dining-room. Now the polished mahogany table was scarred and stained, and the remains of a meal were congealing on the chipped plates. A pack of cards was spread on the seat of one chair, and a dozen empty beer bottles stood by the wall.

With a gesture of distaste Surcon swept the debris from one end of the table, dusted a chair with his handkerchief, and sat down delicately. His companion followed suit without these precautions.

"Where are the others?" asked Ezra.

"They sleep upstairs, *signor*. In an hour they relieve those who are working now."

"There is enough room for the earth?"

"Barely, *signor*. Much will have to be spread on the floor of the tunnel and in the cellars. A little will go in the upstairs room where the relief are resting."

They spoke in Italian, for Mr. Surcon was a linguist.

He took out a bulging wallet and counted out a large sum, and passed the notes across the table.

"There is the pay," he said, "and there is a hundred per cent. bonus for finishing so soon. You will go from here to the other foremen, and tell them to promise their men the same if they complete their work at the time I have ordered."

"*Grazie, signor—subito.*"

"When they finish, they will return to headquarters. Only two need remain—yourself and one other. It is understood?"

"*Perfettamento.*"

The reason of his visit disposed of, the whim seized him to make a second tour of inspection below. This time he did not penetrate the tunnel, but sat on an up-ended packing-case in the cellar, gazing down towards the winking luminance that showed where his machine ploughed on tirelessly. The clamour and purr of it hypnotised him. He realised then, as for the first time, the colossal daring of his plot, and its immense simplicity. The shaft which faced him was paralleled by six others, in various stages of progress, that were being driven to his command at that moment, by similar machinery. He had a stabbing comprehension of the immensity of the Power he was moulding to his hand....

The man Torino, breaking out of the gloom with one of the waste-baskets on his back, paused at the look of intentness on his master's face.

"It is the plan of a genius," he said softly. "So simple—and so unbeatable! It will mean wealth for all."

Surcon nodded.

"Wealth.... But this little hole will be used last. It is our safety-valve—our trump card. While this remains unused and a secret, there can be no danger."

He followed his foreman back to the sty of a living-room and sat down with his chin in his palms, staring into vacancy. The Italian lighted a rank cigarette and searched among the bottles for an unopened one, which he failed to find. Neither spoke, for each was busy with his own thoughts, and the rap-clang of the brass knocker on the front door made them both start.

"See who it is," ordered Surcon, and Torino nodded and tip-toed from the room.

He was back in a moment with a small innocent-looking man whose china-blue eyes swept round the dining-room in one wary all-embracing glance.

"Morini!" snapped Surcon. "Why the devil have you come here? Fool! Would you lead the police——"

"The bulls aren't after me," said Morini calmly. "Arden was on the spot as usual—damn him!—but your idea of having two cars was a brain-wave. He smashed his car into the Carillon, just as I expected, and I jumped from the Navarre. Gee!—I've never seen a man look so sick! He started gunning from the wreckage—plumb in the middle of West Cromwell Road—but we were round the next corner too quick for him."

He spoke without Mecklen's nasal twang, for "Gat" Morini had once been a gentleman—notwithstanding which fact he was infinitely the more dangerous of the two.

"Did you get Marker?"

"Not fatally, though he may die. I always know to a fraction of an inch where my shots go. Arden was so much on the premises he worried me a little, and I misjudged the speed of the car."

Surcon shrugged.

"It doesn't matter," he remarked. "Gunning is crude—I have a better plan now. A few days——"

"A few days, in which Arden may put you behind bars." Morini leaned against the door and began to pour flake tobacco into a curled slip of paper. "You underrate that man, Chief. He's cool—so cool he nearly gives me cold feet. And tough—he's just a slab of Bessemer on two legs." He fixed his cigarette with one deft twist and lighted it in the same movement. "I've met him before, and it was too even a chance between us to make me feel comfortable!"

"Are you scared?" demanded Surcon malignantly. "Because, if so——"

"*Scared*," said Morini equably, "is a word folks who know old Gat just don't use when I'm around. But I don't mind 'em knowing that a coffin isn't my idea of a good time."

Surcon regarded his subordinate in silence, his big hands locked together on the table, his heavy brows lowered.

"Well?"

"Let me go gunning for him, Chief," begged Morini. "I tell you, I won't feel comfortable in this game till Arden's riding in a black buggy. He'd be easy—he takes any risk. He got Lew, but Lew always was too nervy to be much good at close work. I shouldn't have missed him that night."

Surcon shook his head—reluctantly, one might have thought, but none the less definitely. His fingers untwined, and he flattened his palms slowly on the mahogany in a simple gesture that conveyed better than words the utter finality of his decision.

"No. I'll deal with him. He needn't be killed. We can hold him until the Government have paid up, and then he can go."

"You seem to have a soft spot in your heart for that guy." Morini flicked up an interrogative eyebrow. "Is he your long-lost brother or something?"

Surcon ignored the question.

"How's Rodriguez?"

"Nearly dead. He'll go out tonight for a certainty. Trouble is, we can't have a doc. in with that place looking like a cross between an arsenal and a barracks."

"I'll give instructions about him by telephone."

Surcon rose and buttoned his coat. He picked up his hat, and Morini stood aside to give him passage.

Surcon paused in the doorway, and his eyes fixed the gunman with a cold warning in them that was more acidly menacing than his words.

"You understand?" he said. "Leave Arden to me. If you kill him, you will die. That's all."

Morini showed his teeth.

"*Is* he your brother, Chief?" he taunted, and then the flame of concentrated venom that licked out of the big man's eyes made him shrink back. In that moment, with that one level gaze, Surcon, unarmed in the presence of a professional killer, showed who was master.

"No—he is my son," he said simply, and was gone.

An hour later he sat at ease in an armchair, reading over the proclamation that was to appear in every London newspaper the next morning. It was a notice absolutely without precedent in the history of crime—an ultimatum set out with all the cold-blooded arrogant effrontery of a Note from an unscrupulous Great Power to an insignificant Power—a manifesto that was staggering in its presumptuous authoritativeness, before which the imagination reeled away with uneasy incredulity.

CHAPTER 12

TOURS IN BILLINGSGATE

Respectable young ladies of gentle nurture do not as a rule haunt the obscure purlieus which lie east of London Bridge, down towards the river, at one o'clock in the morning; but then, although Susan Hawthorne might have pleaded guilty to the gentle nurture part of the clause, it is doubtful whether she would have admitted her respectability. Respectability and old Smiler, her beloved father, tutor, friend, and companion in the all-important years between fourteen and twenty, were two factors which in the eyes of the initiated were about as likely to merge successfully as oil and water. Certainly, when Adventure loomed ahead, the teaching of old Smiler took no stock of convention.

"If there's Trouble with a big T at the end of anything," was his oft-inculcated maxim, "life isn't worth living unless you're making a bee-line for it. And if, on the way, you come up against something you know you CAN'T do, and it's in the way, well—DO IT, and hell to the consequences."

A pernicious doctrine by almost any ethical standard, but one which by frequent repetition had become as much a part of Susan's life as old Hawthorne himself. Which goes to explain why she sauntered down Lower Thames Street on a certain evening on felony bent. There was no hesitation in her lissom stride—she even hummed a little tune. Nerves? You don't know her! Susan Hawthorne, who on one occasion had stuck up His Excellency the President of Olvidada at the end of a six-shooter, in his own Illustrious Palace, for six measured hours, what time she—er—persuaded him to issue divers orders anent the constitution of that misruled Republic—orders which made His Excellency shudder and gasp and fume impotently—Susan Hawthorne, I say, and nerves? Not in your sweet natural, stranger! Nothing so amateurish as taut muscles, quivering ganglions, and a disconcerting void in the gastric regions—nothing more tremulous than a faint pleasurable tingling of anticipation.

To the casual eye she was simply a weedy youth trudging towards his favourite pub. A moist and melancholy-looking cigarette dangled from the corner of her mouth; her face and hands were convincingly grimed; her shoulders slouched. The corduroy trousers were artistically torn, the ill-fitting coat dusty and clumsily patched, the tweed cap pulled down over her eyes in the approved rakish manner. There were only two things about her attire to distinguish her from the original of the part she was playing, and neither of these obtruded itself. One was her shoes—light black pumps with soles as thin and flexible as rubber wafers, which made no sound as they plodded lightly over the cobbles—the second was a little instrument of blued steel which nestled against her hip, for Susan Hawthorne had spent most of her unusual adolescence in those parts of the world where, the wise go heeled and the foolish are all dead.

So Storm had decided that she wasn't to be in the Triangle picnic, had he? Well, he'd got another guess coming, she reflected grimly. Keep her out of it, when in her time she'd been through more hair-raising adventures, in company with old Smiler and Kit Arden, than she could remember in detail? Not much!

She was swift on the uptake, was this slim girl. Storm had rambled on unsuspectingly about the mysterious warehouse in Billingsgate, and Uncle Joe had spoken sombrely of the mysterious Mr. Raegenssen. The faculty of adding two and two, and unfailingly producing a tentative dozen, was hers in a marked degree, and a few discreet investigations had done the rest. Oscar Raegenssen himself, that eccentric gentleman, was the worthy burgess who numbered that curious "saw-mill" among his goods and chattels, and the coincidence required closer scrutiny. There had remained only the minor problem of the escape from the watchful eye of Terry Mannering, and from the even more intent care of the plain-clothes watch-dog whom Storm had set over her.... To one of her breed, that difficulty was exceeding small. She chuckled reminiscently as she recalled the simple ruse she had employed to circumvent it.

The Sud-Scandinavia Sawmill stood a little way back from the narrow street, occupying a whole block, and fronted by a wide stretch of pavement, not a hundred miles from Nicholson's Wharf—a gaunt sooty building from which by night and by day issued the muffled swoosh and clang of a tireless plant. A forbidden place—glancing up as she approached, she took in its massive dullness; the intangible air of secrecy; the barred and shuttered windows placed high up in the walls; the single narrow rat-hole-like entrance with its steel-mounted door. The demesne of Sud-Scandinavian Wood was going to be difficult.

But it took a lot to daunt Susan, once she had definitely embarked on an enterprise. In one lightning summary of the situation she laid hold of the fact that nothing short of dynamite could force an entrance into that building, if so be the occupants earnestly desired to prevent ingress. Dynamite, or low cunning. Dynamite being clearly out of the question, stealth became the order of the day.

All this she had grasped and docketed in the couple of dozen paces it took her to reach the place, and she never paused as she approached the small door. Under the light of the lone flare which guttered over the lintel, she studied the masonry on either side and located a bell. Her finger pressed it with a firm touch.

A while she waited, and when no response came she pressed again. Straining her ears, she caught the tread of heavy feet coming towards her. There was something threatening about their slow progress which would have alarmed most people—it was as if the janitor knew that the one outside was no regular visitor, and was suspicious. Came the gentle slither of bolts in well-oiled grooves—she counted four of them—and then the protesting snap of a big lock. The door swung back a couple of inches, and part of a scowling face appeared in the gap.

"Vat ees?"

"An urgent message. Hurry up and let me in, you fool!"

As the man perceived her slightness and the fact that she was alone, the door creaked open a further six inches.

"Hom from?"

"The Chief."

"I know no Cheef," said the man, and began to close the door again, but Susan already had her foot in the jamb.

"The Triangle, you infernal idiot," she hissed.

"Vich Triangle?"

She played her trump card. Something silvery glittered in her open palm as she thrust it towards the man's eyes—Joe Blaythwayt had begged it from Mr. Teal as a memento, and Susan had abstracted it from Uncle Joe's treasury without that formality, in preparation for just such a contingency. The charm worked. The door opened wide enough for her to pass.

"Com."

She entered, and heard the door close and the bolts snick back into place. The darkness closed down inkily, and then the shuffling of the janitor's feet stopped and a switch clicked. Over her head a frosted bulb broke into a dim radiance.

Without embarrassment she crushed out the stump of her fag on the dusty floor and took another from a gaudy packet. She knew that she was being inspected closely, but, secure in the efficiency of her disguise, this fact troubled her not at all.

At length the man seemed satisfied.

"Vid hom do you vish to spik?" he queried deferentially.

This was a development which she had not had time to reckon with, but her brain moved fast, and she covered up her slight hesitation by striking a match and lighting her cigarette before replying.

"Is Prester John here?" she asked.

She was bluffing desperately on the fragmentary and secondhand knowledge of Joe Blaythwayt, and prayed that Prester John might be absent. Even if he was there, however, she had her plan mapped out by this time, and she knew her escape was certain—which it assuredly was not if Prester John were away and she went on with her attempt as she had planned.

"I vill see," said the man, and she braced herself up to the knowledge that it was now a case of no retreat, no retreat.... "You haf not been 'ere before?"

"No. I'm always with the Chief."

"Ze Cheef, *hein*? A graate man, but he hass not enof time for ze ladies, *non*?"

He leered at her, and for a moment she dreaded that he might have penetrated her make-up. And then she realised that he took her for a lad of his own type and leanings, and she smiled. What was more, she entered her part so thoroughly and she permitted herself a coarse reply which would have sent the simple Joe, had he been there to hear, purple to the ears.

"In zat room"—he jerked his thumb—"you vill find friends. I vill present you."

"Right you are," she agreed gruffly. "Oh, listen. If John isn't here, you needn't bother to tell me. Just send him along as soon as he arrives. The Chief wants him in a hurry. If he doesn't turn up in half an hour I'll have to leave a message and go along and try to find him somewhere else."

He nodded, and turned to her as though an idea had struck him.

"Zere is somzing beeg an' secret—'ow you say?—in ze air tonight, *n'est-ce-pas*? You air ze second urgent messenger ve 'ave 'ad. Not ten meenits ago zere com a beeg man viz 'urry call for Morini, but Morini is not yet arrive, so 'e attend him."

"There is something in the wind," Susan said easily. "But the Chief doesn't like questions."

The man shook his head.

"Somtimes I 'ave fear of 'is secrets. Even ve do not know quite 'ow beeg are 'is plans. Zere is zis tunnel, now. Even zose 'oo work do not know vhy for eet ees mak'. Zere ees a new *ingénieur* down zere now 'oo mak' inspection. Ze Cheef send 'im wizout varning—a clevaire *Espagnol* 'e 'as recruit. *Mais que faire? 'Y'a du pèse—nous sommes ses esclaves.*"

The Latin's halting speech broke into a torrent of grumbling French, accompanied by much head-shaking and gesticulation. He was still babbling on volubly as he opened the door he had indicated and waved her in.

She found herself in a broad, low-ceilinged room that looked as if it had been rigged up as a doss-house at short notice—which was the fact. Around the walls ran a double tier of bunks on which men slept or smoked or read according to temperament, while others carried on a low conversation. In the centre of the room, under the hanging oil lamp, stood a greasy table about which sat a dozen toughs gambling. The air was thick with smoke and heavy with the nauseating reek of stale beer. It seemed as if no window had ever been opened upon it. Few of the men spared her a second glance. The alert silence which had succeeded her entry dissolved into a murmur of talk.

She crossed the room to a row of barrels which seemed to do duty for chairs, and sat down, blinking through the smoke which wreathed before her eyes from the dangling fag-end in her mouth. Her hand came in contact with a bottle. She picked it up by the neck and drained the small quantity of bitter fluid there was left in the bottom, and set it down again with a clatter, wiping her lips on the back of her hand.

After a while she strolled over to the table.

She recognised the game they were playing, and was amazed that they should know it, for thugs of that class do not as a rule patronise Monte Carlo, and yet they were undoubtedly on familiar terms with chemin-de-fer. While she watched, a burly ruffian in blue jeans swung round and caught her arm.

"Comin' in on this yer game, cuddy?" he asked.

"Don't know it," she answered, playing her part smoothly.

"Come on!" he insisted boisterously. "Yer c'n learn, same as I 'ad to. It ain't much of a game, but there's dam' few Britishers 'ere an' it soots these bloomin' furriners."

She understood then that the cosmopolitan crowd who provided the majority of the gathering in the room were the cause of the departure from the time-honoured gambles of the Englishman, and to save trouble she took the place the patriotic tough made for her.

It was getting her no farther in her quest, however, except that it gave her time to deduce that the French janitor had not found Prester John. In a few minutes the gamblers were deep in a hated wrangle about the destination of certain stakes, and, taking advantage of the diversion, she slipped from the bench and sidled unostentatiously to the door.

The passage outside was in darkness, but in a moment a thin pencil of light flicked out from her hand, roving across the walls. The man who had admitted her had not entered the doss-room, so she gathered that other rooms were similarly equipped. It would be necessary to proceed warily. Directly across the corridor her torch revealed a door like the one through which she had just passed, and, stealing forward, she heard through it a subdued hum of talk. That, at least, was a spot to avoid. Turning to her right, the beam showed that the far end of the passage twisted abruptly to the left, and she crept towards the bend, using the flashlight sparingly.

Round the corner the corridor widened out into a spacious hall. To one side a flight of stone stairs ran upwards; opposite these, another flight ran down into blackness. On each side were two doors, and a fifth door faced her—an incongruously elegant portal of polished oak adorned with grotesque carvings and half masked by rich velvet hangings. The soles of her supple shoes made no more than a soft slithering sound on the concrete floor as she moved forward. At the end she paused undecidedly. That fifth door was intriguing; intriguing also, after the janitor's vague references to a tunnel, was the flight of stairs that disappeared in the direction of the vaults. Susan solved the problem in a reckless way that would have earned the admiration of Smiler: she took a coin from her pocket and held it between her palms.

"Heads the stairs, tails the door," she murmured, and opened her eyes....
Heads.

A whiff of dank, clammy air met her as she felt her way over the first step. Luckily, the stairs were concrete, as was the upward flight, and there was no danger of creaking boards or a rotten tread. Her light showed her a small landing where the direction reversed. She took the corner and continued downwards.

The cellars seemed to extend over the whole ground space of the building, most of the weight of which appeared to be taken by a number of massive pillars. She could only guess at the actual area, for little but the ceiling was visible. Every available cubic inch of space was filled from the floor with great mounds of earth, tightly packed. There must have been tons of it, piled and compressed into stacks. All the thoroughfare that remained was a narrow lane which wound between the huge dumps, and these had been buttressed up on either side of the path so that the last fraction of volume might be utilised. Down this lane danger lay, for in that insignificant width there was not much chance of avoiding anyone who happened to be coming towards her. Moreover, the path was lighted at intervals by electric bulbs fixed to the side boarding. Switching off her torch, she transferred her automatic from her hip to her jacket pocket, where it would be quicker to reach, and went on.

There was a silence in that weird cavern, which was accentuated rather than relieved by the dull rumble of the plant overhead. That the true purpose of this plant was to provide power she gathered from the insulated cables which snaked along on each side.

Presently a yawning hole, fitfully lighted by bulbs suspended from its earthen roof, confronted her. So this was the tunnel of which the Keeper of the Door had spoken. She entered it resolutely. The quality of the air had altered subtly: it had taken on a puzzling, faint, acid tang, which she could not account for until she came to the exit. She must have travelled three hundred yards before that, and then she noticed that there was only darkness in front, and the bulbs no longer hung from above. She switched on her flash again, and a moment later she left the tunnel.

A blank, tile-faced wall was before her, and she looked from right to left in surprise. She was in a second tunnel which ran almost at right angles to the one she had left, and at distances lights hung on the walls. She bent the rays of her torch downwards, and they were reflected by three parallel ribbons of gleaming metal.

And then she understood. She was in the Tube!

CHAPTER 13

INTEREST IN "H"

Making a closer examination with the aid of her flash, she realised her good fortune, for a heavy circular door hung back against the tiling of the tube tunnel. Swinging it cautiously, she found that when closed it fitted snugly into the round gap where the Sud-Scandinavia burrow debouched into the City and South London Railway, so that without a minute study of the surface it was impossible to know that a door existed at all. Remembering that between the hours of two and five ack emma, when the Tube is closed, there are repair gangs moving about its subterranean ways, she realised the necessity for some such camouflage, and guessed that the door had only been left open by an oversight. Scrutinising the inside of it, she found that it was fitted with a strong iron bolt.

There was nothing to be gained by remaining, and she retraced her steps with all speed. On the return journey she noticed that two irregular ruts ran on either side of the earthen floor of the boarded lane. Some heavy-wheeled vehicle had made that trip frequently, but what it might be she had no notion.

As she went, her head was whirling like a ball-race. A clean-cut tunnel down which ran power cables, which came to a dead end in the Tube! The enigma was to her temporarily insoluble, and she had no time to sit down and make a calm, collected study of the facts from all their angles. All she knew was that she had stumbled on the trail of something big, and the most imperative thing at that moment was to get clear with her knowledge and pass it on to more brilliant and capable heads. At least, she would have a short laugh over Storm—he would have to admit that even in circumstances of the magnitude of the Alpha Triangle she had her uses. But, after that brief period of exasperation on the one side and self-congratulation on the other, she had no doubt that Storm was the one man to deal with the situation accurately and efficiently. The steel-keen precision of his mind, no less than the steel-strong virility of his physique, brooked no uneasiness on that score. If she got out, of course, and when....

At the top of the stairs she paused, but it was only a momentary hesitation.

There remained still that intriguing door, and, anyway, she was fairly and squarely in the swim by now. "When you're in the soup, get all the nourishment out of it you can," was another of Smiler's adages, and on it she acted. Having commenced the reconnaissance in such style, one might as well conclude it thoroughly.

The door opened so lightly to her touch that for a second she was suspicious. An instant later she was reproving herself in no uncertain terms for this tentative sign of waning determination, and, taking a grip on the butt of her little automatic, she pushed the door wide and entered. And then she had her work cut out to suppress an exclamation.

The room in which she stood was spacious and roughly square. The walls were hung from ceiling to floor with luxurious curtains of royal purple velvet embroidered with golden arabesques. The orange carpet underfoot had a wealth of soft pile that was indescribably pleasant to tread upon. A double rank of cushioned chairs ran the length of the room, and a broad gangway paved with costly furs led between them towards the far end. The restful half-light which showed her all these things was supplied by three magnificent chandeliers ranged overhead. It was a room like nothing she had ever seen or even imagined, something that in its splendour suggested a mingling of the essentials of a temple and of an Oriental palace. It was an outrage at the same time—an outrage against all preconceived standards, against all logic and all norms. It was a concrete paradox that mocked comprehension and yet was fascinating by sheer daring originality. Its gorgeous simplicity—its ascetic voluptuousness—its Philistine reverence—these were contradictions which numbed understanding and defied criticism.

Dumb with wonder, she simply stared. Her awed gaze travelled again and again over every detail, and then she looked at the opposite wall—the one facing the door—towards which she had not yet looked. And there she saw something which harmonised so perfectly with the atmosphere that it was evident that the room had been designed and decorated to house it, and which at the same time explained the perplexing counter-impressions.

At that end of the room, facing the banks of seats, was a daïs hung with black, and in the centre of it stood a huge gilded throne. And to the right of this throne was the keystone which held the whole architectural monstrosity together and gave its reason and its justification.

It was a gigantic equilateral triangle of silver which seemed to be suspended in vacancy without material support, being probably braced by brackets concealed behind the hangings. It must have been fully five feet of base, and in the centre of it was a Greek *alpha*, similarly made of silver.

She was in the council chamber of the Triangle—that exotic room which nothing but the brain of a madman could have visualised and brought to substance—the cathedral of a megalomaniac....

And then she saw something else, which up to then had not caught her eye, for the shadows at that end of the room were deeper and the interior of the throne itself was shrouded in gloom. But he moved, and she saw him—the man who lounged on the throne—and then he spoke.

"Hullo, Susan—what do you want?"

Her eyes dilated, for although the figure and face of the man were the figure and face of the tousled scoundrel who had invited her to play *chemin-de-fer*, the voice was the voice of Joe Blaythwayt.

"Uncle—Joe?" she breathed.

He lumbered ponderously off the daïs and came towards her.

"I recognised you in that other room," he said, "and I've been looking for you. What on earth did you want to come here for?"

"What did you want to come for?" she parried.

He waved a hand.

"Men are Different," he said grandly. "How did you get in? Oh, I suppose you were the little devil who pinched my badge?" He wagged a fat forefinger at her. "Naughty! I had no end of a job getting in without it."

"Have you seen the tunnel?" she asked.

"Only a bit of it. I was exploring down there when I heard someone padding towards me, and beat it back. It must have been you. Tunnel? That's interesting. Where does it go to?"

"I haven't the foggiest." Her amazement abated, she took command of the situation automatically. "What we've got to do is to get out of here quick, and talk afterwards. Rustle! Storm's got to hear of this at once."

"And Teal," put in Blaythwayt loyally.

"And Teal, if you like. Come along—behind me," she directed impatiently, and the docile Joe followed her.

They were nearing the door when there came heavy footsteps behind them, and the light of a hand lamp swept the corridor just behind them. There were men talking, also, in a language she did not understand. Blaythwayt stopped in his tracks, apparently frozen with terror, and she gripped his arm.

"Into that room!" she whispered. "They know us there."

She was opening the door when the approaching rays veered upwards and fell full on herself and the trembling Joe. A hoarse challenge echoed down the passage. Unconcernedly the girl took her yellow packet of gaspers from her pocket and began to light one as she waited for the men to come up with them. And then, as they arrived and grouped themselves about the door, she returned the box of matches to her right-hand jacket pocket—and kept her hand there.

The bright light searched their faces.

"Who are you?" demanded a cultured voice with only a slight accent. "I don't know you."

"I know 'em," said another, and added a few words she could not interpret.

The frosted bulb overhead woke to life, and they were relieved of the merciless glare of the interrogator's spotlight. She looked about for the one who had claimed to know them, but none of that dishevelled dozen seemed likely to possess so smooth a voice. And then he spoke again—a man clad only in his trousers and a greasy singlet, who stood half a head above the rest.

"They are special messengers of the Apex. Who admitted them?"

"I did." It was the janitor, whom she had not recognised through the smears of engine oil which disfigured his face, who spoke. "Zat was 'ow zey zemselves called. Ze beeg one 'ave ask for Morini, and ze mignon for Prestaire Jean."

"That's in order. John and Morini won't be here tonight—I know where to find them. You'd better go."

It was a miracle to Susan, for the man's face was unknown to her. And yet there was something vaguely familiar about the cast of it. Just that indefinable carriage of the broad shoulders, the lithe swing of the powerful arms—and yet the lank, oily black hair struck no chord in her memory. She looked at his eyes more closely ... *gun-metal grey*....

Surely only one man in the world had eyes of the curious tint, and, taken with the other resemblances in poise of head and general bearing....

He met her gaze calmly, and she could have sworn that the flicker of a smile feinted at the corners of his mouth.

"I'll go with you, if you like to wait a minute," he said. "I'll just get my coat."

A few seconds later he was back, folding a scarf round his bare throat and buttoning his coat tightly around it. Only one man returned with him, as if receiving his final instructions, and now that she had caught an answering "*Si señor,*" she gathered that they were speaking in Spanish.

The man unbarred the front door for them, and they passed out, Storm going last. A curt exchange of "*Buenos noches,*" and the bolts slithered home on the inside.

Storm led them briskly to the corner of the block and halted.

"Now," he ordered, "you can get in a taxi and go home, and thank your gods you're going to bed alive!"

"There's a tunnel," Joe began excitedly, but Storm cut him short.

"I know all about the tunnel, and about the synthetic mosque, and about the power plant, *and* about the doss-house crew, and about the arsenal," was his categorical retort. "I also know that there isn't going to be a second Battle of Sidney Street if I can help it. Our separate bluffs may be shown up at any moment, and then there'll be Hell to pay! I've got to get busy, and you'll hinder me. Step on it!"

"But can't I stay and see the——"

"Nope! Vamos!"

Joe looked hurt.

"This is the first time I've ever been near any excitement," he protested weakly.

"*Get—in—a—taxi—and—beat it,*" snarled Storm, and Blaythwayt moved aggrievedly away.

The girl had watched this brief encounter in amusement blended with annoyance. After all, it was only luck that had put Storm on the spot at the same time as herself, and it wasn't fair. She had taken exactly the same risks as if he had been a hundred miles away, and she wasn't going to be cheated out of her reward.

"All right—we'll beat it," she said defiantly. "But we'll come back!"

"Let me see you, and you'll spend the night in a police station!" Storm flung at them over his shoulder as he strode away.

From the Custom House he phoned the nearest Division and rapped out his requirements in terse, staccato sentences. Then he got through to the Yard, and tried to get Inspector Teal, but Teal, tired of waiting, had gone home to bed. Storm called a third number, and presently the detective's drowsy grumble answered him.

"Come right down to the Sud-Scandinavia Sawmill in Lower Thames Street," he directed. "There's going to be fun!"

"Is that Raegenssen's place?" Teal's voice took on a more alert note.

"Yeh! I've sent a man round to take him, though I doubt if Olaf's still rooted in Finchley. Flying Squad and all divisional reserves are on their way. Bring a gun. The mill's like a fort, and there's over a hundred roughnecks inside. Now burn the roads!"

In less than half an hour the first detachment of urgently summoned men had arrived, and thereafter reinforcements kept coming in batches—broad-shouldered, phlegmatic men who took the unusual circumstances with great philosophy, as though it were merely a slight deviation from routine. Some were in uniform—these had been hurriedly called in from minor duties—the rest were in plain clothes. All were armed, in accordance with Storm's tele-phoned warning.

Knowing that precipitancy might be fatal, he waited until he had mustered a hundred men. Seventy of these he told off to draw an inconspicuous cordon round the whole block, and thirty he sent down to cover the Tube bolt-hole at London Bridge Station. A batch of twenty of the Flying Squad arriving in a van at that moment, he sent them on to occupy a similar position at Bank Station. The mention of the word flashed a blaze of inspiration across his mind.

"Bank!" he repeated to himself. "Jerusalem, what a man!"

It would be some time before the men could take up their stations, and he filled in the period of inaction by smoking a cigarette with calm enjoyment, and discussing the probable result of a local bye-election with a night watchman.

On the stroke of 3.45 he trod out his cigarette end, bade the watchman a cheery good-night, and made a supplementary disposition of the men who had reached the Custom House in the meanwhile. He was just leaving when Inspector Teal dashed up in a taxi, the disarray of his attire testifying to the haste of his start.

"In time?" queried that officer swiftly, and Storm nodded.

"To the tick. We are now going into action."

They walked together to Raegenssen's block. It was just getting light.

Storm paused before the door and lighted another cigarette. Then he jerked back the jacket of his automatic, slipped the safety catch, and pushed Teal to one side.

"No use both of us being shot up," he said, and pressed the bell.

This time there was little delay. The muffled foot-steps of the French janitor came down the passage; the three-inch bars swished back in their steel grooves; the lock clicked. As before, the door swung back a bare, suspicious two inches.

Storm moved so that the light from the gas jet overhead fell across his face, and the door opened wider as the man recognised him.

Storm pushed into the gap, blocking the door open with his foot. The surprised janitor felt a sinewy hand grasp his windpipe caressingly, and a menace he understood equally well glinted before his eyes.

"*Sois sage—et vis!*" hissed Storm in his ear, and the man signified his acceptance of this advice.

He was handed back to Mr. Teal, who in turn passed him on to a bulky shadow which rose from the ground.

Storm, with Teal hard on his heels, led the way into the building, and a number of dim shapes materialised from the adjoining alley and followed them. So far, all had been admirably plain sailing, but luck was not with them that night. Storm was groping round for the switch which controlled the corridor light, when an over-eager constable tripped over the doorstep and crashed down among his fellows. The thud sounded like a detonation in the silence, and Teal turned and cursed the offender in pregnant whispers. Storm found the lever he sought, and pulled it down.

"Teal—left-hand door," he called. "This way, some of you boys!"

He himself turned the handle of the right-hand door and kicked it open. The men were pouring into the passage behind him.

He saw how much that fall had cost them, and sprang into the room. There was another door to it, and most of the roughnecks had already passed through it. Scarcely half a dozen were left, scrambling to get through. Storm caught the hindmost and tripped him. A couple of burly forms promptly sat on the prostrate one.

The next instant something banged close to Storm's head, and he felt the wind of the bullet and jumped back, drawing as he did so.

The panic had stopped suddenly. The half-dozen who had been fighting to get through the second door were now filing out in an orderly manner, and every one of them was armed. The men behind Storm hesitated for a second, for the London bobby is not anxious to use firearms, and it seemed to be the only course left open. They were waiting for orders, and Storm, having none of their scruples, roared them on.

"Feet—first round—don't hit 'em!" he snapped, and a volley rang out.

The retreating men retaliated on the echo, shooting in deadly earnest, and Storm heard the cries of the stricken men behind him. He fired back himself, gunning now to wound, and saw a man drop with a scream. But the retaliatory salvo had done its work; and in the momentary consternation, before the officers could return the fire, those who were left of the half-dozen won through the door.

Storm reached it a second late, and it slammed in his face. On the other side a bar thudded home.

"The table—smash it in!" he ordered.

While they battered at the thick wood he left the room and crossed the passage to see how Inspector Teal was faring. Teal had been more, and at the same time less, fortunate. He had no casualties, but the reason was that those who had occupied the room had escaped too swiftly for him, and the way of pursuit was barred by a door on which his men were already working.

"Heaven knows where these let out," said Storm. "It may be the tunnel, of course. Here—bring three of your men and we'll go and see."

They sprinted down the corridor, and so bore the brunt of the flank attack which the Triangle, with amazing daring and presence of mind, had organised. Just as they turned the angle of the passage an armed mob streamed from a side door and let fly at them on sight.

The five dodged back behind the bend, and, leaning over each other, fired from cover. The police were shooting to kill now, and in the face of that withering hurricane of death the assault faltered and broke.

The survivors retreated to the door through which they had come, and Storm caught Teal by the arm.

"Great stuff! Go back and get the others; just leave a few on guard in the rooms. Oh, and whistle more men in from the outside."

Teal departed obediently, and Storm coolly reloaded. He was breathing evenly, and there was hardly a flush on his face. On an impulse he decided to reconnoitre upstairs, and thereby saved his life.

He was half-way up when the door below him opened and a man appeared. In a moment the apparition had vanished again, but Storm had seen the round black object that had been flung towards the angle he had just quitted. He yelled a warning, and at the same time fired through the door. He heard a bellow of pain, and gathered that his random shot had found a billet. Then the bomb exploded.

Lying flat on the stairs, he blazed between the banisters at the second mass which crowded out to attack, until his automatic clicked on an empty magazine. By this time a fresh contingent had arrived under Inspector Teal, and once again the onslaught was repulsed with losses on each side. But now, instead of retiring to their door, most of the party broke for the stairs, running the gauntlet of the police fire.

Storm leapt up ahead of them, for there was no hope of resistance: there must have been fully eighty men in that solid pack. He had hoped for a single door which he could have held against them, but a long passage fronted him as he reached the top. A side door which was ajar showed a bare room, and he dodged into it, barring the door behind him, and heard the mob go pounding past. Reloading at speed, he opened the door again and fired low as the last of them disappeared through another opening, and two fell to his shooting. Then Teal and a number of men arrived, and he led them in a rush to the door and tried the handle. It was locked.

"There may be another bomb coming, so look out!" he warned, and promptly disregarded his own advice.

The lock burst out under the impact of a bullet, and they charged in.

The place was beautifully empty.

"This is annoying," said Teal with staggering restraint, and walked to the only window.

Hanging out, he looked to his left and saw that the wall continued over to the next block, with an archway below at the street level. He pointed this fact out to Storm, thereby annoying that young man considerably.

"The place is marked as an island site on the surveyor's plans," he said. "They must have sent me an old set. You can see the bridge is newer than either building. I suppose there's a secret panel somewhere, but we needn't waste time looking for it now. What about the birds who didn't get away?"

"The boys have got 'em—thirteen. They were unlucky, all right."

"And eighty-odd have slipped the cordon, you long-tailed land-ape!" snarled Storm with pardonable heat. "Your sense of proportion makes me want to scream!"

His first thought was for the men under him, but he found that an ambulance had been sent along by a thoughtful authority, and Red Cross men were already tending the casualties. Six of the constables were killed, and a number were more or less seriously wounded. Then he went along to the room where the thirteen unlucky ones were under guard awaiting the arrival of a van. Their spirit left nothing to be desired.

"You might as well let us go, guvnor," said one hefty specimen. "It'll only mean trouble if you take us to the station."

"Yeh!" agreed Storm ironically. "And the trouble will be right up under your hats!"

The man looked at him queerly.

"D'you really think you'll get us to the station?" he asked, and Storm showed his teeth.

"I'll think more than that, for your benefit," he said unpleasantly. "I think in about two months' time you will all hang by your necks until you are dead!"

Teal, on a round of inspection, stopped Storm to air a theory. The detective was taking the set-back with great patience. He stripped the wrapping from a wafer of chewing-gum and inserted the sweet in his mouth with care.

"Has it occurred to you," he said, "that even a lot of thugs like that bunch wouldn't be armed to the teeth, every man of 'em, in the ordinary way, if they'd thought they were all snug and chummy?"

This was a far-fetched suggestion, Storm opined, but Teal's confidence was undamped. He went to the telephone in the hall and called Exchange.

"Central-Inspector Teal," he introduced himself. "Has this number been called in the last hour? ... Thank you.... Ah! ... public call box at Monument Station you said? ... Thanks."

"Three bluffs were put over in this shack tonight," Storm murmured thoughtfully as Teal replaced the receiver. "I don't think it matters which one that call gave away." He looked at the detective sombrely. "Teal! This is Hell's own song and dance act! They were waiting for us, and they guessed they could make a slick enough getaway when the time came; they just stayed on to liven things up a bit for us. That's nerve! I wish the swine didn't seem so damned sure of themselves."

"You surprise me—after that speech of yours at the Enquiry," Teal said drily.

Shortly afterwards one of the Flying Squad's vans arrived with the detachment which had guarded the Bank Station. The officers were unloaded, and the captured members of the Triangle shipped instead, with two armed men for company. A third armed man rode beside the driver.

Huge drays with their attendant school of porters were already about, blocking the narrow street, and the van made slow progress. Storm watched it go with a frown, for the confident words of one of the prisoners stuck in his head. A second van arriving at that moment, he sent it on the trail of the first for additional security, but by that time there was a thick jam of slow traffic between the two, and in those circumstances he had some doubts of the efficiency of his precaution.

"If they do get away, I'll believe I'm dreaming a detective story," he told himself.

Nevertheless, the prisoners did escape, and by a ruse so simple that it was almost certain to succeed.

The leading van made for Headquarters via Tower Hill and Eastcheap, to avoid the obstructions of Lower Thames Street as much as possible—a move which the strategist would have foreseen. At the turn into Tower Street it encountered a lorry laden with men, who to the casual eye were navvies on their way to work, but who must almost certainly have been a section of the crowd which had made its getaway through the secret door in the upper storey of the sawmill. As the van containing the prisoners took the bend, its escort being still held up in the wedge of Billingsgate traffic, the lorry seemed to get out of hand, and swerved across the road. It caught the Flying Squad van squarely across the bonnet, throwing the whole vehicle round in a complete circle which fetched up in a smash against a lamp-post. The driver of the police van and the man who sat beside him were thrown out and dangerously injured; the two armed men inside, half-stunned by the shock, were quickly overpowered by the "navvies" who swarmed from the lorry. The rescue party and their friends then reëntered the lorry, which in the meantime had been backed out of the wreckage, and which by reason of its superior weight and the angle of impact had suffered no great damage, and were driven off. The rescue was conducted with such well-organised speed that it was obvious that some such contingency had been feared and prepared for, and the proceedings rehearsed beforehand. From start to finish the incident took no longer than three minutes, and the lorry was rushing away through the deserted streets before any of the few spectators could recover from their astonishment. The lorry was driven round the Tower and across Tower Bridge, and later in the day was found abandoned outside a builder's yard in Bermondsey.

All this, of course, neither Storm nor Inspector Teal heard until some time afterwards.

"There's two more bits of news for you," Teal said in his homeward taxi. "One is that Miss Hawthorne's slipped her man and disappeared."

"I knew that," said Storm, although for the first time since the opening of that brief, hectic battle he remembered Susan's threat to return. "What else?"

"This." Teal fished in his pocket and brought out a grubby scrap of paper on which a message was typewritten. "Birdie tried to get this put in the *Era* agony column. The clerk smelt rats and phoned us."

Storm read:

Allay contemptible inanity. Groan in it ping, correct, a a

a, ping, a a a. Attaboy consuming, brass band ping, a, loving wine. Cry alas, glory me, ping. Alone. Weeping, days are long, 2. Try again, a ping, presumably futility. A ping a ping. It is hope, frustrated, pong sadly, ping, drying tears. Inside, to see pong ping, a, come and be blest.

"Has Birdie taken to free verse," he asked mildly, when he had perused the amazing document a second time, "or are we both mad?"

Teal shook his head.

"Nor is Birdie in love, as far as I can make out," he said.

At the Albany, Storm invited the detective upstairs, for he felt like anything but endeavouring to put in a few hours' sleep before commencing the next day's work.

"You may as well wait a bit and have breakfast with me," he said as they went in. "Has anyone else been getting busy on this little puzzle?"

"It's a code, of course," said Teal unnecessarily, and Storm stopped in the hall to wring his hand in mute admiration.

"You're a genius!" he declared brokenly when he had found his voice.

Comfortably ensconced in a deep armchair, with one of Storm's cigars between his teeth, the somnambulous Mr. Teal became less trite.

"Our tame expert's on the job, but he's nowhere near it yet. Said it was like nothing in his experience. It's something absolutely new. I suppose it's simple enough really, but these experts have such conventionally eccentric minds that the obvious always gets by them."

"Thank God I'm not an expert," said Storm fervently.

He mixed himself a drink, carried the cigarette box over to the centre table, lighted a smoke, and began to work.

He was silent for a long time, and then he leaned back, staring at the ceiling. The pencil in his hand drummed against his teeth, began to beat out a meditative tattoo. The sound interested him, apparently, to the exclusion of everything else, and then suddenly he brought his chair back to the vertical and permitted himself a soft "Jerusalem!" of satisfaction. He wrote swiftly for a few moments, and then turned to the expectant Teal.

"Who are the H's we know in this case?" he asked.

Teal pondered.

"There's Harry the Toff—I think he's in. And Horring, the hold-up man—he's reformed lately, which always makes me think of Triangles these days. Oh, and Hannassay; but Hannassay's dead and buried. That's all I can remember off-hand."

"I can add one to that list," said Storm, and crossed to the telephone.

There was a short silence, and then he was speaking into the instrument.

"Hullo—Terry? What on earth are you up for at this hour? ... Oh, I see.... Yes, I'll bet there was some vertical breeze! Got home all right, though? ... Mmm—alone? ... Not even Uncle Joe? ... Lazy piker! Look here, can I speak to her? Is she up still? ... Right." He covered the transmitter with his hand while he waited, and addressed Teal. "This is the H you couldn't remember off-hand," he remarked. "I want another man to watch her, and I'll have the coats off their backs if she slips 'em again!"

"Miss Hawthorne?" queried Teal, mildly interested.

"That same.... Hullo. Yes.... Splendid! But listen, Susan, I'm coming round right after breakfast, and I'm going to get your goat! ... No, but you've got to play the game! Now look here, where did Joe leave you? ... Tower Hill? ... So you didn't keep your promise? ... Jerusalem—who? ... Damn it.... Oh, all right. S'long!"

He hung up the receiver.

"Saw the getaway and recognised someone," he explained as he came back. "This code, now. It's Morse. Short and long syllables equal dots and dashes. But some of the signals are too long to get into one word, so *ping* or *a* equals *dot*, and *pong* equals *dash*. When more than one word or letter goes to make up a signal the phrase is enclosed in commas. Groan in it ping, for instance, is *dash-dot-dot-dot*. The words are easy. *Allay: dot-dash—contemptibly: dot-dash-dot-dot*—and so forth. Here's the whole shoot, in case you can't read Morse."

He tossed over a slip of paper, and Teal read the scribbled words with interest.

"All bases. Urgent. Take A. No. 2. Kill H. Urgent. Apex."

"Clever," was Teal's grudging comment. "What do we do about it, Chief?"

"Give it back to Birdie and try to kid him you've decided it was innocent. That'll be a job, but it'll have to be done. If the orders don't go out through the Era, they'll go out some way else, and knowing their code 'll be useful if they try it on again. I'm A, of course, and I'm to be taken. But who is 2—or is it a place?"

"Most likely another nest of theirs. There are probably several—the Triangle wouldn't risk everything on one being unsuspected."

"Probably," Storm agreed. "And H is to die—being apparently more dangerous than me. There's a bouquet!"

It was nearing seven, and he went up the outside stairs to call his manservant and order breakfast. Cork was already astir, and in an astonishingly short time steaming coffee and delicate slices of golden-brown toast were on the table, and a great dish of fried eggs and bacon was set before them, still sizzling seductively from the pan.

"This will about save my life," Teal said appreciatively, and heaved himself from his chair.

Across the food Storm regarded him.

"If Miss Hawthorne is the H referred to," he said, "there're going to be a whole lot of three-cornered funerals in the near future. And the Big Triangle 'll be among those present! From now on I'm going gunning for Triangles!"

The detective stared, for if he had seen the words in cold print he would have refused to believe that they could be invested with such a crisp, arctic, incisive malevolence. Storm's voice was very quiet, very suave—but the quietness was like that which comes between the flash of lightning and the answering crackle of its destruction; and the suaveness was not of velvet, but of polished metal....

"The Law," began the respectable Mr. Teal feebly, and then stopped, having met the frosty gaze of those level grey eyes.

"Skunkrot the Law!" said Storm, very gently.

CHAPTER 14

EXASPERATION OF MR. TEAL

James Mattock read the second proclamation of the Alpha Triangle in his morning paper.

It was headed in the flamboyant fashion of the first, but it was much less circumlocutory. Its comparative brevity lent it a force which had been lacking in its predecessor—a force which gained much from the incidents which had come between the two, and which was emphasised by the account of the Battle of Billingsgate and the subsequent escape of the thirteen prisoners, a scoop that occupied the place of honour next to the manifesto itself.

SECOND MANIFESTO
by the Lord of the Alpha Triangle, in Council, to the Parliament and People of the United Kingdom.

WHEREBY it is announced as follows:

Seeing that Our first Manifesto has been ignored, We find it necessary to increase the arguments we have already advanced, why it will be advisable for the Government to accede to Our Terms. And this We do according to this Warning: That, until Our receipt of official notification of the Government's acceptance of the aforementioned and previously detailed Terms, We shall destroy the undernamed Objects of Public Property, at intervals of two days from the date hereof, in the order given below.

The New Underground Junction at Piccadilly Circus.

The Albert Hall.

The National Gallery and the Nelson Monument.

The British Museum.

St. Paul's Cathedral.

The Houses of Parliament.

Concurrently with this Campaign, Our already initiated Policy of Terrorism will be continued and augmented.

GIVEN by Our Hand this Day,
(Signed)

Followed, in the facsimile which was blazoned across the front page of the *Mercury*, the sign of the Alpha Triangle.

Mattock read the whole epistle through a second time. Not that it interested him—he already knew it by heart—but because for the first time he had been struck by an almost insignificant detail of the layout. Searching in his wallet for the clipping of the first manifesto, he compared the two, and the confirmation of his idea made him sit very still for some time.

When he reached the Cockspur Street office that morning, he found that Raegenssen had not arrived, and the police were in possession. Shortly afterwards, Inspector Teal himself entered, and promptly buttonholed the ex-convict.

"The last time your boss was in was yesterday, wasn't it?" he drawled.

"Yes."

"What business did he do that day?"

Mattock looked at the detective.

"I've no right to talk about my employer's business," he said.

"No-o?" Teal's voice was silky. "But we want to know all about it—we're just buzzing with interest, in fact—and you look most like the man who's going to tell us."

"I'm sorry about that."

"What did Raegenssen do yesterday?"

"Rotten weather, isn't it?" said Mattock absently, and turned the papers on his desk.

Teal shifted his chewing-gum with a deliberate clamp of his jaws.

"Did he go to the bank by any chance?"

"I suppose," murmured Mattock, staring reflectively out of the window, "I suppose the ducks like it."

"You listen to me, and look at this! You know a warrant by this time, don't you? And d'you know what you'll get, with your record, if I use it? Marchmont Avenue, Hampstead, at the house of Oscar Raegenssen—burglary and assault—five years."

Mattock regarded the paper in the detective's hand calmly. Then he looked at Teal. James Mattock, convicted criminal and sometime jail-bird though he was, had once been a gentleman, according to Teal's own description, and the fact gave him an immeasurable pull over the detective. Teal, blunt and burly, a man of the people who had won his rank from the academy of the beat, felt uncomfortable under the steady once-over of the self-possessed clerk.

"You know," said Mattock kindly, "your tact would make an angel weep."

Teal had one pose which never failed to conceal his embarrassment. His heavy-lidded eyes half-closed, his whole figure relaxed—he looked as if he were on the point of falling asleep on his feet. Everything in the world seemed to bore him to tears.

"All right, Jimmy," he said wearily. "We can't make you squeal if you don't want to. The only thing that struck me was that giving us a bit of help now would cut a lot of ice. I mean, we could give you a hand in return—maybe go blind a trifle the next time you skated near trouble."

"There won't be a next time," was Mattock's uncompromising retort.

"All clear, then, Jimmy. But don't forget what I said. The offer's always open."

It seemed to Teal that Mattock had watched the whole performance with cynical enjoyment, and the clerk's answer verified that impression.

"If *you're* ever in trouble, Teal," he said, "go along to a music-hall manager. If you get an audition, and your form's up to today's, your fortune's made."

Feeling that he had not had the best of the encounter, Teal stalked into the inner office, where detectives were already at work examining the filing cabinets and the drawers of the roll-top desk. Mr. Teal's attention, however, was attracted by the massive safe, and he stood for a time before it, hands in the pockets of his waterproof, his lower jaw functioning monotonously.

Then he turned to one of the men.

"Has this been touched, Topham?"

"No, sir."

"Not a hand been laid on it?"

Topham appealed to his colleagues, and the reply was a fairly confident negative.

"Of course, it's difficult to swear that nobody's touched it without thinking."

Teal nodded.

From his waistcoat pocket he produced a powerful lens in a chamois bag, polished it on his handkerchief, and subjected the surface of the door to a prolonged scrutiny. Secondly, he studied the lock, and then he called one of the men over.

"Take a look at it," he advised. "Now, you see the faint scratches by the keyhole? D'you notice any new ones?"

"Two or three," was the result after a short examination. "There's also some marks inside the edges of the keyhole itself. They're all very new; in this weather the brass would tarnish quickly, and these marks are perfectly bright."

"Would a key be likely to leave those inside scratches?"

The man shook his head.

"I'm not an expert, sir, but I should say not, unless the original key had been lost and a carelessly made substitute used."

"Thank you," said Teal, and sank upon his knees as if in prayer.

He made a number of deep obeisances before the huge steel box, and then regained his feet with a sigh.

"Keep off this bit of carpet," he ordered. "We shall want an expert on this."

The expert was on the spot within fifteen minutes of Teal's telephone summons, and he came to a decision in a very short time.

"This is either Prester John's or Grantor's work," he pronounced, and Teal was too hardened to the daily miracles of the police records department to show any surprise at the definiteness of his Holmesian piece of deduction.

A number of micro-photographs were taken, and the fine specks of metallic dust which Teal had discovered on the carpet in his supplicatory attitude were carefully brushed up and placed in an envelope. The safe was also tested for finger-prints, the expert in that science going over it minutely with his grey powder and camel's hair brush, but nothing whatever rewarded his labours.

"The extraordinary thing," he said, "is that there's no mark of any kind. If Raegenssen had touched the safe at all recently, he either wore gloves or wiped it with a rag afterwards."

In an hour the plates had been developed and compared with similar close-ups classified in the colossal card-index system of the Records Office, and the unhesitating verdict was phoned through to Mr. Teal.

The vote went to Prester John, and the somnolent detective became a perplexed and irritated man, for the fact upset every single one of his theories and dizzied him completely out of his bearings.

After three thoughtful slabs of chewing-gum he rang up Storm, obtained permission, and then got through to the Yard and demanded the attendance of a third expert—a gentleman who in the past years had earned a comfortable income from his knowledge of safes until a false step and a term of confinement at His Majesty's expense had exacted from him due labour of hire already received, and (unusually enough) instilled into the said gentleman an enthusiasm for a more restful, if less remunerative and spectacular, employment on the lee side of the Law. On occasion, however, the ex-yegg had opportunities for the exercise of his craft without fear of retribution, and this was one of those occasions.

"Open that money box," commanded Teal without preface, and the expert, after a practised survey, grinned superciliously.

"This is degradin' an honourable perfession," he complained. "A blind elepeptic palarytic could open this tin wiv an 'air-pin an' a corkscrew. I suppose," went on the uncertain vocabularian, warming to his topic, "it ain't to be dammagid? Becos, if you ain't particulant, an' there 'appens to be a sardine opener on the presimes——"

"Get on with it," said the detective testily, for he was not feeling humorous at the moment.

The expert got to work with a pained air, first experimenting with three skilfully twisted lengths of steel wire, and then filing a key with the result of his investigations to guide him.

At the end of half an hour:

"An' 'ere we are. All chynge for Charing Cross an' the Pink Elephant an' Castrol. Pass dahn the car, please! An' I may say, Mr. Charman, that a softer crib 'as yet to be builded. Why, if the game 'ad bin so elemtenary in my days, when I was an exterp at the skience, I'd've bin a blinkin' millionanthropist by now, I would. Drivin' abaht Myfair in a calabriot, wiv all the flatties touchin' their 'ats to me an' 'opin' I'd put a monkey in their Christmas Box. That's the narks all over. One lore for the rich an' another fer the porous. An' no gratootooies—'cept from those 'oo make them big enough." He regarded the confounded detective in wonder. "Well, well, Mr. Teal—wot's the matter? Ain't nothink there? Well, wot did jer expect ter find? A leopotamosceraffe or a box o' pink pills? This ain't Masculine's, yer know. No conjuratin' in this gallery."

"Shut up, Nosey," said Teal rudely. "You can leg it now—we shan't want you any more. Oh, leave that key behind you. I want to shut this thing up again when I've finished."

When the "exterp" had taken his departure Teal sat back on the desk and stared at the open safe. Empty, vacuously empty, it stared back at him—one of the most annoying voids he had ever seen. The rows of steel shelves were bare. The only souvenir that Prester John had left behind him was the cardboard replica of the Triangle badge which Teal had managed to conceal from the roving eye of the ex-yegg.

Teal went back to the outer office and interrupted Mattock from the work of balancing a bulky ledger.

"When were you last here?" demanded the detective.

"Yesterday," said Mattock, without looking up.

"Did you go into that inner office?"

"Yes."

"What time was this?"

"About eleven-thirty."

"P.m.?" asked Teal sleepily.

Mattock raised his eyes with a tired expression.

"Oh, are you still here?" he sighed.

"Pip emma?" repeated Teal.

Mattock closed the ledger and pushed back his chair. His face was a picture of long-suffering tolerance.

"Is this a new kind of round game?" he inquired politely. "Because, if so, can't you get a detective or some other imbecile to play with you?"

"No—you'll do. Is Prester John a friend of yours?"

"I seem to have read about him. Did he write a book or something?"

Teal played his penultimate card.

He leaned over the desk and addressed Mattock in a confidential undertone.

"Listen here," he said. "Joan's in the Triangle—you know that, don't you? And you're fond of a Joan. So am I. A nice kid. It's only circumstances make a crook of her. I'd hate to see her follow the rest of the Triangle into stir, and she will, in time, if one of you hasn't a pull somewhere. You're independent now, but I guess there's a day coming when you'll be glad of a friend or two on the Embankment.".

Mattock studied his finger-nails.

"When we sink as low as that," he said carefully, "I'll let you know."

Inspector Teal straightened himself and shrugged. He walked over to the door of the inner office and called one of his men, and together they returned to the clerk.

"Arrest that man," said Teal, and Mattock rose to his feet with a charming smile.

"The charge?" he asked pleasantly.

"Burglary and assault at the house of Oscar Raegenssen on the fourteenth instant. Accessory before and after the fact in the burglary committed in this office last night. Suspected of concealing knowledge of the whereabouts of Oscar Raegenssen, who is wanted on a warrant issued last night. I warn you that anything you say may be taken down and used as evidence against you."

Mattock bowed.

"Thanks for being so lucid. But you've got the last part of it wrong, you know. The correct formula is, *used as evidence at your trial*."

"As evidence at your trial," Teal corrected himself testily. "Take him away."

"One moment." Mattock stopped him. "The third charge falls to the ground, naturally. You've only asked me about Raegenssen's past movements—not about his present whereabouts."

"That'll keep," said Teal viciously. "Try it on the jury."

He was feeling rather fed up with Mattock's imperturbable assurance.

They took Mattock to Headquarters, and the formal charge was made. The same mocking tolerance permeated the man's demeanour when the usual questions were asked.

"Name?"

"James Norman Mattock."

"Age?"

"Fifty-seven years, eight months, one week, four days"—he looked at his watch—"eleven hours and about forty minutes."

"Address?"

"I decline to answer that question."

His tone encouraged no insistence on the inquiry, and they let it go at that.

They were taking him to his cell when he called Inspector Teal.

"I suppose I'll have to stop behind bars for a bit to satisfy your vanity," he said, "but I don't want it to be too long. So you might get hold of Captain Arden when you have the chance, and ask him if he'll see me."

"I'll find out how his temper is this morning," Teal promised him, and Mattock passed on with a courteous word of thanks.

In Storm's room, however, the detective found something else to occupy his mind, and it temporarily eclipsed his concern as to the fate of James Norman Mattock.

"I've got hold of a copy of the deed of sale of that sawmill," Kit said. "It's signed by Raegenssen, more or less, but there's something wrong with the signature—it doesn't agree with the writing on the papers they brought in from his office. Men with two handwritings make me take notice!"

Teal looked at the parchment, and particularly at the date.

"Two months ago. That's about when the reformation set in," he observed.

In the City and Continental office, Joe Blaythwayt was inclined to be taciturn about his client's business until the importance of his coöperation was pointed out to him, and duly signed authorisation produced.

"No, that's not his ordinary signature," he said as soon as he saw the conveyance. "I'll get you some genuine specimens."

He returned almost immediately with a bundle of cancelled cheques, and these Storm compared with the signature of the deed. The two were totally dissimilar. Whereas the writing on the parchment was small and neat, all the cheques were signed in a thick, sprawling hand.

The latest cheque attracted his attention for another reason.

"That's a lot of money to draw in cash," he remarked. "How did he take it?"

"Fivers. It wasn't the first time—I think you'll find two others made out for large sums, though that one is easy the largest he's ever put through."

Teal nodded.

"One way he is Triangular, the other way he isn't," he said peevishly. "That man's the two horns of a fat dilemma, all right. That sawmill wasn't really his, then!"

Storm rang up the other party to the sale, and found him after some trouble—the managing director of a firm of paper manufacturers with an office close by. Having found that the man was disengaged, Teal and he went round and interviewed him.

The result was not satisfactory.

"I remember the transaction distinctly; I should have remembered it, anyway, even if it hadn't been so recent, because of the way payment was made."

"How?" asked Teal perfunctorily, for the trial did not seem to him to be leading anywhere.

"In notes of four different countries," was the reply. "All denominations, big and small. United States dollars, the new Reichmarks, Spanish pesetas, and Italian lire. I didn't want to take them because of the Exchange risk—something considerable in a sum as long as this one—but he promptly added a five per cent. allowance to cover that."

"That must have cost him something."

The director nodded.

"Next, I was afraid of forgeries, but there again he met me. He went round with me to the bank and was present while the notes were examined and passed."

Teal, interested, suspended chewing for a moment while he put a question.

"Hard to describe," said the director. "Nothing noticeable about him, except his height. Past middle age, I should say. Grey hair, eyes light blue, lined face, walked like a much younger man. Very well built, small iron-grey moustache——"

"Beard?"

"No."

"Any kind of accent?"

"None at all. He spoke English perfectly. I'd take my oath he was an Englishman."

"Raegenssen himself without face fungus!" exclaimed Teal. "I always thought that accent of his was a fake—it sounded too much like the cheap revue idea of a Dutchman. It was Raegenssen."

"Or Mattock cleverly padded," added the sceptical Kit. "If you were going to do a deal in my name wouldn't you try to make up to look like me in a general description?"

The mention of Mattock recalled to Teal his prisoner's request, and he would have mentioned it as they returned to the Yard, but Storm was already off on another tack.

"You remember Miss Hawthorne told me over the phone she'd recognised someone in that getaway? Well, she won't pass the glad news on unless I promise she's to have a part in the play. Rat all women!"

"Arrest her as an accessory," suggested Teal sardonically.

"I'd be happier if she was inside! *Kill H*.... Teal, if you go down and break the neck of that constable who fell over himself last night I'll guarantee to rescue you from the gallows! He's put everything back by weeks. By the way, did that ad. go in the *Era*?"

"Tomorrow," said Teal. "I put it over on Birdie all right. Mattock said I was a great actor," he added reminiscently, and recollected his promise.

Teal waited in the charge room while Storm paid a visit to the clerk's cell, and picked up a newspaper to while away the time.

In those days the Press was so full of the Triangle that most other information was crowded away into obscure paragraphs in small type which few people ever read. Teal, having a single-track mind, rarely had time to assimilate any news which did not bear directly on the case in hand, and politics concerned him not at all.

But he already knew the Triangle news by heart, and the second manifesto was by then as familiar to him as his own face. Consequently, he broke his usual habits and cast an eye over the other happenings of the world. And one section fairly leapt to his eye.

DEATH OF A GREAT SCIENTIST
DEPORTED AUSTRIAN CHEMIST COMMITS
SUICIDE
UNCOMPLETED WORK

(Daily Mercury Special Correspondent)

VIENNA, Tuesday, June 3rd.

A drama of real life is locked up in the news of the death of the Austrian scientist, Carl Schewesen, who was deported from England some years ago. Schewesen's clothes were found on the banks of the Danube, together with a note explaining that he was taking what seemed to him to be the only way out of a hopeless existence.

Schewesen was known to have been making researches into the possibility of stabilising Nitrogen Trichloride (NCl_3), the most powerful explosive known to science, but, as far as contemporary methods of preparation have progressed, entirely without practical use, since even particles of dust settling upon it from the atmosphere are sufficient to detonate it. Schewesen had announced a few days before his death that his experiments promised an epoch-making success. He has left no notes behind, however, and it is to be feared that his knowledge has died with him.

Teal read the paragraph a second time, for this premature obituary notice did not appeal to his sense of humour. He was quite certain that Carl Schewesen was alive and in London, and, Storm returning with Mattock at that moment, he pointed to the column and vented his surmise.

Storm read it through, and looked grave.

"NCl_3," he murmured. "That sounds like more fun!"

"Is it very powerful?" asked Teal, and Storm smiled.

"If a small saltspoonful went off between us now, they'd be able to bury us in matchboxes!" he said.

It was then that Teal noticed the presence of Mattock, and turned to scowl at the man. Mattock had been looking over the detective's shoulder unobserved, and his smile showed that he had heard the conversation.

"I know all about Carl," Mattock said. "But the problem ought to amuse the flatties for some time. Flatties, I think, was the term Nosey used?"

Teal was struck by the change in the man's manner since he had met him in Walton Street Police Station. Then, Mattock had had the truculence which comes of an inferiority complex; but that had now dispersed as though it had never existed. In spite of the shabbiness of his clothes and the ugly lines which prison had cut in his face, he bore himself with a calm confidence that annoyed Teal. It annoyed him because he could not understand it. It was so out of keeping with the part of the lag under supervision. Truculence was regular, and cringing was also in order, though less common. So, too, was friendliness. But superiority—no.

"You look pleased with yourself," said Teal glutinously, falling back into his *rôle* of *ennui* personified.

"So I feel," agreed Mattock. "Captain Arden has very kindly permitted me to be released." He glanced at his wrist. "It's just lunch time. Thank the Lord I'm spared the culinary abortions you serve to persons in custody."

Teal's jaw dropped.

"Is that true?" he asked, and Storm nodded.

"I'm sorry, Inspector," he said officially. "I don't think any of the charges against this man will stand. You will, however, keep him under observation."

"I will!" asserted Teal grimly.

Mattock raised his hat and sauntered to the door with a smile. There, he paused.

"I should keep an eye on Uncle Joe, too," was his parting shot.

Teal stared sombrely at the door through which the man had passed. He shook his head sorrowfully.

"And there, by the Grace of the Devil," he muttered, "goes a man who knows far, far more about the Triangle than I shall ever find out."

"I've also cancelled the warrant that's out against Raegenssen," Storm said. "I don't think any charge will stand against him, either, yet. It's easy to prove that the signature to that deed isn't his, and there's no chance of tracing those foreign bills. You won't even get him by identification—nor will you get Mattock, for the matter of that. Neither of 'em fit exactly."

He was tapping a cigarette on his case when the telephone rang, and he was told that the call was for him. When he came back, the light of war was in his eyes.

"Now we shall see some more battle, murder and sudden death!" he said. "That was to say Mecklen's better. I'm going to get him to court tomorrow, if there's a whole army of Triangles in the way! And then we'll see if he'll squeak."

"He isn't the Triangle, anyway," said Teal gloomily. "Is it Mattock?"

Storm did not answer.

"Or is it Uncle Joe?"

Storm was intent upon the feat of throwing his cigarette high in the air and catching it between his lips—a piece of amateur juggling which he performed with skill.

"Then it must be Raegenssen," Teal said dreamily.

"Keep on guessing," Storm encouraged.

Mr. Teal shook his head and nipped the end from a rank cigar.

"You're so close, you'd make an oyster look like a yawning whale," he protested in despair. "Now, why let Mattock out? I'll bet that man knows all the things we want to know about Alphas and Apexes."

"Speak for yourself," murmured Storm, concluding his exhibition of sleight-of-hand by throwing his cigarette over his shoulder from the back and trapping it faultlessly.

Teal did not applaud.

"He must have had something exciting to tell you," he pondered aloud. "Was it absolutely necessary to release him?"

Storm, who was striking a match, watched it flare, and then looked up with his quick smile.

"Oh—sure!" he drawled. "He's going to kill Raegenssen!"

CHAPTER 15

ONCE A GENTLEMAN

Storm being an unconventional young man, it was not to be expected that the private report on the Battle of Billingsgate which he sent to Sir John Marker would be strictly in accord with conventional ideas on the correct composition of such documents. Kit Arden had no manner of use for formulas; jargon made him feel ill; in the presence of the bugaboo of official phraseology he positively writhed. He banged out his points with crisp simplicity, and framed them in sentences like bullets.

The letter is worth quoting *in extenso*, for reasons which will be apparent at sight.

When once the door of the sawmill had been opened, and the janitor removed without noise, the fate of the Alpha Triangle hung by a hair. In spite of the telephone call which told the men in the building that their heavily armoured bag had lost its cat, they could not forecast the minute in which the information so gained would be acted upon. The future of the organisation was suspended by that slender thread; our hope of being in amongst them, raising Hell, before they could collect their wits. You already know how that thread was snapped.

> Whatever a man's genius, he cannot dream of terrorising a city—as the Apex intends to do—without a large number of assistants. With his young army of helpers locked away, he would have been crippled—perhaps irretrievably.
>
> However, we failed—so that's that. Anyway, all we made was an attempt to maim, when our object is to kill.
>
> One or two details stand over.
>
> (1) Besides myself, two others got into the sawmill. One was Miss Hawthorne, secretary to the late Lord Hannassay, who went simply in search of adventure. The second was Joseph Blaythwayt, manager of the City and Continental Bank, Lombard Street, who in his spare time aspires to sleuthship. He is a friend of Inspector Teal, from whom he had heard unpublished facts about the Triangle which (on his own account) fired him with thoughts of honour and glory as

an amateur Sherlock. He is also one of the lives threatened by the Triangle, which fact does not perturb him unduly.

(2) In my opinion, the telephone call which followed our departure came by chance, and was not based on knowledge of any of our plans.

(3) Raegenssen's office was burgled last night, and the safe opened, but I don't know if the men found anything. A lot of attention has centred round Raegenssen lately, so I expect his obituary notice is only a matter of days.

The Billingsgate raid having failed, I am basing my next move on the Era advertisement. It will, of course, be risky; but if anything goes wrong you will know what to do.

I can only guess how the Triangle will continue its campaign. I probably have a better appreciation of that colossal mind than anybody else; but if I gave you a logical prophecy, even you might begin to regard me as an imaginative alarmist. The solid *fact*, which you and everyone else has got to get hold of, is that for the time being all the odds are on the Triangle. They have all the advantage of surprise. Just now, the police aren't prepared. Violent crime isn't familiar to them yet. They can't quite adjust themselves to it—it'll catch them napping, and they'll take time to get busy. There's a genius at the top of the Triangle—or a lunatic, whichever you care to call him—and the police are neither geniuses nor lunatics. They're just plain ornery men dealing with plain ornery crooks, with all the odds on the crook. Crooks catch themselves and each other, but there'll be no nosing the Triangle. It can pay too well, and the little twisters follow the big money. Gangs in the past have gone just because discontented members shopped them. There will be no discontented members of the Triangle—why, their chief can even pull them out of the hands of the police! The rescue of the Billingsgate prisoners will add tremendously to the prestige of the Apex.

I promised you the head of the Apex on a Triangle in a fortnight, and that fortnight still has some time to run.

The brain of the Apex moves in such great leaps that nothing less than genius could anticipate it from pinnacle to pinnacle. Against that there is only one card to play—fear. Even genius has nerves. Even genius can be made to worry about its neck.

I shall win.

The removal of Lew Mecklen from St. George's Hospital to Marlborough Street Police Court was not advertised, but Storm did not doubt that the Intelligence Bureau of the Triangle had its own sources of information. He had asked for, and secured, a special escort from Wellington Barracks, and they were served out with ball ammunition. It was a wise precaution, for the soldier, being a lethal machine, is less chary of using firearms than the London constable, who is a civil institution into whose routine the more effective forms of violence rarely enter. Apparently the Triangle admitted that Mecklen was well guarded, for no attempt was made on the armoured car in which the gunman rode with platoons of scarlet-coated men marching in front and behind.

Lew was taken into the tiny court-room, and a stream of detectives followed him and filled the rest of the space. Outside, uniformed men blocked the tiled hall, and the military escort stood at ease in the road.

The proceedings were brief, for attempted murder offers no option of summary jurisdiction. Mecklen pleaded not guilty and declined to instruct a solicitor. Evidence of arrest was taken, to which the prisoner paid little attention. The verbal proceedings seemed not to interest him, but he studied his surroundings curiously. He did not cross-examine, and made no statement, and the whole business took no more than ten minutes.

"Without a hitch," remarked Storm, in grim reminiscence of the formal Press account of executions—"thanks to the Army!"

Mecklen was committed for trial, and, whilst the necessary papers were being made out and signed, he was taken to a cell in the adjoining police station. It was when they removed him and told him that he would be taken immediately to Brixton Prison that he showed his first sign of uneasiness. He asked if a message had come for him, and, when informed that none had arrived up to that time, he asked to be allowed to see a newspaper. On Storm's authority, the request was refused, and Mecklen was handcuffed and led out between a double rank of policemen. Teal went in front and Storm brought up the rear, and as the cortège came into view of the street Teal halted so suddenly that Storm trod on the prisoner's heels.

Pushing his way to the front, Arden found the detective staring up and down the street with a ludicrously blank expression on his sanguine countenance. Storm looked also, and his lean face hardened. There was a cab rank in the road, and he went over at once and asked a question of one of the drivers.

"About arf an hour ago," said the man. "Just after the man'd bin taken in. A cop comes out an 'ands a note to the orf'cer, an' walks away, an' then the orf'cer shouts '*Shun!* an' off they goes."

"Did you see the constable's face?" asked Storm, and the chauffeur scratched his head.

"S'pose I must 'ave, but I didn't take much stock of it. You don't inspect every copper's dial wot yer sees—you'd get 'eart failure! Just looked an ord'nary pleeceman to me. 'Ulkin' great feller, oldish, walked as if 'e owned the earth—like they all do."

"Thank you," said Storm bitterly, and returned to the waiting group on the station steps.

By that time the escort would be back in barracks. In the first instance, there had been more than enough red tape, and no little grumbling in high places about troops being called upon to do the work of the police. A fresh escort would not be procured without considerable delay, and perhaps not even then. And yet a military guard Storm was determined to have. As it turned out later, he had made a grave mistake in jumping to the conclusion that the dismissal of the soldiery by means of a forged message was simply a ruse to make him send Mecklen to the prison in the ordinary van and under police escort only. Bearing in mind the Tower Hill affair, this was the explanation he had reached, and it made him doubly set on attempting no such hazard. He had Mecklen taken back to his cell, and ordered a special watch to be mounted over him. Then he rang up the C.O. at the barracks, and found that the two platoons had just returned.

"You might find out if the officer kept my note," he said, and waited until the requisite information was forthcoming. "He has? ... I'm sending a constable round for it now; he'll give his number, which is C2447.... Oh, no, nothing whatever, except that the note happens to be a fake! ... That so? Well, you're not half so sorry as I am."

He listened for a moment, and then replaced the receiver with great care.

"Started to quote me: *If you want a thing done well,*" he explained. "On the whole, the observation's appropriate, but not the way he meant."

Teal was looking glum.

"I don't like it," he confessed. "And yet, on the face of it, Lew's almost as safe here as he'd have been in Brixton. But this Triangle's a shade too snappy for Claud Eustace—they think of things the ordinary crook'd laugh at, and they do 'em, and so far they've got away with them every darned time by sheer nerve."

"There's a special guard," Storm said, "and you can spend the night here yourself if you like. I'll see if I can see Marker and get a special order for another parade tomorrow. We can't do any more. Either the Triangle's thinking of raiding the station, or they're planning to hold up the prison van, and I think the first is the least likely to succeed."

Teal shook his head.

"I agree; but it doesn't make me happy. Triangles have three corners, so I guess they might manage to have a prick waiting in two places," he said prophetically.

Down at the Yard, however, a slight ray of hope awaited them, for the call put out the previous day for Prester John had been successful, and the burglar was even then being detained in Cannon Row pending audience.

The man who had made the arrest foreshadowed the result of the interview in his account.

"I took John in a bar in Camden Tower, where he often goes. He didn't deny the charge, and said he was coming along to see Captain Arden today, anyhow."

"He's got his wish, then," said Teal. "Send him up."

The facetious parent who, while replete with beer, had bestowed upon Mr. John the prænomen of Prester must have been gifted with second sight. The celebrated infringer of the laws of property resembled nothing so much as an elderly parson. He was lank and lofty, sallow-complexioned and blue of chin. He affected clothes of clerical hue, wore a high Gladstonian collar and a black bow tie, and generally gave the impression of sanctimoniousness incarnate.

"Good morning, brethren," he said politely. "I heard that my Lords had need of men, and I came."

It was his invariable greeting when summoned before the police to account for his lapses, and he accompanied it with an equally automatic gesture, holding his elbows in to his sides, bringing his forearms horizontal, and spreading out his flat palms in the same plane, a mannerism which the irreverent Inspector Teal described as "John's lo-and-behold mitt-flap."

"Acoustics excellent!" commented Storm. "I hear you visited Mr. Raegenssen last night."

"On business," nodded Prester John.

"And was he pleased to see you?" asked Teal.

"He was—er—unfortunately unable to attend."

Storm passed his cigarette case to the pious one and, when John declined, lighted a cigarette himself.

"How much was Mattock paying you?" he asked, waving his match in the air to extinguish it.

"Mattock?"

"Raegenssen's clerk. He put you on to the job, didn't he?"

"Not that I know of—although, of course, since the name is unfamiliar to me, he may have been the man. May I sit down? It assists the train of thought."

Permission being granted, the man seated himself with a sigh and hitched up his trousers fastidiously. Leaning back, he fixed his eyes on the ceiling and pressed the tips of his fingers together like a pedantic schoolmaster, and after a dramatic pause he deigned to continue.

"The circumstances are—to say the least of it—curious," he said. "To commence, then: I am, as you probably know by now, a member of the society called the Alpha Triangle. You have heard of it, of course?"

"No," said Teal, *sotto voce*.

"Not, you understand, that I associate myself in any way with the outrages which they propose to commit," John explained hastily. "No. I am simply a wage slave—an employee—an hireling. And, in passing, the hire is worthy of the hireling. My employers pay me a salary, which is very comfortable—thank you—and in return I undertake to deal with such refractory locks and so forth as they wish to penetrate. So far I have had little to do, although I was given to understand that there would be an important piece of work for me in the near future. The Bank of England, I think Surcon said—Surcon is the name by which the Apex is known to his men. An assumed name, of course, but we are not encouraged to discover his real one. There was a man named Rodriguez—a Portuguese—who said he was going to find out the real name and put the black—I believe that is the correct slang, Mr. Teal?—and—er—where had I got to? Oh, yes, put the black on. Polite people call it demanding money with menaces. Rodriguez died the other day. Enteric, you know. I'm sure of that, because I was able to take a swab from the hypodermic syringe Mr. Surcon used when he treated Rodriguez to a shot of morphine. Surcon says he qualified as a doctor. So did I. In my leisure moments, I still dabble in bacteriology, and *bacilli typhosi* are easily recognised under the microscope by the trained observer. So—er—one is not encouraged to be inquisitive, is one?"

"Quite," murmured Storm.

Inspector Teal cleared his throat noisily, fumbled aimlessly in his pockets, and came across a battered cigar. He nipped the end from it, and sought for matches. Instead, he found a virgin packet of spearmint, and abandoned fumigation in favour of mastication. Then, having returned the weary weed to his pocket and posted a wafer of chicle in his mouth, he struck a match and absently wondered why there wasn't anything to light.

Which seems to indicate a certain perturbation.

It does. Mr. Teal was familiar with the vanity of criminals, their affectations and their powers of plausible invention, but the yarn of Prester John was something which failed to enter the borders of his experience. The germ of truth in it stuck out like the Eiffel Tower: he had always known that Prester John had drifted to burglary, not from Borstal, but from Balliol, solely because of the moral kink in his nature. But the lying of criminals—which psychologists will tell you is "pathological," whatever that may mean—is expressly designed for the covering up of their defects and defections—not the revelation of the same. Wherefore Prester John became an interesting specimen.

A fact which seemed to have entered the mind of that oleaginous man, for he allowed an appreciable time to elapse before he resumed his confession—time during which the theatrical atmosphere piled up hand over fist.

"Well—to return," he went on at last. "Last night I received a telephone call in the name of the Apex, instructing me to proceed with all speed to Scandinavia House, Cockspur Street. My lord had need of me, so I went." Interval for the lo-and-behold mitt-flap. "Entering the office to which I had been directed to proceed, I found seated at a desk a masked man—that sounds a bit thick to you, I suppose, Mr. Teal, but you've got to take my word for it. Er—a masked man, as I said. Most extraordinary."

He had a trick of affecting to have lost the thread of his discourse, and finding his place with an exaggerated effort of concentration.

"This man—masked, as I told you—er—where was I? Oh, yes; this man explained to me that in his *rôle* of Ezra Surcon—did I tell you that the Apex called himself Ezra Surcon?"

"You did," assented Teal patiently. "He explained?"

"That he was, of course, disguised when he appeared before us, and he had not had time to assume his disguise that night. Therefore, with a solicitude for my own safety which, I may say, touched me to the heart—therefore, he had donned a mask. And that was that. He indicated a safe, and invited me to open it. Which, reasonably enough—you understand—I did. And, when I got in"—lo-and-behold—"the cupboard was bare!"

Storm tapped the ash from his cigarette. The revelation affected him less than it did Inspector Teal; for he had already deducted much of what he now heard, and the criminal's story came as little more than a confirmation.

"Well, Mother Hubbard?" he prompted.

"And that was all," Prester John concluded with an eloquent wave of his hand. "Shall I ask you to picture the scene? My masked friend, shaking with baffled rage—quite upset, you know. Some people take things to heart so. It's a thing I—er—as I was saying, shaking with baffled rage; myself, calm and serene, rather like a turf accountant's clerk as the horses pass the post, knowing that whoever may have lost money his own wages are secure.... There's an extraordinary attraction for me in gambling—I've always wanted——" He caught a murderous gleam in Inspector Teal's eye, and tactfully returned to the point. "So that was that. Shall I endeavour to picture for you the scene—to—to delineate, so to speak, the situation? Shall I——"

"No," said Teal with determination. "What happened after the tableau?" John shrugged.

"What would you? I went. My Lord's manner did not give me the assurance which every gentleman requires before he continues to inflict his company on a comrade, that he is welcome. You follow? The moment did not appear propitious for bringing up such sordid topics as my own remuneration. I folded up my wallet and silently stole away."

He uncrossed his legs as though, his mission accomplished, he was about to repeat that man[oe]uvre, but Teal's curiosity was no more than whetted.

"Did you see any Triangles that night?"

"Er—no."

"Not this?" persisted Teal, and produced from his wallet the cardboard insigne he had found in the safe.

Prester John examined it with interest, but he shook his head as he handed it back.

"This is one of the badges which are issued to the inferior members—the rank and file, so to speak," he said. "The higher members have tokens of silver and enamel. My own—er—have you finished with it yet, by the way?"

The question was ignored. Teal and Storm were busy with their own thoughts, and both these ran in the same channel. Storm, who was watching the methods of the two men dispassionately, allowed the detective to give tongue.

"Why have you spun us this yarn?"

"Why? I—er—thought it might possibly be of some assistance," said John deprecatingly. "As a matter of fact, I am giving up my illegal activities altogether, and resigning from the Triangle. I heard this morning that some obscure relative had died and left me money—nothing great, you understand, but sufficient at least to enable me to inhabit once more those haunts of culture and respectability after which my soul hankers."

Teal grunted non-committally and made a mental memorandum to verify this glad news. Prester John read the disbelief on the round red face, and smiled faintly.

"That happens to be true," he said.

"Then can you help us to locate any other members—silver badge size members, I mean—or any boltholes?"

John made a negative gesture regretfully.

"I wish I could," he said. "Unfortunately, I was never taken to any rendezvous but the one at Billingsgate, of which you already know. As for members, I have never—er—been in the habit of associating with gentlemen in the same—er—line of business as myself. Now that I am meditating a return to the straight and narrow path, my chief ambition is to—er—rehabilitate myself with the police, bearing no malice for the many tussles we have had in the past. But my acquaintances are unhappily so useless for your purpose."

Teal knew that this was the truth, for one of Prester John's many peculiarities was that he never mixed with other criminals, planned and executed all his coups single-handed, and disposed of the proceeds through channels unknown to the underworld.

"There's no clue you could give us about the masked man?" said Storm.

"Nothing. In fiction, a scar—a limp—a missing button. In real life, nothing. Tall, and I should think well-built; but since he wore an overcoat I shall not take the risk of—er—perjuring myself on that point."

Storm himself opened the door to the reforming burglar, and, receiving an almost imperceptible signal, followed the man out into the passage.

"All I've told you is blowed-in-the-glass," said Prester John in a rapid undertone, his pose having dropped from him like a cloak. "I am really going straight, and I know no more than I've told you. Except this. I know how it is between you and Miss Hawthorne—why, if a split sneezes it's known all over the underworld in half an hour. The order went out that she's got to go, and Lew's been told off to do it. He's going to escape tonight—I suppose you knew that? But that isn't Lew's way." He looked at Storm steadily. "The difference between Lew and me is that I was once a gentleman—whatever that may mean. But I was. Lew never will be. His mind is so ... vulgar. Take a stable tip."

He held out his hand a little hesitatingly, and smiled when Storm took it.

"Thanks," said Storm. "But why couldn't you say that in front of Teal?"

"My—er—dear sir, one must make good exits—intriguing curtains." He swung his stick, and once more his face was sanctimonious and his voice treacly. "The worthy Inspector Teal has, in his blundering fashion, crossed swords with me on many memorable occasions. Once, he even succeeded in obtaining my—er—incarceration for a period of three years——the only time I have ever been inside. Painstaking—slow and sure—but not brilliant. I have taken a number of years convincing him that the Church was my proper *métier*. His mind is not elastic. I feared that if I—er—removed the mask of the musical comedy parson the shock, you know—terrible, terrible, terrible—all one's ideas dislocated—and so forth. You appreciate my point?" he pleaded, and there was a peep of laughter in Storm's grey eyes as he watched the lank figure pass mincingly down the stone corridor.

CHAPTER 16

SENSATION OUT OF COURT

Storm returned to meet the lazily inquiring gaze of Inspector Teal. Teal was far too ponderous a man to be swayed by the emotions of the thin-flanked herd, but it was obvious that puzzlement was seething within his placid bulk—the symptom was the exaggerated precision with which his jaws chewed from side to side the plastic sweetmeat of Mr. Wrigley—and Storm was privately amused.

"What was his secret?" demanded the detective with assumed languor, when after some time the information had not been volunteered.

"Oh—Prester John sent you his love," Storm replied truthfully but uncertainly. "He didn't dare give it you in person!"

Mr. Teal's recumbent mountainousness heaved with an explosive grunt which registered unbelief.

They parted, for Storm had a luncheon engagement for which he did not wish to be unpunctual. He met Susan at the portals of the Regal, and thought that he had rarely seen her looking so beautiful. Being gloriously ignorant of the niceties of feminine apparel, he received from her dress no other impression than that it suited her to perfection. In her smart costume of plain bisque, relieved only by the daring splash of green where a flowing kerchief was knotted loosely at the throat of her white silk undertunic, she was piquantly beautiful. The bright sunshine lit up her smiling face, and its searching brilliance at once absolved her red lips and the faint flush of health on her cheeks from all accusation of artifice.

They made a striking couple.

Her loveliness was none of that pink-and-white fragility to which a certain type of Frenchwoman aspires—prettiness which is at one and the same glance irresistibly attractive and yet so obviously unfitted for any locale but the drawing-room and the Poiret gown. She was essentially a girl of the open spaces, with the lithe, free grace of carriage and the delicate browning of a clear skin which come only with a perfectly functioning body bred of, and to, the love of plenty of exercise in the eye of the sun and in the breath of the wind. And Storm fitted her perfectly, being a man good to look upon and finely built, and having a boyish love of laughter always lurking in his steady eyes to counteract the first impression of hardness you got from the square-ness of his jaw and the vigorous set of his mouth. Outstanding at once by the lissom poise of his athletic figure, with just that indefinable air of restraint about him which is the infallible sign of a tremendously dynamic vitality controlled and directed by a dominant will.

He had meant to talk to her gravely, warning her of the dangers she was running, and pointing out the foolhardiness of her last night's adventure. She, for her part, had made up her mind to laugh at his fears and complain of his selfishness in keeping all the thrills for himself. He had meant to be firm: she had meant to be defiant. Somehow, neither programme produced according to schedule.

"Who was the man you recognized last night?" he asked her point blank, and her resolutions crumbled so weakly that she hated herself.

"The man we saw when we had that motor accident," she answered meekly. "Mattock, I think you called him."

Storm had known that, unless she was bluffing, it must have been one of three men, and he annoyed her afresh by the coolness with which he received the report.

"He's an enterprising man," he murmured, passing his cigarette case across the table. "One of these days there'll be trouble for James—you wager the haberdashery on uncle!"

"Aren't you interested?"

He raised his eyebrows.

"Fairly! I know nearly everything there is to be known about Mattock. At the moment, I'm betting in my mind which'll die first—James Norman or Oscar Siegfried. That problem, however, is reserved strictly for office hours, and this is my lunch interval. What're you going to do about a job now Papa Hannassay is with the majority?"

"I don't know that I need one," she said surprisingly. "He's left me everything. I heard from the solicitors this morning."

Storm bit his lip.

"How much?"

The bluntness of his question made her stare at him. She found him unaccountably irritating that afternoon, and had half a mind to snub him, but she decided that that might be a failure. He had an amused way of laughing at people who stood on their dignity which was absolutely impossible to deal with.

"Ten thousand odd—if you're so desperately interested," she said frigidly, and was speedily disconcerted.

His eyes danced with quiet mockery.

"I am. Desperately interested," he assured her, and his smile swept pettiness out of existence. "Susan, don't be small! It's an important question, because I always understood old Pop Hannassay was rich."

"Don't be irreverent," she said severely. "*De mortuis*——"

"*Nil nisi ludicrum*. And how about the dead what die in their sins?"

She opened her bag and handed him the letter. He read it through carefully, and then made a note of the address of the solicitors.'

"Bylom, Craill and Bylom, Suffolk House, Lester Street, Strand. I'll see 'em this afternoon. Ten thousand! Jerusalem—a few years ago old Daddy—sorry, Susan!—Lord Hannassay was worth about half a million. You ought to be rich, instead of the unreasonably proud heiress to a paltry ten thousand!"

"How do you know all this?" she asked in wonder.

He was not disposed to enlighten her at that moment.

"There's damn little I don't know!" he boasted airily. "The snag is, it's going to take me all my time to remove just those little scraps of ignorance!" He looked at her for a moment, frowning thoughtfully, and then dropped a bolt from the blue: "When can you be married?"

Her face went blank.

He disregarded all the time-honoured laws governing the proper setting, manner and preliminaries for such questions. Twice he had made love to her—once, years ago, in his breezy, inconsequent manner in the kitchen of the Presidential Palace of Olvidada; for the second time, on that night when he had driven her home from Raegenssen's. And when he made love he was irresistible. On the whole, it was a proposition he should by rights have put forward long ago; yet, now that he had put it forward, the suddenness seemed alarming. It caused a queer constriction about her heart, and at the same time it brought to a head the vague and formless anger that had troubled her all day. He had been almost insulting—he broke every accepted canon for proposals. In fact, he did not propose at all: he took her for granted, and she was furious.

"Married to whom?" she asked with dangerous obtuseness.

"To me, of course."

The perplexed lift of her straight brows was perfectly done.

"I don't understand. Why should I marry you?"

His eyes held hers, and at the back of that clear gaze she saw a glint of comprehension and, coincidently, of good-humoured reproof which was maddening. Without batting an eyelid, he suggested a sympathetic elder amusedly tolerating the peevishness of a child.

"I really don't know," he said coolly. "It occurred to me you might like to. Besides, you love me."

The man's audacity stunned her. In her consternation it was some time before she could find suitable words wherewith to administer a stinging rebuke, and the effort was not diminished by the knowledge that he had spoken nothing but the truth.

"You flatter yourself," she said coldly, and he smiled.

"You flatter me," was his quick response. "Now, for the love of Mike don't boil over with rage—not till we've finished eating, anyway. Squabbling at meal times is so horribly bad for the digestion! You wouldn't like me to utter a loud shriek and collapse on the floor, clasping my diaphragm—a young man stricken down in his prime with dyspepsia—would you?"

Her retort had simply glanced off the armour of his confidence. The edge of it had cut rather less ice than would cover a sixpence. He might have done no more than ask her to go to the theatre with him, and agreed to wait for an answer until she had consulted her engagement book. He was—Good Lord! He was actually *humouring* her!

"You're mistaken—you won't refuse ever to see me again," he said, and, looking up, she saw that his eyes were still upon her, and knew that he had read her thoughts. And then he switched from the subject with the abruptness of the turning off of a tap: "How's Terry these days? D'you remember the X Esquire case? Old Terry was in that, though it never came out."

He continued blithely to recount the story in that staccato, jerky way he had of speaking, and she had to listen in spite of herself.

He could be a delightful *raconteur*—he had the happy knack of coining spontaneous phrases which had the punch of mule kicks. Gradually, so gently that she never noticed it, he thawed her out of her attitude of barely polite attention. Coffee was on the table before she realised how the time was flying. And, as she took the final cigarette he offered her, light dawned. Why had she been snappy? Because she had had so little sleep the night before, and tiredness had frayed her temper at the corners. Why should she vent her bad temper on him? Because ... because she'd read in the morning paper about the fight in Billingsgate (and she'd never even asked him about it—what must he think of her for that?) ... and she'd had her eyes opened to the danger he was in—and because there was some of *her*, something infinitely precious, going with him into every peril he encountered.... *Because, for days, she had longed for him to want to marry her....*

*U*nderstanding of herself came as a shock, but it did not break her resolution—merely turned it in another direction. He must have his lesson. He must learn that methods which battered a Board of Enquiry into submission (she had had that anecdote retailed to her with great gusto by Bill Kennedy himself when that genial Assistant Commissioner dropped in for a nightcap with Terry) would not have the same effect upon her.

She was still strong in this decision when they prepared to leave, and, when he had paid the bill and was waiting for his change, he had this fact demonstrated to him.

"For the last time but——" He paused and studied the end of his cigarette meditatively. "But two—for the last time but two, Susan, when will you marry me?"

"Never," she said, and hoped she sounded inflexible.

His eyes danced. His optimistic egotism was unshakeable.

"Sure?"

"I've given you my answer," she said, straining to be haughty in the face of that sunny smile. "So please don't ask me the other two times."

"I shan't forget," he promised ambiguously. "But hear me, Susan! Unless you come and ask me to marry you before midnight you'll sleep in a Vine Street cell, probably!"

She stared.

"What for?"

"Safety," he said soberly. "It all depends on whether a certain gentleman now in custody gets clear as he's promised. Now think!"

That evening, before he went to dinner, he made his last arrangements for the guarding of Lew Mecklen. He made a personal inspection of the cell, "fanned" the gunman himself for additional assurance in case he should have succeeded in concealing a weapon, and appointed three men with over ten years' service to watch the man, with three others to relieve them at 2 a.m. He left a last warning.

"If Lew gets away, somebody's hopes of promotion'll be gone for ever! Anything that's sent in to him is to be kept from him until after I've seen it tomorrow morning. He's not to have the privilege of ordering anything whatever from outside—you can tell him all his money's gone to pay his hospital bill. Nobody is to be allowed to enter the cell—don't even go in yourselves, unless he looks like dying. That's all. If the Triangle scores again, I should say the Chief Commissioner'll crucify every man in C Division with his own hands!"

It was perhaps lucky for several people that Storm had exaggerated the brutality of Sir Brodie Smethurst.

The circumstances, as far as one can collate the depositions of those concerned, were as follows:

About nine p.m. that night Police Constable C811, who was standing at the corner of Marshall Street and Broad Street, was approached by a bulky ruffian whose dissonant caterwauling was clearly a public nuisance. On being requested to desist, the large one smote C811 with some strength and his boot, even upon the shins, and was promptly taken into custody. Leading his captive up Marshall Street, C811 met three other musicians who, linked arm in arm, were making the night air hideous with their attempts to harmonise *Rose in the Bud* and *Annie Laurie*. C811 told them to shut up, whereupon the three ranged themselves in line before him, chorused a hearty *tu quoque* plus a vulgar expletive, and switched over to a pathetic rendering, in comparative unison, of Tosti's *Good-bye*. They also were added to the bag, and the four were shot into the charge room of Marlborough Street Police Station, certified drunk and accused of being disorderly withal, and locked up to await judgment in the morning.

They had scarcely been removed to the cells when Police Constable C796 arrived, having in tow two troubadours looking distinctly the worse for wear, whom he charged with conducting a free fight in Regent Street in the course of which they smashed a shop window. They also were placed in durance vile.

Meantime, four husky specimens, who looked like farm hands in London for the day, had drawn up in line before the station entrance, teetering somewhat unstably on their heels, and had commenced to regale the man on duty at the door with *Pack Up Your Troubles in Your Old Kit Bag*—a subtle jest which was not appreciated until later. After enduring their immelodious advice for some minutes, the doorkeeper descended the steps and invited the four bards to move on. The man who seemed to be the leader of the troupe failed to understand.

"Move on?" he hiccuped, swaying slightly. "Norra bi'vit *hic!* Thish—thish, of'cer—thish"—he tapped the Law solemnly on the thorax—"*hic!* thish commun'ty singin'. Finesthingin—*hic!*—England. Go 'way. Don' spoil gai'ty vnations." He turned to his waiting choir. "Nowthnboys—sh-show thish of'cer wotchen *hic!* do. Now. Al'gether."

Whereon the welkin of Marlborough Street rang with a cacophonous interpretation of *Three o'Clock in the Morning*, the chronological inaccuracy of which ancient ditty they appeared to perceive, for they made of it an apologetically discordant dirge. After three more unavailing efforts to make them cease their serenade, or to inflict it on another thoroughfare, the doorkeeper arrested them, and they were marched into the station still wailing the refrain of that touching ballad *Bye Bye, Blackbird*.

And now a problem arose. No police station has more than seven cells, and by then all those at Marlborough Street were occupied. Appealed to for instructions, the Divisional Inspector scratched his head, for more than one prisoner cannot be placed in the same cell except during riots. The four songsters, having been roughly searched and charged, were now lined up at one end of the charge room abiding the Inspector's decision on this knotty point, and their persistent warbling was not helpful.

> "...When somebaaaady waits for meee
> (Shoogar's sweet, saow is sheee),
>   Baaaye-baaaye, blackburrrd.
> Naowone used to laave 'rr understaaand meee,
> Naowone knows—"

"SHUT UP!" bellowed the frantic Inspector, whom this ghastly vocalism was rapidly driving to the verge of insanity, and added a virulent commination.

He telephoned to Vine Street, only to learn that the more aristocratic police station was already full. Unwisely, he chose to exercise his own authority without appealing to headquarters.

> "... Make maaye bed 'n' laaaight the laaaight,
> Aiyull be home late to-naaight,
> Blackburrrd, Baaaye-baaaye!"

The lullaby howled on to an appallingly strident conclusion, and the chanticleers, without tarrying for applause, swept on to an ear-splitting prayer that they might be permitted to join their lost loves upon the bonny, bonny banks of Loch Lomond.

"If this doesn't constitute a riot, God knows what does," squealed the Inspector in anguish. "TAKE 'em AWAY!!"

The four were sent to join their fellow-choristers in the bonny, bonny cells of Marlborough Street. Even that did not end the torment of C Division, for within the next half-hour they accumulated three more psalmists and two men who had endeavoured to capture a policeman's helmet. Towards ten o'clock, a man in a small two-seater car drove down Marlborough Street, turned his car at right angles across the road, and shouted to the constable at the station entrance to stand clear, explaining that he was going to drive right in. He even tried to carry out his threat, and when they went out to him they found that he was very drunk. What was more, he was the only one of the night's captures whom the Divisional Inspector knew by sight.

"You're James Mattock," he said reproachfully. "Jimmy, we thought you'd gone respectable."

Mattock shook his head, staggering a little. There was a fatuous grin on his face.

"James—sh—nothin'!" he protested loudly. "Lis'en. Tell you ... secret. I'm Queen 'f Sheba."

"You ought to be ashamed of yourself—an old man like you," said the Inspector sadly. "Take him away."

With that the influx ceased, and when a humdrum burglar was brought in the Inspector sent him on to Vine Street, feeling that his own preserves were already overstocked. There were now sixteen men divided in between the six vacant cells, and that their lubrication had been thorough was proved by the fact that muffled yelps of carolling still came through the charge room door. It was impossible to subdue the uproar, and the reserve P.C., whose duty it is to make a round of the cells at half-hour intervals, was pleading to be allowed to use chloroform.

About two a.m., when the vociferation was become slightly hoarse and rather less enthusiastic, the reserve constable was making the round when from one of the further cells came a shuddering cry and the thud of a heavy fall. Running down the corridor, the constable found that it came from one of the cells where three men were herded together. One of them lay twitching on the ground, and the other two were watching him helplessly.

"'Ad a fit," one of them muttered; and, seeing the gaoler, added: "Fetch a doctor—Bert 'as these fits. 'Orrible, it is.'"

It was just at this moment, as far as one can gather, that a powerful lorry drew up by the kerb, almost opposite the station but on the other side of the road, and one of the men descended and lifted the bonnet as though to investigate a breakdown. The constable at the station entrance saw the incident, but thought nothing of it.

The reserve P.C., meanwhile, not knowing what to do, called the relief Inspector, and together they entered the cell.

Both were promptly killed.

The three man who were guarding Mecklen rushed down the passage at the sound of the shots and were faced by the three prisoners—the epileptic having made a miraculous recovery—and threatened with automatic pistols. They were brave men, these three constables. Or else, perhaps, they did not expect the three toughs to shoot. Be that as it may, they continued to advance, and were shot down in cold blood.

The prisoners now moved swiftly. They took the cell keys from the dead bodies and released the other prisoners, all of whom were armed. Already there was a tumult in the charge room, and the sixteen, with Mecklen, burst in upon a dozen or so officers, only two of whom had had the time or forethought to arm themselves. The two died in their tracks before they had time to fire a shot, and the others paused aghast. In another second the seventeen men were streaming across the road to the waiting lorry, the hind-most firing random bullets backwards to discourage pursuit. They piled in, and the lorry moved off, gathering speed, to the accompaniment of a final volley from the escaped prisoners. Before the pursuing constables, who were now armed, could return the fusillade, the lorry had turned a corner and disappeared.

The Flying Squad and all reserves of every Division were called out, and those first on the scene commandeered cars and taxis and dashed off in chase, but the seventeen, with their lorry, got clean away. As has been stated, the P.C. at the door had not taken much notice of the lorry, and its number plates had been so caked with mud as to be indecipherable from across the road, in the dim light. And, standing midway between two street lamps, at night, one big lorry looks very much like another—the doorkeeper was unable even to identify the make with certainty, although he thought it looked like a Rossleigh.

But the most remarkable feature of the crime was its execution. For one thing, it proved that the Alpha Triangle had an unusually accurate knowledge of police station routine. In the first place, ordinary "drunks and disorderlies," being apparently harmless and charged only with minor offences, are not perfunctorily "fanned." As was demonstrated at the subsequent inquiry, it would have been possible for a man not suspected of carrying arms to have concealed a small automatic pistol in a holster strapped to the small of his back, with little risk of it being discovered in a more or less formal search; and in the absence of definite information this theory is the one which is now universally admitted satisfactorily to account for the Triangle's success. Secondly, the locks of the cell doors, and those of the doors leading from the charge room to the cells, can only be opened by a special manipulation of the keys which is a police secret; yet the prisoners had clearly been well instructed in this trick beforehand by someone with an intimate knowledge of that secret, for there was no delay in liberating the occupants of the other cells.

The third curious point was that Mattock was found in his cell efficiently gagged and bound with strips of his own shirt. His explanation that he had been set upon and trussed by the two who shared his confinement, just before the prisoners made their escape, was accepted. Experts declared that he could not possibly have tied himself up so thoroughly, and no one had seen him in the affray; furthermore, the head waiter of the Leroy swore that Mattock had entered the bar late that evening, already more than a trifle "oiled," and had imbibed continuously until closing time. Mattock was fined for being drunk in charge of a motorcar, and was discharged on the other count.

It was a verdict which did not please Inspector Teal, for he could have sworn that the ghost of a wink trembled on Mattock's right eyelid as the clerk left the court.

CHAPTER 17

BIRDIE RECEIVES ORDERS

"We don't want to lose you," said Mr. Brome carefully, "so we think you ought to go."

His pale blue eyes bored inexorably into Mecklen's. Before that stony stare the gunman's gaze fell, and his truculent protest, that had framed itself instinctively, died unvoiced.

"Aw—guess you're right, Chief," he muttered sheepishly. "But, naow I'm hyar——"

"What is it?"

"Et's thet skirt. Chief, haow c'n I look af-ter thet li'l' one-way sweedie when every goldurned bull in this hyar burg is out gunnin' fer mine? I'll say it ain't no cinch. Arden's too fly, an' he's her lovin' sugar-daddy. I reckon he's gotten every lallapaloozer in this deck skinned a mile."

Snooper regarded him contemptuously.

They were in the gorgeous sitting-room of Joan Sands' Cornwall House flat, and the magnificent furnishings were in strange contrast to the group of men who sat around the table. Snooper Brome was the only one of that down-at-heel and flashy convocation who could by any stretch of imagination be said to fit—despite his vulgarian notions of waistcoat design, he had a certain dignity which carried them off rather well. For all his bulk, he had not much superfluous flesh, and he was anything but gross; his big features were clean cut—with his flowery vest and white hands, and the mane of dank black hair that swept back from his high forehead, he resembled a prosperous exponent of Impressionism.

The others were less favoured. Mecklen, standing by the door twisting a greasy tweed cap in his grimy hands, unshaven and coarse of face, was a repulsive sight. The rest of the men, who sat at the long board over which Brome presided, were divided between the extremes of shabbiness and over-dressedness.

"Are you getting panic too?" demanded Snooper, grittily speculative.

"Yew said a canful," agreed Mecklen complacently. "Let me give Arden his fer a start, an' then I'll tackle thet Jane—but while thet perambulatin' hunk of sudden death's still millin' round, this chile's gonna stick close home. Tell yuh what, Chief, ef yew'll give the word I'll glom the first freight fer Ardensville, an' when I git home they'll be liftin' him inter his Kingdom-Come-box wit' a derrick, he'll be thet leaded up. An' *af-ter* thet, I'll go chase yore Jane."

"What is the answer to that?" asked Snooper, turning to Morini.

Gat looked at his friend.

"The answer, Lew, is," he said, "when Hell snows over. Big Chief Triangle wants to save that little baby boy, and what Big Chief Triangle says goes."

Mr. Brome extracted a cigar from a pocket of his flamboyant waistcoat and cut the tip from it with a gold pen-knife. Then he looked up at Mecklen.

"You heard?"

"I heard, Chief, but what I wanna say is——"

"What you're going to do, is—go home, Lew," remarked Eddie sharply. "Go home, and stick close home like you said you were going to. When I want you I'll send for you. Go to Buckingham Gate, and if I hear of you showing your nose outside again unless I give the word—it won't be only the bulls who'll be out gunning for yours. Beat it!"

Mecklen glared. He was not a man of equable temper, and the wintry scorn of Snooper's tone, no less than the consciousness of mastery that literally crackled about the words, got right up under Mecklen's pachydermis and rasped on his vanity. He started forward with a torrid word on his lips and brazen defiance in his mien.

"Yew see hyar..."

Brome did nothing, said nothing. He was lighting his cigar, and he never even looked up. His superiority wrapped him round like a sheet of defensive fire. It was a way of meeting rebellion which Mecklen had never encountered before, and before the Unknown the fear of the brute killer roused. If Snooper had met ferocity with ferocity, if his right hand had dropped the match it held and slid down towards his hip, the Alpha Triangle might have been smithereened at that instant. It was a peril the leaders of the Triangle faced daily—hourly—from minute to minute. Under them were killers, ruthless and inhuman tigers, with the ungovernable passions of the wild beasts; and these a mere handful of men essayed to rule and direct. They did it by setting themselves aloof, enveloping themselves in an aura of superiority, and before their caustic hauteur their hired butchers shrank back in perplexity. Snooper, calm and self-assured, dealt with Lew Mecklen in just that fashion. He ignored him. He appeared to have forgotten his existence, and certainly he gave no sign of considering him seriously. The gunman's words trailed away. He was up against something he couldn't understand, and the ingrained instinct of self-preservation flared a red danger signal before his eyes.

"Guess yew said it, boss," he muttered angrily.

Snooper did not look up until the door had closed behind the baffled Lew. And when he spoke he made no mention of the incident; but its effect was not lost on his audience. Only Morini was not awed—but then, Gat Morini was nearly as intelligent as Snooper himself.

"The bomb goes off in about two hours," said Mr. Brome. "So keep clear of Piccadilly Circus on your way home. It'll be the crowning stroke—and the beauty of it is that we can go on dealing out crowning strokes for weeks. We've fought off the police, we've rescued prisoners twice, and we're killing those we've threatened as well. At midnight we shall have caused an explosion which will startle the country."

He stopped, intent on the vision of power that retrospection gave him. The others, only half understanding, waited for him to speak again.

"Arden must go—and the girl. Those are the Apex's orders. I'll arrange that tomorrow—they're dangerous."

He tugged at the ornate fob which graced the southwest of his abdomen, and brought into view a gold repeater.

"The Triangle's about due to speak to you himself. I've heard all he's got to say, and I've got some work to do tonight, so I'll move off. I'll be back later. Morini can fix the telephone."

He departed, and Morini rose to obey.

The telephone stood on a small corner table. Morini took up the instrument and pulled out the flex from the wall plug into which it fitted. He carried it over to a side shelf and brought back instead a polished box lidded with ebonite, on the surface of which was an engraved dial and two frosted bulbs. From the centre protruded the curved horn of a loud-speaker. He plugged the terminals of a piece of flex, which ran from the rear of the box, into the slots at the end of the permanent telephone wiring, and connected two other wires between the amplifier and an accumulator which he fetched from a cupboard. The ordinary installation had now been converted into a loud-speaking telephone, and the flat nickelled button of a small but supersensitive microphone let into the front of the amplifier case acted as the receptive part of the instrument.

Then the men sat round the table, conversing desultorily, to await the voice of their leader. It is a good example of the cautious foresight of the Apex, that orders which, if they were definitely traced to him, would be of great assistance to the Public Prosecutor, were invariably given by a palpably disguised voice speaking to his subordinates from none knew where.

Presently the loud-speaker broke into that sizzling mumble which denotes the opening of the circuit, and a moment later it spoke, with the muffled harshness that is inseparable from electrically transmitted speech.

"Who is there?"

They gave their names, one by one, and the numbers they held in the organisation. There followed a pause, as though the speaker was checking the list. Then:

"To the sixteen men who accomplished the rescue of Mecklen"—here followed their names, read twice over—"a bonus of one hundred pounds per man. It will be paid in a few days by Brome. I add my congratulations on the efficiency with which the man[oe]uvre was carried out."

A second interval, while the loud-speaker hissed quietly.

"Arden must be taken tomorrow. Brome has all instructions. The following will report to him at Church Street, Kensington, at eight a.m. tomorrow, to receive their orders: Lanzani, Sacco, Coles, Horring, Manuelo, Liebessohn. I'll repeat that. Church Street, Kensington, eight tomorrow morning: Lanzani, Sacco, Coles, Horring, Manuelo, Liebessohn. Arden will be taken to Number Two. As soon as that has been done, the same men will be instructed how to proceed with the removal of Hawthorne. Is that perfectly clear, Lanzani—Sacco—Coles?——"

One by one the six answered in the affirmative, and then there was another silence.

"Sands!"

Birdie looked up with a start.

"Yessir?"

"Go to the cupboard between the windows. Are you there? Right. Open it. Inside you will find a small copper vessel. Take it out—and handle it carefully, because if you dropped it Cornwall House would be seriously damaged. Got it?"

Birdie, after a moment's hesitation, had gingerly removed a little calorimeter, and was holding it as far away from his body as possible. He passed his tongue across his lips nervously.

"Yessir," he croaked.

"You have nothing to be afraid of as long as you're careful," the Voice went on. "I have chosen you specially on account of your delicate fingers——-I shouldn't trust any of the others to move that stuff with safety. Don't be scared. If you tremble it may slip out of your hand. Now look at it. There's a tiny bottle inside, isn't there, and the space between the bottle and the calorimeter is filled with chipped ice? Good. I'll tell you why that is. That phial contains the highest explosive known to science, but by a special process it has been made less dangerous than it is in the ordinary way. The only things that will detonate it now are heat—that is the reason for the ice—or a severe shock, such as you might give it if you let it fall. Is that clear?"

"Yessir."

"Very well. You know the *Daily Record* offices?"

"Yessir."

"You have made yourself familiar with the appearance of John Cardan, the editor, as you were told to—you are sure you can recognise him?"

"Yessir."

"Excellent. Then you will go at once to Ludgate Circus, taking a ninety-six bus, and wait outside the office. Take the calorimeter with you. He leaves the office between half-past eleven and midnight. When he comes out, take the little bottle out of the ice, and slip it into his pocket. Then walk quietly away—the explosive will take a little time to warm, and that'll give you as long as you need to get out of range without attracting attention. Have you got hold of all that?"

"Yessir."

"You can keep the stuff in your pocket—the ice will make it perfectly safe unless you should happen to fall down. Now please tell me exactly what you are going to do."

Birdie licked his lips again, and then recited his orders haltingly. Once or twice he was pulled up, and he was not allowed to go until he had mastered every detail. At last the rehearsal seemed to satisfy the Voice, and he was dismissed. He put the calorimeter with its deadly burden into his jacket pocket, keeping his fingers round it to prevent the ice spilling, and shuffled to the door, white-faced and shaking.

"So long, mates," he chattered with a rickety attempt at jauntiness. "See you all later...."

Then he was gone.

"Martinez will drive Morini down to the Embankment immediately," continued the Voice. "You will try to remove Inspector Teal. Morini will shoot, and Martinez will then drive back to Buckingham Gate via Blackfriars Bridge and Road, Lambeth Road, Lambeth High Street, Broad Street, Prince's Road, Kennington Street, Upper Kennington Lane, Vauxhall Bridge, Grosvenor Road, Chelsea Bridge Road. Go through Hammersmith, circle back via Chiswick, go north through Hampstead, and get to Buckingham Gate by way of Tottenham Court Road, Charing Cross Road, and the Mall. I'll repeat that. Take down the important points on a scrap of paper. Ready? Blackfriars Bridge, Lambeth, Vauxhall Bridge, Chelsea, Hammersmith, Cheswick, Hampstead, Tottenham Court Road. Right. One other thing. Wait till you get Teal alone. If he comes out with Arden, follow and watch your chance. The usual bonuses will be..."

"*Teal! Isn't radio wonderful!*" murmured a flippant voice.

Every man in the room spun round. With their backs to the door, they had been so absorbed in the words of their Chief that they had never noticed the faint creak of the opening door, nor the two soft paces that had brought Storm and Teal into their presence.

They jerked round as though hot needles had been run into them, half rising from their seats, with groping amazement in their faces. The microphone had proved its utility, and the loud-speaker had suddenly gone dead. The men who had been listening to it stood rooted to the ground, petrified, while they strove to whip their minds into grasping the situation. Storm watched them, smiling, a cigarette between his lips, his hands deep in his pockets. Beside him, the torpid avoirdupois of Mr. Teal leaned against the door, expressionless of face, motionless except for the intermittent oscillation of his inferior maxilla.

Storm's lazy grey eyes swept their blank faces.

"I hope we don't intrude!" he drawled politely.

CHAPTER 18

PESSIMISM OF MR. TEAL

Morini was the first to recover his equilibrium. He swept a deep bow.

"You're welcome," he said. "Come right in—how did you get in, by the way?"

"The door was open," said Storm. "So, as we meant to pay you a call, we thought we wouldn't put you to the trouble of locking and bolting it."

Teal was inspecting with interest the playing cards and markers that lay on the table.

"What's the game?" he asked inquisitorially, addressing the redoubtable Horring; but that holdup expert was less suave than his confrère.

"I'd like to know the meaning of this intrusion," he broke out heatedly. "I don't know what sort of a country you call this, if a few friends can't get together for a round of cribbage without policemen——"

Teal cut short his protest with one raised reproving hand.

"I shan't argue," he stated mildly. "I suppose *-age* does enter into it."

He could be subtle on occasions, could Mr. Teal.

Storm wandered over to the loud-speaking telephone and examined it curiously. Eventually he traced the flex which contacted with the telephone plug, and disconnected it. He looked round for the telephone proper, and, locating it, fetched it over and connected it up.

"2 LO seems to have closed down," he remarked. "A pity—I love listening in!"

He looked at Morini with a quizzical smile, as though expecting the obvious rejoinder to come from that quarter; but, if this was his hope, he was disappointed. Then he lifted the receiver and waited with it held to his ear.

"Exchange? ... I've just been called, and I think we've been cut off. Can you tell me where the ring came from? ... What's that? ... Are you stone-cold certain? ... Well, pass me on to Supervisor ... Supervisor? ... I'm Captain Arden of Criminal Investigation Department. I want you to make absolutely certain whether any call has been put through to this number during the last hour...." There was a longer delay, and then he got his answer. "Thanks very much. Good-bye."

He turned his back to the table and lounged against it, his eyes narrowing.

"I'm told," he said, "that this number hasn't been called since this morning. Broadcasting with an ordinary telephone is a joke I'm not going to buy!"

Their dumbfounded faces were his answer. It was as clear as anything ever has been that they were no more able to account for the facts than he was. Even Morini's composure suffered a jar, and the pucker that appeared between his eyebrows indicated that he was endeavouring to reach an explanation.

Storm examined the wall plug, and found two insulated wires running down the wainscot and stretching along the floor in the groove between the ceil and the carpet. They led him halfway round the room and then right-angled round the frame of a door. Trying the handle, Storm found that it was locked.

"I'll have the key, please," he requested.

"We haven't got it." It was Morini who made the disclaimer. In the absence of any acknowledged leader, he automatically answered for all.

"Explain!" Storm rapped back.

Morini shrugged.

"You want a whole lot of help, Captain," he gibed. "I thought you were Mother's Infant Prodigy. If you don't know, I'll tell you that door opens into a flat that's really part of this one, but the dame who lives there's gotten very proper notions about ladyhood, and we poor common folks aren't allowed to go in. She's just the obliging owner who lets us use this room to talk in—there's two entrances, and she keeps her own one private."

"What name?"

"Ask me again, Doc. We've never seen her."

Storm reached to his hip and took out a compact wallet from which he selected a skeleton key of a type appropriate to the make of lock. He was successful at the first attempt, and the door creaked open on unoiled hinges.

"Look after these gay birds, Teal," he ordered, and passed into the other flat.

He found himself in a tastefully furnished sitting-room in the decoration of which the work of a woman's hand was evident. He only stopped to glance behind and under the chesterfield, and then went through the door which faced him. He arrived in a light airy double bedroom, and here again the signs of feminine habitation were not lacking; but this, too, was empty, though he peered under the bed and tentatively prodded the dresses which hung in the wardrobe in quest of a cached fugitive. He moved on to the bathroom, but discovered no one lurking there.

After that futile search he recollected the telephone wire, and went back to trace it. It ran around the sitting-room and disappeared over the sill of a window. Leaning out, he saw that it hitched over a common porcelain insulator—from which it swept off to join the junction of other telephone wires. The result dissatisfied him, and he tracked the wire a second time, and on this journey he found that it was tapped very neatly, the secondary wires running under the carpet out of sight. Without compunction he shifted all the furniture which stood in the way, and rolled back the rugs, disclosing twin threads that crossed the floor. Following them up, he trailed them to a bookcase, and saw that they vanished into a hole trimly bored in the base.

He stood up and scrutinised the shelves. One row of leather-bound volumes struck him as being rather too good to be true, and he essayed to open the glass-fronted door in order to make a closer study, but found that it was fastened. Once again he had recourse to his wallet, and after a few minutes' work with a small steel instrument he had the case open. He now found that the row of books was simply a range of dummy backs, which he could pull wide like a second door, revealing a small cupboard. Within he brought to light what he had more or less expected—a phone transmitter mounted on a bracket, and a pair of radio headphones. These he removed, and then pushed back the secret door and, after some difficulty, relocked the case over it. The rest would keep; and he left the instruments on a chair and went back into the larger sitting-room, closing the partition door behind him.

"What're we going to do with these people?" he interrogated the detective, and Teal spread out his hands.

"Suspected of conspiracy—Vine Street *pro tem*. We didn't hear much of that broadcast sermon, but we did hear somebody telling 'em to express me to a better world," he added with grim amusement.

Morini's hand went to his hip, and in answer to that movement Teal shifted something in his hand so that the light caught it. He did not seem to have stirred a fraction—his jaw still vacillated mechanically, and his tired eyes showed little sign of animation. But the fact remained that a wicked-looking Webley had flown into his right hand and was even then focused upon the gunman.

To his concealed surprise, Morini smiled, and brought up his hand with nothing in it more lethal than a cigarette-case.

"You're too suspicious, officer," Gat observed. "Shooting you with Captain Arden for a witness would be foolish. No. I was just about to point out that police stations and Flying Squad vans haven't exactly proved to be the real original cat's pyjamas so far, have they?"

Storm conferred aside with the detective.

"Would conspiracy to murder be a sound charge?"

"Granted it only gets two of 'em—you've got special powers, haven't you?"

"I doubt if my special powers'd be superior to a writ of *habeas corpus*" Storm objected.

Teal shrugged.

"It's worth trying," he said. "The only thing is, we'd have to send 'em to Pentonville right away—stations don't seem to hold 'em. Even if we put 'em in stir straight off, I shouldn't bet on their staying put—the Triangle might turn up with an amateur Army Corps and besiege the jail," he added morosely, and Storm laughed.

"Pollyanna—you little ray of sunshine—shut up!"

The Triangle menace was festering to a head, and for all the lightness of his tone he knew it. It was the season for striking swift blows, here, there, and everywhere. From then onwards the gang must be attacked and raided wherever and whenever the dimmest spook of half an opportunity showed its tail. The risk of lowering police prestige still further by giving the Triangle the chance to make yet another daring coup must be taken. The Triangle must be set on the run, and kept there—hazed, harassed and bulldozed into confusion, till they didn't know whether they were coming or going.

Storm telephoned the prison and ordered a van with double escort to be sent immediately. It would take some time to arrive, and he followed the order with a call to Vine Street asking for a dozen men to guard the prisoners meantime. He had seen the microphone attached to the loud speaker. Already the Big Triangle knew of his presence, and he did not put it above the capabilities of that stupendous brain to organise a lightning sortie to rescue their captives before a conveyance could reach Cornwall House.

"Put your hands high over your heads and face along that wall," he commanded the prisoners, and they obeyed without demur.

Their position did not seem to trouble them at all, and this earnest of their confidence in the Apex was somewhat disquieting. Storm and the detective watched them, cat-eyed, until the men from Vine Street arrived. Then the captives were searched, and Storm sat down to smoke a cigarette while he waited for the prison van. It came surprisingly quickly. The prisoners were rushed down the stairs into the street, loaded into the Maria, and three of the Vine Street plain-clothes men crammed in on top of them to reinforce the warders. All the captives were handcuffed together in a string and the end handcuffs were locked over staples on the inside of the van.

"They'll be blistering miracles if they get out of that mess!" said Storm, watching the red tail-light speed down Piccadilly.

After that the other detectives were dismissed, and Storm and Teal returned to make a more thorough search of the inner flat. They stopped en route to look over the assembly room, and it was while they were there that Storm distinctly heard the sound of a door closing in the next flat.

Teal's ears intercepted the dull click at the same time, and the two jumped for the partition door. The sitting-room was empty, but in that cursory glance round Storm saw that the headpieces and transmitter he had left on a chair had vanished. He jerked open the bedroom door and ran through into the bathroom, but there was no one to be seen. And then a second door slammed, and he whipped round with a frown. Almost at once he grasped his mistake.

"Je-rusalem—the hall!" he snapped, and led the way back through the sitting-room.

Besides the door into the bedroom there was another which he had missed, masked behind a heavy curtain. He flung it open and entered a tiled lobby furnished only with a hat-stand and an occasional table. Opening the farther door, he found himself in the corridor, and sprinted for the stairs.

He overtook nobody in his headlong descent, and he saw nobody he recognised in the street. The porter's cubicle at the entrance was empty, and while Storm stroked his chin in perplexity that worthy toiler came across the road singing a little tune.

"I run out of fags," he replied to Storm's brisk query. "I just went over to a slot machine up the street. No, not five minutes ago—shortly after all those men came out."

"Have you seen any other guys come out or go in?" asked Storm, and the man shook his head.

Kit climbed the stairs again with a frown, and found Teal ruminating torpidly in the bedroom. The detective was dangling a flimsy article of feminine underwear in one of his vast paws.

"This is embroidered 'J.S.'," he said. "Sounds like my old friend Joan to me."

Storm scowled.

"D'you know we're a couple of dyed-in-the-wool mutts?" he demanded. "I'm willing to bet the Big Triangle was lying doggo in the vestibule all the time I was making that first search—I never spotted the hall. And when I went back to the big room he must have padded back and listened to everything we said.... *God's Glory!*"

The oath cracked out like the lash of a stock-whip, and Teal's eyes opened wide at the sibilant intensity of it.

Storm had picked up a brass candlestick, and he smashed it into the glass front of one of the compartments of the bookcase. He wrenched Open the dummy line of books, and then stepped back with his lips lifting from his white teeth.

The headphones and mouthpiece were back in their places, connected up.

"Great Thor in hell!" he breathed.

In an instant he was back to the outer sitting-room. He grabbed up the telephone and gave a number even as Teal, moving with astonishing speed, arrived behind him.

"Hullo," snapped Arden. "*Hullo* ... Pentonville? ... How long have you been on duty? ... Right. Then what time did you get my order for the prison van? ... I see." Storm's voice suddenly became gentle. "You're absolutely certain no call could have come through and been taken by someone else? ... Oh—about half an hour ago.... Arden, Central Office, five-double-seven—you poor fish. Why not think of asking before? ... Well, get me the Governor.... My dear good soul, I don't care if he's asleep—I don't care if he'll be furious—I don't care if he's dying! *Get—me—the—Governor*.... Thank you."

A lengthy pause, and then a querulous growl:

"Yes?"

"Colonel Dayne?"

The affirmative was unprintable.

"I called you up about half an hour ago and ordered your van to Cornwall House. A van came, but apparently it was a fake. I want you to send a man down to your garage and find out if your van is there."

Storm got his answer in about ten minutes, and then he set down the receiver and whistled musically, strolling up and down the room. The expression on his face made it unnecessary for Mr. Teal to ask any questions.

The Triangle had scored again, right under their noses. The fake van must have been waiting for just such an emergency, and the Apex had had all the odds in his favour—he had heard Storm and Teal come, heard their plans, and was already tapped in on the telephone to waylay their message and send a totally different one along to his confederates. The luck of the game had been his down to the last milligramme.

"The only consolation is that the Press won't hear about our wiped eyes," said Teal gloomily, and Storm stopped whistling to grin.

"Don't bet on it," he recommended. "The Triangle might mail a graphic account to all the News Agencies. If I were the Apex, and I'd scooped the kitty like that with a pair of deuces, I'll say I'd sing about it!"

It took a lot to upset Storm. The inevitable cigarette lofted heavenwards between his smiling lips, his hands were deep in his pockets—that boyish enthusiasm, which nothing could damp, shone in his eyes. It was an attribute of his which, delightful in the ordinary way, could be incredibly aggravating in moments of stress, and Inspector Teal glared at him moodily.

Zzzzzzing! ... Zzzzzzing-zing! ...

Through the other flat the hall bell jingled shrilly.

"One rings!" said Storm brightly. "Teal, be a good boy and come greet the visitor!"

He went through to answer the door, Teal following. As he flung it wide the corridor light outside showed up a stumpy, rotund form surmounted by a chubby pink face which split in a jovial beam as it recognised the two men who stood in the hall surveying it.

Teal reached out a languid arm and took the newcomer by the wrist, drawing him inside and kicking the door shut behind him.

"Come right in, Uncle Joe," said Mr. Teal with savage cordiality. "Come right in and open your sweet heart to old Uncle Claud Eustace. He wants to hear a little fairy tale about loud-speaking telephones!"

CHAPTER 19

NCl_3

Joe Blaythwayt waddled into the sitting-room. He turned and gaped at the detective.

"Loud Speaking Telephones?" he repeated in an awed whisper. "My dear sir—my Very Dear Sir—I—er—I—I—I——" His fishlike mouth closed with a smack. "Why, what a coincidence! Finding you here, I mean. I didn't know you were friends of Jimmy's."

A gargantuan grin overspread Teal's homely features with the slow ponderous momentum of an incoming tide. Jimmy; James Norman Mattock. The connection with Joan Sands had eluded Mr. Teal, but now it had been suggested to him his mind invested it with all the immutable actuality of proven fact. The truth sounds almost sacrilegious, but it is that Claud Eustace Teal, flushed with the joy of discovery, was composing a little song on the lines of a well-known nursery rhyme. It ran something like this—

> *Mattock had a little Joan*
> *Whose soul was blushing poor,*
> *And everywhere lamb Mattock went*
> *His Joan went on before.*

Mr. Teal was not a great poet, but he had a wonderful knack of getting a stranglehold on axioms.

"Funny that Jimmy never occurred to me," he said. "Let's take another look at that flat."

A novel lay on one chair, and when Storm picked it up to read the title a thin yellow envelope fell out. It was addressed to J.N. Mattock, and the postmark showed that it had been mailed in Putney at 2 p.m. the previous day. Storm smoothed put the slip of expensive creamy notepaper which it contained.

> Raegenssen having disappeared, the office can probably dispense with your services for a few hours.
>
> You and Sands will take the Torbay Limited from Paddington on the morning you receive this. You will go to Torquay and stay at the

Spa Hotel. You will return to London by the noon express the next day.

£15 is enclosed for your expenses.

The signature was the device of the Alpha Triangle.

Storm passed the letter over to Teal, and when the detective had read it he pursed his lips.

"He's the sort of snake who would have an alibi handy," was Mr. Teal's sour comment.

The voice they had heard over the telephone was certainly that of a man—but whose? Mattock's? Blaythwayt's? Teal could arrive at no plausible solution. And an odd dozen little Triangles had slithered through their fingers that night, winning clear on the blindest, most hopeless bluff that had ever been put up in the history of New Scotland Yard. The detective was anything but satisfied with his evening's work, and proceeded to vent his spleen on the unhappy Joe.

"Who told you to come butting in here?" he wanted to know. "I'll tell you, Joe, you dillytanty bloodhounds rile me. Now, just you warble me that little fairy tale I asked you for—and put in an opening chorus saying why you come rubing round this manor at twenty to midnight."

"Really, there's no need for you to be so offensive, Teal," Blaythwayt protested miserably. "I happened to be in court when Mattock was brought up after the Triangle got Mecklen away from the station—I go round the police courts when I've got any time to spare. It's the best method of seeing Life in the Raw." Joe's tone suggested the suppression of nameless horrors witnessed in the metropolitan courts of summary jurisdiction. "And I'm interested in this case, as you know, so I shadowed Mattock home. Then I had to hurry away, but I wanted to ask him a few questions, so I came along tonight."

"What questions?"

Blaythwayt waggled a podgy hand.

"Material for Writing," he explained unctuously. "One should strive for Accuracy. I wanted to know what it felt like to be set upon by two scoundrels, how it was to be up before a magistrate, and so on. I have never been before a magistrate, nor have I ever been molested by armed desperados, and so I resolved to get my sensations at least at second hand."

Storm lounged into a settee and put his feet up. His glance commanded Teal to cut short the persecution, for Storm had his own idea of the right way to deal with *l'affaire Blaythwayt*.

"You go steady, uncle!" he warned. "If you aren't careful you'll be sampling sensations at first hand. Teal loves arresting people—if I wasn't here, I'll bet he'd pull you in on the spot!" he added, to the detective's annoyance.

"Arrest *me*?" gasped Blaythwayt as though he could not believe his ears.

"You!"

Storm's manner differed from Teal's as much as the attack of a tiger differs from the onslaught of an elephant. Storm's voice was buttered and honeyed. His words came guilelessly, but there were little knobs and spikes sticking out all over them under the glossy varnish.

"You! Blaythwayt, you're playing around with matches in a gunpowder factory! I'll speak to you plainly, because you're the uncle of a very great friend of mine. And my advice to you is—slide! Light out over the horizon and stay lit until this Triangle cyclone has gone past. You'll be safer. Mess about with yeggs and kiters, if you like. Even plain ornery murderers are fairly safe. But steer wide of Triangles! Triangles have got death dope on every point; they've got edges like Kropps; and there's a big bomb packed up in the Alpha. I don't want any dead uncles-in-law—it kind of pancakes the marriage festivities, to go off on your honeymoon hung round with black crepe. I'll tell you something: you're next on the list! You know too much. Now, be a sensible fellow, and pass on what you know, and then vamoose for the duration. Why did you go to Billingsgate?"

Blaythwayt twiddled his fingers round his umbrella uneasily. Once or twice his mouth opened, and then gold-fished shut again. Storm's tone had been very gentle, disarmingly so, but even the innocent Joe had felt the tang of one or two of those tiny needle-points that prickled through the velvet.

"I—er—well, I'll tell you. Teal told me that Raegenssen was under suspicion. At least, he was mixed up in the business somehow; and even if that 'somehow' was only being one of the men the Triangle was out to kill, finding out more about him might have given me a line on the Apex himself."

"And how did you hear of Billingsgate?"

Joe hesitated, sucking the crook of his umbrella. One podgy hand went up and tilted his pot hat back from his forehead.

"Can I speak without prejudice?" he compromised.

"More or less."

"Er—um!" Blaythwayt scratched his head. "Um!" He caught Teal's dissecting eye upon him, and dithered. "To tell you the truth, I was the second burglar at Raegenssen's," he blurted.

Storm was tapping a cigarette on his thumbnail. Teal was probing for a piece of gum which had lodged in one of his molars. The effect of the revelation was that Teal bit his finger.

"And did you recognise anyone at Billingsgate?" asked Storm calmly, and Joe shook his head.

"Only Susan," he confessed.

"And you didn't get your line on the Big Triangle?"

"No. But I learnt something else, and you know what it was. Susan saw it—I only heard of it from her," Blaythwayt dropped his voice impressively. "The Tunnel!"

Storm looked up.

"Oh, yes! Into the Tube. Did either of you find out where it left the Tube again?"

"No."

"Just by the Bank of England!" said Storm coolly, and the Teal and Blaythwayt jaws sagged limply. "The Alpha Triangle was going to smash the Bank of England—they'd got it all mapped out to a hair! But there was just one place where they got snookered. Tell me that one, Joe."

Blaythwayt nodded sagely.

"The vaults are flooded at night."

Storm struck a match and applied it to his cigarette. He looked at the other two through a long wisp of blue smoke.

"Yeh!" he murmured. "They ought to have tried an easier crib. It must have been ... peeving to have a bloomer like that in your calculations—even if it does compensate for having the whole balloon burst by a police raid!"

He climbed off the settee and stretched himself. His face was reserve itself.

"Just one other thing," he remembered. "How did you find out that 'Raegenssen' was 'Sud-Scandinavia Wood'?"

Blaythwayt smiled.

"That was easy. I mean to say, I couldn't be sure, but I Had My Ideas. Susan told me that you had been talking about a mysterious sawmill, and, as Raegenssen's banker, I knew that he had frequently passed cheques made payable to the Sud-Scandinavia. So I knew he had some connection. I found the address in the street directory."

"Thanks very much," said Storm casually. "I think that's all. Are you going to take my tip?"

"Er—um!" Joe looked mournful.

Storm flicked a short cylinder of ash into a flower-pot. His cigarette twirled skywards, his shoulders squared, his hands went deep into his trouser pockets. He looked down at Blaythwayt with a metallic hardness in his eyes, and the other shuffled his feet uncertainly.

"That's my last word—skid!" drawled Storm in a friendly tone under which only an ear attuned to his mood would have detected the cast-iron core. "Give her the gun, prospective uncle-in-law, and hit her up on all six. Chase yourself, and touch the ground in spots. Go rubbering round Canada, or hunt butterflies in Peru—go any place where they never see Triangles except in geometry books or on beer-labels or the rear wings of autos! Don't forget that warning. I'm serious! During the next two days there're going to be special trains running to Gehenna for everyone who's got a line on the Big Triangle, or who's ever had the chance to get a line on him. The Big Triangle himself included—that's my contribution. You come right into that catalogue, Blaythwayt. Give Sherlock II a rest. I guess he needs it."

Never for one moment had that undercurrent of command broken surface; but Joe felt rather than heard it, and a flush of half-hearted obstinacy stole into his plump cheeks.

"Now, when do you leave?" said Storm.

"I—er—um!" Blaythwayt was dubious. "I really don't see, Captain Arden, that you've——"

Zzzzzzing! ... Zzzzzzing! ... Zzzzzzing!

For the second time that evening the clarion summons of the hall bell jazzed into insistence, and Teal ceased mastication for a couple of seconds to frown. Followed the clattering thump of a knocker plied by no patient hand, and then a short pause....

Zzzzzzing! ... Zzzzzzzzzzzzzzing!

Something quite unrelated to any surmise about the identity of the testy one outside prodded the conscience of Mr. Teal, to his discomfort. The foundation of the fact in his misgivings was not long in receiving demonstration.

"More callers!" murmured Storm. "I wonder who this is."

He opened the front door.

"Thank you," said Joan Sands coldly, and marched past him into the sitting-room.

She stood aside to allow Storm to enter, and then placed herself across the threshold.

"Inspector Teal, I believe?" she said, looking straight at the portly detective.

"That's right," said Teal.

Flabbergasted as he was, he could not deny her dignity. She stood with her legs slightly astride, her white hands loosely holding the belt of her simple tweed costume, and a glacial inclemency had come into her baby blue eyes.

"Captain Arden, I presume?"

"Sure!" Storm bowed.

Her gaze shifted to Joe Blaythwayt, who had suddenly become conspicuous by his efforts to efface himself.

"Who's this, Arden?" she demanded. "Is he a split too?"

Storm smiled.

"He'll bless you in his prayers if you call him that. Let me introduce you," he said easily. "Mr. Blaythwayt—Miss Sands. I expect he knows your name. He's Teal's father confessor."

She looked at him suspiciously.

"What's he here for?"

"I think he dropped in for a chat with Jimmy. Isn't that it, Joe?"

"I—er—um!" began Joe confusedly. "The fact is, Miss Sands, I was especially anxious to have a Private Conversation with your—your—um!"

He broke off and looked about him wretchedly, as though his mind was clawing round desperately for a straw of assistance. His embarrassment, which increased with every second of that awkward hiatus, was positively painful. He almost wriggled in his distress, and for the first time Joan smiled.

"My lover?—I suppose that's the word you're jibbing at?" she prompted without a tremor. "You're unlucky."

"We thought you were away, too," said Storm brazenly, and she swung round on him.

"So that's why you came?"

"Hardly! We didn't think you were away until we'd come."

She looked at him with a frown, as if she thought he was being facetious. He appreciated the genuineness of her scepticism, and took the yellow envelope from his pocket and gave it to her. She read it through, and then opened her bag and took out a telegram.

"I've been spending the last two days at Hindhead," she said. "I got this wire this afternoon, and that's all I knew of Jimmy going away. Read it."

"Thank you."

Sorry dear shan't be home when you return sent Torquay important business back tomorrow.

JIMMY.

Storm folded the flimsy and handed it back.

"I see. The Apex must have thought you were in town." Storm whistled out a long jet of smoke. "Who knew you were going?"

"Only Jimmy," she replied, and then once more she was on her high horse. "But I'm not here to be cross-examined. I take it you've been searching my flat. That being so, I'd like to see your warrant."

There was an interlude of silence. Joe had succeeded in retiring to the ample background afforded by Mr. Teal. The detective, having had the guiltiness of his conscience materialised, chewed stolidly and was tongue-tied. Arden coaxed his cigarette to the other corner of his mouth and met the girl's imperious gaze levelly.

"We haven't got one," he said. "Like Mr. Blaythwayt, Teal and I were going to pay a little call on Jimmy, only we got in the wrong door and found a little mothers' meeting in progress. We were in time for the agenda, and stopped to—er—vote upon the motion."

"Don't be funny," she snapped.

"I'm as serious as double pneumonia," he assured her gravely. "Joan, don't pretend to be dense!"

"I'm only Joan to my friends, Arden," she cut him, but he refused to be high-handed.

"I'm your friend, Joan," he said imperturbably. "Whether you call me Captain Arden or plain Arden doesn't bother me any, because I'm not talking for myself—there's every mite of every law in this country, and all the power behind the Law, concentrated in my two hands! You may or may not be as innocent as you seem. We'll argue that later. But come a little tour of inspection and learn things!"

He led her into the outer sitting-room, and she followed impatiently. He pointed to the chairs drawn up round the long table, and the marks of recent occupation in the ash-trays and scattered cards. He exhibited the loud-speaking telephone, and then indicated the wire which ran into her private flat. He took her back and traced for her its route across the floor, under the rugs, to the ornate bookcase.

She did no more than cast a bored glance at each of the damning beacons of incrimination he picked out for her enlightenment. Her lips were tightened up, her face a mask, her bearing inscrutable.

Then he made her look at the bookcase. She obeyed pettishly, and turned to him again with a mutinous tilt to her small chin.

"Well?" she said. "Is that all?"

"Not quite! You've seen the loud-speaking telephone and you've seen the tapped wires. You've seen how anyone knowing the secret of that bookcase could speak through to the other room. Teal and I arrived in that other room in time to hear two men detailed to murder our one and only Inspector Teal. We think those orders were given from your flat. So we're healthily curious!"

"Well?"

"Anything but! It isn't every day you hear the order given for your own execution!"

She faced him boldly.

"Do you think I was the speaker?"

"I don't," said Storm. "For one thing, the voice I heard was too deep for the best woman mimic on earth to have produced. For another, you hadn't a key—you had to ring for us to let you in. Why did you come back if you knew Jimmy was away? Who was going to let you in?"

"I forgot I hadn't a key. Jimmy lost his the other day, and as I was going away I left him mine. He was going to have another key cut."

"Uh-huh. Rather absent-minded of you! What'd you have done—slept on the doorstep?"

She pulled off her hat and shook out her hair. Walking over to a side table, she helped herself to a cigarette from a silver box. She turned round with the lighted match in her hand.

"My God—are you *still* here?" she exclaimed.

"That's real Mattock," Teal said, addressing Storm. "He tried that on me the other day."

"I'm sorry—we are," said Storm. "Now hear me, Joan! Who else had keys besides you and Jimmy?"

"No one that I know of."

Storm took a promenade up and down the room. She had rested against the table, and he stopped in front of her, eyeing her steadily and forcing her to meet his gaze. He said nothing, simply riveted her with that thoughtful stare. And he saw that tense silence rasp her nerves—saw her go a little paler under the paint and powder, and saw the quick straining heave of her bosom. Saw her mouth twitch ever so slightly, and saw the reflex, spasmodic jerk of her hand.

He smashed through her barricade of haughtiness by the sheer relentless battering of his will, and at last she turned her head away with a short shaky laugh and put a little distance between them, placing herself on the opposite side of the table as though to break away from that intangible attack.

"I hate talking like a detective story," Kit Arden said slowly, "but—if you've told me the truth—it looks ... bad ... for Jimmy, doesn't it?"

The blow that her intuition had sensed, namelessly and without logic, had fallen. He saw her wince and grip the edge of the table for support.

"I don't ... understand..."

"I'm sorry." Storm relaxed. The bombardment was lifted. His smile was as light and care-free as if there had never been an Alpha Triangle mentioned in that room. "That's all there is to be said, then. Except that I'll ask you to pass on to Jimmy the advice I gave Blaythwayt just before you came in. And that advice is, let up! Play with fire if you must get a kick out of life, but never do acrobatics on the chute of a blast furnace!... We'll move along now—I expect you're tired."

Blaythwayt, squirming and panting for relief from those taut surroundings into which he had stumbled, was in the van of that withdrawal. He made for the door as a scared rabbit scuttles to its burrow. Inspector Teal, more phlegmatically constituted, followed him with less speed and more self-possession.

Kit was the last to go, and he stayed behind for half a minute. He went up to Joan and held out his hand. She looked up at his face in uncomprehending surprise, and saw that the hard lines had gone and the flinty glitter was no longer in his eyes.

She put her hand in his, and he gave it a little squeeze.

"Kid," he said, "there's a lot of good in you. And one hell of a big brick of courage. I won't preach—I know you'd hate that. But you know what I mean."

How infinitely sweet and gentle his voice could be!

"I am sorry—honest!" said Storm. "But there's quite a way to go between saying you're sorry and coming round with a wreath. In a very few days the Triangle's going to smash, and you don't want to be part of the bang. So don't be silly. Get Jimmy away…. Good luck!"

From the doorway she watched him stride down the corridor. She was conscious of a vague, indescribable feeling deep within her. Something that troubled her, that she could not understand and yet was on the brink of understanding, seemed to have awakened against her volition. Something pleasant and yet rather frightening. Something that kindled up with the promise of a sweeping flame ... something that had died, was reborn.

"Captain Arden!" she called, and he stopped.

"Hullo?"

"Captain Arden." Her speech was a little faltering, a little tremulous. "You—you're the only busy I've ever met who was—pure white—all the way through."

He smiled and waved his hand cheerily; and then he turned to the stairs and ran down.

He found Teal and Blaythwayt waiting for him in the street, and the detective had his friend's arm in an ominously professional grip.

"Joe and me," said Teal, oblivious of grammar, "is going to have words!"

"I hope you won't be rude to each other!" said Storm piously.

They walked down Piccadilly together, and they had almost reached Burlington House when all three of them saw an amazing sight.

Down in Piccadilly Circus, where the statue of Eros once stood, there flickered into being for an instant a terrific blinding blaze of violet light. It seemed to lurch up from the roadway in one colossal wave of whirling, jagged, eye-tormenting luminance—a Cyclopean flood of flaring amethyst which stunned vision and paralysed the brain. In a thousandth of a second it was gone, splintering into a star-searing burst of intolerable dazzling white radiance shot with zigzagging streaks of orange fire. And right in the flash of that fearful disintegration came a shattering, detonating thunder that rocked the very earth under their feet and pounded and pulverised the senses into an agony of quivering helplessness. And then, on the heels of the awful reverberation, followed a mighty rushing wind which reeled them out of all equilibrium and hurled them dazed and breathless to the ground.

CHAPTER 20

MECKLEN IS DISOBEDIENT

On a hot summer night the library of Terry Mannering's house in Brook Street was a cool alluring room.

Susan sat there, cosily stretched out in a deep armchair placed by an open window. At the big centre table Terry was engaged in the arduous task of selecting the probable winner of the St. Leger; and a litter of sporting journals, both pink and white, a much-thumbed copy of *Racing Up-to-Date*, an open volume of Ruff's *Guide to the Turf*, and sheets upon sheets of notepaper covered with abstruse calculations involving such weird factors as weights, lengths and seconds—testified to his earnestness. His wife was sewing in the chair opposite Susan. At times Terry would sit up abruptly and explode into a concentrated malignant malediction upon every congenital imbecile who ever had, ever did, or ever intended to essay the unravelling of equine form; at other moments he would lean back with a resigned look of martyrdom on his face, heave a long sigh, and offer a fervent prayer to be caught up to heaven in a fiery chariot before he reached the stage of dementia where it would be necessary for him to be hailed to a lunatic asylum—which anguished vociferations only served to convulse his audience with unsympathetic hilarity.

Susan had been trying to read, but her mind refused to converge on the printed word. It kept straggling off into other channels, and she would recall herself with a start to find she had skimmed through half a dozen pages without taking in the meaning of a single line. At length this continual absentmindedness forced her to admit that the effort of literary assimilation was, for that evening at least, a hopeless failure. She looked at her watch. It was nearing midnight—in spite of her abstraction, the time had flown past unnoticed—yet she felt in no mood for sleep. Following another outbreak of blood-curdling fulmination from Terry, she laid her book down on her knees, clasped her hands behind her head, and decided to give her imagination the rein it was straining for.

Her thoughts sped instantly to Storm. She strove to picture him in her mind's eye, and discovered to her surprise that she could form only the vaguest possible image. Little mannerisms of his, his swinging gait, snatches of his staccato conversation, vivid expressions he had invented—these were all the material she found to her hand. The complete design eluded her. Even the attempt to visualise his face resulted only in a mental blur. Being no psychologist, this disability irritated and puzzled her.

But at least she could remember nearly every word of their exchange that afternoon, and a soft smile curved her lips. Yes, she loved him—loved him with all her heart and every atom of her being…. But her smile was not of motherly affection. (God help the man who inspires that watery form of love!) It was a smile of pride, of clean, wholesome, exuberant joy that he was hers and she his. He was so fine, so sunny, so eminently sane and vital, so masterful—and yet without any artificial, self-conscious, diluted, drawing-room, flapper-thrilling, synthetic-cavemanishness about him—so dynamic, so fresh and savoury—both intellectually and physically…. And she was going to marry him. That pride she felt whenever she was with him was to be hers always….

And so, after moments of delicious day-dreaming, her fantasy carried her reluctantly to his immediate work—the Alpha Triangle. When would the menace of that dread organisation be lifted from the city? What was the secret of the Apex, that secret which if broadcast would mean the lightening of the shadow which loomed over London—the secret to preserve which the Apex was prepared for murder? The thought recalled to her his threat to have her arrested unless she married him that day. She had believed at first that he was joking. The idea was too preposterous…. And yet, was anything preposterous in those days, when a gang of killers such as one expects to encounter only in the pages of the sensational novelist were trying to blackmail the Centre of the World to the tune of fifteen million pounds sterling—and were, moreover, almost daily giving convincing evidence of their mercilessness and their ability to carry out every threat they made? But why arrest her? The answer was easy: that she might be more efficiently guarded than she could be in a private house. And the alternative, marriage to Storm, would make her nearly as secure. But the day he had given her for making up her mind had gone by, and she had not married him—he had left the choice open to her as if he expected her to ring him up and say: "Kit, old man, I've changed my mind. D'you think you could spare the time to drop into a registry office with me this afternoon?" Everything that was romantic in her revolted from the cold-bloodedness of the idea. It was unthinkable, and yet there had been a substratum of seriousness underlying his light tone. What was the second condition? "*If a certain gentleman now in custody escapes…*" Of course—but no; even that didn't exceed the bounds of possibility, when already the Triangle had rescued thirteen of its members from the Flying Squad van in which they were being hustled to a police station. Who was this man who might escape? And what was his particular importance?

She had no data for the solution of that problem, and branched from it on to another tack.

Why should she be in danger at all, from any member of the Triangle? What did she know, or what had she had the chance of deducing, which might imperil the secret of the Apex? Here at least she had a little knowledge to train on the question. She knew some people who were connected with the mystery: Lord Hannassay, Mattock, Raegenssen, and—Uncle Joe. The inclusion of her uncle amused her; but she left him in the list because he had received one of the Triangle cards. Now, what did she know about each? She took them one by one. Lord Hannassay? The Triangle had murdered him. She knew little about him, except that he held a minor position in the Home Office. Was he connected with any of the other three? ... The recollection of his interest in Mattock, to which Storm had attached some import, came to her in a flash. She wrestled with the circumstances of that case. Mattock had been Hannassay's secretary, and had forged his employer's name to a cheque; Hannassay had prosecuted him without mercy, and Mattock had gone to prison. Therefore Mattock had a grudge against Hannassay. Then how did the others fit in? She was certain that Raegenssen belonged somewhere in that complicated jig-saw—she had a distinct recollection of the afternoon when the Hirondel had skidded into him. Raegenssen had been knocked half unconscious, and she had heard him speak as he was coming round: if he had been partially stunned, his brain would have functioned without the restraint which his caution imposed upon it in ordinary life, and he might have let fall a hint of Something. And that Something had had an astounding effect on Storm, Mattock, and Uncle Joe. She could even picture their different expressions—Storm's tense inscrutability, Mattock's passion, and Uncle Joe's excitement. What was it Raegenssen had mumbled? Some girl's name ... *Sylvia*! That was it. Then where did Sylvia come in, and who was Sylvia—why should she have such an incredible influence upon three men brought together practically by a fluke?

Another idea came tapping at Susan's brain. She could not quite place it—it was something which hammered at the doors of her conscious mind and yet just missed gaining ingress. A cold wind seemed suddenly to lap her spine, sending a shiver up her back to the nape of her neck. She had a numbing sensation of being on the verge of a bottomless precipice, of being on the threshold of some terrible realisation. There was something enormously significant attached to that name, and yet it was only a superficial association. It wasn't the name itself, but ... but ... but the way it was said—Raegenssen's voice!

For a space the fog that had thwarted her memory rolled back and blotted out understanding in a maddeningly, impenetrable vapour of obscurity; and then, through the mist, dawned a slow nimbus of realisation. Raegenssen's voice! Never in her life, she would have sworn, had she spoken to a man named Raegenssen, and yet the remembered timbre of his incoherent mutter "*Sylvia ... Sylvia ...*" struck a responsive chord which vibrated through her consciousness with ever-increasing assurance.

Conviction came against her will, fighting for expression against all the massed forces of logic and reasoning. It was ridiculous, smacking of hallucination, incredible—and yet, pluck that awakened chord ever so distrustfully, it rang true every time. Millimetre by millimetre, battling doggedly against the overwhelming odds, common sense gave ground before the onslaught of primeval instinct. She was sound of mind and body, had never had cause to doubt the stability of her senses; therefore, insane as the idea might seem, it must be granted due audience. And so, with every breathless second, that clear, single note of belief sang in greater and greater volume. She knew she was right, knew she could rely on the combined depositions of hearing and memory ...

She knew Raegenssen's voice, and it was the voice of a man who had spoken to her recently!

The full light of understanding blinded her, and her hands came down suddenly to grip the arms of her chair. Now that all darkness had been swept away by that last swift incandescence of knowledge, she was amazed that she had never seen and gripped that stark fact before. Perhaps it was because she had not thought to place sufficient importance on the incident, and therefore had not turned it over in her mind and inspected it from every angle. Certainly, circumstances had allied to lull her into accepting the salient, startling truth as a thing of no account. Of course, one may always find a full-grown African rhinoceros in a soap factory, but the possibility falls short of the commonly endorsed probabilities of normal life, so that anyone seeking African rhinoceros heads automatically for Africa instead of taking his chance in an expedition to Port Sunlight. In exactly the same way, her subconscious mind had so scoffed at the idea of Oscar Raegenssen being no more than the Mr. Hyde of somebody else's Dr. Jekyll, that the censor on guard between conscious and subconscious had barred out the suggestion. Nevertheless— and, now, she would have sworn to it—Raegenssen was somebody else. Or, conversely, somebody else was Raegenssen. In dress, deportment, face and figure there was only the most far-fetched possible similarity; in the ordinary way, that difference was likely to extend to voice also; all the same, there remained one dogmatic heads-I-win-tails-you-lose certainty by way of bedrock on which to start rebuilding every theory about the Alpha Triangle. And that that certainly had some very intimate relation to the Triangle was an assumption which brooked no question.

Her head was spinning like a high-pressure dynamo; the glimpse of infinite leagues of the Unknown which her new-found wisdom gave her was appalling. She had a grip on one salient fact, and she was sure that attached to that fact was the thread which, properly trailed, would lead to the centre of the labyrinth. Whose, then, was that momentous Voice? She racked her brain for inspiration; but having obliged so far, memory baulked at that last fence. She realised the difficulty of divorcing voice from all association of appearance and demeanour. Storm might have the various compartments of his reminiscence more efficiently docketed and cross-indexed than hers were—but how could one describe a voice? It seemed hopeless unless one happened to be an expert imitator, and that ability was not among her talents. Still she thought she should get in touch with him: even while he was on his way she might succeed in remembering the owner of the Voice. She had a ludicrous vision of herself seated in the Chief Commissioner's room at New Scotland Yard, her head swathed in ice compresses, what time the heads of the Criminal Investigation Department hovered and tiptoed around her, waiting in anxious silence for a clue to fall from her lips ...

She smiled to herself, but the impulse to ring up Storm persisted. Where would he be at that hour? Most probably at his flat, she decided promptly.

She was on the point of getting up from her chair to fetch the telephone, when——

BOOM! ... —*oom!* ... —*oom!* ...

The muffled thunder of a distant explosion came echoing and reëchoing through the ether. And not so very distant either, for the thud of it was louder than anything she had ever heard—it shook the earth and rattled the windows in their frames. She sat up with a jump, and saw that Ann had dropped her work and was staring about in amazement. Even Terry looked up with a surprised expression; and then he leaned heavily on the table.

"Concentration!" he breathed reverently. "What absorption! What industry! I hope you're all takin' a lesson from me. I'm goin' to register a Deed Poll changing my name to Rip Van Winkle. When I started this pestilential job it was June, and now they're already lettin' off fireworks and burning the image of Mr. Fawkes. Still, I suppose to anyone of my vast intelligence——

"Shut up!" commanded his wife rudely. "Susan, whatever was it?"

"Fireworks, I tell you," said Terry. "This is the Fifth, and they're celebratin' Brock's Benefit."

And then, stealing through the open windows, from the east, came the dull roar of a hubbub which swelled with every minute. Came, ever so thin and faint, a horrible, sobbing cry.... The racket grew ... not so very far away they heard shouts, a screaming babel of police whistles, and the patter of running feet...

Terry moved over to the window and peered out over their shoulders, but they could see nothing.

"Not an air-raid, surely? Don't say I've slept all through the Great War, daddy," he murmured, but there was not much jesting in his manner.

They listened. Windows were being flung open and people were coming out into the streets. The shouting had come nearer—men were spreading the news to everyone within range of voices, but as yet it was impossible to make out what was being yelled. Until, gradually, to the three of them, came a glimmer of comprehension. The Triangle. That ruthless organisation had been abroad again that night, spreading death and disaster in some terrific fashion at which for the nonce they could only guess.

On the pavement outside the two detectives who guarded the house were staring into the darkness, speculating about the cause of the disturbance.

"What was it?" Terry called through the window, and one of them looked up and shook his head.

"Can't say, sir. The Triangle threatened to blow up some places, and Piccadilly Circus was first on the list—the noise seemed to come from that direction, but I couldn't swear to it."

Storm's flat was near Piccadilly. A little pang ripped into Susan's heart, and she caught her breath. But it wasn't likely that he'd be in the damage, she reassured herself doubtfully. The Albany was some way from Piccadilly Circus, and London was so big that, even if he were out that night, it was umpteen thousand to one against his having been near the explosion. And, anyhow, it wasn't certain that Piccadilly Circus had been mined, although logic was inclined to support that hypothesis....

Still they listened, and while they did so a handful of men and women ran past, laughing, dashing off to "see the fun." And then, through the night air, came an ominous silence, a murmuring stillness which was perplexing until they realised that it was caused by a sudden stoppage of all the traffic running on the near south and east. And through that hush came a new sound, approaching rapidly. It increased, until it could be recognised as the splutter of a high-powered car tearing through the streets towards them. As it sped nearer, it could all but be identified, and the suspicion it roused made Susan clutch the window sill in unaccountable terror. That loud, rising and falling snort and purr was the voice of a Hirondel—Storm's car. Was Storm himself driving? The fear that It might be carrying his maimed or lifeless body filled her with a shuddering dread.

Was it the Hirondel? The car broke into sight now, rocking down the road with its twin headlights ablaze. It drew almost abreast of them, and then swerved across the road and jerked to a standstill before the door with all its brakes screaming in protest at the rough handling.

One of the detectives ran to open the door, and Susan watched, striving not to flinch, to see who should descend.

It was not Storm—-it was a uniformed policeman. The man spoke a curt word to the detective, and then ran up the steps.

Susan had the door open for him before he could ring.

"What is it?" she cried. "*Quick!* Tell me—is he—is Captain Arden hurt?"

The man twiddled a button.

"Yes, miss—er—well, not much." The constable was confused. "He's—er—he wants to see you ... and..."

"Yes, *yes*!" The girl stamped her foot impatiently. "Go on. Tell me the worst—I shan't faint or do anything silly. Is he—seriously injured?"

"Well, miss, you never know," said the policeman huskily. "The doctors say—

"Where is he?"

"St. George's Hospital—on his way there, anyhow. He sent me to fetch you. That's his car."

"I'll come right away," she said pantingly. "Hurry!"

She could not understand his hesitation, until she turned and saw Terry and Ann standing behind her. Terry was looking grave.

"Shall I go with you?" he asked gently, but she shook her head.

"I'll go alone—I'd rather," she said.

He nodded understandingly, and she rushed down the steps and climbed into the car. The policeman followed. In an instant the subdued mutter of the engine had risen to a deafening roar, and, as the man let in the clutch, the Hirondel leapt off like an unleashed greyhound, They swung into the Park at Grosvenor Gate, and as they emerged at Hyde Park Corner they saw that, diminished as the traffic was at that hour, the wreckage of Piccadilly Circus had caused a block which was already spreading nearly to Park Lane. It was with some difficulty that they threaded their way through the press.

To the girl's inquiries the driver answered only in gruff monosyllables, and she was reduced to picturing to herself what might have befallen Storm. It was anguishing to think of—Storm, the debonair and strong and athletic—now, perhaps, only a crushed, mutilated travesty of life. A quiver of fear touched her lips, and then with a conscious gesture she tossed her head erect and sat stiffly motionless. Courage! ... She must have courage.... He had always so despised cowardice, been so scathingly contemptuous of people who trembled and shook at the knees and whined whenever they came up against the toughness and ugliness of the world.

She had hardly noticed their man[oe]uvring through the gyratory system at the triangular junction of Piccadilly, Knightsbridge and Grosvenor Place; but the lurch of the car turning suddenly recalled her to her surroundings. And with a shock she realised that they had diverged to the left and were racing down Constitution Hill with the Hirondel's cut-out closed down until the engine made no more than a whispering drone which attracted no attention.

She caught at the arm of the uniformed man beside her.

"What's the idea?" she demanded sharply. "You said St. George's Hospital——"

For answer, his left hand came off the steering-wheel and his arm whipped behind her shoulders. His hand came under her chin, and she felt his thick fingers close upon her throat.

"Never yew worry what I said," hissed Lew Mecklen in her ear; and, now that he made no attempt to disguise his voice, his nasal twang shrieked a heart-stopping menace at her. "Yew're comin' whar I want yuh, an' ef yew scream I'll throttle yuh!"

CHAPTER 21

FOUND DEAD

Storm got to his feet somehow, shaking his head like a dog that has been for a swim. He felt sick and giddy, and the blood was buzzing through his head with the whirr of a dentist's drill. The shock had been terrific. Years ago, in Flanders, he had gone through the appalling mill of artillery barrages, intensive bomb-dropping, and the earthshaking fulguration of tons of H.E. sparked off in land mines; but he had never even in a nightmare gauged the possibility of such a stupendous cataclysm as had just taken place within a quarter of a mile of him. Comparatively great as the distance was between himself and the explosion, its force even at that range had been so daunting that it seemed miraculous to have survived it.

He looked around for the other two, doubtfully, as though in his bemused condition he hardly expected to find that the phenomenon had been repeated. But they, too, seemed to be unhurt. Inspector Teal had already regained his feet and was swaying to and fro with one hand clasped to his head, muttering white-hot profanities; and Joe Blaythwayt was sitting up gazing from side to side, his mouth open and his whole face smudged into one incredulous gape. And even while Storm tried to convince himself that the whole thing wasn't a delusion, Teal staggered over to the bank manager and held out a hand to help him rise.

Approximately at this time, John Cardan, editor of the *Daily Record*, left the offices of that enterprising newspaper. He turned into Fleet Street and walked briskly down towards the Strand, for it was his habit to utilise the space between Record House and Charing Cross Station, where he took a late train for his suburban home, to get the necessary exercise his sedentary occupation denied to him. And, as he walked, humming a little song, he was blissfully unaware of the skulking figure that slunk along behind him...

Birdie was more than a trifle scared. He did not fully understand what he was about to do—he could not possibly have had the foggiest inkling of the volcanic power that had been compressed into the few drachms of viscous yellow liquid which swilled about in the tiny phial on which his fingers rested. He had about as much chance of appreciating anything so vast as he had of comprehending the metaphysical conception of infinity. All he knew was that he was carrying a very small quantity of the most powerful explosive known to science—whatever that might mean. Thanks to his weedy frame, he had not had the experience of high explosives which was presented *gratis* to some millions of men between the years of 1914 and 1918. All he knew about explosives was that they went off with a bang, and that they couldn't be so very terrible. Thinking things over, he was at a loss to account for the fear he had when his hand first touched that precautionary calorimeter. No; what scared Birdie now was the knowledge that he was about to commit a bigger crime than any in his petty, sneaking career. What he thought was that his boss had a grudge against Cardan, and that the mucid amber in the phial would simply injure the editor enough to make him sorry for whatever he had done to the Apex. Birdie hadn't any idea what size crime that might be, or how long a stretch he would get for it if he was caught, but he was sure that it would be something pretty nasty.

Like a furtive shadow he began to quicken his steps so as to catch up with Cardan. One hand, resting in his pocket, held the copper ice-box steady, while his finger and thumb grasped the slim neck of the phial. It must be a quick job, and a quick getaway to follow—be the explosion ever so small, he was too well known to the splits to risk being seen loafing anywhere around when the bang happened. His fingers shook a little, and he strove to hold them still. It would be fatal to bungle during the couple of seconds the bottle would take to flash from the calorimeter to John Cardan's waistcoat pocket. By an effort of will he got his hand back to rock-like firmness and throttled down the twitching of his nerves, but he could not control the chilly perspiration which broke out on his palms.

Nearer and nearer he drew, his shifty eyes on the alert for exactly the right combination of circumstances for the fatal movement. It came when they had nearly reached the law Courts—in the shape of three men who were approaching abreast. Birdie came level with Cardan at precisely the right moment, so that for a moment the five of them were in line, so close together that their shoulders brushed....

It was all over in the twinkling of an eye, with just one lightning flicker of Birdie's slim, trained fingers. And then Birdie had ducked down a dark side street and was running for dear life, gasping painfully with the reaction from tension. The copper vessel in his pocket held nothing more dangerous than some clinking chips of ice. With a cry that was rather like a strangled sob, he dragged it out and flung it far from him, and ran on.

And the tiny tube of death reposed in John Cardan's pocket, the warmth of his body slowly thawing out the oily fluid to the temperature at which it would detonate....

Birdie found himself abruptly faced by a solid brick wall. He stopped in horror, and looked around him. He had taken the wrong turning—fear had deadened his judgment—he, who in the pursuit of his craft had long ago familiarised himself with all the back streets which would provide a sound prospect of shaking off his pursuers if he were ever spotted and forced to cut and run. There was nothing for it; he must retrace his steps, go back to the vicinity of the Thing! He hurried through the darkness, stumbling, panting with apprehension.

Birdie had run fast; as he reëntered Fleet Street, he looked in the direction of the Strand and saw that Cardan had not gone more than fifty paces. And while Birdie looked, the last essential fraction of a degree centigrade percolated through the thin glass to the charge of nitrogen trichloride....

Five ghastly seconds later he was racing up Fleet Street, careless of who saw his headlong flight, reckless of the inquisitive glance of any busies who might be prowling the neighbourhood. His breath came in harsh wheezing groans; his eyes were dilated with unspeakable terror; in his face was the ashen pallor of death. He didn't mind where he went—he scarcely knew where his feet were taking him. All that mattered was the placing of leagues and leagues between himself and the awful thing he had seen; for every devil and fury from the Pit was shrieking at his heels....

"They've done it! Blast 'em—they've done it!" said Teal muzzily.

Already people were rushing up towards Piccadilly Circus, and from Piccadilly Circus itself others were fleeing in all directions as though expecting a second explosion. High and shrill above the tumult of shouting came the scream of a man in mortal agony....

Storm set off at a run, Teal lumbered along close behind him, and Blaythwayt tagged short-windedly in the rear. Storm covered that quarter-mile in something close to record time, and Teal was not very far behind when he fetched up almost on the rim of the huge crater which had been blown into the heart of the Circus.

Ezra Surcon had had a good return from his property in Great Windmill Street.

It was an amazing cavern. The charge must have been placed below the deepest Tube cuttings, and experts calculated that to blast a hole of that size must have taken nearly five gallons of NCl_3. The crater measured roughly fifty yards across, and in its depths was laid bare the whole warren of subways that had taken years to construct—there were even scraps of twisted wreckage from the higher level lines tangled up among the debris of escalators and elevators. Also, the Tube had been open at the time.... People had been in those subways, had been walking upon the ground that had been blown away, and omnibuses and cars had been driving over it.... There were things in that trough which had once been human, living, sensate.... In it, too, and around it, were things which had once been living and were not yet dead....

"My God!" muttered Teal hoarsely. "Why can't they *die*?"

His ruddy face had blenched, and Storm himself had gone grey under the tan. The only man who seemed unaffected was Blaythwayt, who stood a little to one side, staring about him in wide-eyed curiosity.

Already ambulances were careering through the streets with their right-of-way bells clanging, and constables were pouring on to the scene to attend to the injured and hold back the crowd of morbid, pale-faced sightseers. Storm and Teal went through the cordon and did what they could for the sufferers. It was a horrible and often hopeless task, but both had had their baptism of blood, and had learned to steel themselves against sights and sounds which would have made many men helpless with nausea.

Doctors were soon on the scene to help both voluntary and official workers, and the first two of these that Storm saw he sent hastening back to fetch hypodermic syringes and—morphia. These he commandeered, and then constituted a panel of himself and their owners. And when they saw what he proposed to do, they said nothing.

"I shall ask you to give me your opinions on the less certain cases," he said steadily. "There are some which you don't have to be a doc. to diagnose. I shall give the shot myself, and I take full responsibility..."

It was an hour before all the human scath which could ever hope to live had been removed in the ambulances, and the dead decently laid out.

Storm was weary of body and soul by that time, and when he found Inspector Teal he saw that, husky as the detective was, he was in no better case.

"I've killed seven men tonight," said Storm heavily. "It was God's blessing to 'em. But I'm—sick! This is worse than war."

Teal was silent. Then:

"What do we do now, Chief?" he asked.

"Go home, I suppose. We can't do any more here. Where's Joe?"

"Somewhere round—I saw him lending a hand with the best of 'em, soon as he'd got over rubbering. He's taken it better than either of us. He must have nerves of ice!"

Blaythwayt came up at that moment, wiping his hands on a stained handkerchief. He was still round-eyed with interest; but otherwise, except for an excusable excitement, he was remarkably self-possessed.

"An Extraordinary Experience!" he said. "Of course, one's very sorry for all those poor wretches; but still..."

He broke off with a shrug, as though to imply that the scientific mind transcended such mundane considerations.

"I ought to drop in at the Yard," Teal said with a sigh. "You've got an advantage over me, Captain Arden—you're not a regular and you don't have to bother so much about routine." He yawned. "Lordy! I seem to average about ten minutes' sleep per night these days," he complained somewhat paradoxically.

"You'll average less for the next seventy hours or so!" Storm told him. "I'll come with you—I might find the Commissioner in."

Joe Blaythwayt was skipping eagerly in front of them.

"D'you think I could come too?" he pleaded wistfully. "I've never had a chance to see inside Scotland Yard, and after what's happened tonight it seems as if my Luck Is In—I don't mean to be callous," he excused himself incoherently. "I'm sorry, as I said, but——"

Teal shook an admonishing finger at him.

"Joe, you go home to bed," he commanded sternly. "You're a blood-thirsty little man, and I think you've had all the horrors that's good for you tonight."

"Oh, let him come," Storm interrupted wearily. "What the devil does it matter, anyway?"

They found a taxi in Trafalgar Square and piled in. Joe Blaythwayt, still clasping his umbrella, which somehow he had managed to retain throughout the proceedings, was all agog with anticipation. Decidedly, one would have thought, he regarded it as His Evening.

Storm was less cheerful.

"The hell of it is that I feel responsible," he explained bitterly. "I deliberately let the Triangle get away, and now he's made tonight's mess. Selfishness—or quixoticism, if you like—I don't know. Listen, Teal, and I'll tell you something! I've known the Triangle for days, but I wasn't going to show him up in the usual way, as I told the Inquiry, for the reason you know."

"You know the Triangle?" broke in Teal incredulously. "I thought that was a bluff you put up for the Board."

"Yes, I know him. I'll tell you what my idea was. I'm a fool, maybe, but because he's my father I didn't want any publicity. And by the same token, I couldn't very well kill him myself. So what I intended to do was collect so much evidence that I could go to him and lay it before him so definitely he'd see the only alternative to hanging was—suicide. I know what his choice'd have been."

"Have you got that evidence now?"

"No," said Storm bitterly, and was silent all the rest of the way to Cannon Row.

They left Blaythwayt in charge of the reserve sergeant and went up to the Commissioner's room. Smethurst was away, but they had not been there five minutes before Bill Kennedy came in for first-hand news of the Piccadilly Circus explosion. Storm left Teal to give the account, and himself went over to the window and sat down on the sill, smoking a cigarette.

Storm's face was chiselled out into grim lines, but behind its inscrutability and actuating the leisurely precision of his movements was a hurtling mill of mental concentration. What was the next move to be? He strove to grapple with the problem, but his over-tired brain refused to function with the methodical accuracy he demanded of it. Teal had complained of the curtailment of the hours of slumber, but Storm himself had had little sleep that last week, and mind is not tireless like machinery. Yet he kept on, keying his already taut faculties almost up to snapping pitch, calling up all his reserves of energy, and struggling with their aid to outline a practical plan.

Teal had just finished his account when the telephone rang. Storm, who was nearest, took the call.

It was the City Commissioner speaking.

"You've had a blow-up in Piccadilly Circus, haven't you?"

"Oh—er—yes! I believe we have!" said Storm ironically, and the Commissioner snorted in disgust.

"Well, we've had a smaller one in Fleet Street. Just one man—blown to crumbs. There's no hope of identifying him. I just thought you might be interested. Sands, a pickpocket belonging to the Walton Street manor, was seen haring away from the scene as if he'd a big scare, so you might put out a call for him."

"I will. Fleet Street, I think you said?"

"Yes."

"Uh-huh. The dead man is John Cardan, editor of the *Daily Record*," said Storm calmly, and hung up the receiver.

After what had happened that night, such minor details as solo murders seemed things of no account. Storm had reached the stage where he was beyond the reach of agitation.

He gave the Assistant Commissioner a brief account of the conversation, and he was still speaking when the telephone bell shrilled again. This time it was the Thames Police depot on Victoria Embankment.

When Storm put down the instrument a queer flush had come into his face.

"A body's been taken out of the river," he said slowly. "Head smashed to pulp with an axe. The tailor's tab in the breast pocket, and some papers in the clothes, say that it's Oscar. I guess this is the end of the world!"

Storm and Teal went off to view the corpse, and the detective was surprised to see that Storm hailed a taxi in Cannon Row instead of setting out to walk the short distance along the Embankment. Mr. Teal, however, was too well trained to make any demur, and he had just got in when Blaythwayt came rushing up.

The bank manager climbed in as the taxi started off, and sat down beaming. The other two let him stay—it was amazing what a fixture that plump little man had become that night. In normal times he would probably have been unceremoniously ejected, but both Storm and Teal were too tired and too occupied with other matters to take the trouble of arguing him home.

The taxi drove to a house in Harley Street, and Storm had to ring for some time before he could get an answer. At length a dishevelled butler swathed in a grey flannel dressing-gown over lamentably striped pyjamas opened the door. When he had heard Kit's business, he began to shut the door again, but Storm kicked it wide and entered the hall. A moment later the Home Office pathologist, himself awakened by the noise, appeared at the head of the stairs and inquired sleepily but with some mastery of expletive, what it all meant.

Storm presented his credentials.

"I'm sorry to turn you out at this ungodly hour, but it's very important. I may not need you at all, but there's a big possibility that I may, and if I want you I shall want you at once!"

"All right," said the doctor peevishly. "I suppose it's all in the night's work. The butler'll give you a drink while I'm dressing."

He was down in an astonishingly short time, and the four of them entered the taxi. The pathologist seemed surprised to see Blaythwayt, and Teal was in a quandary until an idea seized him.

"Mr. Blaythwayt is Raegenssen's banker," he explained. "He's going to identify the body."

Joe stood by while the sheet that shrouded the dead man was removed, and then peered interestedly into the battered face.

"I couldn't swear to it," he said at last. "But I think it's he—that yellow beard of his is so distinctive."

"That's half the trouble," remarked Storm cryptically.

Blaythwayt was then shown the clothes that had been worn by the body, and these he declared without hesitation to be Raegenssen's. Apparently the Swede had possessed only one lounge suit, for Blaythwayt said that the garments were those which Raegenssen had been wearing whenever his banker had seen him.

Storm turned to the pathologist.

"Set up the gadgets!" he ordered curtly, and the doctor, after a glance of surprise, began to unpack the large black bag he had brought with him at Storm's request.

In the small room, besides Teal and Blaythwayt, was also a sergeant of the Thames Police, and to these three Storm addressed his next command.

"There's to be no dispute about this," he said, "so to make everything trebly sure you'll all do your bit. I want each of you to take two hairs from Raegenssen's beard, and lay them on the sheet of paper Dr. Malleson has laid out for them."

Wondering, they obeyed.

"Now stand by while Dr. Malleson makes his tests."

The pathologist bent to his work, while they waited in a mystified silence. It was half-an-hour before he straightened his back with a sigh and indicated that he was satisfied.

"Well?" asked Storm, and Malleson looked at him curiously.

"Peroxide," he replied. "The hair was originally black, and I should say that it was the hair of one of the more southern races—several Spaniards and Portuguese are diluted with Moorish blood. What made you suspect bleaching?"

But this was a question that Storm was not for the moment disposed to answer. As a matter of fact, all that he had suspected was that the body was not Raegenssen's, and the rarity of beards of that Nordic hue was great enough to arouse the suspicion that a black-bearded man would have had to be found and disguised in order to provide a substitute.

He led the way into the office, and a combined deposition was made out and signed. It was an interesting document.

> We, the undersigned, do hereby attest and swear that at 1.30 a.m. this morning we did, in the presence of each other and of the undersigned Dr. Malleson, pathologist to the Home Office, and Captain Arden, temporarily attached to the Special Branch of the Criminal Investigation Department, remove from the beard of a cadaver taken from the Thames last night and so far presumed to be that of Oscar Raegenssen, agent, of Cockspur Street, S.W.1, each of us two hairs; and, further, that the said Dr. Malleson made the examination of these hairs, which is the subject of his appended affidavit in our presence.
>
> (Signed)
> C. E. TEAL, Inspector, C.I.D.
> J. CLAVER, Sergeant, T.P.
> J. BLAYTHWAYT.

> And I, Soames Malleson, pathologist to the Home Office, do hereby attest and swear that in the presence of the above-named witnesses I did examine the said beard hairs, and did find that they were the hairs of a dark-complexioned man which had been bleached with peroxide of hydrogen to give a similitude of fairness. I further add that, from an inspection of other body hairs of the deceased, and from such cranial characteristics as can be observed, my sworn opinion is that the deceased was not Scandinavian, but of the Latin type, and probably of Moorish extraction.
>
> (Signed)
> SOAMES MALLESON, M.D.

And I, Christopher Arden, of Albany, W.1, having been present during the operations specified above, do hereby affirm and support the statements of the above-named witnesses.

(Signed)
CHRISTOPHER ARDEN, Capt.

"That's simply for the official record," Storm said as he blotted his signature. "I want a copy for my own use, also signed by all of you."

When the facsimile had been made out and witnessed, he went back to make a fresh inspection of the clothes that had been taken from Raegenssen's body. This time he made an interesting discovery, for a more careful search of the coat revealed that there were some papers sewn into the lining. Storm slit the silk with his penknife and drew them out—four photographs.

For a while he stared at them, standing as if he were carven out of granite. Every face that was there he knew, and the realisation that he had stumbled upon the last secret of the Alpha Triangle thundered through his head like the roar of a cataract.

"Je-rusalem!" he breathed.

At one stroke all the handicaps that had been piling up ever since the disappearance of Raegenssen, and that had culminated in the Piccadilly explosion that night, were swept away. Just by that one slip. The body which lay stiffly stretched out on the stone slab was not Raegenssen—was not even the man who had impersonated Raegenssen—but it was simply the corpse of an unknown man of similar height and build, and similarly bearded, with his hair and beard bleached to the likeness of Raegenssen's Viking crop and Raegenssen's clothes upon him to assist the identification which the terrible mutilation of the features prevented. And, in putting his clothes upon his substitute corpse, Raegenssen must have overlooked those photographs stitched for safety into the lining. For the third photograph was the face of a man whom Storm knew well by sight, and had also known to be associated with the Triangle—but never had he dreamed that that man was none other than the Triangle himself! The other two—and Raegenssen was one of them—were mere effigies, shadows, puppets that danced to the bidding of the Apex and served to screen his own importance; but the third man was the Apex, the keystone upon which the whole edifice depended....

Storm became aware that someone was breathing down his neck, and swung round sharply. It was Joe Blaythwayt, his cherubic pink face gone livid, his baby blue eyes almost popping out of his head.

Storm stepped pointedly away from the banker, and a crestfallen Joe resumed the nibbling of his umbrella handle. Kit put the three photographs together and buttoned them into the safety pocket on the inside of his waistcoat; and as he did so the fourth fell from his hand.

Teal picked it up and glanced at it before restoring it to his chief. It was the picture of a girl of about twenty, and even the hideous Victorian high-necked, leg-o'-mutton-sleeved blouse she wore and the ugly, old-fashioned arrangement of her fair hair could not disguise her striking loveliness. Even the impassive detective drew in his breath with a quick hiss of admiration. And then Storm gently took the print from him and put it away in his wallet.

"Who was that?" asked Teal.

Kit looked him straight in the eyes.

"That," he said evenly, "was Sylvia Mattock—my mother!"

CHAPTER 22

STORM GOES GUNNING

It was not until they were about to leave the Thames Police Station that the absence of Blaythwayt was noticed. The little man, after being detected in the act of prying over Storm's shoulder, had faded self-consciously into the background; and, from that obscure retirement, he seemed to have sunk through the floor or dissipated into air. Certainly he had subsided completely out of the tableau, and Teal scratched his head in perplexity; for it was not to be expected that Joe, having at last succeeded in getting his nose on to an official scent, would make for home and a comfortable bed with a feeling of sensatory repletion. There is no bloodhound so hot and indefatigable on a trail as your enthusiastic amateur, whether he be a collector of postage-stamps or particularly gory murders, and the evanescence of Uncle Joe in those circumstances was provocative of thought.

"I only hope the little goop hasn't gone off to try and pinch the Apex himself," said Teal gloomily; but, knowing the sensational leanings of his friend, he was none too easy in his mind on that score.

No one was to know that, even as Teal voiced his prayer, an asthmatic and flustered Joe Blaythwayt was panting out instructions to a taxi-driver and scrambling into the cab to be driven swiftly westwards....

"Never mind Uncle Joe," advised Storm. "I guess he'll keep—and he's old enough to be loosed off without a chaperon."

They saw Malleson off in a taxi, and then hailed a second cab for themselves. Storm, nearly worn out, was making for the Albany and a long overdue rest; and Teal, beguiled by the promise of a strong nightcap, accompanied him. They hardly spoke on the drive back, for each was busy with his own thoughts. Teal's, it may be said, mostly ended in question marks, but nevertheless the detective had acquired a number of facts that night which opened up a maze of speculations and startling possibilities. As for Storm, he was wondering vaguely if he would get any sleep at all from then on until the Triangle had ceased to be—so far-reaching were the results of his investigations over the last two hours. His head still throbbed painfully from the concussion of the Piccadilly Circus explosion, but his mind had taken unto itself a new lease of energy. Everything had clarified suddenly, partly through the stimulus of those four photographs, partly because excessive weariness was already entering upon a reaction—that reaction which takes one to a quality approaching brilliance, when the whole body has become so tired that there are no restraints whatever upon the heights which may be attained by the feverishly soaring brain; a reaction which is very short and transitory, and which is followed by a long period of even greater lassitude than that which led up to it.

The taxi stopped in Piccadilly outside Albany Court Yard, and they got out. Storm paid off the driver, and, as the cab drove off, went after Teal, who had gone on ahead.

Teal was at the foot of the Albany steps, and Storm was well inside the Court, before either of them noticed an extraordinary thing. It was very dark, for the electric light mains had been wrecked by the land mine, and one almost had to grope one's way along, foot by foot. And then the moon came out from behind a bank of cloud and drenched everything under its eye in a flood of nebulous silver light, and Storm yelled a warning to Teal which made that slothful man spin round with the agility of an antelope.

The deep shadows cast by the three walls of the Court were alive with men!

Teal took in the situation at a glance. In a fraction of a second he had leapt up the steps, obeying Storm's shouted command, and as he sprang he jerked his automatic from his pocket. In those days, Storm did not rely upon one gun—he carried two, and both of them were in his hands now.

The promise of action had driven the last vestige of sluggishness from Arden's brain, and almost without conscious thought he had remembered the words of the Era advertisement and the orders of the Apex given over the loud-speaking telephone that night. Teal was to be killed, and he, Storm, was merely to be captured. Therefore Storm had roared to Teal to make for cover and not stop to give battle; and Teal, being a law-enforcing machine whose first instinct was obedience, had obeyed automatically before he even grasped the significance of the order.

Crack!... Crack!...

The enemy fired the first shots, and the din double-echoed resonantly in the confined space. Storm retaliated with one gun at each of the two flashes he saw, and a yelp of pain told him that at least one of his bullets had found asylum. Teal had halted at the top of the steps, and his gun blazed back at a third flash which barked in the echo of Storm's twin reprisal. By then, the detective's intelligence had made itself heard above the commands of discipline, and Teal was not the man to run away from a fight to save his precious skin and leave another man to face the music.

Teal's stance was simply asking for trouble. He stood exactly in the right place for the moonshine to pick him out as a beautifully illuminated target.

Storm saw the danger and yelled another order as he raced across to join the detective. But the smell of battle and the sight of those sinister shadows closing in upon his chief had made Teal go pig-headed, and he stood his ground obstinately.

In Piccadilly a police whistle screamed.

Teal fired again into the murky shapes which rushed upon Storm from all directions. And then one of the shapes turned its course and shot back twice at the detective. Storm saw Teal stagger and go down.

An instant later Storm himself had other things to think of.

There must have been fully thirty men lying in ambush along those treacherous patches of blackness. The odds were hopeless. When he started running, Storm had been making for the Albany entrance; but there had been men hidden in the darkness on either side of the steps, and now these barred his way and their fellows hemmed his retreat via Albany Court Yard. There was only one horse to back. The fact that all the shooting had been aimed at Teal seemed to indicate that the order not to kill Kit still applied. Storm's only chance, then, was to bank on the men obeying orders and try to put the fear of God into them with merciless gunning from his own quarter. Storm took that chance. His two automatics rattled like machine-gun fire, and he saw one after another of the men in front of him go down before that leaden scythe until he had cut a lane through the blockade. Others were already closing in to fill the places of the fallen, but, running like a sprint champion, there might be a thin hope of breaking through before they could take up position.

What Storm hadn't—couldn't have—allowed for was the fact that there must always be men behind him. Therefore he didn't see the arms of the two men behind him swing up, didn't see the two skilfully-thrown sandbags hurtle through the air—only felt the dull, sickening impact of something heavy and yet yielding upon the back of his neck, before he crashed to the ground and everything vanished in a whirling infinity of blackness....

He came to on a sofa, with his head throbbing horribly, and his first surprise was to find that he was in his own flat. The second was the presence of a man he knew, who was binding up an ugly wound in Teal's shoulder.

"Terry!" called Storm. "How did you get here?"

Terry Mannering looked up and smiled, but the haggardness of that ordinarily cheerful young man made the grin unconvincing.

"That's all right, brother. You sit tight for a bit and get the bump off your cranium. Havin' a solid ivory skull, you're still livin' when by all rights you ought to be dead—in a large experience of sandbaggin' and divers kindred sports, I may say I've never——"

"Cut out the bedside manner, Terry, for the love of Mud!" snarled Storm weakly. "What's happened?"

He tried to sit up, and had to make several attempts before he could overcome the sick giddiness that the effort caused. Terry went on bandaging Teal, and tried to infuse flippancy into his tone as he gave the account.

"Havin' missed our tame policeman," he said, "the Triangle coves had rather come a mucker. Far as we can make out, the idea was to pip Teal first bang an' then grab you in the same bar, so to speak. Unfortunately, you two warriors put up such a scrap an' made such a row about it that half the Roberts in London were chargin' on to the field before you'd been downed and outed as per invoice. Therefore, realisin' that dispersion is occasionally the better part of valour, your adorin' playmates legged it through the Albany an' out the other side, where the Roberts ceased from troublin' an' the policemen were at rest. They got away, leavin' your bodies on the plain an' a number of short-winded bobbies pantin' in their wake. Really, you know, you want to enlist a few Olympic runners in your comic copper battalions, if you want to catch young Pegasi (or is it Pegasuses?) like our friends——"

"Oh, cut it out!" snapped Storm. "What brought you here?"

Terry gave the finishing touches to Teal's bandages, and then left the detective to put on his coat and himself lighted a long cigar and puffed thoughtfully.

"I suppose you'll have to know," he murmured at length. "Though, as a qualified physician whose disgustin' wealth has stopped him from practising I'll warn you that if you go dashin' off doin' anythin' silly you'll be knocked up for weeks. Well, to put it briefly, at home we thought you'd been knocked out in the firework display. An' Susan thought so too. You were on your way to St. George's Hospital, and had very kindly sent your bus round to bring the chief mourners to your deathbed. A uniformed Robert was drivin', so everything in the garden looked lovely—barrin', of course, your own impendin' demise..." Terry studied the end of his cigar intently. "D'you get me, little one?"

Storm sat still for some seconds. He might have been graven in bronze for all the emotion he displayed; and yet, behind that mechanical masquerade, he was suffering the tortures of the damned.... Susan, his Susan ... in the Power of the Dog.... "*Kill H...*" At that moment, for the first time in his life, he knew the meaning of utter hopelessness. Nothing mattered in the whole world, nothing existed but that hideous fact. The Triangle might blast London off the face of the earth, might blow to atoms a thousand more John Cardans—it wouldn't count a lonely Continental cuss. Susan was gone.... The only ray of hope came from the implied assertion that she'd been kidnapped instead of murdered on the spot, and even that knowledge was fraught with fears too horrible to contemplate....

Put into the balance in Storm's favour that in the last seventy-two hours he had had less than seven hours' sleep, and perhaps you will understand

and forgive him for plumbing such abysses of despair. And that spineless despondency was only momentary. Before it could consolidate the position it had gained, Storm hurled up every supporting mote of fighting weight that was in him to hold the breach. With a clinched effort of will which racked and locked his nerves in positive physical anguish he focused all his strength upon the one object of getting his mind and body back to par. His face remained inscrutable and all his muscles were relaxed, but the sweat broke out in glistening gouts on his forehead. And, gradually, inch by painful inch, he scourged himself into cool, calm reason. Watching him, few would have known that in the fleeting of those few seconds he had gone down into Inferno and dragged himself back again into the world.

Storm raised his eyes. His hand went slowly to his pocket and drew out his cigarette-case. With leisured care he selected a cigarette, tapped it on his thumb-nail, and put it between his lips. Still with the same Alpine steadiness, he took a box of matches from his pocket, struck a light, and held it to the cigarette. He extinguished the match with one flourishing sweep of his hand and broke it into little tiny splinters, dropping them one by one on to the carpet. And then, sitting with his elbows on his knees and his hands cupped boyishly under his chin, he took the cigarette from his mouth and blew out a long blue trail of smoke.

"Yes?" he prompted, and his voice was as coldly level as a frozen tarn.

Terry fastidiously preserved the cone of ash that was accumulating on his cigar.

"Well, I offered to go with Susan, but she wanted to go alone. Still, I'd gathered from the Robert's not very snappy backchat that you were more or less lyin' on the banks of the Styx waitin' for the ferry; so, for the sake of old times, after allowin' Susan half an hour's start to get through the last fond farewell"—Terry grinned wryly—"I tottered along myself. Had the jolly old Sisters of Mercy heard of Captain Arden? They had not. Had the worthy chirurgeons? *Non plus*. I combed every ward myself, and when we hadn't located you I remembered the Triangle's interest in Susan and began to get a whiff of *Mus decumanus*, or the common rat. Toddlin' round to Scotland Yard, I was told you'd just left on a morgue tour along the Embankment. So I came toolin' on here to wait for you. *Et voila!*"

"I see," said Storm. "Can you get me some real eighty-over-proof dope? Snow for preference. I'm about done in, and my acquaintance with rest cures looks like being not yet."

Terry looked at him for a moment, and then nodded.

"I'll knock up a chemist myself," he promised. "But you'll try to get some sleep, won't you? Tumblin' into the arms of Morpheus, and so forth?"

Kit nodded.

"I can't do anything tonight, but God knows what I'll feel like tomorrow. I won't use the stuff if I can help it, but I want it for a stand-by. Push off now like a good fellow, and get Teal home right afterwards, will you?"

Terry went, and then Storm crossed to the telephone and called Scotland Yard. He was lucky enough to find the Assistant Commissioner still there.

"I want Prester John," said Storm. "Get him to my flat by nine tomorrow if it's humanly possible. And Birdie, if they can find him. Have men out after the two of 'em all night, and hogshave all search warrants! Also Snooper Brome—add him to the list. Got me?"

Then Storm went wearily to his bedroom. He wound his alarm clock and set the bell at 8.30; and then, only removing his coat, collar and tie, he fell into bed and was almost instantly asleep.

The buzzer awakened him after an all too short rest, and his first impulse was to shut the darn thing off, turn over, and sink back into the delicious Nirvana from which its clarion call had roused him. And then he remembered everything…. With a sigh he flung off the sheet and got up. His head ached appallingly, and for some unknown reason he was stiff in every limb. He undressed and made for the bathroom, and under the invigorating chill of a cold needle spray a good deal of the muzziness cleared away. A brisk rub down restored him still more; and, so great were the recuperative powers of his robust health, he finished dressing again with the feeling of being little the worse for the strain he had been through. A slight thickheadedness and a heaviness in the eyelids—that was all.

He burst into the sitting-room to be greeted by the yawning visage of Mr. Teal.

"Je-rusalem!" he said. "What're you about so early for?"

"I haven't been away," replied Teal, stretching his sound arm. "Your sofa's pretty comfortable, and I don't like being sent behind the lines when there's anything doing on the front."

Storm turned to his manservant, who was laying the table for breakfast.

"We'll start with a double Colonial breakfast," he said briskly. "And make your coffee black and strong!"

He was gulping a Horse's Neck into whose composition very little ginger ale had entered when the Assistant Commissioner arrived.

Bill Kennedy was alone, and the scowl which invariably disfigured his face before breakfast was more worried than usual.

"I haven't got either of your men," he confessed bluntly. "Prester John's left the country to make a new start in Canada, and Brome's vanished. We never knew much about Snooper, anyhow, and the lag who runs his fencing store in Kensington when Eddie's away hasn't seen him for days. What's the particular hurry?"

Storm told him in four words, and then—

"Did Mr. Mannering turn in that dope, Teal?" he asked.

For answer, Teal pointed to the cellarette, and Storm went over and opened the small parcel which lay there. He took a glance at the hypodermic syringe it contained, and the two phials packed into the metal syringe-case, and slipped the box into his pocket.

He carried writing materials over to the breakfast table and wrote while he made his meal. When he had finished there were five closely written pages which he checked over carefully and then sealed into an envelope, scribbling his initials on the flap.

He gave the package to Bill Kennedy.

"I put you on your honour not to open this unless I fail to report at the Yard by midnight," he said. "It gives you the identity of the Triangle and a string of substantial evidence against him—enough to hang an army! If I don't turn up you'll know what to do. Secondly, I'll bet you've had men put on to guard me after last night?"

"Yes." Bill nodded.

"Take 'em off right now! Bill, I guarantee that if I see anyone that looks like a nursemaid in trousers tailing me around when I leave here I'll wring his neck! I *want* the Triangle to catch me—that's the only chance I've got left of cleaning up this mess outside of the Old Bailey. You put that right up inside the big bone you wear under your hat, and let it dig itself in!"

Even as he spoke Storm was stripping off his coat and shirt, and they had a chance to view his magnificent torso. The muscle just lay on him in slabs, writhing and cording under the satiny skin with every movement he made. He was ribbed out and sinewed up like a thoroughbred racehorse— he might have served as a model for a statue of Apollo, with his perfectly proportioned, splendidly supple and yet immensely powerful development. Storm was always trained to a hair; and, at that moment, as he stretched and limbered up, he looked fit to fight for a kingdom ... whereas he was going to fight for something which, to him, meant more than all the cities of the world and their glory——

He disappeared into his bedroom and returned a minute later with a heavy bundle in his arms.

Against each bicep, by means of straps fastened above and below the muscle, he fixed neat leather holsters which carried compact small-calibre automatics. Against his right calf he laid a small thin razor-sharp poignard which was held in place by his sock and sock suspender. Thus secretly armed, he pulled over his head a jerkin of pliant deerskin which laced up to the collar-bone; and over this he put on a singlet of the finest steel mesh.

Kennedy and Teal observed all these accoutrements with unconcealed interest, and Storm smiled.

"Courage gets medals," he remarked as he resumed his shirt, "but people who sail into typhoons without taking in canvas, battening all hatches, and rigging life-lines, just get what they deserve—and that's Hell!"

He completed his reclothing, slipped another automatic—to be found if and when he was searched—into his hip-pocket, lighted a cigarette, and picked up his hat.

"So far I've been the world's premier boob," he said—"the most paralytic fall-guy that ever wore pants. And I'm going to get even or bust!"

He was in high spirits. In spite of the ever-present fear for Susan which haunted the back of his mind, he was totally unable to repress his cheerfulness. The scent of battle always got him that way; and it was a trait of his which caused him great annoyance, for, when sparring and waiting about turned the corner into the straight run home of action, breathless and perilous, he seemed incapable of seeing things in their true values. But this callousness was only superficial. The real fact was that a high incentive whetted and honed the edge of his deep-rooted fighting instinct, making it seem predominant.

"Where're you going?" asked Bill Kennedy.

Storm paused at the door, and a reckless smile, reminiscent of the Viking warrior whose idea of heaven was a Valhalla where daily warfare provided eternal bliss, touched his lips.

"Looking for trouble!" he said grimly. "And I think it's coming good and fast!"

CHAPTER 23

PANIC OF BIRDIE

Susan sat quite still. The tension of Mecklen's fingers about her throat and the ferocious look on his face left her in no doubt but that he would carry out his threat if she gave him the ghost of an excuse. Besides, Susan wasn't the sort to go into hysterics when yammering for help didn't offer any reasonable hope of help being forthcoming. There were a few pedestrians about and not another car in sight—anyway, even if she did shout, and were heard, her would-be rescuers would have about as much chance of stopping that flying Hirondel as they would have of hopping over the Woolworth Building.

"You needn't get excited," she said coldly. "I haven't screamed since they took me out of long clothes."

Mecklen said nothing. Still retaining that menacing grip on her windpipe, he was hunched up over the steering wheel with his eyes glued to the road in front, pushing the car along as fast as he dared.

"You can take your hands off," Susan added. "Someone might see us, and"—she groped about in her vocabulary of American for a phrase the Bowery boy might understand—"I don't want to be mistaken for the Sheba of a roughneck like you. I promise not to yell."

Lew hesitated, and then withdrew his arm—not because her gibe cut any ice with him, but because he'd remembered his uniform and didn't want to make himself conspicuous if anyone *should* happen to see them. Tough-looking policemen don't as a rule drive round in expensive cars with their arms round the necks of fashionably dressed girls; and Mecklen realised that he'd left enough tracks behind him already that night without adding to the number.

"Yew'd better not squawk," he assured her, to make it plain that he released her for his own reasons and not because of her command.

They swung round the Victoria Memorial and entered Buckingham Gate. The car ran down the deserted thoroughfare and tacked down a side street on the left and left again into a dark mews.

Mecklen stopped the car and took Susan's arm in a vise-like grasp.

"Git outa here," he ordered. "An' jest yew see yew don't fergit wot I told yuh. One yap, an' yew git yores."

She got down from the car, and he followed her. In the darkness he shifted his clutch to her left arm, and she felt something prick her breast, and saw the dull shimmer of steel.

"Jest a *ree*minder," he said. "Move!"

He unlocked a garage door and pulled her inside. She heard two bolts clang into place behind them, and then a switch clicked down and the place was dimly illuminated. She saw that what had seemed to be one solitary lock-up was in reality a huge garage which ran the whole length of that side of the mews behind the other dummy doors. Stored in it was a wonderful collection of motors—two aluminium-finished racing cars, four Rossleigh trucks, a Navarre limousine, a Carillon cabriolet, and one black closed-in van which she could not identify although something about it was vaguely familiar. And the noticeable fact about the collection was that none of them carried number plates; she saw the reason a moment later, in the shape of a stack of detached plates of different numbers from all counties, ranged along the wall.

Mecklen dragged her across to what looked like a big tire cupboard. This he opened, revealing it to be empty, and fumbled with a bracket at the back. In a few seconds the false back slid sideways, laying bare a faintly lighted passage. Lew extinguished the garage light and made the girl precede him into the tunnel, while he shut the cupboard doors and slid home the inside panel.

There were only a dozen feet to go, and they emerged into a spacious cellar. Here Mecklen paused, rubbing his scrubby chin as though wondering where to go next. At length he went over to a door which led off the vault in which they stood, and he seemed surprised to find it empty. He came back and seized her arm again.

"In hyar," he rasped, and almost flung her inside.

The door closed again, and she heard a bar thump into its socket on the outside.

An electric bulb glowed in the ceiling, and she was thankful for it. She took stock of her position as calmly as she could. The room was more like a cupboard than a cellar—it could have measured no more than eight feet by six. It had held a great deal of earth recently; the stone floor was half an inch deep in it still, and small clods of damp soil adhered to the walls. There was no window—no outlet of any sort except the door through which Lew had pushed her—but the door itself fitted loosely in its frame, so that there was no lack of air. She went to the door and ran her fingers under it. Despite its clumsiness, it was fashioned of three-inch oak. It might have been three-inch boiler steel for all the hope of escape it offered her; and, shoving her hardest, she couldn't make it budge against the heavy outside bar that held it shut.

Leaning against the wall, she thought out the circumstances methodically. For armoury she had the pin of a small brooch and her two hands. Expectations—what? The story about Storm being injured might or might not be true, although now she was inclined to regard it as nothing more than a cock-and-bull yarn invented to decoy her. Strangely enough, her first emotion was of exasperation; she, old stager that she was, to have been caught on the hop with an antediluvian parlour trick like that! Well, how long would it be before she was missed? Terry, being an old friend of Storm's, might go down to the hospital himself later on, and then the fraud would be exposed. Or, if he didn't do that, and Storm was safe and sound, Kit'd be sure to ring her up in the morning; and, once he'd absorbed the news of her abduction, he wouldn't be likely to let grass grow under his feet. Extraordinarily comforting was that thought. Within a few hours—she looked at her watch—within eight hours at the very limit Storm would know all about it, would be out scouring the metropolis for her. The last feebly rising bubble of panic collapsed. She was sure, now, that Storm hadn't been smashed up. He'd be On The Job, moving heaven and earth to find her, and every Triangle in Christendom massed up in one big wad all round her, with barbed wire in front and a company of field artillery behind, wouldn't stop him....

Her day-dreaming was interrupted by the return of Mecklen, laden with a rough straw-filled mattress and a couple of coarse blankets. He dumped them on the floor and went out again. For a fraction of a second she had meditated attacking him from behind when his hands were full and his head turned, but the thought had died as quickly as it was born. She was strong and supple as a young mermaid, but she knew that against his rugged bulk such crude methods would be wasted. She might have got him in a ju-jitsu grip—she knew one or two——

He came back again that minute, carrying a small table on which was an enamel mug of water, a loaf of bread, some fried bacon congealing on a cracked plate, and a hunk of butter wrapped in a scrap of newspaper. Her chance of springing on him unawares was gone now, for he kept the table between them all the time.

"Make yoreself at home," he invited. "Sorry I cain't stay an' wait on yuh jest naow, but yew're supposed ter be dead. The boss might think et kind o' queer ef I stayed grubbin' 'round these hyar cellars, an' it don't pay ter git the boss's goat. But I'll see yuh later—don't yew worry!"

His foul leer struck a qualm of terror into her heart, but she faced him boldly.

"I don't worry," she said acidly. "What's your name?"

"Mecklen—but yew kin call me Lew, honey."

"Well, Mecklen, I've heard of you. You've killed a good many people in your time—have you ever wondered what it's like to die?"

He lounged against the wall, grinning.

"Huh—yew li'l' cougar! So yew're gonna make ole Lew pass in his cheques, air yew? Gee, baby, I'll say yew got sand!"

"Oh, no, I'm not going to kill you," said Susan. "But I'll tell you the name of someone who will. Ever met Captain Arden, the man they call *Storm*? He's out hunting you by this time, Mecklen, and d'you know what he'll do to you when he gets you? He did it to a man outside Valparaiso once—a man rather like you, Mecklen—staked him out and flogged him to death with a stock-whip! How does that appeal to you? And he'll get you, Mecklen—there's no hole and corner on God's earth you can hide in where he won't find you one day. Storm never gives up! Think it over."

There was no idle threat or bravado in her tone. She stated the facts simply and cold-bloodedly, so that the smooth venom behind them would have stabbed horror into the soul of most men. But Mecklen's imagination was that of the untamed brute—he had to feel the lash before he could flinch from a sight of it.

"Storm!" he scoffed. "I'll tell yuh something. That sheik o' yores'll eat his breakfast right in this hyar shack. Now think thet over!"

And then with a cat-like spring he rounded the table and caught her in his arms in a bear's hug. His fetid breath stung her nostrils, and, before she could move, her lips had tasted the gross contact of his mouth.

He jumped back, breathing heavily, one fist stuck out in front of him.

"Keep off," he warned. "Thet war jest something ter go 'long wit. I'll kiss yuh—properly—later. See yuh again soon, honey. Yew'll larn ter like ole Lew—he ain't no amachoor!"

The door bumped shut behind him, and she was alone again…. But now there was a new fear to face—something that she'd never thought would come into her own life, often as it occurred in the pages of the novelist. The tightest corner she'd ever been in…. She tried to stay the involuntary quivering of her lips. The hot defilement of Mecklen's embrace seemed to sully them still, and she got out her handkerchief and rubbed them with it. Death itself she could have met with a proud contempt, but that…. She sank on to the mattress he had brought and buried her face in her hands. She was … desperately … *afraid*….

Lew went stumbling up the cellar stairs with a burning exaltation skipping about like a lump of molten lead in his rotten heart. He passed through the stairs into the back hall, and was confronted by a small man whose ferrety face was drawn and haggard.

"Lew!" The little man grabbed Mecklen's sleeve convulsively. "Lew—I—I saw yer go dahn wiv a bundle 'f beddin' an' then yer went agayne wiv a table 'n' grub. I was on the front stairs, an' I saw yer!"

Mecklen rested his hands on his hips.

"So li'l' Birdie sore ole Lew," he grated. "Did yew!"

"Yes. Wot's it mean—wot's it *mean*?"

Birdie seemed almost frantic. His normally sallow complexion was ashen, and he was shaking horribly, like a man with ague, and an ugly look came into the gunman's eyes.

"Air thet enny perticlar concern o' yores?" he drawled, leaning forward so that his out-thrust jaw almost touched Birdie's nose.

"Yes—I don't understand! *Lew*! Why're yer lookin' at me like that? My Gawd...." A shifting light of madness was coming into Birdie's staring eyes. "Lew! *'Oo's dahn there? ...*"

"Yew li'l' four-flushin' piker!" snarled Mecklen.

His huge hands were clawing out for Birdie's throat. They found their hold and, crushing the pickpocket's scraggy neck in that boa-constrictor twist, Mecklen shook him as a Great Dane might shake a poodle.

"Yew li'l' *runt*!"

"Lew!"

It was Morini's voice, hard and imperative. Mecklen took no notice until the butt of a gun struck him a stinging blow between the eyes.

Lew staggered back and Morini fronted him, having reversed his automatic to the business position.

"Gat, yew vamoose! Wot's bitin' yuh——"

"You've gone loco," Morini cut in with no suavity. "What're you fightin' for? If the Chief heard of this you'd be fired right out into the streets, where half the bulls in London are watching to draw a bead on you. Out with it—what's the trouble?"

"Thet li'l' critter——"

"Well?"

But Mecklen, aware that he had made a blunder in saying even that much, had relapsed into a glowering silence. Morini turned to Sands, who was cringing against the wall, grasping and rubbing his throat where Lew's fingers had left thick scarlet weals.

"What did you do, Birdie?"

Sands was crouching back, and then he made a sudden dive for the door. "I'll show yer!" he cried, and bolted down the cellar steps.

Susan sat up with a start as the door of her cell burst open and Birdie, wide-eyed and choking, crashed in. An instant later Mecklen's huge form loomed in the gap, and then Morini pushed past him.

"Don't yer worry, missy," Birdie got out tremulously. "I'll see yer fru—I 'ad a sister, once...."

"What's this?" snapped Morini, wheeling on Mecklen.

"Wotcha think?" growled Lew surlily.

His raging eyes were alert for Morini's every movement, for he was twice the size of the other, and the broadcasting of Susan's presence was going to spoil Lew's plans considerably. But Morini still had his gun, and he never gave Mecklen a chance to catch him off his guard.

"This is the Hawthorne girl." Gat's voice was fiery. "You were told to leave her alone. And, anyway, she was to be killed. Instead of that, you've showed her our headquarters, and you're still keeping her alive, so that if she got away we'd all be dished! Lew, I've a good mind to give you yours!"

All unobserved, Birdie had edged along the wall towards the open door. Lew and Morini stood just inside. And then Sands leapt through the narrow gap like a fleeing rat, and was halfway up the stairs before the other two realised that he had gone.

"Keep yer pecker up, missy!" he bawled. "I'll get the pleece!"

Morini flung up his gun, but Susan kicked the table against him as he fired, and the shot went wide. The next moment Birdie was out of sight, with Lew in cursing pursuit.

Susan caught Morini's wrist and wrenched it round with all her strength. His gun clattered to the floor, and he closed with her in a short, whirling, hand-to-hand tussle. Susan fought back at him furiously, but the man was wiry and as slippery as an eel. In less than a minute she found both her elbows locked behind her back.

"I know ju-jitsu too," he grunted, and kicked his fallen gun out into the passage.

He threw her from him violently, and the door was shut and barred from outside before she could rise again.

Birdie could run! He made the front door before Lew had reached the head of the cellar steps, and Mecklen was left gaping at an empty hall. Birdie had got away! Fear of what would happen if the pickpocket reached a police station and squealed had temporarily paralysed Lew's faculties. It took him some seconds to soak up the immense significance of the disaster, and in that time Morini, more agile of mind and body, had passed him at a sprint.

Birdie had tumbled down the front steps, moaning aloud with apprehension. There wasn't much mettle in Birdie Sands—gutter-born, gutter-reared, and gutter-minded, he was totally unfitted to play any more blackguardly part than that of the petty sneak-thief. And what he'd gone through that night had shivered his brittle nerves to fragments. He'd killed a man, and you could be hanged for that.... The ghastly sight he had seen in Fleet Street haunted his vision. And then the girl—that had been the final straw that broke him down. The splits'd say he was a party to that crime, too. And he knew, or divined instinctively, what fate was in store for her....

"Gawd, let me get aw'y!" he mumbled, panting. "P'r'aps they'd let me off wiv a laggin' if I syved 'er.... I 'ad a sister once...."

His chest felt as if it was bursting, and a steel band seemed to have tightened round his heart. His legs were like lead. He was travelling terribly slowly now, as though in a nightmare. Athletic training had never entered his life, and chain-smoking had ruined whatever natural stamina he had ever possessed. He couldn't keep up that killing pace....

Would they follow him through the streets? The thought almost made his knees give out like over-heated bearings. For some unknown reason it didn't occur to him to shout for help.

Morini opened the front door and looked up and down the road. He had moved fast. Birdie was not seventy feet away, running flat-footedly, with his elbows splayed out and his head down, all but done in already.

To shoot would be suicidal—it would bring the whole neighbourhood about their ears in two shakes. Morini knew a better way than that. He dropped his gun into his pocket and brought his hand out again with a long, heavy, but beautifully balanced knife. He poised it in his palm; and then, as Birdie passed under the full glare of a street lamp, Gat's arm went back and came forward again with amazing speed....

The knife flashed out with a low *whuu-uit*! He saw the flickering sheen of it as it skimmed away like a darting splash of quicksilver, saw Birdie go down with the haft of it sticking out between his shoulder-blades, heard Birdie's shuddering scream gurgle away into an awful sob....

Morini stepped back into the hall and closed the door without a sound.

CHAPTER 24

VISITORS FOR JOAN

Long after midnight Joan Sands had sat curled up on the chesterfield. Through the open window had come the thunder of the Piccadilly explosion, but she had not even gone to the window to try and find out the meaning of the noise and shouting. Something dreadful had happened, and the Triangle was in it. One didn't have to be a clairvoyant to realise that without making a personal inspection. And where the Triangle went Jimmy went—even to the gallows....

She consumed cigarette after cigarette, without tasting or enjoying a single one, and her eyes were bloodshot with the smart of straying smoke. It was a purely mechanical process, a device to assist thought or to prevent it—she was not sure which. At least the narcotic had a soothing effect on her overwrought nerves, and having something to manipulate with her fingers kept her within certain materialistic bounds. The same applied to the stiff whisky-and-soda she had mixed herself; half of it was still in the glass beside her—she had gulped half of it down, and had not touched the rest since.

A queer, hectically coloured jazz-pattern mind had this slim, fluffily beautiful girl. Now those jazz-patterns had kaleidoscoped into a medley of nightmare imaginings. The only light in the room came from the red-shaded reading lamp behind her head, and the shadows around her, with their crimson high-lights, grouped themselves into the real semblance of her dire grotesque visions. She would have sold the world for company at that hour, for the comforting presence of someone strong and calm and friendly who'd hold her in his arms and scare away the bogeys with a cheery word. Jimmy, for instance. In those last few days he'd shown a sympathy one wouldn't have suspected him of possessing and a strength of character which was the last thing on earth an ex-jailbird waster ought by rights to have trumped out. Or Storm would have done. She wished she'd made him stay—bar Jimmy, he was the only man who'd ever had a kind word for her, who'd ever treated her four-square, with no *arrière-pensée*. And the realisation that she no longer felt capable of standing on her own feet and facing things out alone was the hardest of all to bear—she, the ice-hearted, cool, calculating adventuress, was getting soft; while even jelly-spined sops like Jimmy were suddenly sprouting shells. The fact that Jimmy's new-found backbone had awakened in her a genuine respect—something that was tending to passionate love—didn't enter into the balance sheet for the moment. There were weaknesses and tender patches in her armour that she'd never encountered before, and the discovery of them was a salutary lesson to conceit. Joan failed to derive any enjoyment from the revelation. Shock education takes some standing up to. She preferred the Montessori system.

Anyway, all recrimination and sentiment aside, the fact remained that she felt intolerably lonely and unhappy. For the second time in her life she was utterly sincere, and she was unable to decide whether her primary reaction to this unaccustomed attitude was shame or—fright. Not, of course, that she figured the whole thing out in such a precise scientific manner. Her introspection ran on lines which combined the antics of a giant switchback and a roundabout, but the general trend of them was much simpler.

She must have dozed at last, for a stealthy movement beside her recalled her to objective thinking with a big jump. She looked up, shaking the hair out of her eyes. There was a man standing beside her couch.

"Jimmy!" she breathed. "How did you get here?"

She was getting up, but he put out a hand and gently forced her back, sitting down beside her. He looked very tired, but he was smiling.

"I couldn't stay away. I was supposed to stay till tomorrow, but I'd done my—business—and there didn't seem to be any point in sticking on. So I came back on the night train. Why're you up so late, Joan?"

"Oh—I don't know," she said petulantly. "Why can't I sit up if I feel like it? I didn't feel tired."

He was gazing fixedly at her, and then he took her face between his two hands and turned it so that the light fell full across it.

"That's not true. Something's happened—I can see it in your eyes." His finger moved and brushed two little drops of dew from her cheek. "You've been crying. Joan! What is it?"

She said nothing, pulling his hands away and bowing her head again into the darkness.

"Have the police been here, Joan?"

He was looking about the apartment, but she had replaced the rugs and furniture so that there was no trace of Storm's visit.

"The Triangle have blown up Piccadilly—my taxi driver told me about it," he said. "Is that it? Or did the men come through from the next room and—and annoy you?"

He could hear the quick hissing intake of her breath. And then, with a little gasping cry, she drooped into his arms.

"Joan"—fiercely—"*Joan!*"

"All right, boy." Her hands went up and passed behind his head. "I was worried—because of you. And crying—because of you. Because—because—oh, Jimmy, say it for me!"

"Because you love me," he said unevenly. "Joan ... my darling girl...."

Somehow they had both come to their feet. Never in all Mattock's flabby life, never in Joan's hard life, had either known a moment to compare with that one. She had married him to please him, and she'd never made any secret of it. But now...

He kissed her lips, her hair, her eyes, straining her to him. Heaven lay around him like a flame; the glory of it eddied through his veins like fire.

"Joan, I'm a rotten old buffer for you to fall in love with," he muttered. "But I'll try to wash that away. We'll go on a proper honeymoon—anywhere you like—out of here—give up this flat——"

"No—no!" She broke away from him almost savagely. "You've got to listen. The busies've been here tonight. Arden and Teal. They searched the place—look!"

He pulled her roughly back into his arms.

"What does that matter?" he demanded. "What does anything else in life matter besides this?"

"Nothing.... But you must look, Jimmy."

She forced him to turn so that he faced the damaged bookcase. He stared at it dumbly, and she felt him go stiff, but he shook his head.

"Have you broken it or something?"

She pulled open the hidden door, showing him the headphones and transmitter.

"This is your bookcase—you had it sent in, though I've never seen you go to it. It was always locked. Arden showed me—that's a cut-in on the telephone in the next room, and Arden said the Triangle gave orders to his men *from here*. There was a letter for you from the Apex. Arden showed that to me too. You left it behind. Jimmy, I know what your business was in Devonshire! What's the use of keeping up the pretence?" She looked straight at him. "*What time did your train get in?*"

He said nothing, and there was a long silence. His face was working strangely. She saw the old devil rousing again in his staring eyes, and ran to him in a panic.

"They may be back any time—maybe they were watching and saw you come in! I've got two bags packed. I had them ready waiting for you. We've got passports—we've got to get away! Jimmy——"

Zzzzzzing!... Zzzzzzing!...

The strident voice of the hall bell cut short the incoherent stammer of words that tumbled from her lips, and for a space of time it seemed as if her heart stopped beating. And when it moved again, it pounded like a two-stroke piston. The busies had seen Mattock come in…. They were going to arrest him…. His face went white; yet still he stood motionless as a statue, gazing at the bookcase with unseeing eyes.

Zzzzzzing!... Zzzzzzing-zing!...

"They're here! Jimmy—what's wrong with you? Why don't you do something?" She glanced frantically about her. His immobility was maddening. His brain seemed to have gone dead. "The other room—they mightn't look there——"

Zzzzzzing!... Zzzzzzing-zing!...

It was the flimsiest of flimsy hopes; but if she could stall them off for a couple of minutes he might have time to break away before the cordon closed. She must centre all their attention on the one door while he got through the other.

The bag she had packed for him stood in one corner. She thrust it into his hand, and his fingers closed on the grip mechanically. The partition door was still ajar, but she had almost to barge him through the gap. He was gone at last, and with a gasp of relief she closed and wedged the door and hastily tidied her hair. Then she went unsteadily down the hall.

"I'm sure I Beg Your Pardon," said Joe Blaythwayt politely.

So great was the shock that for a moment she just gaped blankly at him, while he came inside and wiped his shoes fastidiously on the mat.

"A most irregular hour for calling, madam," he remarked. "I trust you will Forgive the Intrusion, and—er—Feel No Alarm on account of my Presence. I am a Widower, and therefore not Impressionable. The Urgency of my Business is my excuse."

When Joe was excited the intangible Capital Letters which decorated his pompous speech multiplied exceedingly. He was clearly excited at that moment. A light which in anybody else would have been called martial shone in his eyes and his grasp on his umbrella was fidgety.

Recovering slightly she closed the door behind him and led him into the sitting-room. There had been nobody else to be seen in the corridor.

"Now what d'you want?" she asked sharply.

"I want to see Jimmy," he replied, so bluntly that she was taken aback.

"Jimmy's in Devonshire—you know that," she said.

His cherubic blue eyes wandered round the room, and came to rest at last on a felt hat which lay on the floor by the chesterfield. Before she could stop him he had picked it up and seen the name written in the lining.

"This wasn't here when I was!" he squeaked excitedly. "Jimmy's been here since we left! Where is he?"

"I brought that in to clean a stain off it," she told him calmly. "Jimmy won't be back till tomorrow. If you want to see him so badly try again tomorrow evening."

He wiggled a fat forefinger all but in her face, literally dancing in his agitation.

"Woman, Do Not Lie To Me!" His flustered effervescence resulted in speech that fairly bristled with capitals. "I Want The Truth. Jimmy Has Been Here. Jimmy Is Here! Where's he hiding? Where's he gone? What've you done with him? Answer Me!"

Question overflowed question in one delirious cataract but Joan had recovered her composure to some extent by this time.

"What's your game?" she demanded hotly. "Coming into my flat at this hour of the night and making a scene! Get out, Blaythwayt. Who d'you think you are? Who are you? Some fly cop—one of these clever busies out of a serial?"

"No, madam—my Warrant!"

With an air of a conjuror he produced from his waistcoat pocket a glittering silver and enamel badge, and she recoiled in horrified amazement from the sign of the Triangle.

It is doubtful if he observed her perturbation at all. At all events he ignored it. His blue eyes swept the room again, peering at every nook as though he expected to find Mattock concealed behind a flower-pot or cached behind a picture. He saw the closed partition door, and let out an electrifying squawk of eagerness. She saw the inspiration dawn in his brain, and made an instinctive movement to block the way—a rash step which she instantly regretted.

"Stand Aside, Madam," he commanded tremblingly; and, when she did not budge, he pulled her rudely away and kicked open the door.

She tried to hold him back, impelled by she knew not what fear, but he flung her off like a child. He dashed into the other room and she followed him to find him blinking open-mouthed at emptiness. Mattock's bag stood on the table but Mattock himself was gone and the door leading into the passage stood wide.

For some seconds they were both petrified. And then Joe Blaythwayt gave vent to one strangled yelp of apprehension and rushed across the room, and she heard him go blinding down the corridor towards the stairs.

CHAPTER 25

MAHOMET AND THE MOUNTAIN

Susan had thought she would never have been able to sleep that night, but she managed it somehow. She had waited for an hour and a half after Morini had dashed out of the cellars, and, when he failed to return, she lay down on the mattresses and pulled a blanket over her. For a long time her thoughts gave her no rest. They milled and clamoured tumultuously through her head, whirling her through mazes of doubt and perplexity and conjuring up hideous visions to line the route. And then, in some miraculous fashion that nevertheless seemed eminently natural, the hullabaloo merged into a dull monotonous humming blackness, and with a detached, infinitely distant interest she observed herself sinking into great dark depths of fathomless quiet....

She awoke with a start, roused by the sound of someone unbarring the door, and looked at her watch. To her surprise she found that it was nearly nine o'clock.

The man who entered was not Mecklen, but Morini. She was glad of that, illogically, for, although the gentle Gat was probably as sinister a scoundrel as Lew, he was far less obtrusively so. Mecklen had never been a gentleman, and was therefore inclined to be somewhat vulgar in his villainy; Morini might be more dangerous, but he was less repulsive, and she felt more in the mood for tackling a Morini than a Mecklen.

As it happened, however, there was nothing menacing about the educated Gat that morning. He was carrying a tray which had been decorated with a clean white cloth and which was laden with much more attractive fare than Mecklen had brought her the previous night. The coffee-pot was silver, and the jug of steaming milk was spotless; there were two slices of toast in a rack, and eggs and bacon reposed on a plate that was neither chipped nor cracked; he had added an immaculate cup to replace the battered enamel mug which Mecklen had given her, and had even remembered to include a napkin.

He gave her a polite "Good morning," and smiled as he noted her puzzlement at the stainless furniture of his burden.

"These things belong to the Chief," he explained. "He isn't home for breakfast, so you're in luck."

He leaned against the door and watched her eat. She was able to muster a respectable appetite, and was especially grateful for the refreshing heat of the coffee, for the cellars were none too warm. The only other discomfort she had felt was a certain stiffness from her cramped bedding, but a little free movement would soon remedy that.

She became aware that Morini was looking at her curiously, although he never descended to the Mecklenian coarseness of a stare, and when she had finished she sat back and returned his gaze inquiringly. For answer, he smiled again and extended a gold cigarette case.

"Thank you." She helped herself, and accepted the proffered match. "The last gasper before execution, Morini?"

"It is rather like it," he admitted coolly, and glanced round the tiny room. "Condemned cell and all—except that real condemned cells are cleaner. I wonder if you will die today?"

He posed the contingency with a speculative air that was terrifyingly humorous.

"Last night you were cursing Mecklen for not killing me," she remarked. "Why haven't you rectified the omission?"

He twisted his mouth.

"You'd better see the Chief first, now you're here. He's due to arrive at any minute."

He was preoccupied, as though some big problem filled his mind, and she saw that it was useless to attempt to discover what plans had been made for her disposal.

He picked up the tray and left her. A strange unreality had overcast everything with a haze which prevented her from working things out collectedly. This dispassionate discussion of murder jarred against all canons of actuality. Even in a court of law there was some emotion about a death sentence—one couldn't, somehow, flurry up any panic about a threat delivered in such a matter-of-fact tone....

Morini was back in a quarter of an hour, and his face was woodenly expressionless.

"The Chief's arrived," he said. "He wants to see you. Come along, please."

As in a dream she followed him. He took her through the hall, and she saw little mounds of dry earth untidily swept up into the corners. Halfway down he opened a door, and she had a glimpse of luxurious velvet hangings which had something familiar about them: royal purple with golden arabesques. Suddenly she realised where it was she had first seen those exotic decorations—the sawmill at Billingsgate! So, somehow, the conceit of the madman had made him take the enormous risk of stealing his gorgeous trappings away from a place over which the police still kept watch. He had carted away the earth that had filled the house in Buckingham Gate, packing it in crates and removing it in lorries at dead of night, to be dumped in the deserted quarries around Purley, simply to gratify the vanity of his megalomaniac mind. The method of his accomplishing the feat, of course, she could not know, but the completed fact gave her yet another queer sidelight on his weird mentality.

Morini slipped into the room, leaving the door slightly ajar, and she heard the brief conversation which passed between him and the man who sat in the room.

"Here she is, Chief."

"Bring her in, then."

"Right…. Oh, by the way, Chief, Lew went slinking out to a coffee-stall just before dawn—the darn chaw-bacon!—and he came back through the garage. He said there was somebody skulking round in the mews, and somebody else busy doing nothing in a doorway on the street outside. I don't see how the 'tecs could've got a line on us, but Lew swears to those two rubbernecks."

"There wasn't anyone about when I came in."

"Maybe it was just a couple of hoboes, boss. Lew ought to dilute it. Just thought I'd mention it."

Morini appeared in the doorway again and beckoned the girl in. She entered with her head held high, walking as coolly as if she were strolling into a hat shop to take a look round. She only gave one glance to the furnishings of the room—enough to see that it had been fitted out into an exact replica, on a smaller scale, of the council hall in Lower Thames Street.

Another thought occupied her mind. Two men had been stalking round the mews early that morning, if Lew were to be believed…. Already Storm was on the move, though she couldn't imagine how he had managed to locate the house of her imprisonment. That was an awkward snag in the way of rescue which hadn't occurred to her until that moment, and she was glad it hadn't cropped up before it had been surmounted. She had always been blessed with nerves of ice; even before the peril of Mecklen's innuendoes she hadn't wept or gone into hysterics or lashed around the cellar beating frantically on the walls in an ecstasy of terror, and, now that the clouds looked like breaking in the near future, her heart even sang a cheery refrain.

Storm was getting busy, and Storm was no moss-harvester when the fur promised to fly.

Susan smiled in confident bravado as she turned towards the daïs she knew she would see at the far end of the room. As in the sawmill, the huge emblem of the Triangle was suspended a little to one side of the throne; and, on the throne itself, sat a big built man, shabbily clad in rough grey tweeds. She did not recognise him, for a black felt hat was pulled down over his eyes and a black silk handkerchief folded diagonally was tied round his head, hiding his features from cheek bone to chin. All she could see of his face was the pale luminous glint of his blue eyes as he gazed fixedly at her. He sat back, with his gloved hands clasped on his knees, moveless as a sculpture in tinted marble.

All those details she took in in that first fleeting glimpse. It was half a second later that she saw that the Triangle was not alone on the platform. Another man stood beside him....

It was an immaculately dressed man, tall and broad shouldered. One hand rested arrogantly on his hip, and he was smiling a trifle grimly. She recognised him with a thrill of amazement, which changed instantly to a qualm of incredulous fear....

Storm came out of the Albany swinging his stick, the inevitable cigarette lofting jauntily between his lips. To have seen him, you would have taken him for an unusually athletic specimen of the Idle Rich, and you would have jeered lustily at the mere suggestion of his having any heavier cares in the world than the selection of elegant shirtings and tasteful hosiery. In fact, an ideal model for a portrait of one of the *jeunesse dorée* sallying forth in quest of the matutinal cocktail.

Huh!

Well, you hit the bull with one shot—his cares lay lightly on his muscular shoulders; for, big as those cares were, he possessed one of those pigeonholed minds in the various compartments of which the fortunate owner can always hermetically seal away anything with which he does not want to be bothered at the moment. Storm's plan of action was already mapped out and blue-printed; and, granted that the other side played up in accordance with the laws of probability, that plan was bound to succeed as far as he had designed it. True, his scheme didn't take him all the way home; but, there again, sufficient unto the hour was the worry thereof. Doubtless the god who watches over all merry fools who go pelting in where archangels would hesitate to show the tip of a wing would provide for the aftermath. Theoretically speaking, the man who can wedge his head into a lion's jaws can get it out again. A somewhat risky theory to put into practice, but Storm happened to be the sort of intrepid scapegrace who gets a kick out of fool gambles like that.

And it was all so beautifully simple. Thus far, the Mountain had shown great enthusiasm for the company of Mahomet, but Mahomet had steadfastly declined to visit the Mountain. In its eagerness, the Mountain had even detached portions of itself to go in search of Mahomet and convey him into the Presence; but Mahomet had remained obdurate—even violently obdurate—and kept his distance. And now the Mountain was more zealous than ever, with the difference that Mahomet had changed his mind and had been seized with an overpowering desire to pay a call on the Mountain. Therefore, the transition into the presence of the said Mountain should be easy....

In Piccadilly a taxi was crawling along by the kerb very conveniently. Behind it followed another, also seeking whom it might transport; and, behind that one, trailed a third. In the offing was a fourth. The ghost of a smile hovered on Storm's mouth. Verily, the anxiety of the Mountain appeared to be exceeding great....

Without hesitation, Arden waved his stick at the leading driver, and the taxi swung into a stop with commendable promptness. As Storm opened the door his keen eye detected the automatic lock which nine hundred and ninety-nine ordinary passengers out of a thousand wouldn't have noticed; he marked also the steel netting between the double panes of the window, and observed how neatly the sash had been screwed up so that nothing less than a jemmy would open it. Leaning over to give his instructions to the driver, he saw that steel shutters had been fitted inside the cab against the glass partition between the driver and passenger, so that the chauffeur would be in no danger of being stuck up with a gun smashed through the glass by a refractory prisoner.

"Number Ten, Downing Street," said Storm solemnly, and climbed in.

The driver himself, with a courtesy unwonted in taxi-drivers, got down to make sure that the door was properly shut, and Storm guessed that when the driver returned to his perch the automatic lock would also be efficiently latched.

They moved off towards Piccadilly Circus, where perspiring constables were struggling to man[oe]uvre a dense millipede of cursing traffic round the narrow gallery which was all the route that was navigable until the hordes of navvies who were even then at work had repaired some of the damage done by the last night's explosion. Kit sat back comfortably, crushed out the butt of his cigarette beneath his heel, and lighted a second. Looking through the wire-netted window at the back, he saw that another taxi, empty but with its flag down, tailed along in the rear. He could identify the chauffeur—an unsavoury-looking thug whose license had been suspended indefinitely some months ago after a curious accident which had attracted the fruitless attention of the Public Prosecutor.

Satisfied that his head was well and truly padlocked between the jaws of a particularly ferocious lion, Storm searched the interior of his own cab for any possible booby traps. A careful examination, however, disclosed nothing more deadly than a small spanner under the carpet, and the speaking tube which communicated with the driver. He did not put an agile employed of chloroform, or even some more subtle gas, beyond the resources of the Triangle, and therefore he plugged the mouthpiece of the tube with a handkerchief packed in as tightly as his strong fingers could jam it. So far everything had been admirably plain sailing, even if a shade too close to the wind to suit the nervy, and it wouldn't do to have everything messed up by sleep dope. But, now that he was sure there was no secret gas inlet, he composedly devoted himself to blowing smoke rings and wondering—the truth must be told—exactly how long it took one to get married in England. The precariousness of his present position left him unruffled. He was virtually a captive, on his way to a personal interview with the Big Triangle, and that was exactly what he had wanted; for Mahomet hadn't the foggiest notion where to find the Mountain unless he was taken there. Storm had got his ambition, and the Apex had got his—whether the Triangle would be satisfied with the one hundred and seventy pounds of consolidated Gehenna they had collected remained to be seen....

"We are now," mused Storm lightly, "fairly and squarely in the cart. It happens to be a non-stop bus, and only runs one way.... *Jee*-ru-sa-lem!"

He was not interested in their progress down Haymarket and into Trafalgar Square, but when the taxi cut round into the Mall he sat up and began to take notice. It occurred to him that a little realism might be introduced into the entertainment at this juncture, and he began to hammer on the steel shutters and rattle the locked doors. The taxi continued on its way unheeding. After a moment's thought he pulled his big automatic, smashed the right-hand window with the butt, and got his fingers behind the netting which intervened against the second pane. Strong as he was, he could not dislodge it, so, instead, he twisted the muzzle of his gun through the mesh and sent a bullet snarling past the chauffeur's ear. The cab swerved and then accelerated vigorously, and he sank back on the seat again with a soft laugh.

He had not fired to raise an alarm, but he saw immediately the measures which had been provided to deal with him if he had attempted to do so in earnest. The taxi which followed them drew quickly abreast, and he caught sight of Lew Mecklen leaning out of the window. He thought of pipping Lew through the neck, *pour encourager les autres*, but before he could put his idea into effect Mecklen swung up a syringe which resembled a chemical fire extinguisher. There was a sharp hiss, and a cloud of acrid spray billowed into the cab.

For a moment nothing happened, and then Storm reeled, gasping, into the far corner. His nostrils stung with the pungent fumes of liquid ammonia, he choked and coughed and writhed, his eyes were a streaming agony of blindness. "Yew try again, ya big cheese," taunted Lew from the other taxi. "Try again, ya big stiff, an' I'll flop yuh wit' anot'er squoit—jest fer bendin' some lead into ole Lew's leg, youse!"

"All right, ole Lew," muttered Storm, panting. "We'll argue about that later! Hully gee—that stuff's worse than slumber mixture!"

He took no more pot shots, but concentrated on getting the pain out of his eyes and regaining vision, for he badly wanted to know where they were taking him, and he had no wish at all to be helpless when they brought him into the presence of the Apex. When he could see again, he found that they were travelling down a street of imposing, austere houses, and it was only a couple of seconds before he had oriented himself. He saw Wellington Barracks on his left, and half a minute later the taxi whisked down a side street and turned into a mews, Mecklen's cab following. The second cab stopped, Lew got down and opened the door of one of the garages, and Storm was driven right in. Through the back window Kit saw the door barred behind them, and then Mecklen came round and poked the nozzle of his ammonia syringe through the broken window.

"T'row out yore gat," he commanded.

"I can't unless you open something," Storm pointed out.

This fact hadn't occurred to Lew, and after a while the door was moved a cautious three inches.

"T'row it out."

Storm obeyed, and the door was fully opened and the ammonia jet stuck into his face.

"Git down—an' no rough stuff, or I'll draown yuh wit' this."

Storm got out, smiling amusedly at the apprehensive care with which Lew trained the spray on his every movement. Storm's jaw was thrust forward, his cigarette canted almost vertically, his lips, drawn up at the corners, showed a gleam of white teeth. Everything functioned exactly as per invoice. He was in the enemy's camp, and every muscle in his body was tingling with joyous anticipation.

"Frisk 'im," snapped Mecklen.

Arden opened his arms as a habitual criminal does in the police station, and the first taxi-driver came up and searched him. The taxi-driver was not gentle or squeamish, for the bullet which had zipped past his ear had alarmed him considerably, and he made what he thought was a thorough fanning. That he found nothing was not his fault; he even prodded Storm in the small of the back, doubtless with memories of the Marlborough Street episode, but drew blank. Storm had sixteen-inch biceps, and the chain mail he wore effectively disguised the outline of his arm-holsters. At length the chauffeur stepped back and signified that he was satisfied, but Lew did not lower the squirt.

"Over thar—by thet cupboard," he ordered. "Start anyt'ing, an' I'll douse yuh!"

"You're mad as a meat-axe, Lew," said Storm commiseratingly. "I want to see the Big Triangle first. You flatter yourself! I guess I can kill you any time."

"Yah!" sneered the gunman, and Storm winced.

"You do make vulgar noises, Lew," he protested mildly.

Mecklen leaned over the syringe he still pointed at Kit's face.

"Listen, buddy. Thet heavy date o' yores is hyar, an' yew kin tell her ole Lew's sweet on her. We got the moll right hyar, an' she'll never git out again."

"That's why I came," said Storm calmly.

Mecklen scowled. As we have seen, he was not a man of high intellect, and Storm's frigid imperturbability made him uneasy. Like the armour of assurance which enveloped Snooper Brome, it was something which he couldn't deal with. It was as hopelessly out of his depth as the fourth dimension. Every way of attack he tried he came up against those invisible spikes, and bafflement filled him with futile anger.

"I was told ter kill her, but I jest brought her home an' necked her. Don't that make yuh feel glad?"

"Not half so glad as you'll feel when I shoot you through the stomach instead of through the heart!"

"Last night she gimme the air, but before I'm t'rough she'll be proud ter marry me," persisted Lew.

Storm rolled his cigarette across to the other corner of his mouth.

"Loud cheers!" he drawled. "Going to reform, are you?"

One of the chauffeurs had opened up the panel at the back of the tire cupboard, and was standing waiting by the gap. Mecklen jerked his head towards the tunnel.

"In wit' yuh!"

"Sure!"

But Storm paused before stooping in, for the glaring hate in the gunman's eyes had roused in him an irresistible temptation to add a final tab to his brief baiting of that unlovable murderer.

"You know, Lew," he murmured affably, "every day and in every way you grow more and more like an overfed dog-louse!"

Then he entered the passage, and as he went Mecklen landed out a vicious kick. Storm never stopped or looked round. Mecklen would keep a little longer. Kissed Susan, had he? Arden reckoned that that kiss would turn out to be the most expensive one in Lew's amorous career. As for the kick, that would only add extra zest to the extraction of due payment. Lew's shins were within easy reach of a smart backward hack, but Storm deemed it inadvisable to court a fresh shower of ammonia, for he knew he would need all his faculties to be at concert pitch during the next hour or two, and his eyes were still twinging from the effects of the first dose he had received.

They emerged into the cellars, and one chauffeur led the way to the stairs. Halfway across, Storm's foot brushed against something which went rattling across the stone floor, so that Lew and the other man pulled up with a start.

"Only a mouse," said Storm genially. "I'll hold your hands if you're scared."

"What was it?" demanded Mecklen sharply.

He was peering around fearfully, and presently he saw what had made the noise—a fountain pen heavily encrusted with gold work. He picked it up and looked at it suspiciously.

"Thet yores, Arden?"

"Oh, yes," said Storm boredly. "Combination turnip-slicer, gramophone, trouser-press and portable aeroplane."

He reached out a hand for it, but Mecklen thrust the pen into a pocket and pushed him away.

"Keep movin'," he growled. "Funny, ain't yuh? Mebbe yew'll be sick presently."

"I shall if I see much more of you," remarked Storm crudely.

"One day," threatened Lew sullenly, "I'm gonna make yuh wish yew'd never bin born. Yew flap yore mouth too much. I'm gonna——"

"I'll be there," yawned Storm, and Mecklen relapsed into a pugnacious silence.

As Storm climbed the steps an odd, dancing, metallic laughter glittered in his grey eyes. That fountain pen had given an entirely new twist to the situation, and as yet he was unable to gauge whether the twist was going to be big or small. For Storm knew and had recognised the ornate filigree with which the pen was embellished, and he wondered what business James Norman Mattock might have in Buckingham Gate that morning.

CHAPTER 26

SECONDS OUT OF THE RING

"Believe we've met before, Captain Arden," said the Apex. "Somehow I can't get into the way of calling you Kit."

"Don't bother to try," advised Storm. "Somehow, I can't get into the way of calling you father."

Ezra Surcon sat down again on his throne, taking in every detail of Storm's appearance with a keenly appreciative eye. It was a strange meeting between father and son, that. Family love is mostly a matter of long proximity, and there had been none of that between those two. No affection was in their clashing glances—Storm's interrogating, half-mirthful, accusing, dangerous, assured, level; Surcon's full of frank admiration blended with a trace of fear. Neither hate nor love was in the air, yet the atmosphere bristled with something far more potent. Circumstances had thrown them together to do battle on opposite sides of the law; battle to the death, fought out with words alone right up to the final *mêlée*—surely the strangest encounter in the annals of crime.

"You're like your mother, son," said Surcon slowly. "You've got that cornfield Saxon hair of hers, and her eyes. And yet you're *me*.... I used to stand up that way, once—that proud, reckless way...."

There was a short silence, while Storm met his father's gaze inscrutably, and Morini propped the door, an automatic swinging unobtrusively in one hand. "You're clever—like I am," said Surcon. "You found me—probably nobody else could have."

"Yeh!" agreed Storm. "But you're like Lew—you flatter yourself. You weren't so very difficult, although I grant you—every time—there was a lot of luck in it. And now the game's up. I've got you. What're you going to do about it?"

Surcon raised his eyebrows.

"Do about it?" he repeated.

"You said it! You're right where I want you. Hear me! I'll tell you a home truth you missed through not bringing me up yourself instead of slinging me into a workhouse when my mother died. And that home truth is that there's one big wad of conceit swollen up above your ears, which same has just landed you in the fishiest kettle of fish you ever dived into in your sweet life! You think you're sitting on several square miles of velvet. You've got me, you've got Miss Hawthorne, and you figure it out you've got every card in the pack neatly stacked up in your own private mitt. Guess again! Maybe you think I'm bluffing. Guess twice more! I never put up a bluff unless I've got an even chance of pulling out if it's called. That applies now. Scotland Yard have got your little dossier nicely tied up in pink ribbon, just waiting to travel along to the Public Prosecutor. And d'you know where you'll be when that dossier makes its speech? On the drop, Big Triangle, plumb on the drop! It's all sealed up, because just now this game happens to be a private one, and I don't want any policemen sitting in if I can help it. But if I don't rock into Scotland Yard by midnight—the witching hour!—the seals'll be broken, and that means the hangman'll be earning big money about eight weeks later. Which prison'd you fancy? Pentonville—Wormwood Scrubs—Holloway—Brixton? ... I expect it could be arranged."

Surcon stared as though he could not believe his ears. Here was his prisoner talking calmly about executions, and all the minor troubles that were coming to the Big Triangle, when all the time Morini had the bead on him, and would use it at a word! And, in spite of their terse, slangy phraseology, Storm's words carried conviction in every ice-flecked syllable.

"When I say I know everything, I'm understanding the case," Storm went on. "God Himself couldn't raise a longer charge sheet than I'm going to hand out to you right now. We'll take it in tabloids. All clear? Then I'll shoot. One: I know all about your treble life and your fake deaths. I know the beaver who was hoicked out of the Thames last night was no more Oscar Raegenssen than he was the King of England. There never was an Oscar Raegenssen—except you in fancy dress! I've proved that, and there's a little *billet-doux* from the Home Office pathologist himself to prove it twice over. Not to mention Miss Hawthorne's little piece. I know why you loved that tin can you called a safe in your office—I've slid out the shelves and opened up the dinkiest little cubby-hole any crook could want for a lie-low. Why, I've even got your photographs in your two side-line costumes. Olaf the Seabird, complete with false beard, comes into the picture gallery. Just to show you there's no ill-feeling, I'll give you a free tip which I'm afraid you'll never have a chance of using. Here it is. If you must disguise yourself like a dime-novelette detective, never get in the way of an auto. You're liable to be knocked silly, and then you forget to fake up your voice—suppose anyone's snooping around who knows both of you, that kind of lets a whole menagerie of cats out of your bag."

"I'm glad you allowed the element of luck," remarked Surcon ironically, although a certain tenseness in his voice spoilt the effect.

Storm flicked some ash from his cigarette.

"Share and share alike! If I was lucky in that, you were the most doggone lucky crook that ever went on a jag. Suppose the man detailed to look after your mischief had been anyone but me? Think he'd've let you go off smiling? You get a third free guess! Only I don't like my relatives being pushed through traps in execution sheds—it's rotten bad for the health of the genealogical tree. Besides, the papers'd make such a song about it. *Apex Caught By His Son…. Captain Arden, Police Hero, Gets Father's Death Warrant….* Thanks all the same, but I don't laugh at jokes like that!"

"And what is your alternative?"

"You'll hear that all in good time," said Storm. "Wait till I've finished my speech, and don't interrupt. It's rude. Right! Item Two: I know exactly why you sent your cheap Bowery lead-slingers clinking for the men you did. I know why Cardan was killed, and Marker nearly, just like I know why Hannassay died. Why, I've seen plate glass less transparent than you! The amazing, everlasting, all-fired and brass-bound miracle is that even a mutt like old fat Teal didn't have the bracelets on you days and weeks ago. I could've done it; except that, as I've explained, it'd've been embarrassingly public. A day or two late, you decided it was time one of your incarnations faded out, and you got away with it. You kidded Teal, but you'd have to put up a bit of whole cloth big enough to cover the world before you got me guessing! And I think that tots up to about *that*. You never did anything particularly mysterious. I saw you stick up Moraine's, and all the world knows how you wangled the getaway from Marlborough Street Police Station. That was smart, I'll say. But it didn't matter. A few little fish don't matter when there's a whacking great whale jumping round the net. And that net is now blocked in with sheet iron and reënforced concrete tough enough to hold even you! D'you doubt me—d'you think I'm bluffing still—or shall I fire off another tankful?"

Surcon said nothing. As Storm's staccato sentences shot out their deadly burden, the Apex had receded further and further into his throne, his jaw thrust out, his pale blue eyes gleaming like pin-points of azure flame, his whole crouching position resembling the compression of a wild animal about to spring. A crackling electricity had oozed into the air. The trace of uneasiness which had been in Surcon's eyes from the first had grown now into a raging devil of fear, with hate, desperation, and fury leaping in to join forces with it and bolster up its fundamental weakness. Storm's gun-metal grey eyes, drilling without a waver into his father's blue ones, were hard and pitiless.

"The Roman father is an old *cliché*," continued Storm's quiet, even, compelling voice—quiet enough it was in actual physical fact, but the explosive, dominating exclamation marks stabbed everywhere, relentlessly, through the superficial placidity. "But I'm on the road with a new line of goods: the Roman son! You can't expect mercy from me. If you do, you're wasting good day-dreams. You've killed men. One man you killed with your own hands, so Prester John told me, and I'm inclined to believe him. Loonies—conceited loonies—like you, don't take much stock of a human life or two when their own hides are in danger of being tanned. I've killed men, too, but not to salve my head-swelling. Because you're a murderer you've got to die. That's the law, and in your particular case I think it's a damned sound law. So sound that I'm here to supervise, personally, the carrying out of the sentence. Maybe you thought you were one hell of a bright boy catching me first shot with that taxi gambit. Your fourth guess! A babe in arms 'd've seen that springe. It stuck out ten miles! I let myself be roped because I didn't know where to find you, and finding you happened to be the most important act in the play. You thought you'd got a sucker, and now you've got to get it into the ivory over your ears that I'm a red-hot Tartar. I'm out gunning for Triangles! Once you're off the map I'm going to bounce Lew, and anyone else who horns in on the bouncing 'll get a free passage to Hell along with him. Lew won't be the only one. I guess the world can muddle along well enough without Gat either, for that matter, and there're a few others who'll share the same cemetery."

Morini himself was erect now, and the finger which crooked round the hair-trigger of his automatic quivered eagerly. His baby blue eyes were cold. A man of good education and more than average intelligence, he was able to judge exactly how risky every second of Storm's continued life was. Morini wasn't fool enough to mistake case-hardened facts for an empty bluff.

"Say the word, Chief," he grated. "You can't keep him now. He knows too much. If he gets away we're all done, and he's so slippery you can't guarantee to hold him till he's dead."

"Yeh! You Gat!" Storm swung round. "Shoot and then get measured for a coffin! You poor damned goop! Haven't you got it into your bony coconut yet that I wouldn't have come rubing into this party without being sure I was going out again O.K.? I've told the Assistant Commissioner that if I'm not back in his office by twelve tonight he's to open the envelope I've given him and act on what he finds in it. By eight o'clock this morning there was a watch on every port in England. An armed watch, Gat, with photographs and descriptions of every big fish in the Triangle pond. You're on that list! And you're not a Big Triangle—you'd want more savvy than you're ever likely to have before you could disguise yourself so's they wouldn't recognise you. Take it from uncle! Try not to be a worse oaf than God made you, for the love of Mike! Hear me! This is the way you get out of the mulligatawny. Make your boss see the game's up. Once he's gone you stand a chance of staying. Without him there'd be no Triangle. It takes a porky slab of hot dog like he's got to run a bucket shop as big as this. And once there's no Triangle I might feel kinder and more loving towards my fellow-men. Which I don't mind telling you I don't at this moment. You've got a gun. Take your choice. Certain death or an even chance!"

Then Storm turned his back on the gunman, as though he were never in doubt of the alternative that gentleman would select, and faced Surcon once more.

"Suppose you kill me," he rapped out, "Teal'll get you—sure! Maybe you'd like to hear exactly what evidence Teal's got to hang you with? Well, take it in pills again. One: he knows now you're Oscar Raegenssen. Two: I've left him data enough to prove you're Snooper Brome too! Chew that bullet, sweetheart!"

Surcon half-rose from his chair, white to the lips. That was a shot he had never expected to hear blazed at him. The one secret he had thought he had held even against Storm's acumen had been flourished as certain knowledge with a calm assurance which staggered him. It was uncanny. Yet he did not lose hold of practical thought. Almost in the same flash his brain had seen and seized upon the only way of escape which now lay open to him, and already he was whizzing it through his imagination, moulding and developing it.

"That gave you a jolt, I'll bet!" Storm continued. "I guessed when I saw you in Raegenssen's house the night I burgled it. I was sure when I found you were the man who'd raked Mattock and Joan Sands into the Triangle. Gosh! you're so easy, I wonder you've got this far! Right. Let's get on. Three: given the first two scoops I've mentioned they can prove you were the man who directed the sticking up of Moraine's. Four: they won't be bothered much with proving you ordered Miss Hawthorne to be killed by Morini after she'd seen you that night in Hamilton Place and your Raegenssen costume. Five: Raegenssen was the registered owner of the Billingsgate sawmill. Bad break of yours, by the way, forgetting to sign the Deed of Sale in the Raegenssen handwriting. I suppose you bought the place before you'd fixed up what handwriting Oscar was to have. Six: Prester John's evidence that you murdered, with typhus bugs, a man who wanted to know too much about you. Seven: having proved you *are* the Big Triangle, you're therefore responsible for the deaths of several people in the Piccadilly Circus beanfeast. I guess that little bunch'll weigh heavy enough in the scales to send you to Hell express, as soon as they can get you convicted and string you up. Now crow!"

Storm paused and reached for his cigarette case. He gave one glance at Morini, and saw that the gunman was leaning against the door again with his automatic directed straight at his, Storm's, heart.

Storm lighted a cigarette and splintered the match between his fingers, watching Surcon intently for every sign of the effect his incisive sentences had had. Surcon's head was bent forward, so that he looked at Storm from under the rim of his prominent brows.

"Understand me?" asked Storm softly. "Got that little mouthful under your hat? Is it walking around squeaking at you? ... It's your cue. Do you kill me and Miss Hawthorne—and hang? Do you lock us up and try making a bolt for it—and hang? Or do you walk out into the next room and shoot yourself without any fuss? Once upon a time your family name must've meant something to you. D'you want the initials on a prison wall, just over an inconspicuous grave, and your own life history minutely recorded in every book on crime that's written from now onwards? Or have you got a spark of decency left in you? Have you got guts enough to stay dead like a gentleman? It's your shout. Pay up, and nobody'll ever see the bill. Don't square it my way, and you go to Tophet through a mud bath."

It seemed for a moment as if Surcon was searching his son's face for any trace of relenting, but Storm's features were set in a granite, ruthless, inexorable mask. And then the burning rage crept back into Surcon's eyes.

"Are you much better than a parricide?" demanded Surcon fiercely, literally shaking with passion. "Isn't your idea just to shelve the responsibility for the act—and be the cause of it just the same?"

"Put it that way, if you like," returned Storm icily. "It happens to satisfy what conscience I've got. And since I hold the whip hand, what I say goes!"

The effrontery of his manner passed over the heads of his hearers. They were becoming inured to it. His crisp, self-possessed manner had ladled them out such a succession of incredible blows that their senses were growing numb. He coolly usurped the position of dictator, when all the time he was at their mercy—domineered, bullied, insulted, mocked them until their wrath towered over him in great boiling waves. And through it all he smiled serenely, punching home the facts he had to deliver with the efficient force of a piledriver. He didn't play his part as by rights an unarmed prisoner should have played it—didn't give a hoot for the superiority of their position—didn't give a damn for their spleen. One might have thought he had the entire British Army drawn up in a hollow square round the house in Buckingham Gate, just waiting to rush in if anybody started rough-housing. Storm was his nickname, and now they had some idea how he had earned it. He was Storm. It didn't count with him that several unpleasantly large hornet's nests were jazzing round his ears. He played out his lone hand with a blithe confidence they couldn't cope with.

And he had got under Morini's skin.

"You've got to give him his, Chief," snapped Gat. "He said the instructions to the bulls won't be opened till midnight—that gives us more than twelve hours to make our getaway. We can go down to one of the Channel seaside places and go off in small boats. We ought to be able to make the French coast. It's risky, but it's been done before. He may be your son, but you needn't see him shot. I'll do it. You can't cling on to that stunt of locking him away—he knows too much."

"You said it!" murmured Storm. "And I know a whole lot more than I've spilled this morning. Shall I go on? If you'd like another dose, you're welcome! You moron! Hear me, Gat! Don't you think I'd seen that getaway scheme years before it ever penetrated your maggoty skull? Keep on hoping! Why, you cheap C_3 cretin, by this time the whole Channel Squadron and the North Sea Fleet are ranging up and down looking for just such an easy get-away. Think again, Gat, and think fast!"

"I'll give you my answer, Captain Arden," said Surcon. "Morini, bring Miss Hawthorne here."

As the door closed, Storm sized up his father. Surcon seemed to bulk bigger than ever, huddled up in that ornate throne; and Storm knew that, immensely strong as he was, he would stand no chance against such a giant of a man. Surcon must have read his thoughts, for a bitter smile touched the thin lips.

"No hope that way, Captain Arden. You get your strength from me, and the tree is bigger than the branch."

Storm smiled back, and for a second a ray of humanity relieved the stern set of his face.

"Sometimes you appeal to me—your nerve's nearly as good as mine," he said.

Nevertheless, Surcon's action gave him furiously to think. The Apex hadn't reacted according to schedule. Somewhere up that enigmatic sleeve was a trump card, and Storm had an uneasy suspicion that he could guess what it was without much chance of error. As he had said, he never put up a bluff without having an even chance of pulling through if it crashed. That even chance had suddenly tumbled down the market to about three to one against. And yet, for all that momentary misgiving, he never changed his calm, arrogant poise. No need to show your bluff till all the other cards are on the table, if you can avoid it...

Surcon had put on a black silk handkerchief by way of a mask, and was pulling his hat down over his eyes.

"A slight precaution, though I doubt its necessity," he explained, and then Susan was outside the door.

Storm recognised her footsteps, but Morini came in alone. Affecting lack of interest, Storm heard every word of conversation which passed between Morini and his Chief, and Kit's brow furrowed for a second as he endeavoured to account for what Mecklen had seen.

And then Susan was in the room, and a little of Storm's grimness relaxed as he heard her gasp of surprise.

"Hullo, kid," he drawled cheerfully. "Sleep well? I hear Lew was a naughty boy last night. Don't worry—I'm going to strafe ole Lew very soon!"

"How did you get here?" She had taken her cue from him, and was smiling, playing up gloriously to him. "Don't say they got you after all?"

"I think not," Storm said carefully. "The general impression at the moment is that I've got *them*!"

Surcon's smile distorted his tight mouth into a cryptic grimace.

"Morini—fetch all the men who are in the building. Make sure Mecklen comes."

Once again Gat departed.

Storm stepped off the daïs and went to Susan. His back was to Surcon, which fact gave him an opportunity to wink encouragingly at her. His grin was cheerfulness itself, but she did not like the metallic light which lay behind his expressive eyes. He took her arm and led her back to the platform, and she thrilled to the cool steadiness of his hand.

Men began to file into the room, taking their places at the benches without speaking. Clearly the vanity of the Triangle had made him summon such portentous assemblies before, for the men moved like a well-trained company of soldiers at Church Parade. Storm had time to be amused.

"Mecklen!"

All the men were in their seats, and the Apex spoke out resonantly. Lew came forward sheepishly.

"Take that girl!"

Two men in the front jumped up and caught Susan by the arms. They hurried her on to the platform, against the huge silver triangle, and began to tie her wrists to two of the corners, so that the base ran across her back. She fought desperately, striking out at their faces with her clenched fists, but with a couple of sulphurous ejaculations as the first blows got home they closed in and gripped her arms, holding her helpless.

Morini was standing beside Storm, his automatic swinging ostentatiously at the "ready" in case of any attempt to go to the girl's assistance. But Storm made no move to attack. He stepped back, folding his arms so that the hands came in the armholes of his coat, and under cover of the cloth he was working away at the sleeves of his bullet-proof vest.

And all the time he cursed silently, although his face never betrayed his kindling fury. He'd been caught! His precious plot had had a link in it so weak it wouldn't have carried an emaciated guinea-pig, and he'd never seen the flaw. He'd plumbed the uttermost profundities of multitude; he'd attained dizzy pinnacles of boobery; he'd wallowed in oceans of sublime insanity. To Bill Kennedy that morning he had confessed that in the past he'd been a mug, and he'd sworn he was going to atone for it—instead of which he'd rolled out of an ordinary frying-pan into a fire that was more like a roaring blast furnace....

Susan was bound, now, and the two who had done it were back in their pews, rubbing bruised shins and muttering luridly.

"You have a gun, Mecklen," said the Apex. "You were told to kill Miss Hawthorne, and you disobeyed. There is still time."

Lew took his revolver from his pocket and looked from it to his leader. Brute as he was, there was something ghastly about such a cold-blooded murder which he found hard to stomach, and he frowned doubtfully, as though unwilling to comprehend. Surcon returned the look with a remorseless determination gleaming in his blue eyes. Slowly Mecklen raised the gun....

"One moment!" The Apex turned to Storm, and that deep, sonorous intonation filled the room like a chant of doom. "You may be less sure of yourself now, Captain Arden. It is now my turn to offer you a choice.... Take Miss Hawthorne and go free to report at Scotland Yard. Resign. And then go abroad for three months and forget all about the Alpha Triangle. Refuse those terms——"

"And——?" prompted Storm, very quietly.

"And Mecklen will not be disobedient a second time."

Storm looked at the girl. She was standing quite still now, her head erect, and a light of proud defiance in her eyes.

"Tell him to go to blazes!"

Her voice rang out with bell-like clarity, and there was not a hint of faltering in it. Storm swallowed a lump that had come into his throat. His head bowed, as if in the agony of making his decision, but all the while his hands fumbled away swiftly and surely at his arms. Another second....

At last he raised his head and his cold eyes swept from Mecklen to Morini, from Morini to Ezra Surcon, *alias* Bulsaid.

"Sure thing—you great little wonderful kid!" he cried, and his hands leapt into view with lightning-like rapidity.

Three shots reverberated as one. The men in their chairs, watching, spellbound, saw Mecklen clutch his chest, sway, and sag to the floor with a long sighing groan. They saw Morini reel back, clawing convulsively at a jaw which Storm's heavy-calibre bullet had smashed and all but torn from its sockets. They saw Storm himself, struck over the breast-bone by Morini's fractional-second-late shot, stagger and then, miraculously recover himself....

And then Storm was on the daïs, shielding Susan with his body. One gun-laden hand, resting on his hip, roved from face to face of the men still sitting as though paralysed, in the body of the room; the other focused on the Apex.

"There's my answer! *Now* crow, you second-hand Gorgonzolas!" he mocked them.

CHAPTER 27

MR. TEAL BUTTS IN

The Assistant Commissioner did not leave immediately after Storm had gone. Instead Bill Kennedy and Mr. Teal sat in the Albany talking over many things. And it was when Mr. Kennedy was taking up his gloves preparatory to departure that the telephone bell rang. The Assistant Commissioner took up the receiver.

"Is that Captain Arden?" asked a voice.

"Yes," said Bill, to save trouble.

"I'm speaking from St. George's Hospital. We've got a man here who wants to speak to you urgently. I'm afraid he's dying—they picked him up in Buckingham Gate last night with eight inches of knife in his lungs. He's only just recovered consciousness."

"What's his name?"

"Sands."

Bill Kennedy whistled softly.

"Any idea what he wants to say?"

"Not much. He'll only speak to you personally. But he keeps muttering something about a triangle and a girl."

"I'll be there in eight minutes, laddie," Kennedy stated crisply.

As he replaced the instrument he saw that Teal was struggling off the sofa.

"Never," said Teal solemnly, "never in my life have I missed anything that was going on worth being present at. If you try to make me break that record, sir, I shall resign this morning. Don't say anything about my shoulder, because there's no bones broken—it's just a flesh wound I'd rather be without, but it doesn't mean I'm going to be tied down in a bath-chair."

Bill Kennedy was an excellent judge of time and space. Exactly eight minutes after he had hung up the receiver he was standing beside the death bed of Birdie Sands, that funny, wizened little man. Teal was with him, and they were hidden from the rest of the ward by the screens which in hospitals are placed about the beds of those whose hours are numbered.

The whizzer looked up with a wry smile. He was pale from loss of blood, but in no pain. His breath came in long, slow, wheezing draughts which scarcely stirred his shallow chest. The clear luminosity of the Beyond was in his eyes, and a strange serenity had smoothed out the wrinkles on his pinched face.

"Where's ... Arden?" he asked, faintly.

Bill Kennedy sat down on the bed, Teal remaining erect.

"Captain Arden's gone to look for Miss Hawthorne," said Bill. "He wanted to settle the Triangle alone and we had to promise not to interfere unless he failed. I don't know how he was going to set about it, but he had some plan or other in his head."

Birdie was silent. Then:

"I never met 'im," he whispered. "But they s'y 'e was a good busy. Listen, Kennedy."

Sands raised himself on one elbow. The effort caused him a fit of hoarse coughing, but he shook off Bill's restraining hand impatiently.

"Yer gotta brike yer promise. Not only fer 'is sike. There's the 'Awthorne girl. She's there—in that 'ouse in Buckingham Gate. They'll kill 'er, sure. Or worse.... That Lew's a swine ... blarst 'im. Dunno w'y, but I 'ate Lew ... poison! More'n Morini, even—an' Morini knifed me. Throws knives like a bloke in a circus.... Oh, yer needn't shike yer 'ead. I know.... I'm not much ter look at—not much ter think of—I'm just a cheap crook, an' a little one at that. But I 'ad a sister once.... Joan.... She's married ter Mattock—strite an' proper, swelp me. She's clean. Teal—yer was always an honest dick—get 'er out of the mess—ter make a man 'appy yer won't never see agine?"

"Yes," said Mr. Teal.

Birdie pawed weakly at his throat, then held out a thin hand. Gravely Inspector Teal took it in a firm grip and held it for a moment.

There was a silence. And then Birdie spoke again. Quickly and breathlessly, his voice growing a shade stronger, for the end was very near.

"Get ter that 'ouse. Black 'ouse. Now. Wiv all the flatties yer can lay yer 'ands on. No time ter lose. Arden can't never win—'e don't know what I know. The Triangle's got a card Arden'll never beat. There's a tunnel—another blow-up, an' it's bigger'n Piccadilly! *'Urry!* ... There's no other w'y ... ter get 'is girl ... out.... Never mind yer promise.... Will yer go?"

Birdie clutched Bill's sleeve earnestly; and, quietly, Bill nodded.

"Yes."

"Then go! Ain't no ... time.... Don't wait fer me—I alw'ys lived alone.... S'pose I can die alone ... I'd rather...." A shrill, feeble cackle of laughter broke eerily from the dry lips. "Oh, yer damned Triangle! I got yer—Birdie, little crook Birdie.... An' I got yer ... smashed yer!... Blarst... yar!" ...

And then the voice fell so low that Bill Kennedy had to lay his ear almost on Birdie's mouth to catch the gasping words.

"Put on the lights…. I'm afraid of … the dark…." Birdie's hand went groping for Kennedy's fingers. "Joan … Joan … Birdie's goin'…. Never was much use to yer … But yer … all … right … *Joan!* … It's cold…. Kiss me…."

"We'll get in through the mews—most of these old houses have back entrances that way," said Teal.

Unostentatiously a cordon had ringed round the gaunt, sinister house in Buckingham Gate, and the mews behind was thronged with armed men whose rubber-soled shoes had made no sound on the cobbles. Bill Kennedy was in charge of the men in Buckingham Gate itself, and Teal was left to direct the opening of the attack.

A minute study of the tire tracks showed that, although there were six lock-ups along the west side of the mews, all the cars which had recently passed in and out of the garage had entered and left by one particular door. Teal made a careful examination of the lock, and also tested the resistance to a steady, cautious push.

"One bar across the centre," was his expert verdict.

Then he drew up his men and gave them their instructions. There was an odd furtiveness about the proceedings—the thirty men mustered in the mews might have been conspirators meeting at dead of night to hatch some nefarious plot, instead of burly, stolid plain-clothes men with nothing more sensational about them than the police automatic and truncheons with which they were armed. Even Teal, an unemotional law-enforcing machine, found himself speaking in hushed tones, although their danger lay far more in being seen than in being overheard. Nevertheless, all the men were pressed close up against the garage doors on the west side, to minimise the risk of being observed by anyone who chanced to look out of one of the upper windows.

"… And if any perishing sinner falls over his own feet this time, like one adjective noun did in Billingsgate not so long ago," Mr. Teal concluded, with whole seas of incandescent vitriol bubbling up in his measured delivery, "I promise him he won't only wish he'd never been born—he'll pray that there's no such thing as reincarnation, when I've finished with him!"

With which horrific prognostication Mr. Teal moved off to take up his position.

He glanced round, and made certain that the twelve men whom he had detailed to assist in the breaking in of the door were stationed ready on his heels; and then he took a Smith-Wesson from his hip pocket and thumbed back the hammer.

"Ready?"

The question ripped out in sibilant warning, and a second later things happened.

Teal's revolver thundered, and the heavy bullets shredded the lock completely out of existence. Simultaneously, Central Inspector Teal and his twelve good men and true hurled their total three-quarter ton of bone and brawn against the barred door. And, with one prolonged, rending, splinting crash, the door simply was not....

They burst panting into the garage, and might have come to a check there among the miscellaneous assortment of trucks and cars but for the spectacled man who happened precisely at that moment to be emerging from the secret panel behind the tire cupboard. In an instant he was whisking back, like a startled mouse which has peeped out of its hole and looked straight into the eyes of a hungry cat; but Mr. Teal, moving at a rate of knots which his weight and inertia made to seem positively supernatural, crossed the concrete flooring like a whiff of smoke. He reached out a long arm and grabbed the horn-rimmed gentleman before that blushing violet could obscure himself behind the closing slide.

"Carl, darling," hissed Teal, "why did you leave your happy home? And how's Mr. Nitrogen Trichloride this merry morning?"

Before Mr. Schwesen could utter a suitable reply, Teal had yanked him halfway across the place and smothered him in a stifling bear-hug. And thereafter, while practised hands clicked gyves upon floundering wrists, the eminent Austrian chemist found it necessary to reserve all his energies for the task of avoiding suffocation. It was all over in a trice, and, even as the remainder of the thirty poured in through the broken door, Mr. Schwesen was on his way to the police van which waited in Petty France.

The fat being thoroughly in the fire by now, speed became the order of the day. Headed by Teal, whose injured shoulder was by this time troubling him far more than he would ever have admitted, the constables rushed through the cupboard and down the short tunnel to the cellars. Two men were left to guard the end of the passage, and the rest raced up the stairs.

The hall was deserted.

Moving as silently as they could, the detectives opened each door in turn, finding large volumes of vacancy at every attempt. Two doors only were left for investigation when Teal, issuing his orders in a hoarse whisper, detached half his force to make a round of the upstairs rooms and guard against an escape, similar to the getaway the Triangle had brought off in Billingsgate, by means of an opening into an adjoining house. At the same time, the front door was unbolted without noise, and Bill Kennedy, together with some of those who were watching Buckingham Gate, came in soundlessly.

And then Teal silently turned the handle of the first of the two remaining ground-floor doors. A dark, narrow corridor fronted him, and he signalled for only six men to accompany him. There was no window or light of any sort in the runway, and when they had gone twenty paces the faint light which filtered in from the gloomy hall ceased to be of any assistance. As quietly as he could manage, Teal kindled a match, and found that the passage terminated in a dead end, the only outlet being a low door which opened off on the right.

Teal laid a cautious hand on the knob, and suddenly a tremor ran up his spine, for the handle was turning of itself under his light grasp....

Breathlessly he mouthed his men back out of the passage, and flattened himself against the blind wall so that the opening door would hide him from whoever came out. The oak swung back by inches, nervously, and it was nearly half a minute before it closed again and Teal saw a stocky, crouching shape silhouetted against the nimbus of twilight which came from the hall.

Holding his breath, Teal leapt silently as any pard. His big hand tightened round the man's throat before so much as a whimper could disturb the stillness, and Teal lifted the furtive one bodily from the ground and padded down the corridor with him.

"There's a long, long jail a-waiting—for you—dearie!"

Teal's voice stole to the man's ear drums in a husky pianissimo, and Teal's ungentle fingers forced a scared face round to meet the light.

And then Inspector Teal, that sedate apostle of tranquillity, let out an involuntary gasp of amazement, for the man he carried was Joe Blaythwayt!

CHAPTER 28

LAST ROUND

Storm's face was bleak, but his two guns might have been gripped in vises mounted on rock-based foundations for all the quivering they showed. He thought that the colossal impact of Morini's bullet must have broken a rib, for, although no revolver in the world loaded a charge heavy enough to penetrate that wonderful steel-chain armour, the imperviousness of it was no defence against the sheer shock of the blow. Every breath he took stabbed an excruciating pang through his lungs. Yet his gay, reckless fighting smile was on his lips; and, when he spoke again, his voice was still deadly even, still rippling so deceptively smoothly over jagged slivers of quartz.

"Free Tip Number Two—straight from the stable—Big Triangle: When you flick out the king of trumps, never start in gloating until you're dam' sure the other man hasn't got the ace tucked away in his fist some place! This is where you look round for your umpteenth guess! All of you. And listen—just bat so much as an eyelid, one of you frogricked horse thieves, and you'll find out where fleas go when they've dined off a dope-soaked suicide! Anybody care to try it? No? Nobody curious? I'll say you're a crew of unenterprising sons of a Port Mahon baboon! And I'll bet less than twelve hours ago you were all scratching each other's backs and telling yourselves what a tough lot of hell-for-leather fire-eaters you were. Je-rusalem! You make me tired. What about it—huh? Can't you even raise one lone cuss-word among the lot of you? Tough? Gosh! I'd like to have the whole boiling of you aboard a good old-fashioned windjammer with a hard-case bucko mate to help me teach you real toughness."

They said nothing. One or two were on their feet, but even they remained safely motionless, having apparently no wish to court the certain death which lurked in the breech of the automatic that roamed so hopefully from head to head. And Storm went on baiting them, playing for a few minutes' grace in which to recover slightly from the stunning results of the shot he had taken and to formulate some scheme for getting Susan loose from the ropes without exposing himself to attack.

"You poor wet fish!" The tang of his whiplash contempt bit tellingly into the raw ends of their vanity with every measured stroke. "A suckling could boss a gang of white-livered slum rats like you! Hold up London itself for fifteen million? Take an expert's advice and go off and practice on hen-rabbits till you get stringy enough to hold up a hysterical old woman for fifteen cents and get away with it. I'm disappointed. I'm a plain ornery fighting machine—I'll fight anyone, any time, any place, and any old how—and I thought I'd landed the goods when I picked on you. Instead of which I find I'm bullyragging a grownup Sunday School. This is my second guess! After grubstaking a stumer like this, I'm going fishing for tadpoles next time I feel bored. It's more exciting, and a heap more dangerous."

He had them writhing under the scourge, knew that every iota of the smart sank right in where it was meant to go—but still they stayed their hands. Tenacity of life, for the moment, held them at bay. Only for the moment. Storm knew that it couldn't last. It was only a question of time before someone gave the cue for the next movement of the ballet, and that time wasn't likely to be over-long elapsing. Very soon they must realise their strength, just as he realised his weakness. He was alone in the house, and no one knew where he was. No rescue party had been arranged for at the critical moment. If they attacked him in one concerted mob, he might kill half a dozen of them if he were lucky, but after that they'd have their revenge. And Susan would be left to face the final racket....

Zero hour.

Already he had pondered every detail of the room. As far as he knew, there was only the one exit—the door through which he had entered. There might be others—in fact, there probably were—but those hangings which surrounded the room were as bad as a fog. There wasn't a hope of gaining sufficient time to poke round all the four walls until one spotted the necessary bolt-hole. Therefore....

"Big Triangle, this is a private bus," Storm said. "Get off! Go and play with your friends in the audience."

One gun motioned him away from the platform, and then returned to aim on Surcon's heart. The Apex hesitated, but there was a flaring menace in Storm's grey eyes which brooked no refusal.

"And keep those hands of yours miles away from everything!" added Storm.

Slowly the Apex stepped off the daïs and walked towards one wall in the body of the room. Then Storm dropped one gun into his coat pocket, stooped swiftly, and gained possession of his knife. Backing in front of the silver sign to which Susan was bound, he felt for the cords which held her. Once found, a couple of rapid slashes, and she was free....

His luck had held—incredibly—but he had no leisure to waste on applauding his good fortune. Quick as light, he slipped the automatic from his pocket again and placed the knife in her hand; and even as he did so he saw that the pent-up torrent was on the point of breaking. The men were looking to the Apex, waiting tensely, keyed up for the signal to let fly. Storm could almost see the squall careering up to engulf him. Only a few seconds more—if that—but Heaven grant him the respite of those few seconds!

"Big Triangle!" Arden's voice clipped out again, and this time he glutted into it every fierce, rampaging demon of savage command he could concentrate on the words. "You're my hostage. Freeze on to that! It's no bluff this journey! The first man who makes a threatening movement'll finish it after you're dead! I've got you covered, and I never miss. Look!"

And then Storm diced everything on an even chance. Either his action would win the few seconds' cowed stillness he needed, or it would be as a spark to the over-dried tinder which was only waiting for its opportunity to blaze up and wipe him off the earth.

He made the gamble without a flicker of an eye.

Two vicious little tongues of orange flame spat out of his automatics, and the two shots rattled like the sharp rat-tat of a drum.

And Storm was sidling towards the door with Susan following him. And Ezra Surcon had sprung back a pace, clapping shaky hands to his ears, for Storms' bullets had grazed under the lobes like two hot searing irons scraped across the skin.

"That'll show you whether I've handled gats before!" Storm challenged, frostily as a Siberian zephyr. "And next time it won't be fancy shooting you'll see demonstrated. Now think again, all of you, before you cut up crusty with me!"

Susan's hand was already on the door, and in the tingling silence Storm heard her catch her breath. The next moment she was whispering in his ear.

"There're men moving about outside—creeping around. I can hear them."

"Hell!"

The word murmured almost inaudibly in Storm's throat. More mess! When he had heard the Apex summon to that room all the men who were in the house, he had naturally assumed that the order would be obeyed. With the only exit he knew ruled out, they were in the most ghastly blind alley two people could have strayed into. And once again the effect of his arrogant threatening was wearing off—more quickly than before, now that the men he was dealing with had grasped their own danger as well as the precariousness of his position. They would never let him get away if they could possibly prevent it, even though they ran the risk of being shot down in the attack. Each one of them would hope to be lucky and escape the few rounds Kit could loose off before they reached him, and each would be aware of the havoc which would be running amok once he got in touch with Scotland Yard. The Apex most of all. Surcon's hands were coming slowly down from his face, and a fiendish lustre burned in his pale blue eyes. His voice rang out suddenly, breaking in on the sizzling intensity of Storm's thought.

"Wait, Captain Arden!"

Surcon, too, could move like an arrow. And the shock of Susan's discovery had taken that last, infinitesimal perfection of keenness off Storm's alert brain—such an all but imperceptible blunting, yet great enough to make an incalculable difference.

Ezra Surcon had flung up his hands and parted the hangings behind him. They saw that screwed to the wall was a small switchboard of porcelain from which protruded two six-inch levers of ebonite. And the Apex had one of these firmly gripped in each of his upraised hands.

"Now listen to me," he shouted. "Haven't forgotten Piccadilly Circus, have you? Well, try to imagine twice that amount of NCl_3 under—*Buckingham Palace*! Why else should I make my headquarters here? There's a tunnel from the cellars—or was, before the explosive was tamped in—and the Palace isn't far. The stuff's packed in huge blocks of ice, but when I pull down this switch it'll close a circuit, and this heat's a network of platinum wires among the charge. Shoot me, and the weight of my body'll pull down the switch. I'll prove to you I'm not bluffing, either. See the other switch? That connects with a tiny tube of nitrogen trichloride upstairs. Show you——".

He dragged down the second lever. From over their heads came a dull, ear-numbing thud. The ceiling cracked, and little fragments of plaster broke away and crumbled to the floor....

The explosion, small as Surcon had said the charge was, shook the house. Came a hoarse exclamation outside the door, and someone barked out two words ... then, the muffled patter of feet stumbling up the stairs.... The Apex looked drawn and haggard suddenly, and an almost childlike puzzlement crept into his eyes.

"What was that?"

"More of your friends, I expect," remarked Storm coolly, for he had recognised the voice outside in the hall. "Susan, get the door open—hustle!"

"It's locked!" screamed Surcon. A mad triumph shook him. "Locked—locked—locked! No escape! Get after him, men! *Get on—get on—what're you waiting for?* Watch, Captain Arden!"

Storm saw the knuckles of Surcon's right hand whiten over the lever they still held. Storm blazed away—carelessly, with one gun, into the ugly surge of men who hurled themselves at him; accurately, with the other, at Ezra Surcon. And Storm thanked all his pagan gods that his boast had been a sound one—that he never missed. Three bullets sped like three crashing thunderbolts into Surcon's right wrist, smashing flesh and bone and sinew to a spurting crimson pulp.

Storm saw the Apex drop his hand, and then Captain Christopher Arden, trouble-hunter, was slap in the middle of as big a slice of trouble as any Hotspur could desire. With two empty guns clenched in his hands to add weight to his blows, he was battling for dear life against a horde of raging maniacs who, fortunately for him, were too closely packed to be able to use their weapons without risk of killing each other, were hampered by their own numbers ... men who used tooth and talon like wild beasts ... men, like animals, thirsting for blood....

No giant of legend could have stood up to that terrible onslaught for more than three minutes. Human muscle and nerve, however willing, were physically incapable of sustaining the fearful pace of such a fight. Storm slogged away with the powerful precision of the fighting machine he had called himself, but he felt his strength going and the *sog* of his sledge-hammer blows into contorted faces growing less potent with every punch. His fists catapulted out from all angles—he still smiled, but grimly—and all the time he knew it couldn't last. A red mist shot with eddying whirls of black and silver swam before his eyes nauseatingly; his chest was a hive of toiling agony; he wondered wearily how long it could last. But he never let up. He knew he was going out, knew that his hour had struck ... a great and worthy end to so wildly glorious a life. He knew no fear—only a strange, primitive exaltation.

Battered, bruised, and torn, thereafter he fought on in silence. He knew that he had been fighting for no more than half a minute, yet in that short space he felt as if he had lived through an eternity. As though separated from his body, his mind stood out clear as a crystal globe in sunlight. He could think coldly, calmly, and work out exactly how much longer he could keep going. Another half-minute, perhaps, and then—*finis*....

And then a new voice broke into the tempest. A familiar voice, preternaturally excited. Teal! How had Teal got in? Had he found the secret entrance, or broken through the locked door? Funny, that—Storm hadn't expected rescue. All the odds had been against Teal getting in before it was too late. But it was Teal's booming bass all right—no doubt about that—and Teal himself, ploughing like a cruiser towards him.

"Hold on, Captain Arden! ... Hold on! ... Come on, boys!"

And Storm managed to cheer back:

"Atta baby, Teal! Give 'em Hell!"

CHAPTER 29

BREAK AWAY

They got him away. Somehow, after a second eternity of effort, he was free of the swaying, cursing throng. Leaning against the wall, panting, drawing a bleeding, aching hand across his filming eyes. Susan clutching his hand, straining herself against him. Teal's arm around his shoulders, supporting him.

Out of the Valley of the Shadow…. Homeric….

Men were still pouring through a door which had been knocked off its hinges, struggling in scattered knots to overpower the last stand of the Triangle. The Apex himself was not among them.

"The Big Triangle!" gasped Storm. "Teal—get him! Black mask ... he's gone!"

"It's all right," soothed Teal clumsily, and Storm shook him off with an impatient shrug.

"It's all wrong! You've got to get him! Tear down the hangings! There must be another exit."

Teal obeyed, Storm helping as best he could. Other detectives were at work immediately.

And so they saw that at the end of the room where the dais was, the curtains hung three feet off the wall, leaving a hidden alley at the end of which was a door. Teal was the first through, and when he saw where he was he nearly choked, for it was the narrow passage where he had caught Blaythwayt.

When they reached the hall they found it deserted, for every man on the job was by then crowded into the throne room to help the fight. In a sudden flash of intuition Teal raced for the cellar stairs, and, as he opened the door, he distinctly heard the clatter of shoes on stone slabs die away.

"Through the garage!"

They could be but a little way behind. Teal pounded down the steps, with Storm hard on his heels. Even as they reached the cellar level, they caught a glimpse of a tall figure sprinting down the gloom of the short passage towards the now open panel in the tire cupboard. Storm kept up with Teal in that hectic chase—how, he never knew. He was tired unto death, but a superhuman will-power kept him going when every fibre of his body shrieked for rest. And they were in the tunnel when they heard the roar of a racing car's exhaust.

An instant later a second exhaust stammered into life!

Storm remembered the two silver racing cars he had seen when they brought him into the garage in the taxi.

"Who in glory's that?" Teal's amazed ejaculation as he ran.

Then they burst into the garage itself. The first car was already in the mews, and they were in time to see the tail of the second disappear round the smashed door of the lock-up. There was no chance of starting up another of the cars to follow in pursuit—even assuming that one of those which were left would be capable of overtaking either of the first two lean, speedy super-cars, which was unlikely. Teal and Storm sprinted down the mews, Teal dragging his revolver from his pocket as he went.

They saw the hinder car turn right as they entered the mews, and as they reached the end they saw it skid round into Buckingham Gate, with the driver hunched up over the wheel in an attitude of desperate concentration.

Then they were in Buckingham Gate themselves, and, standing on the kerb, they witnessed a play which might have been lifted from a sensational movie scenario.

The first car had a lead of about fifty yards, and was increasing it. And then they heard a hideous, clanking grind. The driver had missed his gears. The racking, tortured noise went on, mingling with the deafening drone of the racing engine, as the masked man strove frenziedly to force the cogs to engage. And while he did so he turned in the seat and they saw a gun in his hand. The second car was gaining ground rapidly now, and then the revolver cracked, and the second driver's cap went spinning. Again the masked man fired—twice—and Storm and Teal heard the whine of the bullets passing over their heads.

"Je-rusalem—he's shooting at us!" Storm exclaimed, and began running towards the two cars.

The leading racer was slowing down, for the almost continuous grating which came from it showed that the masked man had still failed to get in gear again. The distance between the two speedsters was lessening swiftly— twenty yards ... fifteen ... ten ... and the second car moving like a streak of light. For the last time the masked man fired, practically at point-blank range, but although his bullet might have stopped a charging man it could not stop a charging car. And charging the second car was, heading straight for the decelerating racer.

And the pursuing car must have been travelling at over sixty miles an hour....

Teal and Storm came up some minutes after the collision. A mangled wreck of twisted machinery and rent and crushed aluminium—that was all. With two bodies jammed in the ruins, weltering in a spreading pool of petrol tinted with something red.

It was some time before they could get at the two men. One was James Norman Mattock—dead, with the masked man's bullet through his brain. Death had wiped the hard lines from his thin face, taken the prison bitterness out of his glazing eyes. It seemed as if a faint, peaceful smile lay on his lips.

Mechanically Inspector Teal doffed his hat in the presence of death—for the first time in his life. It was not because of James Norman Mattock.

"Poor Joan—poor kid," he muttered under his breath.

And then they turned to the second body. The black felt hat had fallen off, and they saw the greying hair which had once been Saxon yellow.

Storm, knowing that the man was dead, turned and walked slowly away.

It was the detective who bent and unfastened the black silk handkerchief. And one long, dazed exhalation whistled through the teeth of Mr. Teal, that bored and placid man.

"Great Kippered Herring!" he breathed. "Lord Hannassay!"

CHAPTER 30

TIME!

Four people went back to the Albany that night, and sat in Kit's snug den smoking and clearing up the odd threads which remained of the Triangle mystery. Bill Kennedy; Inspector Teal, once more phlegmatic and somno-lent; Susan, a trifle pale but very lovely; and—Christopher Arden Bulsaid, Storm, Lord Hannassay.

"*Curtain*—and an effective tab, too," murmured Storm.

His face was considerably damaged, and every limb ached, but he felt supremely happy. He smiled. Between his bruised lips a cigarette canted sky-wards at the old optimistic, devil-may-care angle.

"Yeh! Lord Hannassay the late was the Alpha Triangle. You all know how he got the bug of revenge in his brain, and you can all imagine how it grew up till it filled his whole mind with ideas of making himself a tyrant over all London. He might've done it, given complete sanity to add to his genius. Lombroso'd tell you that wasn't possible. I hope Cesare's right—it's lucky for all concerned if he is. Hannassay couldn't put his scheme into prac-tice till he had money. He got that when his father died in India, leaving him the title and bags of cash. Then Hannassay got busy. Created a Mr. Brome, in which *rôle* he got in touch with the underworld; and an Oscar Raegens-sen to handle the financial side of the organisation. Things got a shade too warm around Lord Hannassay, so we had Fake Death Number One. Later on, things began to hum around Siegfried the Pelican too, so Hannassay trot-ted out Fake Death Number Two and just carried on as Snooper. You can write in most of the rest for yourselves. Among other things, you'll be keen to know why Hannassay fainted when he saw me the day—night, rather—Morini went gunning for Miss Hawthorne. You remember there was only the reading-lamp on in the library? The shade was turned up, and the light came on my face. He thought he was seeing the ghost of his wife, Sylvia Mattock, Jimmy's sister. Hannassay started off his campaign of revenge by shopping Mattock over a forged cheque. Hannassay was rather a brute to my mother, so when Jimmy came out of stir he had a double grudge to settle off his own bat. Hannassay made his second bloomer when he took Mattock on in Raegenssen's. His idea was, of course, to stop him again, since the first shopping hadn't functioned strong enough. But Mattock got wise to a thing or two—one of them was when Raegenssen got in the way of my auto and spoke with Lord Hannassay's voice. That leaves only the Alpha part of it—a bit of supplementary evidence. You mayn't know it, but the Greek *alpha* was supposed in its original form to represent the head and horns of an ox. Bulsaid—*bull's head*…. Got it?"

Storm stretched himself.

"And I think that's the complete rehash, according to Cocker," he remarked after a pause. "Oh, except for Uncle Joe."

"There's a great detective lost in Uncle Joe," said Teal sadly. "D'you know, he cut the wires connecting with the charge of nitrogen trichloride under Buckingham Palace? He heard the Apex threatening you with it and crept along behind the hangings till he found 'em. Uncle Joe's got nerve—he'll be able to write a wonderful book after tonight. By the way, somebody's going to have a ticklish job digging all that H.E. out before the ice melts off it," added Mr. Teal lusciously.

"I'll tell you how I figure it out that Uncle Joe found the house," said Storm. "Mattock, I think, must've joined up in the Triangle, once he got a line on the big boss, in the hope of finding out enough to put Hannassay in the Awful Place. Hannassay'd 've been glad to have him in, as it'd make shopping him easier. Matter of fact, Hannassay didn't go on with that scheme—he was too busy trying to get his fifteen million thick 'uns out of the Treasury. Before that, he'd also got Joan Sands in, to give him a bigger hold over Mattock than ever. That was all done through Snooper. Snooper had the telephone tapped and the bookcase put in, and told each of 'em separately not to touch it or talk about it. Mattock didn't associate Snooper with the Triangle at that time, or we'd have been saved a lot of trouble, so he obeyed orders. God knows why! Anyway, after the Piccadilly Circus explosion, Mattock got less dumb. He put two and two together and made—Snooper! So he went chasing Snooper last night, and Uncle Joe trailed *him*. They went down Buckingham Gate in procession, and all landed up in the right place. If we owe something to Uncle Joe, we owe a darn sight more to Jimmy! I said he was going to kill Raegenssen, and, by hookey! he did. What's happened to Uncle Joe, by the way?"

Teal grimaced.

"Last time I saw him, he was rushing round to talk to Joan. He's been talking to her and pulling the sympathy gag nearly all day. How any man can be so keen on studying criminology," said Mr. Teal, wilfully dense, "beats me."

The four of them had dined together, and the silent-footed Cork had not long cleared the table and taken his departure. The coffee cups in front of them were still warm, and yet already a subtle restraint had forced itself into the air. Two of the guests began to wonder if, even in that short time, they had not overstayed their welcome.

Mr. Assistant Commissioner William Kennedy glared at Mr. Central Detective-Inspector Teal, and Mr. Teal stared sombrely back at Mr. Kennedy with sleepy eyes. Solemnly each of them nodded to the other.

As one man, they rose to their feet.

"I've got a lot of work to get through before I can seek my well-earned rest," said Bill gravely. "Your own particular jaunt may be over, but crime goes on for ever."

"I," said the drowsy Teal, "have been working all day, and I'm very tired."

In the sacred cause of Accuracy, one must put it on record that Storm lapsed lamentably from strictly good manners. He expressed no regret that they could not stay longer, nor did he beg them to remain. In fact, he bade them farewell in haste, as if he were afraid that they might change their minds. Only when they were irrevocably hatted and gloved did he become aware of his duties as a host.

"Not even a quick one before you go?" he suggested half-heartedly.

Mr. Teal shook his head, shifting his gum to the other side of his mouth.

"It's bad for the heart," he said. "Fat men didn't ought to drink...."

Storm closed the door and came back into the sitting-room. He sat on the table, swinging his legs and singing a little tune. Deliberately he crushed out the stump of his cigarette in the ash tray.

Susan got up.

"I suppose I ought to be going, too," she said.

But she did not go.

THE END

www.ingramcontent.com/pod-product-compliance
Lightning Source LLC
Chambersburg PA
CBHW011717240626
47153CB00009B/2891